Sally on the Rocks

WINIFRED BOGGS

First published in 1915

This edition published in 2021 by
The British Library
96 Euston Road
London NW1 2DB

Cataloguing in Publication Data
A catalogue record for this publication is available from the British Library

ISBN 978 0 7123 5304 5
e-ISBN 978 0 7123 6708 0

Text design and typesetting by JCS Publishing Services Ltd
Printed in England by CPI Group (UK), Croydon, CR0 4YY

Contents

❁ ❁ ❁

The 1910s

- In 1910, the average salary for a man is around £70 a year.
- In the 1910s, the average age at first marriage in the UK is about 26 years for women and 28 for men.
- During the 1900s and early 1910s, emigration is very high in the UK – as many as 8.7 per 1,000 people in England and Wales, and 18.7 per 1,000 in Scotland.
- **1914 (July):** The First World War begins. A week later, Great Britain officially enters the conflict.
- **1915:** *Sally on the Rocks* is published.
- **1915 (May):** RMS *Lusitania* is sunk by a German U-boat off the coast of Ireland, with the loss of 1,198 civilian passengers and crew. With American passengers among the dead, the incident is considered a major factor in building support for America's eventual entry into the War.
- 1915 sees the highest number of marriages in England and Wales to date (360,885), though this record is beaten in 1919.
- In 1915, infections account for the most deaths in every age group for men under 75, and for almost all women's age categories. Antibiotics would not be discovered until the late 1920s.
- **1916 (January):** The Military Service Act is passed, conscripting single men between the ages of 18 and 41 (with some exceptions) to the

army. This was extended to married men in May 1916. When *Sally on the Rocks* is published, recruits are still voluntary.

- **1919 (December):** The Sex Disqualification (Removal) Act 1919 enables women to join the professions and professional bodies, sit on juries, and be awarded degrees.

❁ ❁ ❁

Winifred Boggs (1874–1931)

Winifred Boggs was the popular author of more than a dozen novels in the early twentieth century, but her reputation appears to have been short-lived and very little is now known about her life. During her lifetime, many of her novels appeared simply as 'By the author of *The Sale of Lady Daventry*', her sixth novel, from 1914, described by the publisher as 'the novel that made a reputation'. Few biographical details were included alongside the early editions of these works, and it has not proved easy to discover much else about this elusive author.

What is known is that Boggs was born in 1874, and published under the pseudonyms Edward Burke and Gloria Manning, as well as under her own name. She was a frequent contributor to *The Lady's Realm*, a woman's magazine that targeted upper-class women readers and which closed in 1914 or 1915. *Sally on the Rocks* was originally published in 1915. The *Times Literary Supplement* said, 'It is difficult now to give a fresh touch to satire on village life, but Miss Boggs has succeeded'; while another contemporary reviewer commented, 'Sally is a personality in herself, one whom every reader will like, if only for her breezy charm and honesty'.

Several of Boggs' novels were translated into Spanish, including *La Ruina de Sally*. Her final novel, *The Romance of a Very Young Man*, appeared in 1930, and she died the following year.

Preface

Sally on the Rocks seems to have all the tropes we might recognise from a romantic comedy: a love triangle, a waspish spinster, a broken heart. But this novel has many hidden depths. The First World War and a meddling letter from the village troublemaker are what propels our heroine, Sally, towards Little Crampton, the village at the centre of the story. Winifred Boggs finely draws the characters we recognise from other village stories. The gentle clergyman, the officious bank manager and the ambitious widow are all present, but not as they first seem. Boggs' description of the village and its inhabitants draws us into a novel which is so much more than a comedy of manners.

At 31, when Sally arrives in Little Crampton she is not only on the rocks but on the shelf. She believes that marriage will be the only thing which can save her. But regardless of that possibly unpromising premise, *Sally on the Rocks* is an unexpectedly feminist novel. At different turns the usual stereotypes are upturned. Despite the love triangle, the female rivals find a sisterhood. The differing consequences of men and women's behaviour are discussed. Even the baddie of the piece is recognised as an intelligent woman without a real outlet.

When so little is known about an author, perhaps there is a tendency, particularly with women writers, to try and learn something about them from the characters in their novels. Winifred Boggs remains an enigma known only by her novels. Would she be a Miss Maggie? Or a Mrs Dalton? Or the eponymous Sally, who is so generously depicted?

We can only draw our own conclusions about the author who writes such strong and nuanced female characters.

Above all, *Sally on the Rocks* will make you laugh. From the schemes Sally dreams up in pursuit of her quarry to the interior monologues of the bank manager in thrall to his dead mother's book of aphorisms, there is so much warmth and light in this novel. With Sally we have a complicated and endearing character you cannot help but root for.

Lucy Evans
Curator, Printed Heritage Collections
British Library

Publisher's Note

The original novels reprinted in the British Library Women Writers series were written and published in a period ranging, for the most part, from the 1910s to the 1950s. There are many elements of these stories which continue to entertain modern readers, however in some cases there are also uses of language, instances of stereotyping and some attitudes expressed by narrators or characters which may not be endorsed by the publishing standards of today. We acknowledge therefore that some elements in the stories selected for reprinting may continue to make uncomfortable reading for some of our audience. With this series, British Library Publishing aims to offer a new readership a chance to read some of the rare books of the British Library's collections in an affordable paperback format, to enjoy their merits and to look back into the world of the twentieth century as portrayed by their writers. It is not possible to separate these stories from the history of their writing and as such the following novel is presented as it was originally published with minor edits only, made for consistency of style and sense. We welcome feedback from our readers, which can be sent to the following address:

British Library Publishing
The British Library
96 Euston Road
London, NW1 2DB
United Kingdom

Sally on the Rocks

Wealth lost, something lost;
Honour lost, much lost;
Courage lost, all lost!

CHAPTER I

"The new bank-manager is a bachelor, and simply rolling"

The successful little Cramptonian is born, not made, as strangers coming to the place soon found to their cost, for even the Cramptonians themselves had to be careful, on account of Miss Maggie Hopkins.

The 'white flower of a blameless life' availed you little; sooner or later Miss Maggie got hold of it, threw it in the mud, said in effect, "Just look at this beastly thing!" and held it up to the shocked gaze of the neighbourhood.

Most people have something they would prefer to keep to themselves, not so much sin as folly—some miniature skeleton. Whatever it was, Miss Maggie with her gimlet eyes and corkscrew methods 'got it out of you.'

It was she who discovered, within three days, that the new doctor and his wife had emerged from 'shops,' and Mrs. Hill, who was given to what is called 'swank,' had to walk humbly in Little Crampton thereafter. Miss Maggie also discovered—though this took longer—that the lawyer's new wife, who seemed so modest and quiet, had once kicked a lavish leg before the footlights.

As a matter of fact, Miss Maggie's discoveries would need a volume to themselves, and may be dismissed.

The stranger had pitfalls to right of him and pitfalls to left of him; all of them unpleasant, and some of them fatal. If you fell in and crawled painfully to the top, you encountered Miss Maggie's pole, which thrust you down again. As you floundered in the deepest mire you condemned Miss Maggie to a yet deeper Pit, but you had to leave Little Crampton just the same.

You might think that when you had successfully passed the test of the gentry all was well. You were very much mistaken. There remained High Street. You must buy only in High Street, and 'the best of everything,' which really meant the worst of everything—at village prices.

If you failed, then High Street insinuated to your face that you were no lady, and your house was to be let at a sacrifice. The greeting of Mr. Alfred Bingley, bank-manager and lay-reader, denoted the temperature of your banking account and was a useful chart with its 'set fair,' 'very warm,' 'cool,' or 'heavy fall,' as the case might be. If your banking account was not up to the Little Crampton standard, it behoved you to bank elsewhere.

Yet it was a place of unrivalled beauty, a garden in the heart of a garden. There were long stretches of moors, where, unless you had spent your boyhood upon them in getting lost and found, you were swallowed up by a maze the moment you left the beaten tracks. Short cuts led to miles and miles of despairing search—and to scandals.

In the autumn Little Crampton flamed in crimson and gold and purple. Acres of corn tossed their heads in the breeze, rustled in the silent night watches, whispering of strange things. There were defiant poppy faces laughing here and there among the gold, cursed at by the farmers, uprooted and forbidden, yet living their radiant hour just the same. There was a mantle of purple heather on the moors spread flat for all to tread on, and wrapped closely round the hunched shoulders of 'The Mountain.'

The Mountain really represented an object lesson, since it showed that in Little Crampton it was the habit to make mountains out of mole-hills. Neither was 'The River' as important as it sounded. There were other rivers in Europe, some of them larger. There were even people who had not heard of Little Crampton.

There was the strangest, most wonderful sea, for though by climbing The Mountain you could get sight of it, sometimes hear a low murmur, and it seemed within a walk, yet it never was, and there was no road to it. It lay, like the magic of to-morrow, always just a trifle ahead.

Maybe those of Little Crampton who had grasped the Great Adventure, and laid hands upon To-morrow, had reached its shimmer of gold and grey, but no living tongue claimed this feat, and many held that it was but a mirage. At any rate, it was only the very young, or rather foolish, that went on trying to reach it.

If you were a male Little Cramptonian, you fared forth to make your mark in the world; if you made it, you returned, still 'in the prime of life,' to retire. If, on the contrary, the world made its mark on you in the shape of painful dents, you still returned, though only to await that magic To-morrow.

If you were the common or garden non-adventurous woman, you stayed, waiting for things to happen. When you awoke to the fact that 'things'—for the best of reasons—hardly ever happened in Little Crampton, it was always too late. The tide of youth and hope, coming in with a clamour, had gone out swiftly, leaving a long stretch of barren grey shore behind it. No longer the flow, only the inevitable dragging ebb. Little Crampton had its tragedies, tragedies of duty, of foolishness, of inefficiency—that greatest of all tragedies. They were written in the faces of those women who had lacked grit or opportunity to break away, but still asked themselves that "Dare I ?" which never had an answer; they were dying in the dead faces of those who had ceased to ask even that question, because they no longer cared. That final dreadful thing called 'resignation' lay behind those hopeless eyes now.

Linked with tragedy walked comedy; tragedy laughing, comedy weeping; bound together for all time, and sometimes hard put to it to say which was which.

If you came in the guise of a lady, and especially a young widow, it was ages before people called. Miss Maggie was finding out about you.

If you came in the guise of a bachelor—unusual and thrilling—Miss Maggie had still to find out about you first, only it would not take so long as if you were a young widow of pleasing exterior. You would get an invitation of some sort before she got her first call, but if you and the young widow 'happened' on the same day, it was simply all over with both of you—especially with the young widow.

The sooner you discovered that Miss Maggie was neither to be defied nor ignored, but appeased, the better. Also that it would save time and trouble to tell her your own version of the worst. No matter how small the skeleton she pounced upon, the lady could make its bones rattle so loudly that you would be deafened yourself.

If you were a curate she invariably had you removed by the bishop under the most scandalous circumstances. Not that you were likely to be a curate; to go to Little Crampton had become equivalent to being unfrocked. Instead of the curates there were 'helpers' and 'lay-readers,' but even they knew Miss Maggie would find out about them if they were not very careful. Happy the immaculate Alfred Bingley, who could positively invite inspection of his past and his present.

The Reverend Adam Lovelady did his best against Miss Maggie, but he was only a man, and she was a woman. But for the curse of sex she must have been famous as a ruthless criminal barrister or investigator. As it was, she made the foolish as infamous as possible, and had a malicious joy in life. When anything was brewing, or had just brewed, she was overwhelmed by invitations to tea and the very best cakes, which she devoured with appalling voracity. But it was worth it; she invariably knew the most dreadful details.

If you were a male stranger, 'passed for the present' by Miss Maggie, you would be sure to receive an invitation to dinner from Mr. Alfred Bingley—provided of course your balance at the bank was all it should be. After dinner you would probably have to hear about Mr. Alfred Bingley's wonderful mother, and the wonderful book she had left behind her. You might even be favoured with extracts, after which it depended upon your own cook and your carnal appetite whether you ever accepted another invitation. On the whole, Mr. Bingley's dinners were considered the best part of Mr. Bingley. When he was not thinking them out, or exercising to get an appetite, or eating them, or banking, he was acting free curate for the good of the souls of Little Crampton.

Even so a dull time had fallen upon Little Crampton, so dull a time, in spite of the war, that Miss Maggie Hopkins wondered if nothing could be done to introduce a certain liveliness.

Suddenly she thought of Sally Lunton.

Sally Lunton had been very lively indeed six years back, and made the tongue of gossip wag fast, for the Reverend Adam Lovelady's black-eyed ward was quite the liveliest specimen Little Crampton had ever found in its midst.

Without a moment's hesitation Miss Maggie took up her pen and wrote:

DEAR SALLY,

Mr. Lovelady says he hardly ever hears from you now, but that you are still at the same address, in spite of the war. How attractive you must find Paris to remain at such a time! There's no news. Mrs. Randal is ill, and as usual will see nobody but Mr. Lovelady. I expect she will leave all her money to cats.

By the bye, the new bank-manager is a bachelor, and simply rolling, quite fifteen hundred a year, and most of it private means. There's influence, and he's sure to get a big London bank. He's about forty and gives very good dinners, and is quite presentable for a man with his prospects. His mother was an *awful* woman, but she's dead. I suppose he'll be married now. There's a new widow, Mrs. Dalton, with a little girl, who seems the leading candidate, but it's a 'poor field,' as Mr. Paton would say.

I suppose this war will do away with your livelihood. It's not any easier when people get older, is it? I'm sure it doesn't seem like six years since you were here and celebrated your twenty-fifth birthday. Mrs. Dalton makes out she is only twenty-seven, but I should say she was as old as you are, perhaps even older. I have very nearly got it traced. Her father was that man who shot his wife showing how to shoot rabbits, and swore it was an accident, and married a very pretty young girl soon afterwards.

What are you thinking of doing next? Dreadful how the war is taking all the marriageable men, isn't it? We had quite an argument about it the other day at the Patons', and Mr. Paton was rude, as usual. I said that I thought the bachelors should be saved and only the married men sent out, Mr. Paton having been married twice, as you know, and not minding if he's married a third time either. Mrs. Paton is certainly getting on. The 'getting on' stage is the most trying, don't you think? After you are past it, well, people leave you alone; but till you are you *must* keep on struggling. The trouble is, so few women seem to realise when it's decent to cease struggling. They think they may as well go on for another year or two while they are about it.

Mr. Bingley is simply invaluable to Mr. Lovelady, and always at the Vicarage. He gets his money's worth by reading the Scriptures at anybody he thinks they suit. Last week it was about women attiring themselves in an unseemly fashion; he looked at Elizabeth's hat. I am sure you would like him if you happened to meet him, though his name is Alfred. He's so safe, and of course there's the house and 'perks,' as well as the fifteen hundred. They say he asks a blessing at every meal, even at afternoon tea, though he always takes exercise for his digestion to be on the safe side. He reads prayers at the servants morning and evening. Unfortunately another housemaid has just run away.

Mrs. Dalton goes in for being the womanly kind. The little girl is a great help. If such a nice little girl, why not an equally satisfactory little bank-manager? One knows how much he would love to have a little bank-manager—and that Mrs. Dalton would rather have a motor-car.

We want somebody to liven up things dreadfully. What a lot of exciting things must have happened during the six years you have so mysteriously disappeared from our ken! You must tell me all about them; as you know, they would be safe with me. Why shouldn't women sow wild oats too when they get the chance? Of course, the nuisance is, they mostly don't. Still, you were the kind to make your chances, and that's always something.

I never knew such a Grundy-man as Mr. Bingley. Still, I must own that as far as *outward* appearances are concerned he has lived up to it—so far.

I have my doubts whether Mrs. Dalton's comfortable income is anything of the sort, and not a lack of real principle. I don't want to make a pun. *She doesn't bank here.*

Lydia is mopy, as usual, but you can't if they won't. Grace as jolly as ever. She spends her days over pigs and manure-heaps and other disgusting details no lady ought to know exists, and reads poetry in the evening. Mr. Boliver got married soon after you left—on the rebound. He's fatter than ever.

One thing is pretty certain: Mr. Bingley will never be disappointed in love, not only because of the fifteen hundred, etc., but because he cares for himself with that highest, holiest passion that remains faithful throughout. His mother *was* a woman. Such a mercy she's dead; unfortunately her book still lives. However, as it's the one privately-bound copy something might happen to it some time—one never knows. It's full of advice on how not to get married.

Of course, like everybody else, he started to walk to the sea, but, unlike them, he gave it up at once as useless. He has decided that it is a mirage. Nina, Mrs. Dalton's little girl, is *absolutely devoted* to him. She's very well brought up. I always think that widows are twice-armed, don't you? Well, if you can't come to cheer up poor Mr. Lovelady you can't, but I'm sure he would be awfully pleased to see you, and so would

Your affectionate friend,

Maggie Hopkins.

P.S.—Mr. Paton says he'll lay two to one on Mrs. Dalton any day.

This letter reached Miss Salome Lunton when she was in serious straits; things were looking grim and grey, and the shadow of the gaunt wolf lay athwart the threshold. The Paris she had known was dead, her chance of livelihood with it. A strange and rather terrible city had arisen in its place.

"They may be here to-morrow" was in the eyes of all, though on the lips of none. They had heard what had been done in Belgium; they did not even whisper what might be done in Paris; they knew.

The tense city seemed to hold its breath; any day it might become the city of dreadful deeds. The dog, who had known the whip before, bared its teeth at the menace, but was well aware how little those teeth counted. The preparations for defence—which all in their heart knew inadequate—proceeded feverishly. The beautiful trees had to go; Paris crouched like a woman robbed of her bright tresses, her crowning glory, and set her teeth against the morrow. Already the hordes were thundering at her gates.

And then—a sudden change of 'tactics.' On September the sixth Joffre halted his spent and retreating army, and three times were his words passed from rank to rank, and men fainting, dropping in their traces, dying of exhaustion, heard that clarion call to a desperate stand:

"Let all advance who can; let all who cannot advance die where they stand!"

All stood, and many died. The German tactics also changed. Their festivity in Paris was 'unavoidably postponed.'

So the tragedy of the city was averted, but not the tragedy of Salome Lunton and those in like case with her. Thirteen years to build up just enough to keep body and soul together—all swept away at the sound of a drum! While nations were locked together in a strangling grip, dealing death, finding death, she had still to fight her own battle of ways and means. After thirteen years she was further from the goal than when she had started, gay and confident, at eighteen. Whatever came or went she would never sight that goal, for in a world where many were talented and a few had genius she had only a cheap mediocrity. It was not the conditions without that flung her on the scrap-heap—though they hastened that flinging—but the conditions within. The divine spark was absent.

Hers was the tragedy of doing without most of the things that made life worth living. There was luxury as an accepted standard in her blood; in her art little, and in her purse even less. Others, mushroom growths, most of them, lingered at the feast; she was sent empty away. There were times when her whole being revolted and the thing became unbearable. At such times she asked herself strange questions, terrible questions. …

Most of her life had been spent in the grey underworld, a place neither reputable nor disreputable, mainly sordid and uncomfortable. What a far, impossible climb to the world of ease and reputation, but how short and easy a step to that other world below! Emptiness in the life she knew; in the far place above, pearls and peace of mind; in the place below, diamonds and satin and laughter—and the years that the locust hath eaten.

She always looked in the glass at such times as these, though not in vanity. She was merely tracing the history of her black eyes and little pointed chin which had descended to her from countless Luntons, and remembering the history of this ancestress or that; none of them respectable. Everybody knew the Lunton tradition, that 'the men are bad, but the women worse.' She had only to follow that tradition, 'go the Lunton way,' and find the primrose path.

Flaming yellow hair, flaming black eyes, a mouth a little bitter, cheeks too sallow and thin for perfection, but cheeks that could blaze to a strange arresting beauty. A figure long and lean—too lean—but sinuous and graceful. All the assets, or nearly all, for something held back, something proud and fastidious and clean. But then her whole heart and soul held back from poverty and stress. One was too difficult, the other only too easy.

"And we Luntons always travel the easy way in the end," she reminded herself. "I shall come to it unless another road opens before me. I will not be ground down in the very dust any longer. I will and must have money and ease—some way."

She laughed, and then she wept. It was her pagan philosophy to live only in the present, to snatch at the pleasure of the hour lest that pleasure should never come again, but the past crushed her heart in its hand, and just for once she did not tear those fingers away. They hurt, yet it was not an agony she would willingly have foregone. If it had spoiled her life it had at least meant one month's wild happiness, and it is not everybody who can look back even to that. Happiness! It had gone beyond that. It had been magnificent, something that had borne her aloft on radiant wings. Her heart had sung with joy; her feet had seemed scarcely to touch the earth. But it was finished.

A voice that she had stilled for six years rang through the attic studio and through her heart. "Sally Lunn, Sally Lunn," it called lightly and laughingly, "let's see what else we can find for tea!"

She leaned her head wearily against the dilapidated arm-chair. "Oh, Jimmy, if you could have cared more, or I less, how much easier to bear now!"

She pulled herself out of the chair, and thrust her face out of the window. Then she drew it quickly back. The wounded were being carried past. The awful pity of that procession!

Her thoughts came quickly to the things of the hour, the tragedy of nations. "To be a woman at such a time," she thought, "useless! Just an incubus! If only I could overcome fainting at the sight of blood and be taken into a hospital! Oh, that poor boy! …"

She shuddered, choking a little as she pulled down the blind. Life finished before it was well begun; one of the most awful sights—and one of the commonest!

"I must get away or I shall go mad!" she thought.

It was then that she opened Miss Maggie's letter.

"She can't be so bad at heart," she thought, almost ashamed to think how she had disliked Miss Maggie; "here she is practically making me a present of her frightful Mr. Bingley—for of course he is frightful, that sort of man always is."

Fifteen hundred a year, a house, 'perks,' and prospects! A glimpse of the respectable world, and not too far a climb, surely. "I believe I could get him; I'm sure I could get him," she thought; "just the type to fall to the unknown quantity. Possibly he has never met a girl like me before, certainly not in Little Crampton."

She laughed at the thought of Little Crampton. She remembered it so well. How absurd she had always found it, and yet somehow so restful. Yes, she would visit Little Crampton again, not for a rest this time, but for a husband.

"Mrs. Alfred Bingley," she thought mockingly, "wife of a man who reads prayers at the servants twice a day, and 'asks blessings' at afternoon tea!" The thing seemed so incongruous and so ludicrous that she began to laugh, and laughed till the tears streamed from her eyes. "Alfred Bingley! Yet what's in a name? Doubtless the John Joneses get somebody to love them; then why not the Bingleys with fifteen hundred a year? Really, it's rather decent of Maggie Hopkins to make me a present of the Bingley man."

She had not quite grasped Miss Maggie's intention. For Mr. Bingley to have fallen to Sally would have been neither interesting nor exciting. Miss Maggie's idea was rather to dangle the rich bait before two eager fishes, and then snatch it away from both at the last moment. It was the pursuit, not the capture of the prize she sought to witness. She would have Mr. Bingley free for many a long year to come, and damsels, faint but pursuing, on his tracks. That was life—in Little Crampton.

Sally's face softened at the reference to Mr. Lovelady, and she was ashamed and remorseful. "What a selfish beast I am," she thought, "what a worthless little beast! I am fond of Lovey, and yet when have I ever bothered about him? Only for my own sake now and then, or because I wanted something. Why, I deserve the very worst that can happen to me, yes, the very worst! In all my life I have never thought of anybody but myself—and Jimmy; and even that was a selfish love. What a prize for Mr. Bingley!"

Her mobile face changed again. "No, I won't—at least not if I can help it!" She would give herself another chance, postpone the evil day and the evil choice. "I'll give London a chance. If it lets me pick up a decent living, lets me be really decent a little longer, I'll resist the temptation. If it doesn't—." She did not finish the sentence, but her mouth set into grim, unlovely lines.

She went to London, telling Mr. Lovelady her intention but not her address. There were reasons for not giving that; her friends were such a 'shady' lot. It would hurt him, "and poor Lovey has been hurt enough, Heaven knows!" she thought pitifully.

For months of the wettest, most dreary winter she had known she gave London its chance to save her, but that city of dreadful night politely but firmly declined to do anything of the sort. Thousands were sinking to destruction; why not Sally, worthless child of worthless parents?

Sally, however, had a tenacious mind, and no wish to be swallowed up; she wanted money and ease and pleasure before the morass covered her, and she merely reread Miss Maggie's letter.

"That woman hasn't married him yet or I should have heard," she thought. "It's Fate, and why hesitate any longer? It's either Mr. Bingley or—"

She paused, and then added quickly, "I mean, of course, it's got to be the pious bank-manager. God help him—God help us both!"

Her laugh was not very successful.

As winter's stern face was softening before the coy advances of spring, 1915, Sally Lunton came to Little Crampton.

She arrived dramatically, expected of none, heralded by crashes and bumps, by the boxing of an ear, the objurgations of Elizabeth, and the emphatic oath of a man.

CHAPTER II

"I am absolutely on the rocks, Lovey"

The Reverend Adam Lovelady was buried deep in his arm-chair and a book on his pet hobby—roses. His study was shabby, but cosy and most scrupulously clean. Elizabeth saw to that—a trifle drastically, her master thought.

A faint breeze, sweeping across from The Mountain, stirred the curtains and ran its cool fingers through the parson's plentiful grey hair. Mr. Lovelady, an inhabitant of Little Crampton if not altogether of it, was sufficiently Cramptonian to call it a 'sea' breeze, and believe he could taste the salt on his lips.

Outside blackbirds and thrushes were very busy with their courting songs, and, swaying on the branches of the trees, were the first to flavour spring. If the Reverend Adam was without an Eve, for them there was a sufficiency of Eves, and a paradise without any serpent that they knew of.

During the winter Mr. Lovelady fed the birds, very wastefully, Elizabeth considered. During the other seasons they repaid him by robbing him of his seeds, green shoots, and fruit—and by their songs. The Reverend Adam considered himself their debtor.

Afar off a cock crew—Ananias; an exultant crow enough, for he still had sway over his cherished Sapphira.

At his master's feet, as near as he could get, slumbered Old John. Old John had been Young John once, and rather a gay dog in his day. Now he was rather deaf, rather blind, very tired, and twenty years of age.

Just a peaceful, almost sleepy, English scene.

Into peace swept storm.

First a loud bump sounded in the hall, then a crash, and then another bump.

"Well, Elizabeth will see to it," thought Mr. Lovelady, burying himself deeper in book and chair.

Elizabeth 'saw to it' without loss of time. It was a way she had. Her voice carried to the study.

"Young man," she said, "if you're a bomb-thrower come to break up the house, say so; but if you call yourself a porter delivering boxes, you just mind what you are at, or it'll be the worse for you."

The deliverer of the boxes laughed, an ill-advised thing to do when dealing with the drastic Elizabeth.

The Reverend Adam instinctively clapped his hand to his ear as a certain familiar sound reached him, and tried not to hear the lurid oath which followed from the aggrieved party.

"She's doing it again. I wish she wouldn't!" sighed Mr. Lovelady.

"You run some risks," said the porter sullenly.

Mr. Lovelady could feel Elizabeth toss her head as she retorted, "You can treat men as you like, or ill-treat 'em, long as you ain't married to 'em. Once you are the boot's on the other leg."

"And a damn good thing too!" said the porter. "She's following. I didn't recognise her at first owing to her new hair. You wimmin are that queer and handy at improving on nature!"

"You men are beyond improvement, being hopeless from the first!" snorted Elizabeth.

"Go on!" said the man from the station admiringly.

Then came another voice, gay and careless, and a long, low, delicious laugh.

The vicar flung down his cherished book and pitched himself into the hall. "It's never Sally," he cried joyfully, "Sally at last!"

Something long and lean, with a mop of yellow hair, dancing feet, and dancing black eyes, curled its long length round him.

"Yes, it's the bad penny. I'm absolutely on the rocks, Lovey, so I've come."

Elizabeth stared after that yellow where dead-brown had once been. "Well, I never did!" she exclaimed. "After marryin' this time, or my name ain't Elizabeth!"

Meanwhile the study door clanged sharply, and Sally did her best to strangle her guardian. "Yes, I 've come at last."

"And a good thing too, a jolly good thing!" he cried boyishly.

"Dear old thing! You don't look a day balder! What do you think of my new hair?"

He was too busy kissing the wicked black eyes, pinching the dear little pointed chin, to hear or heed. "It's been a long six years, my dear, and rather a lonely time."

"I'm a selfish beast," she cried, "but I'm dreadfully fond of you, really, Lovey dear—when I think of it!"

"You are a gay young thing, and I'm a sad old thing. Youth to youth, gaiety to gaiety; Nature's law and God's law. But the same Sally, the same happy, light-hearted Sally?"

She turned, her eyes hidden against his neck. "Ah yes, happy, light-hearted," she echoed; "still just dancing through life. Something without much of a soul, and never a heartache!"

"Yet somehow you are changed." His voice was troubled.

She threw her hat across the room and faced him, laughing. "Yes, Lovey Dovey, I've achieved the latest fashion in hair, or what was the latest fashion before the war."

He looked at her and started. The thing was a shock to him. "Your hair has changed colour!" he gasped.

Before dull brown, now radiant, flaming yellow!

She pushed him into his chair. "Dear Innocent! Hair doesn't change colour; it merely 'suffers a change' now and then."

"Oh, Sally, but why?"

"It's nicer."

"No, no! What God has given us is best."

"Sometimes God gives us a squint, dear thing, but we get it rectified if we can."

She shook her yellow mop in his face. It swept across his lips like fine silk.

He kissed it, but murmured apologetically, "It looks so natural."

"Yes, doesn't it?" she cried, delighted. "I would not have used horrid bleaching stuffs or dyes; they never look natural; but when a friend at one of the hospitals told me that hair turned a lovely yellow under the X-rays, well—I was X-rayed. It was before the war, of course, just to see. He was right and I was pleased, and there you are! Everybody said I looked perfectly sweet in my new hair. What do *you* think, Lovey?"

"Well, well, to be sure!" he prevaricated.

"I do look sweet? Can't I see myself in your blue eyes?"

"You are thinner than ever," he said accusingly. "Why didn't you write? Why didn't you come before? Why will you never let me know the worst, Madam Lucifer?"

"Oh, it's the worst right enough, the scrap-heap this time."

He grasped her tightly. His Sally in trouble! "Nonsense, you shall not talk like that! Besides, we've got you now, and we are going to keep you, eh, Old John?"

Old John lifted his head a moment and growled. He hated to see feminine things on his master's knee. He knew what it meant. Trouble, and yet more trouble, perhaps something broken as well. Long ago, when he had been young and gay and rather naughty—as befitted youth and gaiety—a big she-thing and a small she-thing had curled themselves up just like that. And Old John had hated all she-things from that day to this. Then one day they had been planted in the ground, just as his master planted his roses. The roses had come up again; they never had. He was a jealous dog, and not in the least sorry. Now his master would play with him all the time.

But his master had never played again, and even his voice had sounded different. The dog was puzzled. Then he worked it out in his dog-like way. There was something broken inside his master so that it hurt to play. Didn't he know all about that, and how it hurt, by bitter experience? His had been the affair of playing with a bigger dog; his break had been mended, his master's never had, though one could not hear it rattle. But then humans were queer, and perhaps, in their world, it wasn't the thing to rattle. Anyway, the gay young master became all of a sudden a sad old master. He sat with empty arms, with eyes that somehow made Old John feel very uncomfortable, and black hair grey.

Old John had been jealous of Sally on her last visit, and thankful when she suddenly disappeared. He took it for granted she had been planted too and wouldn't come up again. Humans didn't, it seemed. And now here was this Sally-thing installed on his master's knee, calling him names that even a dog knew were silly and undignified. The sickening thing was, his master seemed to like it. It was years and years since his face had shone like that.

Old John considered human females very trying. They made an undignified fuss of you one moment and smacked you the next. If there was a nasty human puppy present, even one without hair, they did not see you at all. They said they would take you for a nice long walk—dear old fellow, now!—and then their silly legs gave way before you were well started. He really couldn't see why sensible creatures like men kept them in the house; the yard, if it must be, but certainly never the house.

His growl died away in a moan. It was difficult to be energetic even in hatred these days; one's bones would ache so.

Sally stopped and patted him. "Old John still alive? How ridiculous!" she exclaimed. "He must be a hundred, surely!"

The Reverend Adam winced. There was not so much left that he could afford to dispense with Old John. "Only twenty," he said hastily; "dogs have lived longer. Perhaps we shall see each other out."

He had his little secret that even Miss Maggie had not discovered. He patted the shaggy old head, and the dog stirred his weary bones, and dropping his head on his master's knee looked up with infinite devotion in his pathetic eyes, but tried slyly all the time to prize Sally off her perch with his nose.

Sally laughed and held on, and because the dog was so very weary he slipped back to his old position. "Oh, it's nice to be back again," she said. "Little Crampton is so safe, so—so respectable!"

It was good to feel respectable again, to come from the grey into the sunlight. One was away from the slime, the horrible things that mouthed in its depths, the shadow-shapes slinking past, the insomnia of a city;

away, too, from that voice that whispered, "There, but for the grace of God, go I," and that other insistent voice that would not be stilled, "Some day, some day … it may be you …"

She shivered, clinging close to Adam Lovelady.

"You always laughed at respectability, you bad girl," he said. "How you used to hate it!"

"I don't hate it now," she said, very low. To be respectably established for life had become the one crying need of her nature, the one escape from a terrible alternative.

"Well, that's a good thing," he said heartily. "So you haven't quite forgotten us, after all, and that's a better thing still."

"Forgotten you! Forgotten our dear Helena and little Nan! I will show you how much I have forgotten!"

She ran into the hall and seized hold of a canvas done up in sacking.

"I could never show you one of my paintings before," she explained on her return, "because they had to be rather naughty to satisfy the firm; but this I did for you." Her hard mouth softened, and her eyes were misty. Her cousin's husband was the best man she knew, perfect in her eyes, but what she called 'Fate' and he 'God' had been very cruel to him.

"It is called 'Broken and Mended,'" she said, unwrapping it, "and it may be true—one never knows." She spoke to comfort him, not for any conviction she held. Sally was without convictions.

The picture represented the Gates of Death. On one side, in all sorts of attitudes, were those who had been broken by sin or loss, circumstances or weakness; on the other side of the Gates were the figures made whole. Inside the Gates a beautiful woman with deep, loving eyes, a laughing mouth, and a chin the counterpart of Sally's own, eagerly awaited someone who would pass within. She held a small replica of herself by the hand. This was Helena Lovelady and baby Nan.

The idea was crude enough, almost cheap, but poor Sally was only a cheap sort of person, and was perfectly aware of the fact; but the execution of it was delicate and appealing. It was, at least, the best thing she had ever done, perhaps the only thing with possibility in it, and certainly the only one for which she had been offered a good price.

She had come pretty close to starvation, but she had not sold 'Lovey's' picture.

"It is beautiful, beautiful! I cannot thank you," he said huskily. "I had not even a good photograph."

"It was as I saw them last," she said simply, "when they were on this side of the Gates."

It was not as Adam Lovelady had seen them last. Two blackened, twisted bodies were all that terrible railway accident had left him. It was the only time they had been parted, even for a day, and his idolised, dainty wife, his tender, toddling child had been broken and burnt and tortured.

For long the red mists of Hell had surged round him; for a time he doubted, and refused to say, "The Lord giveth and the Lord taketh away; blessed be the name of the Lord." For a time his faith had reeled, and then he had bowed his head and but clung the closer to the Cross. Another had said, "Let this cup pass," and it had not passed. Another, sinful man, had spoken of a burden that was heavier than he could bear, yet in the end he had found strength to bear it.

The Reverend Adam, staggering a little in his weakness, followed those others, murmuring with ashen lips, "A broken and contrite heart, O God, Thou wilt not despise!" For Old John was right; there was something broken inside his master.

Sally stood beside her guardian looking on the loved faces. She had lived with them once. They had been so poor they could always manage to help others. Sally had been so much worse than orphaned; they knew of the bad, reckless blood in her, of the murky world from whence she had come, and put all their help and love and wisdom to the task of her salvation.

She leaned her cheek against his, her face somber enough now. "The heart knoweth its own bitterness," she breathed. "You and I know, Lovey. Perhaps we know too much: we have wisdom where we would have ignorance."

His eyes were fastened on those other faces and he did not heed.

Because he had neither eyes nor ears for her just then she could say what lay in her heart. "Lovey, it's as well others can't see inside, and all the little broken bits, and that we don't betray ourselves by rattling." She laughed softly, though she was not feeling amused. "Can every sort of break be mended?" she asked.

He turned at that. "Aye, in God's good time."

"In our own good time, I mean? After all, the present is all that we can be absolutely sure of."

"If I thought like that I could not bear life!" burst out Adam. "You pagans, as you call yourselves, have a terrible courage or recklessness. To write 'finis' to the love that has passed away, soul of our soul, heart of our heart, our flesh and our blood! Who could bear it?"

"We've got to bear it," returned Sally, setting her teeth.

"You will find a better and stronger faith than that, my dear."

She shook her head. "I am a materialist. I prefer the bird in the hand. No, the bad breaks are never mended." She took up an exquisite china cup. "Most perfectly mended by experts," she said, smiling rather oddly; "the break hardly visible unless you look too close—which is bad manners; but broken for all time, my dear, and shorn of value." She put it down abruptly, her eyes very dark and tragic.

Perhaps she thought of the Lunton history; a race born but to be broken. They all came badly to grief sooner or later, and Sally was the last of them. With her an old race passed. It remained with her to be faithful to the old tradition or to inaugurate a higher one. The Luntons never thought of anything but the desire of the moment, to be gained at any cost, or of anybody but themselves, though to do them justice they did not whine about the cost when it came to paying it. They were gay, unrepentant sinners to the end and most excellent company. If the men went to the devil they went like gentlemen; if the women were wanton they were fascinating and beautiful wantons. The motto of both was 'A good time'; they had their good time, which often meant a bad one in the eyes of the righteous, and turned up their toes with a jest.

Sally was the child of recklessness. The last male Lunton ran away with a chorus girl before he was twenty. A hasty marriage had been almost immediately followed by the birth of Sally. The young couple remained together till Sally was three. They lived on the mother's small stage earnings (the woman was pretty, but without talent and absolutely respectable), and what Philip Lunton made by showing pigeons 'life.' They knew a little more about 'life' when they were plucked bare, these pigeons.

Of course they lived in the underworld, that world which, with the exception of her visits to Helena Lovelady, Sally had known all her days. By the time she was three the tie binding her parents had worn very thin. It snapped suddenly; the violent infatuation came to its inevitably violent end. Philip Lunton conceived another passion—the Luntons were usually just in or out of some violent love affair—and departed with a lady to the continent, where pigeons gathered in plenty, and blackguards too.

Sally's mother struggled hard to keep herself and the child on her pitiful little earnings, and prayed God that a livelihood might be granted her. Sally was taken to the theatre and made a fuss of, and, thanks to soft hearts, always had enough to eat. For a time the struggle was desperate, then the woman was always 'resting'; she could get nothing. Others had as much beauty and talent, and were less particular. The years passed slowly, grindingly.

Just as Sally was beginning to suffer, fortune changed. The woman got no better parts, but prosperity smiled upon them; there was always a gentleman, sometimes in a carriage of his own, to drive them back from the theatre. Then came gentlemen with hired vehicles, and then ones without any, and less of comfort. It puzzled the child at first; later she grew to understand as much as a child may, and to take it all for granted. At ten years of age came the final scene: the woman, weary, broken, gasping out her life in a stuffy little room.

Adam Lovelady and his wife went to the funeral; Philip Lunton was too busy. He had also practically forgotten the little episode, or that he had a wife and child. They took Sally home with them. They found her worldly-wise in the worst sense of the word, and without the least idea of right or wrong. She was not immoral, merely unmoral.

"A regular Lunton," sighed Helena. "What a tragedy heredity can be!"

"Environment can work miracles, with love thrown in," Adam had said optimistically, and between them they had gone far to save the child.

But for her father they might have saved her altogether. When she was fourteen her father made a sudden appearance, took a fancy to her, and swept her off to his disreputable haunts. Sally was happy enough.

A year later he had to disappear for a time, and dispatched Sally to the Loveladys without a word. The girl of fifteen knew every form of evil at second-hand, and more or less took such things for granted. There were two worlds: the Loveladys', where one was happy and tried not to show certain knowledge or be too bad; and the other, where one tried to hide any knowledge of good or ideals. She was happy enough in both.

Gradually the evil memories grew dim, when back came her father again—and in funds. Why, Salome was almost grown up, and a beauty! She was wasted in a dull little hole of a village and a stuffy little vicarage. She must enjoy herself, see life! So he took her to Paris, dressed her up, and showed her life. It was all very gay and interesting, and while there was plenty of money she had no regrets, though she thought often of the Loveladys and cherished them in her heart.

Things got less rosy, money became short. It had been all ups and downs in her life, mostly downs, and she took her cheap artistic talent to a firm of cheap colour printers. When her father died, the week she was eighteen, she settled down in Paris with some of the friends she had made, less disreputable than her father's, perhaps, but by no means over-reputable, though kindly and generous. She was young and healthy, had a keen zest of life, and so she was happy.

Here she stayed for seven years, almost forgetting Adam Lovelady, though sighing, and misty-eyed, when she read his letters. She usually forgot to answer them; she was so very busy, working and playing.

When she was twenty-five she found herself badly in need of a rest. Then she remembered Little Crampton. She got fit in no time, but stayed four months, and then returned to Paris, promising to come back within a year.

Up to this time she had been reckless, but no more. In spite of examples all round her she remained immaculate in the one sense. She had flirted; she had never loved. Then the man came, and she loved in the mad, reckless, Lunton way, beyond all reason, becoming at the same time better and worse, happier and more unhappy.

The thing ended suddenly, with it everything in a sense ending, and now she sought no longer delirium, but safety, ease, respectability. If, according to the judgment of some, especially those Nature had placed by reason of appearance or temperament beyond the reach of temptation, she had been 'bad,' surely the wonder was, seeing all things, understanding all things, that she had been no worse! Temptation there had been in plenty, but only one love. To anything else she had not hauled down the flag.

Such was the girl who had come to marry a man she was sure would be dreadful—at the parting of the ways. On one side sordid starvation, or worse, on the other Mr. Bingley of the bank and comparative affluence. Sally was, after all, just like the rest of the world, with good and bad fighting for the victory from the cradle to the grave, somebody always judging or misjudging, but none ever knowing the ultimate gain or loss.

"What a long way off six years can seem," she said at length. Then she seemed to shake her dark mood from her, and tugged at Mr. Lovelady's sleeve. "I'm starving," she said; "what about supper?"

Mr. Lovelady sought Elizabeth. "The best you can do, and at once," he cried.

"I suppose it's love, sir?" asked Elizabeth. "I thought she hadn't got that new hair for nothing. Who is he, and when's it to be?"

"Tut, tut, Elizabeth; your mind is always running on matrimony!" reproved the parson.

Elizabeth, in no wise abashed, stared at him. "And what else should it run on, sir," she demanded, "seeing as how I'm still a spinster?"

Mr. Lovelady left the question unanswered. He never argued with Elizabeth; he knew better.

CHAPTER III

"Isn't there a man called Bingley?"

While Sally ate she asked questions. "Any new neighbours?" she enquired casually. "Isn't there a man called Bingley?"

"Mr. Bingley is the bank-manager," returned Mr. Lovelady, looking surprised; "I cannot understand how you have heard of him."

"Miss Maggie wrote to me, and I think she happened to mention someone of that name."

The vicar made a face. "That woman! Heaven forgive me for saying it, but she makes me think of a snake in the grass. She leaves her loathsome track over the fairest things."

"She hasn't a bad heart," returned Sally, still seeing Miss Maggie as one eager to help the more or less deserving to a prize. "She said he helped you."

"He does," assented Mr. Lovelady, though without enthusiasm; "he is, in fact, invaluable."

The girl's face sparkled wickedly. "He shan't be stopped in his sphere of usefulness," she grinned. "Have no fear. The modern husband and wife bring themselves up happily by seeing as little of each other as possible."

"Really, I cannot follow you," said the vicar, bewildered. "Besides, Bingley isn't married."

"Isn't he? But that's the sort of thing that may happen to a man any moment."

The Reverend Adam laughed. "Not any moment, to Bingley," he said; "he is not in the least that sort of man. He has been paying attentions to

Mrs. Dalton, a young widow, for a year, but he goes no further. Still, of course he—"

"Exactly," agreed Sally.

The man looked at her fondly. How attractive she was with that flush on her face, how unusual looking!

"He is an estimable man, most estimable—"

"As bad as all that! How you hate him, Lovey dear!"

"*Sally!*"

"Oh yes, you do. Even parsons are human. You like a person because you like him, not because he is worthy or unworthy. As a matter of fact the 'worthy' get precious little real liking. Marriage is a cramping little cage, but one's got to play the game inside it. It doesn't do to beat out one's life against its bars; it's better instead to learn to eat out of the captor's hand."

"Inconsequent as ever! What has that to do with Bingley? You used not to talk like that six years ago. I wish you wouldn't."

"Six years can mean so much burying."

He caught the flash of anguish in her eyes before the laughter crept back, and drew her to him. "My dear, tell me. Burying what?"

"Oh, only youth and illusions and a few absurd things like that; don't be afraid; the grave is deep enough."

He made her face him. "Sally, there is something—you have suffered?"

She shrugged her shoulders. "The usual lot, and possibly less than I deserve. How I should like to be done with suffering! There is so much I would like. A rich husband, for instance."

"Not without love, my dear."

"It's so easy to love the well-endowed, the opener of the gates of the world! Of course I should love him—within limits. Some people have a sort of tap inside them marked 'love,' which they can turn on or off at will. Well, I'll turn on the thin matrimonial trickle, not a river, but quite a pleasant little stream. He could hear it go tinkling, tinkling all the time."

"Marriage without love is horrible," said Mr. Lovelady gravely; "just a degradation instead of a happiness."

"The world is full of horrible things," answered Sally, "and after our first youth we've got to realise it, and suffer them all more or less gladly.

It is horrible when the valuable lives, when happy youth is taken, and the others left. This war reaping the youth and manhood and strength of the world, robbing us not only of this generation, but the next, is horrible, but it still rages on. God looks down from His high Heaven, but He does not put back the sword in its scabbard. Death is horrible, and life sometimes more horrible still."

"Sally, Sally, my dearest! What happened in those six years to make you talk like this?"

She laughed. "Perhaps it was what did not happen. Sometimes frustration and futility are the greater tragedies. But those years are dead things, and I am only concerned with the living. What shape is your Mr. Bingley? The name sounds distinctly circular."

"He isn't my Bingley," said Mr. Lovelady in a tone almost of irritation. "Why are you so curious about him?"

"Because he 'lay-reads' so beautifully."

He could have shaken her. "Are you never serious?"

"Not oftener than I can help," she returned truthfully. "It's one of the things I find uncomfortable, and have forsworn. I am a spinster of thirty-one, with the sowing of wild oats rather than the sewing of fine seams to my credit, and it's quite time I did."

"Did what?"

She looked at him under her long black lashes. "Oh, the usual thing."

"Turned over a new leaf?" he asked eagerly.

"Certainly there would have to be a new leaf—and the rest turned down. Is the Bingley fat?" she added inconsequently.

"Sally—"

"He is? Well, one can't have everything in a lay-reader."

"Not fat, a little plump, perhaps."

"Dear Christian, always so merciful! You must really introduce the man to me and I must do the civil to him. After all, it's very decent of him to work for nothing."

Mr. Lovelady looked at the face he found so attractive and lovable, and somehow the thought of introducing his helper to Sally found little favour in his sight. True, everybody expected Bingley to marry Mrs. Dalton sooner or later, but he hadn't seen Sally. In the Reverend Adam's eyes to see Sally was to admire her, as to know her was to love her. Suppose Bingley were attracted to her? Suppose Sally married him for the sake of a comfortable income? The idea was unthinkable. Sally must rise to higher things than this. Besides, she had not yet seen Alfred Bingley; that would be more than sufficient. He could not declare that she was altogether admirable, an angel, such as his wife had been, but she was at least proud and fastidious. Such as Bingley would have to admire in vain. He drew a long breath of relief.

It was then that Elizabeth opened the door. "Mr. Bingley in the study to see you, sir," she announced. "He says it's special."

"What a coincidence, just as we happened to be talking of him!" said Sally, rising and taking her guardian's arm, while to herself she murmured, "Oh, my prophetic soul, my husband!"

CHAPTER IV

"Gracious! What a husband for 'Mrs. Alfred Bingley'!"

"Don't you bother to come, dear," said the vicar. "I expect you'd rather unpack. It's only parish matters."

"Oh, no bother," said Sally; "I may as well get it over." To herself she added, "One likes to see one's relation by marriage at close quarters."

She pressed through the door at Adam's side, her cheeks very flushed, her eyes very bright, her hair a flame over her forehead.

"So this is the contents of the study!" she gasped to herself. "Gracious! what a husband for 'Mrs. Alfred Bingley'!"

Whatever her sense of dismay, she showed nothing of it. She stood with a careless wild grace waiting for the inevitable introduction, her black eyes modestly veiled in the presence of a member of the stronger sex. She had taken the measure of Mr. Alfred Bingley.

He did not quite take hers. He thought she was the most striking-looking girl he had ever seen. Was she not perhaps almost too striking-looking? The presence of the perfect woman should rather be felt than seen. He knew, of course, of her relationship to Mr. Lovelady.

He gave his most courtly, and portly, bow as Mr. Lovelady mumbled a reluctant introduction.

Sally tried to look as much like a clerical relation as possible. It was difficult, but not impossible—for Sally. She became most piquantly demure.

"How odd," she said, and gave her low, delicious laugh. "I have just been hearing how invaluable you are! How good of you to give up your priceless time, and how clever to be successful where so many have failed. You must be quite wonderful."

Mr. Bingley knew he was wonderful, but he sometimes doubted whether others knew it sufficiently well. He had sometimes thought it would be nice to be really appreciated. This girl realised at once; how sharp she must be!

She dropped carelessly, but gracefully, into a chair where she would appear at the best advantage, the light of the lamp shining on her hair, and listened respectfully while Mr. Bingley talked to the rather unresponsive vicar on parish matters. It was quite a lengthy treat. The speaker could feel her drinking in every word, and was in no hurry to snatch the cup from her lips.

With the exception of his wonderful mother, he believed the correct rôle of woman to be that of looker-on and listener. Too many of the modem type sought to seize the reins for themselves, to occupy too much of the stage; but this girl was obviously not of that type.

Sally folded her hands in her lap and showed just as much of her slim ankles as she thought Mr. Bingley would approve and admire, but not an inch more. Her hands and feet were beautiful, and she was quite aware of the fact.

"I am such a good-for-nothing creature," she sighed; "it makes me ashamed when I hear of all the wonderful work you are doing, running a bank—so complicated!—and the parish too!"

This was too much for Mr. Lovelady. "I—" he began.

"Yes, dear, I know," broke in his ward sweetly, "but you haven't a bank as well, you know. Think of all those rows and rows of figures, of adding them up right, of never getting Mr. Smith's account mixed with Mr. Brown's, and of not just using a little from here and there that nobody would miss. Really, it's extraordinary!" And she looked at Mr. Bingley with eyes very bright and reverential.

Though Mr. Bingley did not purr aloud, he knew perfectly well how a cat felt on being stroked the right way. He gave this charming girl an indulgent smile. He could not but feel that if she guessed the real intricacies and responsibilities of his position she would hardly be able to put her amazement into words. As for the matter of using money that did not belong to you because nobody would know, that was the true feminine standpoint. It was not so much that women were dishonest, as that they were not fitted for responsibility. Nature had designed them for other causes. To have given them the highest sense of honour and mentality, equal to a man's, would have been sheer waste. They must be womanly, essentially nice, entirely ignorant on certain matters, and a little dependent. And, of course, they must be attractive.

"One gets accustomed, one gets accustomed," he said modestly.

"If you *will* under-rate yourself—" Then she broke into a laugh; her laughter thrilled him, and made his pulses quicken.

Mr. Lovelady got hold of the conversation; it was obvious he was not pleased.

"Jealous," thought Mr. Bingley, preening himself. "Of course she's young enough to be his daughter. Still, he may think of marrying her, poor girl! Guardians do sometimes marry their wards, and he's no real relation. He plainly resents her enjoyment of the society of a man of the world. How narrow these parsons get; what a false idea of their own importance!"

"I suppose," wondered Sally plaintively, "there's nothing I could do? With the women and children I mean, of course, and the dear little babies. I could learn, you know." She looked engagingly up into Mr. Bingley's face.

Mr. Lovelady could not stand this outrageous hypocrisy. He knew Sally's opinion about young babies. "My dear," he protested, "you used to say that till they got over their 'rawness' they made you think of skinned rabbits."

"How young and crude I must have been!" sighed Sally.

"How ready to own her fault," thought the approving bank-manager. "One could train such a woman to do almost anything. She would be as wax in the hand."

He liked her small pointed chin. Mrs. Dalton had rather a heavy jaw.

A heavy jaw sometimes denoted pig-headed obstinacy, in a woman. He fell into deep thought. Sally had an air of race, of distinction. That lasted longer than mere beauty; it did a man credit. Mrs. Dalton narrowly missed being common looking. Her neck was too short and thick; she was too short and thick altogether, and at the best commonplace. Had he been rash to go so unthinkingly upon his way? It was a relief to remember he had not gone very far upon that way. Still, she was a very estimable person; and an eagle—when that eagle was of the male variety—could not, alas! always find another eagle to mate with; he must stoop to accomplish his matrimonial destiny. With Sally one would not stoop so far.

On the other hand, Mrs. Dalton had an estimable child and an estimable income. Miss Lunton's mouth looked charming when she laughed or smiled, but in its brief moments of repose it was too long and thin, almost determined-looking. Such hair and eyes were a startling combination; he could not feel sure his mother would approve. Then he knew Mrs. Dalton through and through, could read her like a book, and he had only just met the vicar's ward. "Life is very complicated, after all," he thought; "at least, for a man in my position."

Miss Lunton had not come out of a home; she had had her own flat and that sort of thing. It should, of course, make her the more eager and grateful for a home in the only sense of the word. On the other hand, she might have got 'notions.' Once or twice it had occurred to him that she looked like a woman with ideas. A most pernicious thing for a woman, ideas! Now Mrs. Dalton was quite devoid of a single idea. She was all sheer womanliness, tender, yielding. Still, Miss Sally Lunton might be yielding, in spite of the rather hard corners to her mouth; and gentle Mrs. Dalton had an obstinate chin. The one was safe, the other charming, and perhaps charm was a little dangerous—in a woman.

Sally, of course, knew she was being taken stock of, and guessed much that was passing in the bank-manager's mind. She had delivered her own verdict within five minutes of entering the room.

"Awful," she decided, "and not so easy as I anticipated. It will mean the strenuous life and no mistake, and caution, caution all the way. Still, it's got to be done."

She felt sure her future husband had no vices, but then had he any virtues? Was it all weaknesses and limitations? The single vice would have been so much less irritating. A vice usually left intervals; these other things had none. Vanity, egotism, pomposity took no hours off; neither did narrowness, meanness, prejudice. On the other hand she felt sure he was honourable, truthful, and could be 'got at' through the very weaknesses she detested, and perhaps there were dormant possibilities only waiting to be called forth—and perhaps not!

His appearance held no thrills, unless, as far as Sally was concerned, a thrill of aversion. He was plump and thick, and his legs were very short. He had a fat, pasty face, shrewd little eyes, a blunt nose, and a tiny, rather pursed-up mouth. He would have been growing bald if his hair had not been so grown and brushed as to cover the denuded spots.

When the question of heights came up he was in the habit of saying casually, if asked, "Oh, I suppose about five nine or ten," and really managed, by avoiding measurement, to suppose it. If most women over a certain age, flattering themselves they do not look it, will lie deliberately about their age, regarding it as the one lie permissible to the most honest nature, so will most men under a certain height exaggerate their inches. Only the girl not past the summer of her days, or the man close to the six-foot mark, are strictly truthful on such matters.

A shudder seized upon the girl. How much easier if the victim had been young and handsome and delightful, though still the same abomination in essentials! Then she shook herself free of the influence that would hold her back. "One can put up with any decent-living man, provided there's money," she reminded herself; "and he's busy enough and out enough. Kismet! what of the other alternative? Would that be easier, the end a sort of peace?"

Yes, she would go on, and to the bitter end. She was sorry he was no fool; that made it easier, if the other made it seem more creditable. So she smiled up winningly into his face, and encouraged him to talk about himself. Not that he needed so very much encouragement; oneself was somehow so different, almost unique.

Mr. Lovelady broke into a touching discourse rather brusquely, and practically ushered Mr. Bingley out of the house, thereby playing into Sally's hands. He did not wonder that the bank-manager was so attracted; it was just what he had feared, but he resented Sally's attitude. He said as much.

Sally opened innocent eyes. "But I had to be civil to the creature after all he is doing for us."

"You were almost more than civil. I should be sorry if Bingley got—got ideas."

Sally laughed. "Oh, the Bingleys never get ideas," she said, purposely misunderstanding.

"Bingley has been made rather a lot of in Little Crampton. He is not without vanity."

"Are any of us? Well, I must go and unpack."

Mr. Bingley went home treading on air. He was conscious of a spring feeling in the atmosphere, and that he was feeling younger than he had done for some time, almost dashing, indeed. The Reverend Adam had made Sally seem so much like forbidden fruit, and as a strong man who liked his own way, and of course always got it, Mr. Bingley played with the temptation of snatching the apple out of the Reverend Adam's hand.

Not that he was going to do anything in a hurry. Certainly not. He would be most careful in every way, and prove Sally to the hilt before he paid her the least attention. If she were the type that paid the attention he would snub her at once and decide upon Mrs. Dalton.

Secretly he did not approve of Mr. Lovelady. He was too easy with the sinners of the parish, and inclined to let everybody off too lightly. Consequently they went and did it again, and Mr. Lovelady was as much to blame as anybody. The Reverend Adam played with the backslider's child as heartily as he played with others. Mr. Bingley did not hold that these proofs of sin should not be played with, far from it, but he did think they should be played with rather differently. Neither should the unmarried mother be greeted quite the same as the true spouse; she must be chastened.

He thought of Sally all the way home, but, as was seemly, he dismissed her when he rang for the servants and prayers, and thought of nothing but their good, and hoped they were taking advantage of their rare opportunities.

Before going upstairs he opened a fat, beautifully-bound volume, with *The Book* simply and modestly inscribed in big gold letters upon it. To him it came next the Bible and long before the classics. Mr. Bingley could not approve of the classics. *The Book* should really have been entitled *A Son's Guide to Matrimony* or to celibacy. He turned to the page of wisdom that had been allotted to the day. The late Mrs. Bingley possessed the art of being always topical. She was almost too topical for her son's liking.

"*Never trust a woman with yellow hair and dark eyes*" was the first he read; "*either there is something abnormal, and to be avoided, or else art has stolen what nature has forbidden. Such women are dangerous.*"

"Mother was a wonderful woman," sighed Mr. Bingley, almost regretfully; "her genius told her what I should be called upon to face."

He faced the next extract, a facer indeed!

"*Never think of a woman for yourself; think of her first and last as the mother of your children.*"

"Ah!" breathed Mr. Bingley, "how sacred! How like mother!"

He lapsed into deep thought. He manfully acknowledged that he was attracted by Sally, but was it a mere selfish attraction? What about the little bank-manager? A mother with black eyes and yellow hair was a risk. Marriage for a man placed in his solemn position must ever mean duty before pleasure.

Then her age? He was forty-one; Sally, he calculated, only about ten years his junior. A man in his prime does not want a middle-aged wife. In ten years' time Miss Lunton would be middle-aged; he would be still in his prime.

He had discovered, through a slip she had made, that Mrs. Dalton could not be more than twenty-seven, and, also through a slip, that she had a nice little income of her own. Then Nina Dalton would make a most creditable step-daughter, and he was really fond of her. So far nothing had appeared in his mother's book absolutely to dispose of Mrs. Dalton. True she had said, "*Beware of widows who are young, or look it; they soon discover a man's weaknesses,*" but as he had no weaknesses to be discovered, there was no danger there.

He pursed up his mouth till it was no more than a button, dipping here and there, hoping to find something which implied it would be his duty to marry Sally. Instead he found a host of pitfalls.

"*A fat woman is a fool, or she wouldn't be fat,*" announced the drastic lady; "*but it's the lean women who have the devil in them.*"

Mr. Bingley did not say "Damn." He never used such words, but he buttoned his mouth a little tighter, and his small eyes held a resentful gleam. Lean! It wasn't a pretty word; few of the great writer's were. Miss Lunton was slim and tall and graceful; surely that was not equivalent to harbouring the devil. Neither was Mrs. Dalton fat—he hated fat people; Boliver, for instance, was an atrocity—a little stumpy, perhaps. He felt to the full the problems he was called upon to face. How simple for the average man!

"*A woman who will show no more than the tip of her shoe is just as likely to be cursed with big feet as undue modesty.*"

His eyes lightened; his mouth came undone. Sally had shown the perfect mean, modest and yet attractive, and beautiful feet and ankles. On the other hand, Mrs. Dalton had a careless way of catching up her dress on a muddy day that exposed far too much for modesty, her legs being what they were. His great mother was asking him to take Sally to his bosom.

He worked down the page, hoping for further signals pointing the right way.

"*A woman who can't, or won't, say 'boo' to a goose before marriage, will say more than 'boo' afterwards.*"

Mr. Bingley had never met the type of woman that could not say 'boo' to a goose, and did not believe they existed. He was of the opinion that even the most delightful women talked too much. Yet Miss Lunton hadn't; she listened, and how perfectly!

His fat forefinger ran down the index for the word 'Listen,' and of course found it. The index alone comprised a dictionary.

"*They act listeners beforehand who will quickest change the rôle afterwards.*"

That could be stopped almost before it had time to begin. The silent strong man puts his foot down once, and all is as it should be thereafter. Mr. Bingley smiled pursily.

Then he looked at the clock and waited for it to strike eleven. No matter whether he felt tired or extremely awake, as long as he was at home, he gathered up himself and *The Book* at the striking of the hour and went upstairs. He was in bed as the clock struck half-past, *The Book* on the table by his side; asleep as it struck twelve.

Such was the admirable Alfred Bingley.

On this occasion, however, he broke a fixed habit. It was nearly half an hour beyond the usual time before he got to sleep, and even then he dreamt of forbidden fruit in the shape of black eyes, yellow hair, and divine ankles. And a low delicious laugh sounded through his dreams.

He awoke suddenly, shocked horror in all his being. He had been pursuing Sally over moor and mountain, and by the glaring impropriety of moonlight!

"This won't do," he gasped. "What would mother say?"

He switched on his electric candle and opened *The Book* to see, looking up 'Dream' in the index.

What Mrs. Bingley thought, she said, and in no unmeasured terms.

"*When it comes to dreaming of a woman, it's time to beware.*"

He decided to dream of Sally no more, and went to sleep firm in that resolve. Alas, that this godly, upright man should have such an evil dream! He married both the candidates, and was most comfortable! His horror on waking is too poignant for description. He had been so ideally happy, so content! He had not minded doing wrong, or even thought of it; it had merely seemed such an excellent way of solving the problem.

CHAPTER V

"You needn't be afraid your nose will ever be put out of joint!"

Meanwhile Sally, whose ears should certainly have been burning, slept the sleep of the just, or the unjust, digestion counting more than conscience in these matters.

Mrs. Dalton was not asleep; she was doing sums. She found out that her appearance of prosperity could be carried on until about June. Her chin looked very dogged as she shut up her account-book. "By the middle of June at latest," she decided. Then she also slept; she had not yet heard that there was a serious rival in the field. She had kissed Nina, who looked adorable in her flushed slumber. "You shall have that pony and a fair chance in life, my precious," she murmured, "and you needn't be afraid your nose will ever be put out of joint."

It was Mr. Lovelady who got no sleep at all. He could not help worrying about Sally. If anything happened to him—and as he and his doctor knew, something might happen any hour—what would become of Sally? He had nothing to leave her. She never expected to earn another penny with her brush. She declared the war had finished 'the minnows' for good and all. What did become of such women? A ghastly question, and a ghastly problem! Some of them dragged out grey lives up and down the stairs of others. At the thought of Sally's 'old lady' he smiled. No old lady would have Sally, neither would Sally take upon herself, for a few pounds per annum, and board and lodging, a burden few are strong enough to bear. It would be uncomfortable, and Miss Lunton never permitted herself to be uncomfortable. Her flair was all for the flesh-pots; self-sacrifice had never entered into her life.

"Why," asked the Reverend Adam almost peevishly, "aren't there enough good and suitable men for all women? Why have they to marry the others, or remain unmarried?" Then he hurried away from a question that implied discontent with the world as God had made it. Sally was different from other women, so very attractive, and under the cynical surface, he felt sure, lay wonderful treasures of heart and mind.

"If I died to-morrow she would starve, or—"

He traced that 'or' no further. He knew Sally was not of those who starve. She would find some sort of a primrose path for herself, and tread gaily over the hidden thorns, saying with a laugh, "After all, one can't have everything."

He longed to know her safe, to see her rising to her higher self. The Luntons were never safe. It was very wrong of her to have her hair changed, but he had a sneaking admiration for it all the same, and men were men. They always turned to look at Sally, and she was of the type which looks back.

"Why isn't there a good and suitable man?" demanded the vicar again. "It's simply disgraceful!" Then he remembered his cloth, and corrected himself. "I mean most unfortunate." He jerked about in bed and ejaculated, "Oh, bother Bingley! I knew he would be taken with her!"

What would Sally make of her life minus the saving clause of happy love? Soon she would be middle-aged. Middle-age was a drab time for a woman alone, and many a woman's life had been made drab by the lack of her own home, some work and interest, some place to fill in life. "A beastly time" Sally had once called it, and he had not contradicted her. He had seen so many going through it, and it had seemed—yes, beastly. It wasn't a clerical word, but it was a fact. '

Sometimes he wondered if he knew everything about her. She never brought him the depths to look into; she faced those alone. Sometimes she crawled painfully up to the heights, but not for long.

“It makes me feel so winded, dear,” she explained inelegantly; “the air’s too rarefied to keep this Sally alive.”

“She must be good, because she’s always pretending to be bad,” he reflected thankfully. Sally must win out in spite of her family history, somehow ‘make good.’ He would be content to live a little longer if he could see that. “If Helena had been here to help!” he sighed, as he sighed a dozen times a day. Nothing had ever gone wrong when his Helena was alive, or if it had he had not noticed it. But Sally must work out her own salvation. Another could help, but no other could save.

CHAPTER VI

"You can put on your boots without a chair"

On Sundays in Little Crampton everybody went to church in their best clothes. Sally's were Parisian and, though quiet enough, held the gratified eye.

"Nobody could say I don't look suitable for a bank-manager's wife," she told herself, putting a little pink powder on her face and drawing down a coquettish veil. "I'm dying to see Mrs. Dalton and learn the worst. I wonder if Lovey would let me have one of those new short, wide skirts. I believe he'd like it." The 'he' did not refer to the vicar.

Owing to his official position Mr. Bingley had to be early at church. Mrs. Dalton also had to start early, because, of course, Nina's short legs wanted plenty of time upon the journey.

Consequently, as Mr. Bingley passed Vine Cottage it was not unusual to see its inhabitants just ahead. Mrs. Dalton still had her husband's field-glasses. She wished she could take them to church, for Miss Maggie had been telling her about Sally and the length of time Mr. Bingley had spent at the vicarage on the night of her arrival. She was glad to remember that she had a priceless asset in Nina.

Mr. Bingley liked to walk to church between the nice-looking widow and Nina, who adored him. It gave him a sort of sacred sense of paternal and conjugal importance without the responsibility—or the expense. He had played with the idea of walking thus through life—at least, of him and Nina doing so; Mrs. Alfred Bingley would be more often concerned with things of the nursery; that was the true woman's sphere. His love for children was perfectly genuine; to them he could unbend, become a natural man.

Nina was a sharp child and eight years of age, her mother having, of course, married as a 'mere child.' She narrowly missed being stumpy, but one likes little girls rosy and plump and soft. Her tongue was long and pointed—her mother had just such another—and seldom ceased. Though Mr. Bingley liked to talk himself, he would still vacate the stage for the sake of a child's prattle. He encouraged Nina to open her innocent, curious heart to him, and though she sometimes came out with awkward things, as children will, he managed as a rule to stem the worst. To-day he was a little absent; he was wondering if Sally would be in church.

He greeted Mrs. Dalton and captured the child's plump hand. Then he dropped it to tie up his bootlace, giving a faint groan as he essayed the difficult feat.

"Mother creaks just like that," said Nina, interested, "but *she* uses a chair. Don't you use a chair?"

Mr. Bingley did, but he managed to evade a reply.

Nina's errant attention was caught by figures coming round the curve. "Oh, it's Mr. Lovelady," she cried, delighted, "and such a lovely lady with him! Oh, I hope they'll stop! Oh, she *is* nice!"

Mr. Bingley's heart gave a mighty bound; Mrs. Dalton's fell.

Then came the introduction, Sally staying behind, while Mr. Lovelady went on to the church.

The rivals smiled, taking each other's measure in a glance, and fearing it. They knew it was going to be a grim struggle to the death, and yet they were attracted instantly, and wished it might have been friendship. How delightful to have laughed together over the situation, and that absurdity, Mr. Alfred Bingley.

As it was, the chin of one and the mouth of the other showed doggedly. They were on different sides. Fate had made them combatants against their will, and fight to the bitter end they must, but each knew the other would fight fair. Sally already knew what it was like to be on the rocks, and the other woman was not without imagination. She guessed; she could feel them sharp and pitiless, while a wild sea, that meant the end of all, washed ever higher; and she was not only fighting for herself, she was fighting for her child. It was literally victory or extinction.

Sally saw a stumpy woman with a lovely complexion, nice hair and features, and rather shrewd brown eyes. She obviously cultivated womanliness for Mr. Bingley's benefit, but she was essentially commonplace, almost common. She might have come from one of the farms, or out of one of the village shops. Sally could only have come of distinction. After her looks were gone that would go down with her to the grave.

The contrast was almost violent. Beside Sally's long, lean elegance and Parisian clothes Mrs. Dalton looked her very worst; shorter, thicker, dowdy. She knew it, and knew that Mr. Bingley must know it. Still, there was always Nina.

Nina had already made friends with Sally. She knew she must never express an unflattering remark aloud, but she never got scolded for the others.

"I like you," she began instantly, "your shape and your clothes, and your tallness, and how you walk. Don't you, Mr. Bingley?" Her instinct told her that Mr. Bingley did.

Mrs. Dalton sighed.

"I like your shoes," the child went on, "they're so small and high. *You* can put on your boots without a chair. I like your legs," she continued innocently, "don't you, Mr. Bingley?"

Mr. Bingley flamed.

Sally gave her seductive laugh.

"I like your hair, and your big black eyes, though they are just like the wicked fairy's in my book."

Mrs. Dalton felt this was better; she hoped Mr. Bingley would notice that Miss Lunton's eyes were distinctly wicked.

"And I simply *love* your laugh!" added the child.

Sally laughed again. This innocent worship was sweet to her.

"I even like your mouth, though it's dreadful big, isn't it? because it curls up all twisty at the corners. Don't *you* love her mouth, Mr. Bingley?"

Again Mr. Bingley flamed. He would not tell a lie to save himself from disaster, or burden his white soul for a friend in direst need, or to save the Empire. He did love Sally's mouth, and everything that was hers, but he knew he mustn't; his mother's dead, though undying, voice, most solemnly warned him.

"I like everything she is," went on the small enthusiast, "but specially her laugh and her legs. So different to mine—and mother's."

Mr. Bingley, redder than the reddest rose, broke and fled in utter confusion.

The two women struggled for gravity, and then, their twinkling eyes meeting, laughed out loud. They went into church.

Mr. Bingley tried not to think of indelicate matters during Divine Service, yet the contrast noted by the child would occur and recur. He was shocked at himself; he felt almost wanton.

"It shows I must avoid her," he thought. To see what he must avoid his eyes went again and again to Sally, as Mrs. Dalton and Miss Maggie Hopkins knew, without the trouble, apparently, of even glancing at Mr. Bingley.

In the doctor's pew stood a fine, well-set-up lad in the uniform of a private. This was Douglas Hill, the doctor's eldest son. Sally looked across at him and smiled. His face lit up and he beamed back at her.

Mr. Bingley bit his lips. This was unsuitable behaviour in the sacred edifice. Mrs. Dalton would never do such a thing. He forced himself to give attention to Mr. Lovelady's always brief sermon. He did not think very much of the vicar's sermons, and knew he himself could do infinitely better; yet he realised that Mr. Lovelady was doing his very best, that it was not his fault if he was not as highly gifted as some, and listened indulgently. He preferred dogma in the pulpit to humanity, and Mr. Lovelady was distinctly human.

With whom should he walk home, Miss Lunton or Mrs. Dalton? Even Paris had scarce a harder choice. Perhaps, as lay-reader, he had better lend the light of his countenance to Mr. Lovelady. If Miss Lunton chose to accompany her guardian home, that committed Mr. Bingley to nothing. He would not encourage the girl; she should realise it was the vicar he was walking with. She would probably ask him to come round the garden when they reached the vicarage, but he would refuse, firmly, if kindly. He would show temptation what a poor chance it had against Alfred Bingley, Esquire, of the bank. He never had any need to run away from the devil; it was rather the devil who fled him.

He would not exchange many words with her, either; he would be strongly silent, and at the gate almost grim—the silent, strong man, in fact. If Miss Lunton fell in love with him it would be due to no encouragement on his part. To look up to a man is good for women, and they were not always able to realise it; silent strength was ever their ideal. How the men chattered and gossiped at the Little Crampton Club; one was hardly able to get a word in! That fat fool Boliver and disagreeable Paton were two of the worst offenders.

Sally and he, Douglas Hill, and Miss Maggie and Miss Lydia Hopkins came out of church together, exchanging greetings.

Miss Maggie, abnormally thin, with a pinched face, long, pointed nose, pointed ears, thin and acid of mouth, gimlet-eyed, was the first to speak as they got outside.

"Oh, Sally, how pleased you must have been when your dull brown hair turned into that lovely yellow! Was it very difficult?"

"Not at all," said Sally calmly; "I just had my head X-rayed and that's what happened."

"What was wrong with your head?"

"They were afraid of homicidal mania," said Sally gravely.

Mr. Bingley frowned. So, strictly speaking, her hair was partly artificial.

"What a charming sermon," gushed Miss Maggie; "I always say that if people would do what Mr. Lovelady told them, though telling is easier than doing, Little Crampton would be quite ideal. I like that one about Lot's wife best, and never turning back, whoever or whatever you are going for." She looked at Sally.

Then Douglas Hill drew the girl away, and Mr. Bingley, with a sense of outrage, saw them go and sit on a distant stile, and heard her call him "Duggie." He had been quite prepared to remove the temptation from his own path without any outside interference. A raw youth of twenty! True, in the foolish eyes of women, a goodly youth enough, handsome and tall and muscular.

Mr. Bingley had not been pleased about the war. It seemed, and most unjustly, to push him a little out of the limelight. The women became hysterical over khaki. Their eyes never lingered on black coats, did not indeed see them, when the uniform was there! The country went mad over youth and physical efficiency, grit and sacrifice.

He was over the age limit and he had a conscience. To call himself an official thirty-eight, as many men well over forty were doing, was a lie, and one he would be no party to. Imagine being killed with a lie almost fresh on one's lips! He was not a coward, but he was sensible, and not of the stuff from which heroes and sacrifices were made. There is always the man who will cling to ease and the soft job through thick and thin, and while leaving the heat and burden of the day to others, claim the same wages. Of such was Mr. Bingley. He considered he was doing equal service to the State by retaining his easy billet, investing his private income, and drawing his modest salary. He called it keeping his head in an emergency.

He was glad to think that as an observer he could take the wider, more Imperial, view of things, and that he was not cramped by being a mere and prejudiced participator. 'Business as usual' was, of course, his favourite platitude; it never wore too thin for him. In an expansive moment he had tried on a friend's uniform, but he had fitted very tightly in it, and found it neither comfortable nor becoming.

He could not understand why a uniform should transform a man in a woman's eyes. It seemed to go straight to their heads. There was Sally, Miss Lunton, fussing over that swaggering, lanky boy. If only women had more ballast! Naturally every man of sense got himself born a Briton; at the same time the price of greatness left him cold. The clarion call to arms, and yet again to arms, fell on deaf ears. Dash it all, there were plenty of lads without responsibilities in the country, of no economic value; let them go!

If the Bingleys were in the majority, rather than the minority, Britain must have been in the dust long ago.

It is unnecessary to add that he had said that no raid by air or sea of the sacred shores would ever be possible. When the impossible happened he blamed the Government. When disaster on land and sea fell like a thunder-clap on the nation he blamed the leaders. He explained how differently, and much more successfully, he would have carried out affairs, aye, and ended the war by this!

"These raw lads are getting very spoilt, I'm afraid," he said pompously to Miss Maggie.

"They aren't all so raw," she returned. "There are two in Douglas's regiment over forty, men of good position, too."

"My dear lady, you must admit a man of forty doesn't get his head turned."

Miss Maggie tittered. "Perhaps not; only once it starts turning it simply *whizzes*. There's no fool like an old fool."

Mr. Bingley kept his temper. He even condescended to explain that forty was manhood's prime.

Fat little Mr. Boliver, having greeted Sally with enthusiasm, came bounding up to them. Mr. Bingley smiled graciously. He liked standing by Boliver, the fat fool! it made him feel so tall and slim; just as he disliked standing by young Hill, because it was then young Hill who seemed so tall and slim.

"Smart, strapping fellow," said Mr. Boliver, alluding to Douglas; "plucky young devil, lucky young devil! Ha, Bingley, our time is over for that sort of thing," he looked at the figures by the stile and sighed, "if it ever existed."

Mr. Bingley was furious. Mr. Boliver looked every day of fifty, but he was actually the bank-manager's junior by three months.

Miss Maggie was glad she had written to Sally.

"We old fools have to stay at home," complained the man of big heart and little tact, "just cumbering the ground, having had our time, while the bright boys with their careers ahead, and life untasted, go out to face the music. It seems low-down, hardly the game. What use are we ?"

The question was an outrage, and Mr. Bingley was incapable of reply.

What use, indeed! Had the fool no glimmer of intelligence? What of the bank, of the future little bank-manager, that sacred charge? No use, indeed! He made a strange noise in his throat, and met Miss Maggie's gimlet-eyes. *What* a woman!

Miss Lydia looked hopelessly in front of her. She was not listening; she was not interested. She seldom did listen, seldom was interested; she never crossed the threshold of life. She had only wanted one thing, and to her failure had meant an agony and a humiliation that could not be borne. Her history was written in her face, and in a few lines. She had been pretty once. She had looked for this prettiness to bring her everything, and to that alone. It had brought her nothing. Her two plain sisters got their joy out of life; she got anguish.

Miss Maggie pinched her arm. "Do wake up, Lydia!" she commanded.

"Mind you, I tried to do my little bit," went on that absurd creature, Boliver, "but the fellar laughed in my face, or rather, pardon me, ladies, at my stomach. You're not as bad as all that, Bingley—yet; they could train you down a bit, old son."

"You seem to think a bank takes care of itself," remarked Mr. Bingley, grey with fury.

"Well, they could send some old crock to play round with it till you returned, couldn't they?" Mr. Boliver did not in the least mean to be offensive; he merely had rather an unfortunate way of expressing himself. He did not mean 'crock' as Mr. Bingley took it up, merely someone a few years older.

"They don't put crocks in banks, Boliver," almost hissed Mr. Bingley.

"They must put them somewhere at such a time," persisted Mr. Boliver; "stands to reason. Why not the banks?"

Mr. Bingley choked again.

"Then school-mistresses have offered the flappers, nice gels, too—"

This was more than the affronted bank-manager could bear. He turned his back.

Mr. Boliver saw another friend, and rolled off happily.

Then Mr. Lovelady appeared and looked about for Sally. About time, Mr. Bingley considered. Sally came up flushed and smiling, a delightful picture. Mr. Bingley decided to favour her with his company, after all; he badly needed stroking the right way.

"How Douglas grows," said the vicar to his ward; "you found a change, Sally, eh? Just a kid when you used to bowl to him. We must have him up."

This was not stroking Mr. Bingley the right way. "Everybody seems almost too ready to make a fuss, seeing how vain the modern lad is," he said, mortified.

Mr. Lovelady turned on him with most unclerical fire in his blue eyes. "Where would the country be, save for these same 'vain' lads?" he asked; "or you and I, and all of us here? If we cannot go are we to deny them gratitude? Is it vain to offer up the greatest of all earthly possessions? Do they go because they love fighting and pain and death? Is there any greater sacrifice? 'Greater love hath no man than this—'"

"Go it, Lovey," whispered Sally, delighted, "let him have it fairly in the neck!" Mr. Bingley's attitude disgusted her.

The unhappy Bingley felt almost overwhelmed, but he stuck manfully to his guns. "Many of the—the conditions are to be deplored," he began; "drink—"

"The God of Battles will judge them, Bingley," answered Mr. Lovelady, his eyes still blazing, "that's not for you or me."

The poor bank-manager tried to fall into step with Sally. Sally ignored him.

Mr. Lovelady took her arm, marching her on ahead, leaving the lay-reader to escort the Misses Hopkins. "I'm a poor Christian," he groaned; "I could have cheerfully felled that man to the earth, and—and then have jumped upon him." He groaned contritely. "Who am I to preach to others?"

"Oh, Mr. Bingley has his Waterloo to come, don't you worry," she returned easily.

At the vicarage gate the others caught up to them. Mr. Bingley waited expectantly for Sally's invitation. After all, the vicarage garden was very charming.

Sally gave a careless nod to the Misses Hopkins, an even more careless one to Mr. Bingley, and turned to go into the house with her guardian.

There was nothing for it but to depart. Nothing had turned out in the least as the ruffled man had expected. He had been so well prepared to resist temptation, and temptation had not offered itself for resistance. It had hardly played the game.

CHAPTER VII

"I hope I don't disturb your rest?"

Seeing that their ways lay together and Mr. Bingley was always the 'perfect gentleman,' there was nothing for it but to accompany the Misses Hopkins.

Lydia looked on the ground, her eyes hopeless. On her fiftieth birthday she had, to quote her sister, "ceased to struggle—and about time, too!" Maggie had never wanted to marry; she disliked men. Grace had always been set on farming. She was short and fat and jolly, and enjoyed every moment of her hard-working life.

"Sally does look nice in her new hair," observed Maggie, "don't you think so, Mr. Bingley? But how funny she will look when it gets streaky, as artificial hair always does. How thin she has grown, too! She will be as thin as me in a year or two."

Acidity had left the speaker a revolting skeleton. Her bones seemed to clank as she walked.

Mr. Bingley found the prospect unpleasant.

"Of course you know her father was the last of the 'wild Luntons'?"

"Of Castle Lunton? Yes," assented Mr. Bingley; "she must be connected with half the peerage." Surely his mother would appreciate that!

"Not much use when the peerage repudiates you," smiled Miss Maggie, "and there isn't a cent. The castle and everything passed out of the family in Sally's grandfather's time. He was a nice one, if you like, but his son was worse. They always get worse as they go along. Sally is absolutely the last. Besides," this was what she had been leading up to, "her mother was a chorus girl, and *you* know—"

She gave a modest little giggle, but managed to mention the close dates of wedding and christening.

Mr. Bingley's face was reward enough. A chorus girl grandmother for the little bank-manager! A chorus girl with a scandal attached!

"I don't know how they can," went on Miss Maggie; "hardly anything on, and lots of unmarried men there! I should feel so indelicate like that."

She would indeed have been indelicate 'like that,' though perhaps more through lack of flesh than of clothes.

Mr. Bingley permitted himself a quick smile. How humourless women were!

"I don't know what will become of the poor girl if she doesn't get married; and it isn't so easy these days."

Mr. Bingley became a trifle cattish. "It's usually easy when they are young and attractive," he said loftily. "It would be impertinent to doubt Miss Lunton's ability to get married if she wished to."

Miss Maggie was annoyed. Was she helping Sally to her victim? "There's marrying and marrying," she said, "and Sally is such an outrageous flirt. That's how Mr. Boliver got married so suddenly. She makes fools of people. I wonder what she would do if anything happened to Mr. Lovelady? He looks quite ill sometimes, and twice lately I've met him coming out of the doctor's house. She would be in a mess and no mistake, but perhaps she'll think of *some* way out in time."

They came in sight of the Red House, the only property of any size in the neighbourhood. It belonged to a Mrs. Randal, a rich widow.

"Why, the blinds are down," exclaimed the sharp-sighted Miss Maggie. "Then she must be dead at last. I'm sure she's taken time enough, and made fuss enough, too, though of course Dr. Hill would encourage that sort of thing. I wonder where all her money will go? Cats, of course."

"She has crowds of nephews on both sides of the house," said Miss Lydia listlessly.

"She hated all her relations, and would have nothing to do with them. Must be so trying to be disliked by the rich relation, and perhaps liked by the poor ones. She wouldn't even have me in the house; Mr. Lovelady was her only visitor. It's to be hoped he's not counting on getting anything. Parsons are always such beggars, in both senses of the word."

Mr. Bingley flushed with indignation. "Mr. Lovelady is almost too unworldly," he retorted, "and the country ought to give its clergy a living wage."

"Men always count on something; it's not for want of counting they are disappointed."

"And do women never count on anything?" asked Mr. Bingley majestically.

"Only on husbands," snapped Miss Maggie, feeling her sister wince; "and they are usually more disappointed than ever when they've got one." As usual she had the last word.

Soon after the mid-day dinner Mr. Lovelady departed to the Sunday-school.

Sally unearthed a French novel, more witty than moral, and a box of cigarettes, and collecting all the cushions in the room, curled herself up on the drawing-room sofa.

She began to yawn, then she dozed. In her dreams the past gripped her and she sang for joy. Jimmy whistled the tune that came nearest to "Annie Laurie." Then the whistling ceased, and everything else seemed to cease. It would all be silence now, and she knew her heart was broken.

She came out of her dream and the heartache, and wiped her wet eyes and wet cheeks. "Sally, you silly ass!" she cried, "how often must I tell you that the past is without profit, and that you are *not to do it!*" She was resentful, because, though she could command the waking hours, she had no jurisdiction over the others. She shook sleep from her eyelids and, lighting a cigarette, plunged into her book.

It was just at this moment that something pointed out to a very astonished lay-reader that he was entering the vicarage gate, the hall, and, *via* Elizabeth, the drawing-room, to find, most extraordinary happening of all, that Miss Lunton was there, and alone! He had no idea how it had all come about; his legs had simply insisted upon bringing him.

Sally acted with great presence of mind. She knew that Bingleys never permit their women to smoke the mildest of cigarettes or read the mildest (comparatively speaking) of French novels. She crushed the lighted cigarette between the pages of the novel and sat on both.

"How explain it if I catch fire?" she wondered.

Mr. Bingley stooped stiffly over Sally and shook her hand. "Good afternoon. What a lovely spring day!" he said. "I hope I don't disturb your rest?"

Sally looked up at him with eyes that tears had softened, and a flush on her cheeks where the salt tears had stung them. No, Mr. Bingley hadn't disturbed her rest; that part would never be his. She told no more than the truth when she said, "Oh no, I am glad to see somebody." She gave a slight jerk, so that she could come down more violently upon the book. She thought she smelt burning. Ah, it was out now, thank goodness!

Mr. Bingley sniffed. Sally liked strong Turkish cigarettes.

"Yes, isn't it naughty of Lovey? All over the house! But of course one can't grudge men their masculine pleasures," said the noble Sally.

"One respects a lady's drawing-room, though," returned Mr. Bingley, with equal nobility. He would.

He studied Sally, unobserved, as he thought. No, her hair showed no signs of streakiness. It was just untarnished yellow flame. Naturally other women would say things. It was such a petty, jealous sex!

Her pointed chin was absolutely fascinating, and not in the least obstinate. If her mouth was wide the lips were finely cut as a gentlewoman's should be, not in the least thick, and it *did* curl at the corners. Her teeth were perfect, and her own. There was one of Mrs. Dalton's he strongly suspected. His own were all his by purchase, but so well done that he knew nobody could ever discover it. Miss Maggie, however, had said before he had been a week in Little Crampton, "Not one of his own."

What a lovely little aquiline nose Sally had! A sheer delight, neither too large nor too small. Mrs. Dalton's was too large, and of no special shape. His own was short and thick, and rather by way of being a button. Consequently it was necessary to be particular about noses.

Perhaps Sally failed a trifle in her forehead. It was like her chin, narrow and pointed, and too high; it would have been a disfigurement but for the skillful way she trained her hair low down upon it, shortening it by an inch. In her jerk of surprise at seeing him (he had observed the jerk) she had revealed a very long length of slim ankles. Ankles should not be too vital in a wife, but when she crossed a muddy road, or perhaps wore one of the new wide, short skirts he saw illustrated, they would come in rather useful. After all, the right sort of legs were essential in the future Mrs. Alfred Bingley. Slimness was, of course, essential for any mode, and she was just the right height.

Yes, the physical qualities were all he could desire, but they were just those by which he must not let himself be unduly biased. It was the higher qualities that must count. Would she realise that it was in the nature of things he must always know best ? Would she cling, not heavily, but still cling? In a word, would she be the ivy to his oak? He had heard of awful unsexed creatures who actually wanted to be another oak, and refused to be the ivy, keeping none of the solemn vows sworn at the altar. Mercifully there was no trace of the mother who had been a chorus girl, but more than a hint of the father who had been a somebody, if a disreputable one.

She met his eyes with a dependence that thrilled him. She did not seem to want to talk about herself like most women; she only cared to listen. And how brilliantly she listened! How she made one sparkle, give of one's best! Twice he made a joke, suitable for Sunday afternoon, of course, but still a joke. Once he was almost witty, though unconsciously witty. He had tea. Never had tea tasted so delicious before, and how gracefully she poured, as Miss Maggie expressed it. Two hours seemed no more than five minutes. He tore himself reluctantly away, a most buoyant Mr. Bingley.

"I shall see you in church to-night?" he asked eagerly.

Sally seemed to dally with the temptation. "Perhaps," she said at length.

She went to church, but Douglas Hill monopolised her, in his impudent young puppy way. In fact, he bore her off to supper at the doctor's house, promising to bring her back "in decent time."

Mr. Bingley went home to his own luxurious meal fuming. For once he did it less than full justice, and thought of something as much as his food.

"That young cub will make love to her," he muttered, ringing the bell for prayers; "he's just the age when they start, and usually with their seniors."

He read prayers in an exasperated voice.

Sally saw nothing of her guardian till the following morning, then she took the bull by the horns. "The Bingley was here yesterday afternoon," she announced casually, "borne on Cupid's wings, poor panting Cupid! I was smoking naughty cig. and reading naughty French novel, so sat on both. When he sniffed I said what a horrid dear you were, simply doing it all over the shop. I'm afraid he doesn't quite approve of you, Lovey."

The Reverend Adam tried to look disapproving.

"We must, of course, encourage him to go on lay-reading for all he's worth. Some night we must ask him in to supper, and Elizabeth shall do her best. We will, won't we, nice old thing?" She stroked his cheek.

"You make everybody do what you want," exploded the vicar. So the fellow had started his hanging round her. If it had been anybody but Bingley! Of course there was no harm in it, but Sally always must have her meed of male admiration, and if there was nobody else to give it she would take it from Bingley.

Sally winced at his words. "Not quite everybody. After supper, dear, you must lose something and go and look for it, and leave me free to work at being womanly. I should laugh if you were there."

"Sally, a true woman—"

She stopped his mouth with a kiss. "Even true women have to do a bit of pretending, if they're true women—"

"In all these years you must have met somebody who makes the thought of flirting with Bingley impossible."

"It takes two to make a match," answered Sally a little bitterly.

"You cannot mean … ? Nobody could resist you, darling."

"Well, somebody did, once. Anyway it's all over now. It was six years ago, a lifetime. It was bad at first—a sort of toothache in a different place. When I found it unbearable I did the sensible thing, had the tooth out. Now there's only a gap, and I've got a nice new molar to put in its place. I don't suppose it will bite quite so well, but as far as appearance goes nobody will be able to tell the difference. I call it Mr. Bingley. Let's go and watch the things grow."

They wandered round the exquisite garden, Old John at their heels.

The moment Mr. Lovelady paused the tired dog flopped down and rested, but he always got up and crawled along when the vicar moved.

Sally stopped at the fowl-run. "Ananias is a wonder," she exclaimed, looking at the handsome cock. "I notice that it's always a different Sapphira. Is that quite moral, Lovey—and a vicarage garden, too!"

The cock, who had hollowed out a secure entrenchment and had a small immature-looking hen tucked under his wing, looked at them contemptuously. Interfering, greedy, selfish things, humans!

"He must know about the war," laughed Sally; "look how deep he's dug himself in! I don't think much of the light of the harem, though."

"He's a rum bird," said the Reverend Adam. "That hen is worse than useless; lays no eggs, and eats enormously, but Elizabeth daren't kill her because of upsetting him. She says he would never get over it." He took out his watch. "I must be off. Oh, by the bye, I've got to go to Mrs. Randal's for the reading of the will. Can't think why they asked me!"

Sally's eyes sparkled. "Oh, Lovey, if she's left it all to you because she hates her beastly relations!"

"You absurd child! Why, I don't even expect anything for the parish. Why should I?"

"Oh, blow the parish! That's what I call wilful waste. You couldn't buy me even a pair of shoes out of the parish, because you're one of those tiresome clerics with conscientious objections. You were the only person she had round. Of course, if she left it all to some single male relative that wouldn't be so bad either."

Mr. Bingley got his casual invitation, and accepted it eagerly. Elizabeth did them so well that Mr. Bingley was astonished and a little shocked, and rather tempted to overstrain his digestion. That a clergyman, poor and obscure, should sit down to such a meal as a matter of course argued a carnal appetite and love for the fleshpots, ill to see in one of his cloth.

Mr. Lovelady refused to lose anything and go out to look for it, so Sally lost something instead, in the garden, and took Mr. Bingley with her to find it. They did not find it or bother about it very long, but they came upon a most sympathetic moon rising slowly over the trees.

Mr. Bingley flew home. His feet no longer touched the earth; it had got beyond that. He was besotted. How womanly she had been!

Mr. Lovelady came back from the reading of Mrs. Randal's will with great news. He had been left a thousand pounds for the poor of the parish, another for the church, and a rare specimen of an old Bible for himself. Everybody was surprised, but there was another surprise coming.

"All the rest that I die possessed of to James Thompkins," the lawyer read out, "only child of the late James and Margaret Thompkins, because, of all my nephews, he alone answered the call of his country."

Not a word about cats! No legacies! Everything to James Thompkins. And she had never mentioned the war to a soul.

Mr. Lovelady told Sally.

"Two thousand," she pouted, "but none of it for that charity which begins at home. How horrid! Couldn't you put me down as the 'poor of the parish' and buy me one little short skirt? How exciting about the nephew! What's his name?"

"Simpkins, I think. I didn't notice; it was all so astonishing. He was there, a little man with a most taking face. He's the son of Mr. Randal's sister who made the family so angry by her marriage. He's to be called Wilmot-Randal; the old lady's maiden name was Wilmot."

"And this Mr. Wilmot-Randal, is he married?" asked Sally breathlessly. Oh, if a knight should appear to save her from the dragon!

"Oh yes, a wife and two children. He rushed off by the first train to tell them the news. I never saw anyone so excited. He enlisted when war broke out, and is now home on sick leave with a hand that won't heal sufficiently for him to return. Oh yes, he's married, my child." He pinched her cheek, and laughed a little.

Sally's face fell. "No luck," she sighed to herself. "Poor Mrs. Alfred Bingley, how sorry I feel for you, my dear! After all, you had possibilities—once!"

CHAPTER VIII

"Wealth lost, something lost; honour lost, much lost; courage lost, all lost"

The rising tide of spring filled Sally with a restless energy; it blew cold one day, and warm the next, and she was tormented with a desire to be up and doing, and then depressed by the consciousness that there was nothing to do. At such times she would dig in the garden, though only intermittently.

"How pleased Lovey will be when he returns and sees what I have done," she would think, only to add with some apprehension, "That is, if I haven't dug up the things I shouldn't! They *looked* most uninteresting, anyway."

She gazed idly at Ananias and his beloved bride, tucked close together as usual, and made a face of disgust. "If I had known half as much as that sly little cat, things might have been different now!" She flung a luscious worm to the couple. "The sacrifice of the lower to the higher, or is it possibly the higher to the lower?" she asked herself. "One never knows."

Sapphira had it undivided.

"Will Mr. Bingley cherish as beautifully?" wondered Sally, and knew he would do nothing so ridiculous.

A hen came out of the inner house, thirteen golden little balls rolling after her. She swept them before her royal husband's eyes, and looked triumphantly at Sapphira, but Sapphira turned up her beak at them, and the lordly martinet turned his back. They were always coming and going, these yellow balls, shrill, noisy little creatures that grew out of their petticoats to scraggy hideousness in no time! He was bored to death with it. Thousands had gone—he neither knew nor cared where—but there were always thousands coming on. In a bitter moment he had once suspected that that was all 'They' kept him for. Silly old business! Silly old world! He sidled closer to Sapphira; she, thank goodness, did not go in for that sort of thing; she was immeasurably above all the mundane things of the world. Young and old, tender and tough, his wives went to pot in the end, a female fault as well as a misfortune; but himself he knew for an immortal, and variety is the spice of life. On the whole he was fairly satisfied.

Sally was not. She went indoors, and putting on her walking things started for the moors. She loved The Mountain which led straight from the back of the vicarage garden, and its magic sea, and the moors and the wind that swept across them. She did not leave the paths she knew; there was only one end to that.

The Hopkins' house was on the moor road, and Miss Maggie was seated in the drawing-room window. When she was at home she always sat in the drawing-room window, noting who passed to the moors and with whom. When she was not in the drawing-room she was probably in the bedroom above, where she slept. Her ambition was to inhabit the rooms over the post-office in Little Crampton; it stood at the four roads, and one saw life from there, and no mistake!

Sally waved a greeting, and Miss Maggie waved back. "Alone," she thought; "whom is she hoping to meet on the moors?"

Sally was not hoping to meet anybody; on the contrary, she was trying to outpace the self that kept step with her. It was an ideal day and an ideal scene, and she was ashamed of her own discontent and restlessness. Her craving to be alone was satisfied, alone with the wind and the sky, with nature, and nature's shy, wild things.

There came the sound as of horses galloping over sodden turf, and the half-wild ponies, belonging to Gillet of the Moor-end Farm, fled past; lashing tails, dilated nostrils, fiery eyes. A plover circled overhead uttering plaintive prayers that the robber should look in any but the right place for that sacred nest. A new-born lamb fell weakly against its mother, feeling its feet for the first time; a belated spring visitor, this, for the other lambs were frisking madly, and soon many would, alas! cease to frisk, and be associated with mint sauce instead of green pastures. A cow looked up at the stranger out of great brown, dreamy eyes; a litter of small pigs ran squealing to their mother. Sally was at home with all these.

The turf, a little soggy in parts after rain, was dry and springy on the higher levels. There was a sky of flame and glory, but not a harbinger of peace, for biting into the crimson blaze were sharp, black, monstrous shapes. A gay little wind sprinted lightly along.

"It's not a bad old world," thought Sally, drawing a deep breath. "I'm glad to be alive, and lucky to be alive, on such a day as this!"

She came in sight of Moor-end Farm, and Gillet working in the yard. He touched his forehead to her, and went on with his work. He had more than he could even hope to get through now the war had taken his son and labourers. Mrs. Gillet, wringing out clothes, observed that 'parson's Sally' was a rare treat to look at, and began to discuss her chances of Mr. Bingley with her unresponsive husband. Mrs. Gillet had one daughter in service at the great Mr. Bingley's, and the other with the Misses Hopkins. As a gossip she ran Miss Maggie very close indeed.

Her husband, as usual, paid no attention whatever to her remarks. The labour problem alone filled his mind.

Sally looked idly at the workman's cottage, known as 'The Hut.' She noted the window-pane still unmended, and that the place was empty. The Hut belonged to Gillet and was given over by him to whichever of the two labourers did not board and lodge at the farm. Miserable as it was, it was eagerly enough sought after in times of peace.

She left The Hut behind and got out into the wild solitudes. It was not till it began to threaten dusk that she turned. The walk had done her good, strengthened her philosophy. After all, life was bound to be a little difficult; one must just make the best of it, and get what one could. It was absurd to expect too much, and it wasn't as if there hadn't been something priceless—once.

The wind grew stronger, and she bent her head before it. Suddenly a shape seemed to loom up at her, to collide with her, and she gave a startled exclamation.

"I beg your pardon!" said a refined, impatient voice.

Sally found herself looking at a tall, stalwart young man with a set, strained face, and then he had gone, plunging towards the wood, swallowed up by it. She had had a glimpse of desperate eyes.

She stood still for a moment, her heart beating with fear. What had he done, or what was he about to do? Who was he? Why did he look like that?

"Like what?" she asked herself, puzzled, for she could not quite put a name to the sudden thing she had seen, or thought that she had seen. She accused her imagination of trying to make a fool of her.

For a moment she hesitated, then she also hurried into the wood. She had a terrifying sense that something awful would happen unless she were there to prevent it, yet had no idea what this thing could be. It was as if she had suddenly found herself in some intangible nightmare.

When she got to the wood she could see nobody, though the crimson sky threading among the budding trees gave a fiery light. She began to run in obedience to a voice that bade her haste, and her light feet made no sound. Then she was up against what she had but vaguely understood. She knew now what she had seen in those haunted, despairing eyes—the anguish of a lost soul and self-murder.

The stranger stood with his back to her. He had taken a revolver out of his pocket and was raising it to his temple.

Sally realised that what had to be done must be done instantly; that there was no time to think matters out if she was to save his life. It occurred to her that to shout would be fatal; he would start, and the bullet would probably enter some part of his head even if she had spoiled his aim. On the other hand, to jerk his wrist down smartly, so that the deadly weapon pointed in front of them, might still cause it to go off, but not necessarily fatally.

She had to take that risk. She gathered herself together into a lissom heap, and sprang noiselessly forward. Then her hands were round his wrist, the revolver pointing downwards. There was a report that made a startled bird rise with a scream, and the bullet had sped, but harmlessly.

"That was a near thing!" she gasped.

The man wheeled round on her, his blue eyes almost black with rage. "How d-d-dare you!" he stammered, "how dare you, I say! What is it to you?"

"A life," said Sally.

"Mine, not yours, if you will be good enough to remember it." With his left hand he released himself from her clasp. "Go away, go away at once! What are you doing here?"

"I guessed; I followed you."

"Damn your curiosity and your interference!" he burst out, and then added sullenly, "I beg your pardon, but you had no right, no right at all."

"You don't deny what you were going to do?"

"What I am going to do is entirely my own concern, madam."

"But on such a day! I was just thinking how good to be alive, and you—and you. … Oh you must be mad! Such a priceless gift!"

"That is as one finds it."

"Or makes it," she suggested softly.

His handsome, finely-cut face was marred by a sneer. "So you are going to preach? The ever-popular part!"

Sally stared, and then laughed, if only unsteadily. "Me preach!" she exclaimed. "Why, good gracious! What, *me*? Oh, I say, that would be funny!"

"It would be a bore," he said rudely.

"It always is," agreed Sally, "a beastly bore; but people love it so, don't they? I suppose one ought to let them enjoy themselves now and then. You—you won't do it before me, will you?" She gazed fearfully at the revolver.

"Of course not."

"But you'll do it as soon as I've gone?"

He made no reply.

"Then I shan't go, that's all," she announced cheerfully.

"Don't be so ridiculous!" He frowned. He looked round as if intending flight.

"I daresay I can run almost as fast," said Sally. "Do you see what I mean? You'll find me a regular shadow. It'll make you so ridiculous, too, won't it?" She looked at him with very bright eyes, showing nothing of a heart fainting within her. It was so easy to say these things, to sound positive and determined, but not so easy to carry them out. He was long and lithe, every inch of six feet, and had the look of an athlete about him. True, she could run extraordinarily fast for a woman, but not as fast as a trained man. "You shan't do it! I won't let you. You shan't do it!" she persisted.

His face contradicted her. She knew he was just as determined to shoot himself as she was to prevent him. Man's strength against woman's strength—and wits! She uttered a voiceless prayer. To hit on the right note, something to bid him pause, to be able to think of one effective thing to say!

"It's so—so cowardly," she almost sobbed, "and so final. Beyond death there is no appeal."

"Exactly." He spoke thankfully.

She felt it was a losing game that she was playing, and raged that she could only play it so badly.

"Please, please don't; oh, *please* don't!" she implored.

"I wish you would go, and not be so tiresome," exclaimed the would-be suicide angrily.

"I won't go; you needn't count on that. And I shall go on being tiresome till you give me your word not to." Her mouth fell into determined and unbecoming lines.

The stranger looked at her and found her uncomely and very much in the way. What inopportune things women were! Desperate as he had been, it had still taken a little nerving up to set out thus upon the Great Adventure, but he had nerved himself up, and for this. All would have been over now, restfully over, if it had not been for this interfering woman with the long, grim mouth. Damn her! The crimson of the sky blazed into his eyes; it made him think of blood and terrible things. He would for ever have ceased to think by now, save for this girl. Damn her! Damn her!

Sally faced his look, though it was ill to bear. She seemed full of confident courage. He guessed nothing of a madly-beating heart.

"One does what one likes with one's own life," he said curtly.

"Not quite all one likes, surely? A life so seldom stands alone; there are the others. It's such a priceless, glowing thing; nothing can give it us back. Even the old and the wretched cling to it till the last, make a fight to keep it. How can you, young, strong—"

"Youth and strength can make some things worse," he replied.

"Your people? You must have somebody belonging to you?" It had often seemed to her that everybody had but herself. It was not many people who were without a single blood tie in the world. There was 'Lovey,' of course, but even Lovey was not everything, not really and truly her own.

"I belong to nobody," he answered, turning away his face; "they do not wish it. Now do you understand, and will you go?"

"There is always something left. Is it some woman? Oh, it is bad for a year or two, I know, but life becomes worth while again; and there are so many women left in the world, even nicer, more beautiful—"

The man gave a scornful little laugh. "Do you suppose I am the sort of fool that would shoot himself for a woman?"

"Of course not," she said quickly, wondering what had brought him to this pass. "I don't think you are the sort of fool to shoot yourself at all. It's a fool's trick; it leaves nothing to happen, nothing to Fate."

"I've had quite enough happen, thank you. Will you be good enough to leave me?"

"Most certainly not!"

"Will you force me to do it before you, after all? I beg your pardon," he added hastily; "of course I did not mean that, but it would have been over but for you, and now it's all to go through again. After all, it's enough to die once."

"Then you don't exactly like the idea?"

"There is no other way. I should not have delayed so long."

"What have you lost? It must be much, indeed." She had thought she had lost all that suffering humanity could, but suicide as a means of oblivion had never even occurred to her. If there was no genius in her art she had a genius for life, and a zest not easily destroyed.

"I have lost everything," he said.

"Everything?"

"Everything, and under the most terrible circumstances. I have flung away lives. I have betrayed my country. Now are you satisfied?"

She shrank back, and horror filled her. For a moment she was almost sorry she had come in time. There were things she could never forgive.

"You mean you, an Englishman, a gentleman, have acted as spy for the other side?" she jerked out.

He turned on her as if he would strike her. "My God, my God! If only you might have been a man! You should have paid for that!"

"Won't you tell me what it is?" she asked gently.

"Oh, a mere trifle! I led my company to death in the face of direct orders, men who were much to me, believed in me—the fools!—and would have followed me anywhere. Well, they followed me to Hell and failure, and I had all the luck. *I* escaped scot free!" He broke into a bitter laugh. "Fortunate, wasn't it? Two hundred gone, three left, and I one of the three! Of course I was cashiered, and serve me right. I should have been shot—no, hanged! And now I want to run away from my own hell, if you'll be so good as to permit me."

Sally turned very white and could not speak for a moment; then she said, very slowly, "Believe me, I can realise what you feel, but a blunder is not a crime. When you disobeyed orders, as I take it you did, you thought you were acting for the best. Perhaps the orders seemed impossible, and you thought you saw a better way?"

"I had no right to think. I should have acted."

"But you meant it for the best? Please explain."

"I thought I saw the chance of a big and more valuable success, that's all, and not as expensive an action as the one I was told to take."

"And luck went against you?" said Sally. "For, after all, what is it but luck? If you had succeeded, promotion and honour, if a reprimand came first; but failure is the one thing that nobody ever forgives."

"Insubordination must be punished," he returned listlessly. "It's going to take everything we know to pull this thing off, and it won't be so easy then. My God, it's the seething pit of Hell out there! Blunders like mine delay the end, send good men uselessly to their deaths." He put the revolver in his pocket and covered his face with his hands.

Sally noticed that he was shaking all over, and her heart was sick with pity for him.

"Two hundred—two hundred," he murmured, agonised, as if to himself. "Some of them with me for fifteen years … the old sergeant who had helped me as a raw sub, God knows how finely … proud of us all he was—proud of me. God help us both! In the Boer War together, and now this. Distinction there, extinction here. And you want me to stay in my own little hell so that I can go mad, like a man I saw go mad once; the third survivor that was. Day and night I see nothing but those figures trapped by the barbed wire I led them into—the dead and the dying eyes. No brothers could have been more to me—"

Sally's light fingers stole into his pocket. She drew out the revolver without him being conscious of her action, and, thrusting it into her belt, buttoned her loose coat over it. The blood that had seemed frozen began to run through her veins again.

"Oh, I'm sorry," she said," I'm sorry. But in time—in time—"

He did not seem to hear. Indeed, he was unconscious of her presence. He was living that awful scene all over again for the hundredth time. He had stood there looking on his work, realising disaster, but something had seemed to burst in his brain; he had not really felt much. He was like one with a bad hurt, at first no pain, just numbness, and then the slow, ever-increasing agony. He had stared meaninglessly at the sergeant, who had wept like a child, and who refused to meet his eyes.

If only he had felt! If only he had shot himself there and then, been out of it, spared the agony that was to come and grow greater day by day! But he had just been numbed. To have been found dead in the disaster he had wrought! To have spared his family, who had sacrificed so much for him, the last disgrace! But nothing had been spared. They had gone slowly back, the bullets avoiding them. The third survivor had dashed on ahead of them; he was laughing and screaming and singing. It was said his reason would never return. That, too, had been his work; the gallant innocent had had to suffer for the guilty.

Sally tugged at his arm. She was growing frightened, even though she had the weapon of destruction safely hidden.

"Things pass," she said, "and you are quite young. How old are you?"

"Thirty-five," he returned mechanically.

"One can start the world again at thirty-five, make up. You could enlist, make your way up a little, still help—"

"I am too well known. How could I face them? Besides, they would not have me. Sometimes I think my nerve has gone." He took his hands away from his face, and Sally saw that it had turned grey.

"There are other things, other countries—"

"Not for me; the army was my life, my all. I am finished, broken. How should you understand what it means to be flung on the scrap-heap just as everything is promising the best?"

"Indeed, indeed I do!" she cried eagerly; "more than you can guess."

"Pah!" he said contemptuously. What nonsense she was talking! She was well dressed, good looking, had obviously come out of a comfortable, sheltered home free from the storms of adversity, from the fret of ambition, the wild stir of achievement. "Impossible," he said. "I doubt whether the fact that I am what is termed absolutely 'on the rocks' can convey anything to you. How should it? I have no money, no work, no honour—nothing."

"'Wealth lost, something lost; honour lost, much lost; courage lost, all lost,'" she quoted earnestly. The words had revived her courage many a time.

They failed to stir him. "Well, it's 'all lost,'" he said, "and that's all there is about it. I cannot see those sights, hear those sounds, and know that they are the consequences of my madness. The very dead had reproach in their eyes, while those who only prayed for death—"

Suddenly he uttered a hoarse cry, and the next moment he had fallen crashing to the ground, and lay like a log at Sally's feet. She wondered if he was dead, if she had failed to save him, after all.

She placed her ear upon his heart and thought she could detect a faint sound. Then she ran to Moor-end Farm.

Gillet came back with her, and they found the stranger recovering consciousness, but quite dazed, and very meek and obedient.

"I want you to put him to bed and keep him there for a day or two," said Sally.

Gillet scratched his head. "All right, miss," he said resignedly.

"I'll be responsible for him," she promised.

She returned home feeling that the man was safe for a time. As a soldier he would choose the one means to an end; and she had his revolver. He would not be able to get another for a day or two, perhaps not then; they were not picked up as easily as all that, these days. In the meanwhile almost anything might happen, and after the attack he might come round to a more rational frame of mind.

She came up the next day and learned that the stranger was sleeping like a log. "Like one who hasn't slept for a week," said the farmer.

Sally thought it might be possible that he had not. "Look here," she said to Gillet, "this is not going to be so bad for you. Of course he's a gentleman, and he's had some trouble, but he's honest, I can vouch for that, and without work or money. He's strong, and is pretty certain to know something about horses, at least, and can learn other things if he likes. He's not stupid, anyone can see that. Employ him to help on the farm; it might mean a lot to both of you."

Gillet's face brightened. "It would mean a lot to me, Miss Sally, but he's a gent, right enough. Maybe he won't. If he's been a wild 'un and got through his money, well, he don't want work; he wants money to play with—"

"No, no; he isn't like that, I feel sure he isn't. Just you try him and see."

"I'd be only too thankful if he'd try and help; he's a big, strong chap."

"That's right, and don't be afraid of working him too hard; the harder the better. And—don't let your wife talk, if you can help it."

Gillet chuckled. "There ain't a man living as can stop a woman's tongue," he said.

CHAPTER IX

"I am sick of the war!"

Sally told Mr. Lovelady about the stranger at Moor-end Farm, but she did not tell him much. He just knew that she and Gillet had come upon him in a faint, and that was about all. The man's tragedy was his own.

She did not, however, lose much time in finding out all she could about him by way of General Smyth. The old general lived down at the Point and was a walking reference-library in all matters pertaining to the army. If he had not actually met every officer of the British army in his time, he had met their parents or relations, or had at least heard about them. He had a very retentive memory and a garrulous tongue. She met him in High Street and he turned with her. She was a favourite of the old man's, for she had suffered his tedium in times of peace, and Little Crampton hadn't. It was only since the war that the general had come into his own, and been listened to instead of fled from.

She brought the talk to the cashiering of officers, and asked the old gentleman if he thought there would be much more of it.

He at once started off at full swing. "When war breaks it breaks badly," he said, "and there have been some hard cases among them, mighty hard cases, though doubtless some deserved even more than they got."

He began to talk of individual cases. None of them seemed to Sally to apply to the stranger. However, she possessed her soul in patience, and met with due reward.

"Robert Kantyre, now—that was a bad business," he said meditatively;

"fine young fellow, smart as they make 'em, promising, dashing—a bit too dashing, perhaps. Can't understand it."

"Who was he?" asked Sally. "Someone you've known?"

"Met his father once, years ago. Never saw young hopeful, pride of the family, and all that sort of thing. A regular Kantyre. Bless my soul, the Kantyres were giving a good account of themselves in the days of bow and arrows, and one can't have a war without 'em. This boy and his cousin were both at Spion Kop. Robert got a D.S.O. and a bullet that ought to have killed him, and which he's never felt, I believe; and the other got his marching orders, leaving this fellow to carry on the tradition of the Kantyres. It was taken for granted that if he came through this war alive he'd be well on his way to the top of the tree. Instead of that the young fool takes it into his head to think for himself, which wouldn't have mattered if he hadn't happened to think wrong, and to disobey orders. That's the end of the last fighting Kantyre. Good God! the sacrifices they made to put him in the army! His father was a half-pay colonel at the time, and there were five girls ahead of him, but all just set their teeth and gave up something, and the fellow worked hard, and was straight as a die. Smoked very little, and then only the cheapest stuff, and was as near teetotal as makes no difference; paid his way with the most rigid economy, but never a cent for pleasure. Gave up all his time to work, making himself and his men efficient, and, by God! everybody said he'd done it. And now this! Damned if I can make head or tail of it. Beg your pardon, Miss Sally, but I tell you the thing worries me, worries me infernally. It's made no end of talk in the Service. Like a thunderclap it was."

"Poor fellow!" said Sally.

"Ay, he's broken all right. Wonder what will become of him? Can't understand why he turned up alive. Was a plucky one, too, they said. Very rum, very rum indeed. His mother was very ill when she heard, and just didn't bother to get better, and the old boy had a stroke at his wife's funeral, and has turned childish; thinks we're fighting the Boers, and keeps telling the girls how well Bob is doing, and that it isn't everybody that gets a D.S.O. at twenty, and that he's going to be worthy of the best traditions of the family, and so on, and how pleased they all must be that the sacrifice was made."

"That must be hard to listen to, though it's a good thing for the poor old man, I suppose."

"Oh yes, he's happy enough; but those girls—not that they are girls, of course, just five old maids embittered at the thought of what they have given up for this disgrace. They can't bear his name mentioned. You see, they had to live in the dullest hole, for economy, without any social life, and make out to their brother that they liked it; and they weren't bad-looking girls. They might have married with decent chances and had homes of their own. Of course they are bound to take it badly, and I believe they wrote and told him he had killed his mother and destroyed his father's reason, as well as spoiling their lives. A big, handsome fellow, I have heard, a regular Kantyre."

"And nothing can ever put it right again?" asked Sally pitifully.

"No, no; the fellow was in the wrong, owned up at once. Was to have got his majority in a day or two. He had a Field Marshal's baton in his pockets, that boy; everybody said so. Simply a dead cert. The fellow that wrote and told me about it said that for a small engagement it was the most ghastly of the whole war, and that's saying something. Barbed wire, and only three out of over two hundred got back, and the young fool among them. *That* nobody could understand. He must have been dazed, I suppose. Everybody's sorry, he was very popular, but of course he's finished if he's still alive. I doubt it myself."

Sally said nothing.

"That bullet he got in the Boer war was an odd business. By the position of its entry it should have entered a vital organ and killed him, but he felt little or no inconvenience. They probed about as much as they dared, but never located the thing at all, and though when the X-rays came in one of the R.A.M.C. got him to be examined for curiosity, devil a sign of a bullet was there—though, mind you, it was inside all right."

"And won't it ever give trouble—if he's alive, I mean?"

"Not with the abstemious life he leads, or did. I suppose if a chap was a drinker it might set up mischief, but Kantyre mightn't have spent years in India, for all the thirst he exhibited. The Kantyres have all excellent physiques. Well, well, it can't be helped now; battles are the graves of reputations, as well as bodies."

General Smyth always ended up with this remark.

Sally went slowly home. She was sure she had the young man traced, and under the circumstances she could understand his desperate expedient. She thought of his deeply-tanned face, his dark blue eyes, and his magnificent physique, and wondered if she would have felt so very much pity if he had been small and plain and weakly. She did like fine, handsome men, though Jimmy had been small and far from handsome. But then Jimmy was—Jimmy.

The next day she went up to the moors again, and found the stranger sitting on the stone bench outside The Hut. His head was drooping, his hands hanging listlessly; it was as if he had just let go. Young, strong, the ball at his feet—and now this derelict by the wayside!

She took her seat beside him in a matter-of-fact way. "You are better, I hope?" she asked cheerfully.

"There is nothing wrong with me, thank you. By the bye, you took something of mine away with you?"

"I just took a fancy to it," said Sally casually; "it's a way I have. You will let me keep it a little longer?"

"It is kind of you to ask my permission, seeing that you intend to keep it in any case."

Sally did not speak for a moment, then she said slowly, "I will only keep it for two months, then you shall have it back if you ask for it."

"Two months is too long."

"Time soon goes when one is busy."

"Busy! I have no occupation."

"No, but you will have. Gillet wants your help, and wants it badly. It will mean the saving of the farm. The son who took charge of the colts and broke them in enlisted. You could do that sort of thing?"

A faint gleam of interest came into his eyes. "Horses? Oh yes."

"Take it on for two months, and see what turns up."

"What is it to you?"

"I have suffered too," she said simply. "I should like to be your friend if I may?"

"After what I told you! I thought women judged such things hardly."

"I have no right to judge anything hardly. I only despise cowardice, the man without grit who just lets go. You could never be like that after you had once pulled yourself together. If you will let me be your friend there is nothing you could ask of me in vain."

"You are very rash, Miss—"

"Lunton, Sally Lunton."

"Very rash, Miss Lunton. A drowning man catches at a straw; what if I pull you under too? Be wise and let me sink, and sink alone."

"Ah no," said Sally, "that is not wisdom."

"My name is Robert Kantyre, late captain in the —, but I have told Gillet that my name is White. To everybody but you it must be White. If I thought a soul guessed—"

"Your secret is safe with me, Captain —"

"'Mr.' now, please," he corrected, compressing his lips.

Sally went slowly home. She felt easier in her mind, if not altogether easy. Miss Maggie saw her pass, and again wondered what attraction she sought on the moors. Mr. Bingley had not gone that way.

Sally did not notice the sleuth-hound; she was deep in sombre thought. What ruin the war, directly and indirectly, was spreading all around, ruin of lives and hopes and fortunes! The greater the civilisation, so it almost seemed, the more ruthless the struggle. Civilisation lay trampled underfoot, moaning in her dust, her face a bloody pulp, armies hacking their way across her. Robert Kantyre's career and honour had gone, and the wine of youth was spilling on the fields of Flanders, and on the wide salt seas. In its first phases the country had exclaimed at the price of disaster, now it was shocked into silence at the price of victory. Victory and Liberty, fine words both, but being paid for unto the uttermost farthing.

She remembered the fine poem 'To Liberty,' and murmured two of the verses to herself:

"You are hymned by every tongue,
Every harp to you is strung,
Goddess ever fair and young,
Queen sublime.
Yet—your plan we cannot probe,
There is blood upon your robe—
There is blood upon your robe
All the time!

"There's a star above your head,
But—around your feet, the dead;
And your riddle all unread
None can probe.
Still with merciless device
For your gift you claim the price,
And the blood of sacrifice
Stains your robe!"*

She walked faster. Thought was becoming unbearable, and she was ashamed. This war—and the pursuit of Mr. Bingley! How hideous it seemed!

Then she saw him coming towards her, and remembered he always managed half an hour's exercise to give himself an appetite for luncheon. For once she was not pleased to see him, and he missed the fascinating smile, the sparkling eyes.

"The brave lives taken, the Bingleys left," she thought, and her lips tightened.

Mr. Bingley took off his hat with the gallantry he kept for those ladies of his acquaintance who were attractive and 'all right,' a term which covered a multitude of the proprieties.

"Why can't I remember 'business as usual'?" thought Sally. "What a thing it is! What a thing I am! Who bothered to make insects like us, I wonder?"

---

* By F. Raymond Coulson.

"How solemn you look!" observed Mr. Bingley with heavy playfulness. "A penny for your thoughts."

"The war, of course."

Mr. Bingley frowned. "I am sick of the war!" he exclaimed, exasperated. Food prices going up, dividends going down! A nice sort of thing, and in England, mind you, not some mere foreign country! Only that day his cook had come to him and cast that bomb, the domestic ultimatum, right at him. She must have an extra twenty-five per cent for the household books, or he must—yes, she dared a 'must,' and to Mr. Bingley!—be content with a less varied and luxurious diet.

Let those who talk of war problems give a thought to Mr. Bingley's. Was ever soul so rent in twain? Was ever man so hit in his tenderest, most sacred feelings? The unhappy man was torn between the two strong passions of his life, his money and his food. One of these priceless things must be sacrificed to the other. It had been worrying him all day, and he could not make up his mind. It was a most momentous decision.

He was annoyed that Sally should remind him of the war and his unhappy position. It was not like her usual tact. He did try to be thankful for small mercies; the thankless sometimes had even those small mercies rent from them. For instance, for a man in the state of life to which it had pleased God to call him he was well off, and not in the awful position of a tradesman, by which he meant a person who had anything to sell, from pictures to pots and pans, for whose goods the demand had lessened. Still, he had been a faithful steward of his own money, and now he had to be a little false to his money, or to his inner self.

"It's so horrible!" cried Sally, though not the Sally he knew.

"Horrible! Of course it's horrible," he agreed.

"The sacrifices—"

"*Awful!*" agreed Mr. Bingley fervently.

"Courage, sacrifice! If one could rise to either, then perhaps one's life would not have been in vain, after all."

"Very noble sentiments indeed," said Mr. Bingley, pleased. He did not see that his wife would be called upon either for courage or sacrifice, but undoubtedly it was well that women should possess these attributes, as long as it was the courage of endurance and good-temper, and the sacrifices of a willing spirit.

"Strange how war brings out the worst and best of people!"

"Strange that Germany should be allowed to proclaim a blockade, that their submarines should be allowed to go where they like, do what they like, even threaten our food supply!" snorted Mr. Bingley. "What next, I wonder?"

"Perhaps London."

Mr. Bingley snorted again. "What nonsense!"

"One must be prepared for the exponents of 'kultur' to drop a few bombs on Westminster Abbey."

Mr. Bingley looked startled. A thought had come to appal. He waved aside the matter of Westminster Abbey, and said in a horrified voice,

"Suppose it were the Bank of England!"

"Suppose it were Bingley's," thought Sally, and burst out laughing, and once started could not stop. She could see the indignant expression on Mr. Bingley's face as he was blown through the air.

"You astonish me, Miss Lunton," said Mr. Bingley heavily; "you astonish me very much."

She thought how much more she could astonish him by just mentioning her thoughts. Instead she struggled for gravity and a change of subject.

Mr. Bingley had, however, already chosen a subject. "Scarborough was a disgrace," he exclaimed; "I used to go there myself."

"Well, the country turned over in its sleep; even that is something. What right have we to consider ourselves immune?"

"We are British," said Mr. Bingley magnificently.

Sally shrugged her shoulders. Certainly Mr. Bingley was, in the very worst sense of the word. He also possessed the British art of never believing in the uncomfortable thing.

"A glorious heritage," he said pompously, preening himself a little.

"A heritage not all of us deserve, I fear," she returned; "at least I know I don't. What am I doing? Nothing. What can I do? Nothing. Our lives are secured to us at the price of others. We cannot suffer very much except in pocket."

"Is that nothing, Miss Lunton?" demanded Mr. Bingley, growing red with anger.

"Almost nothing, when you haven't a pocket at all, or when you have a sufficient one. We ought to think of giving, not keeping."

Mr. Bingley thought that was spoken so exactly like an illogical woman who had nothing to give. "One seems for ever subscribing to something," he grumbled. He had, in all, given ten pounds, and thought it liberal. "It's we workers and tax-payers, the backbone of the nation, who are paying for this war, though the Government started it without asking our permission. I should never have consented. I should have pointed out what it would mean, have made them realise the thing, shown a little forethought! Then the war is not getting along as I hoped," he went on in a tone of deep displeasure," and not nearly as well as I consider it should. Still not through the Dardanelles! Most disappointing, most unfortunate!"

"Very," agreed Sally dryly, "and most careless when our ships and brave sailors go to the bottom—or even the mere foreigners!"

"I hardly understand you, Miss Lunton." His brow was heavy with displeasure.

"It does not matter. There's plenty of life and courage in the country yet. I cannot understand the free young man who could but won't; but the man who would, but can't, has all my sympathy. He has to keep a stiff upper lip in the face of general misunderstanding. After all, his is the hardest job. He is ready enough to sacrifice himself, but is it right to sacrifice wife and children? Does it pay in the long run?"

"I shouldn't think of doing such a thing!" exclaimed Mr. Bingley in horror.

"Of course not, but what a struggle! The very poor or the wealthy have not that problem to face; all the others have. Don't let's talk of the war any longer. It's too harrowing. I hate to think of the pick of our manhood facing such horrors. What will be left when the war is over?"

Mr. Bingley might have pointed out that he most certainly would be left, and that that was surely something to be thankful for; but he was too offended with Sally to answer at all.

He took a rather stiff farewell, and Sally was too much occupied with her own thoughts to know or care what his attitude might be. She realised that she would care on the morrow, but the morrow had not yet dawned.

Mr. Bingley went down High Street feeling very ruffled. He ran into 'that fat fool, Boliver' and 'that pernicious ass, Paton,' and their conversation did not smooth matters. They were advocating conscription, the raising of the age limit to forty-five, "if only as a shield, d'ye see, Bingley," and sending the bachelors out first.

"If a man hasn't over-eaten and under-exercised he ought to be fit at forty-five," insisted the pernicious ass, who was fifty, but lean and active.

"Of course it would mean some training, a fat lot of training," said the fat fool, laughing at his own execrable jest.

Mr. Bingley came away with his head in the air.

Miss Maggie stopped in front of him. "Have you been smelling the drains again?" she asked, contemplating his attitude.

"I have not," said Mr. Bingley. What a crowd of disagreeable people there were in Little Crampton!

"You looked as if you had. Oh, there's Mr. Paton and Mr. Boliver."

Mr. Bingley looked down at the round little body of the distant Mr. Boliver. What absurd little legs! What a moon-face, and slits for eyes! He thanked God he was not as this man.

"By the bye, did you meet Sally just now? How fond she is growing of the moors! Naughty girl! Did you ask Mr. Paton how his wife was? I'm certain she's dying from the same disease as the first Mrs. Paton."

"What was that?" asked Mr. Bingley, interested.

"Mr. Paton!" giggled Miss Maggie.

Mr. Bingley thought that constant association with a fellow like Paton would be enough to drive anyone to distraction or death.

"He's had a medical training," whispered Miss Maggie, "and they can do it so much easier, and without being found out."

"Do what?"

She sunk her voice. "Inject germs and things."

"Germs! What germs?" asked Mr. Bingley, startled.

"I don't know what are most used for the purpose," she returned. "I will find out. Mr. Bingley?"

"Yes?"

"If you had a wife you didn't like, would you inject germs into her?"

"Good Heavens, no!" gasped Mr. Bingley; "it would be a crime!"

"I mean if you couldn't be found out?"

He eyed her sternly. "What difference does that make? A sin is a sin, whether it's found out or not."

"Yes," agreed Miss Maggie, "but quite a different one. Would you risk letting her inject germs into you?"

Mr. Bingley was even more horrified. "Certainly not! I should not marry that sort of woman."

"But you wouldn't know she was that sort of woman till too late; people don't."

It seemed to Mr. Bingley that everybody had some unpleasant suggestion to make. It was a relief after this to encounter Mrs. Dalton, and in her new spring costume. It was a very well-cut and expensive costume indeed, with an elegant air of simplicity, and of a soft dove-grey that brought out the pretty shades of the wearer's pink and white complexion and bright brown hair and eyes. She had never looked better, appearing engagingly plump rather than stumpy. How dove-like, how womanly, how chaste! thought the enraptured Mr. Bingley; and quite economical, he felt sure. What was meeker, more tender than a dove?

Sally did not in the least remind him of a dove; in fact, only a few minutes back, he had seen in her eye something more akin to the fierce glint of the eagle. He pursed up his small, tight mouth, and his eyes grew cautious. He really must be more guarded about Miss Lunton. Women were so vain. She would be getting ideas in her head if he wasn't careful.

He recalled a line of wisdom from his mother's book. How well it applied!

"*Don't marry a woman with opinions; marry one with a receptive mind!*"

Sally had shown the cloven hoof that very morning; she had had opinions of her own and, not content with that, had stated them only too clearly. On the other hand, what could be more receptive than the mind of a womanly creature in dove-grey?

And here was Mrs. Dalton to his hand, presenting the perfect mean.

Oh, what a wonderful mother he had had! What a priceless guide! Her genius had removed every pitfall from his path! Why, he could not even think of Sally without the consciousness that he was on very thin ice, and far too close to the board marked 'Danger.' True, it was rather an exhilarating sensation, and made him feel very young and just a little dashing. He never felt dashing with Mrs. Dalton.

He sighed. Was he a coward? Only a coward fled from danger. A brave man faced it. Was not this a time to be brave? There was a thrill attached to danger quite lacking in the presence of dove-grey and safety. Far better teach that black-eyed young person a lesson by showing her how very easily he could skate into safety without getting even damp.

Why not—well, there it was. He did not name the thing zigzag, but that was what he meant. He would zigzag a little, and wait and see. Consequently, for the few moments that were left he zigzagged in the direction of Mrs. Dalton, who was most dove-like in every way, and he departed for his luncheon feeling soothed. He was in a less agitated frame of mind than when he had left the house torn between two great decisions.

After luncheon he managed to make up his mind, and announced to Vanner, as she knew he would, that he would prefer the menu unchanged. He hoped to be able to save that twenty-five per cent in some other way, or to make some extra good investment, so as to put things straight.

Still, he was heartily sick of the war. It was not only threatening his country and his countrymen, but it was threatening the peace of Mr. Bingley, and, by Jove! *that* was coming to something.

CHAPTER X

"Stop! ... oh, you little idiot!"

Sally waited till the end of the week before going up to Moor-end Farm to see how her protégé was progressing. She felt a possessive interest in the man whose life she had saved against his will, almost a maternal interest, though he had come into the world four years sooner than herself.

"A kind of step-mother by proxy, say," she explained it to herself, as she took the short cut down the 'cattle way.'

The cattle way was so called because it ran from Moor-end Farm on to the moor road, and was a long, high-hedged, rutty lane with one gate leading into the farm fields and another closing the lane from the moor road. It was used solely for driving herds of cattle to the Farleigh markets, and on Wednesdays a drover was usually waiting by the gate that led into the road, while another drove the cattle from the field-gate into the lane towards him.

Had it been Wednesday, nothing would have induced Sally to venture within a mile of it. Cattle browsing in a field she would pass, at a distance, but cattle being driven on to her in a narrow lane were a terror she could not even think of without changing colour. However, Wednesday had come and gone, and she picked her way among the deep ruts of the lane carelessly enough. She wondered what Gillet would have to say.

He seemed pleased to see her. "You were right, miss," he said slowly; "he can work, gentleman or no gentleman. White, as we have to call him, but I doubt me it's not his name, miss. He's sharp with the cows and the sheep, but with the horses, why, he's just a fair wonder! If only—" he paused, a troubled look on his face.

"You are afraid of losing him," said Sally, very pleased with what she had heard; "but I don't think you need be at present."

"It ain't that exactly—" hesitated the farmer.

Sally read apprehension in his eyes. Had he guessed anything, then? Had 'White' let his secret escape him?

"What is it?" she asked directly. "I would rather know. You see, I—I found him when he was taken ill, and asked you to take him. It makes one feel a little responsible. If there is anything I can do—"

Gillet scratched his head. "I wish you could, Miss Sally," he sighed, "but it ain't young ladies' work. I misdoubt me that parson could do any good, either, or that he was really ill when you found him. Maybe it was that which brought him down-like. Gents take to it same as others. It's easy gettin' in the clutches, but it ain't so easy gettin' out."

Sally's heart sank. Something had obviously gone wrong already. "What has happened?" she asked quickly. Had he made another attempt at suicide?

"Miss, I never guessed it was that. He come regular to work o' mornings, he seemed fair savage to work, not wanting to be stopping nor nothink. He asked if he might have The Hut, and I was only too glad, it going all to rack and ruin. My wife, she fixes it up for him, him to have meals along o' us, and The Hut, which my missus will keep decent for him, such to be allowed for off his wages."

Sally could understand that Robert Kantyre would desire a certain amount of privacy, a place, no matter how poor, he could call his own. It seemed to her an excellent arrangement, and she said as much.

"Yes, if he'd keep off it."

"Keep off what?" asked Sally.

"The drink, miss. He drinks cruel."

Sally gasped. The news was a shock to her, and she could hardly believe it. She remembered his character for an almost austere abstemiousness.

"Surely not!" she cried.

"It's true, Miss Sally."

She wondered how long his habits had been like this. Had he withheld the one vital thing when he told his story, and revealed himself as perhaps only one who believed himself to be on the point of death would have done to a total stranger? Was drink the secret of his downfall, and had she but saved him for death in life, the lowest of all degradations, since out of the one any other may spring? Had he made that horrible blunder because his wits had been fuddled at the critical moment? Then no wonder he had said it was a case of 'all lost.'

"You are quite, quite sure? You have seen him?"

"Aye, Miss Sally, lying there like a log in the hut. I've gone in and blown out the candle. It's gospel truth I'm telling you; he ain't gone sober to bed since he started. Soon it will take him in working hours, and then—" he made a hopeless gesture with his hands. "I have seen so many go the same way, fine chaps many of them, but with the curse on them, and maybe not the mind and the will to fight. It's a cruel thing, eating out the vitals of a man like a cancer, rotting him body and soul. If but they'd stop in time! This chap now: he don't show it yet, but soon it'll come creeping out in his face, and then—"

"We must do something, think of something!" she cried.

"You can't save a man agin his will," said Gillet.

Sally was silent. She knew that perfectly well. If Robert Kantyre had no mind to be saved they could do nothing. She was angry with him, but she had pity, too. Whether disease or vice, the man was in the grip of a destroying fiend, and if he submitted weakly to that tyranny there was nothing to be done. She thought of his unhappy, finely-cut bronzed face. No sign of the enemy had been there. Surely he could still be saved.

"Thank you for telling me," she said at length. "Does anybody else suspect?"

"No, miss, not yet."

"You will not let them if you can help it?"

"If can help it," he assented.

"I will try and think of something," she said; "it will be difficult, but there must be some way. He's on the farm somewhere now, I suppose?"

"Aye, with the cattle."

She walked quickly to The Hut. The door swung lightly open on the breeze. Through the window she could see into the living-room and, since the door to the bedroom lay open, into that also. The place looked very bare, but neat and clean. The portion of the bed that she saw was spotless. It certainly did not look like the habitation of a drunkard.

For some time she stood looking in. Then suddenly she made up her mind and went inside. She went straight to the one cupboard the place contained, and there she found only too much evidence of the thing Gillet deplored.

Robert Kantyre did not trouble to hide his weakness. He drank openly and unashamed. Here were empty brandy bottles, one half-empty, and a glass with a strong mixture of the stuff not quite finished.

Sally's mouth set in its most unbecoming lines. She went to the sink and deliberately poured the contents of glass and bottle down it. Then she put the bottle and glass back in their places and came out of The Hut. As she turned into the cattle way she decided that she would have to have this thing out sooner or later with Robert Kantyre, but she did not relish the idea.

"He's going to be a nuisance, this man," she told herself, frowning, "and perhaps I have bitten off more than I can chew."

Buried in deep thought she passed the field-gate leading into the lane without looking up. She was trying to think of some way to introduce a most delicate subject when next she met the man of the moors. Would it be better to tread warily, or to take the bull by the horns, and be direct and blunt about it? Had she—

Her thoughts broke off abruptly, and panic-stricken terror took their place. The field gate had been opened, and a herd of frightened, charging cattle poured out on top of the luckless Sally. She had never been in such deadly physical fear in her life. All her wits deserted her. She screamed and ran, and the cattle, crowded by those pushing behind, came thundering down on her, dangerous in their panic. The narrow lane became a surging red sea.

The girl tore along the rough, uneven way, keeping just ahead of the herd, but only just ahead. More than once she almost tripped and fell.

She had spoken of being broken, but she was like to be broken in dead earnest if she lost her footing, for numerous powerful beasts would soon have beaten her into pulp beneath their hoofs. Even in her terror she realised that she had not been altogether broken, after all, that there was something unbreakable within her, and that life was sweet. She also realised that the foremost cattle were almost upon her, and that, while she could not go any faster, they both could and would. The smell of the great red bodies, the heat that seemed to come from them, the bellows that sounded to her like the bellows of ravening fury, added to her panic.

The one thing she might have thought of never even occurred to her. The hedge was fairly high, and, in most places, thick, but here and there came a thinning, a gap where the sheep had pushed through. She could have crushed herself into the hedge, have sought such a gap, even though the cattle were also crushed against it behind her, rearing up on it. There would have been a chance that way; there was little or none the way she had chosen. She was just possessed by the utmost agony of terror.

The man in charge of the herd shut the gate to behind him as the last animal was driven through. Suddenly he heard a scream. He looked round, but could see nothing, and in front of him the rushing cattle hid everything. The scream sounded again, and he guessed what had happened.

"Some fool of a woman," he thought, exasperated. "How like 'em!"

He realised the danger and his own difficult position. He was now behind the herd, driving them on to their frightened victim, and he could not get through them as matters were, at least not in time.

He climbed up on the five-barred gate and looked down the lane. He saw the long, lean, flying figure of a woman, but he could not see her face. As he looked she tripped, and he caught his breath as the beasts seemed to come down on her. Then she was up again, but losing ground.

He sprang down inside the field and tore along the hedge till he came to where the girl was on the other side of it.

"Come into the hedge here—quick!" he commanded imperiously, widening a little gap as he spoke and working his body through. "Stop! … oh, you little idiot!"

Being called a 'little idiot' somehow arrested Sally. She turned her head, pausing for an instant, and the man caught her by her skirts and pulled her with violent inelegance through the gap he had made.

"Of all the fool tricks!" he began.

Sally did not hear this last observation. Her reasoning powers had fled. She was only conscious that something had seized her. She thought of the red herd, struggled fiercely, and while she waited for the worst to come, screamed and screamed again.

"Don't be silly!" said somebody, shaking her.

She stopped screaming then, and found herself looking into Robert Kantyre's face. She dropped limply into his arms, fainting dead away.

Robert laid her hastily on the grass. He had not the vaguest idea what to do with a fainting woman, only had a sense of exasperation that they always—so he had been told—fainted at the most inappropriate time and place. As he looked down into the ashen face, a strand of bright yellow hair caught and held his attention. Then he recognised Sally, and frowned. She had saved his life against his will, dooming him to further misery, and now he had saved hers, with, so he hoped, more fortunate results, so that they were quits.

"I wonder how long they take to come to?" he asked himself uneasily, as the girl still lay as one dead.

At that moment Sally opened wide, terrified eyes that looked blacker than ever. "Then I'm not trampled to death?" she asked, surprised. "I thought I *felt* it seize me, fling me down."

"That was I," said the rescuer brusquely.

"Oh! ... was it?" Then her eyes blazed. "Well, it was the least you could do. You drove them right on to me. Why didn't you look what you were doing?"

Robert was taken aback. Here was gratitude! "How was I to know anybody was there?" he asked at length. "When I saw what had happened I called on you to stop."

Sally knit her brows. "I heard someone call me a 'little idiot,'" she said coldly. "Was that you?"

"I'm afraid it was, Miss Lunton. Pray accept my apologies."

"Not at all," replied Sally, her voice like ice. Then she added angrily,

"The idea! To stop under them instead of getting away! Was that all you could think of?"

"It was," said Kantyre laconically.

She got up and shook her dress. "Still, you got me through the hedge. I suppose you saved my life." She did not speak gratefully. 'Little idiot' was still rankling. "I should never have used the cattle way if it had been Wednesday. They only take them on market-day, and then there's a man waiting by the gates on to the road."

"Well, there'll be one about due now," said Robert; "he and I have to take them to Farleigh, as it couldn't be managed on Wednesday. Don't use this place again, Miss Lunton. After all, it isn't quite safe unless you follow the herd."

"I certainly shan't. I happen to be a little nervous about cattle. I don't believe I should mind so much if they hadn't horns, or weren't so red, or didn't bellow, or—"

Robert Kantyre smiled. "In fact, if they weren't cattle, Miss Lunton," he suggested.

"Well, I suppose that's about the size of it," she owned. "Still," more stiffly, "though I'm lots of things, I'm not little, and I'm not an idiot."

"Indeed you are not!" he returned quickly. "It was most unpardonable, but I didn't recognise you, for one thing; the words just escaped me, and I was almost as frightened as you were, and the poor beasts were, for it was fright with them too, you know."

"Oh yes," said Sally in a resigned tone, "of course I know. Cattle, or burglars, or snakes, are always much more frightened of you than you are of them. You've only got to remember that and keep perfectly calm. People always tell you that. Thanks so much."

Robert Kantyre flung back his head and laughed.

Sally stared at him. At this moment it was difficult to associate this man with the cashiered officer, or with the drunken outcast. She remembered that at their first meeting she had something to say which would put him at a disadvantage, but the tables had been turned. He had saved her life, and he quite obviously considered she had acted very foolishly, made herself rather ridiculous, in fact.

"It's odd how things never fit in," she thought.

For his part Robert Kantyre was looking at Sally with seeing eyes for the first time. He liked her black eyes and yellow hair, her slimness, even the angry curl of her mouth as she resented his crudeness. He felt a momentary interest and forgetfulness.

Women had not come into his life; his career had been everything. He was not the type that marries for money, and without money marriage was impossible; therefore he very wisely kept out of temptation. His chief affection had been given to his mother, whose death he had hastened by his disgrace, and there had been a great sympathy between his father and himself. That father had now become a child again, and that thing also lay at his door. His five prim elder sisters he had never understood. Sally struck him as different from any woman he had ever met. Before his disgrace he had been a masterful man, efficient and commanding, and he had not gone to pieces all at once, or completely even yet. It was the accumulated horror of the thing, and the loneliness of his position, that had flung him down.

In this almost ridiculous rescue of Sally he had found something of his lost manhood, been masterful, perhaps even a trifle superior. He had hated her for rescuing him; it was a humiliating turn of the tables that his strong masculine sense abhorred. Then she had lectured him on that black day, affected to understand what no woman ever could understand, and taken advantage of his shattered nerves to get the horrible story out of him. She alone in all the world knew the exact truth, and he had rather she knew nothing. She had looked down on him from the immeasurable heights that day, an imperious goddess pointing out to a foolish mortal the error of his ways. She had taken his revolver from him, as the mother takes the injurious toy from the bad little boy. No, decidedly he had not liked Sally then!

Now she had come off her pedestal with a rush, no goddess looking down on frailty, but something more frail still, and quite as foolish. That side of him that was so eager to get back to the lost place she had helped infinitely more by being saved than by saving. He had not wanted her offered friendship or any help she had fancied she could give, but he had a sudden need for it now. It had seemed but a straw for a drowning man to cling to, now it was at least willing human hands.

"Of course I'm very much obliged," she said, laughing herself. "I suppose it was rather funny, really—most things are; but it will never amuse me personally."

"It must have been dreadful for you," he said sympathetically. "It makes us quits, doesn't it?"

It was the first time he had shown any gratitude, and Sally augured great things from his tone. He was glad, then! Then she thought of the relief in his voice, and wondered again.

"You prefer being quits?" she asked.

He flushed darkly. "I—I should hate to be under an obligation to anyone," he burst out, "let alone to—"

"A mere woman?" she finished for him.

"Oh, I didn't mean that, only—"

"I understand," she returned thoughtfully. Her heart failed her a little at thought of the hateful task ahead. She must say something, tell him she knew, see if he would not try and help himself. Yet what could she say? It seemed to her entirely impossible, almost indecent, to hint at the thing, and hints would probably be of small avail with this blunt young man.

Robert let pass a statement which he considered absurd, but he felt his interest in her deepen. After all, few men were as much alone in the world as he. Mother dead, father childish, sisters repudiating him; it only remained for his godfather and Uncle Robert to do the same. Uncle Robert had been his boyhood's hero, though among the Kantyres he was called 'unsatisfactory,' or 'a rolling stone.' But what true boy doesn't love a rolling stone and his stories of strange cities and strange men? Uncle Robert, his father's elder brother, would descend upon them without notice and leave in the same fashion, giving good cheer and jollity, and asking nothing. It was his son John who had died at Spion Kop, for he had followed the Kantyre tradition and gone into the army. Now John's son, all that was left to the elder Robert, was fighting in the Canadian contingent at the Front. Robert's uncle had taken up Government land in the most desolate reaches of the North-West Territory, and his grandson and he had been doing well there. Robert wondered how the old man got on alone, and above all why he had never written since the disgrace. He felt that deeply, for he had hoped for a less harsh judgment from his godfather.

His face grew very sombre again.

"Gillet says you are a wonder," said Sally.

"So you called about my character? Was that all he said?"

Sally took the bull by the horns. "No," she said brusquely, "and I went into The Hut and poured it down the sink."

There was rather a tense silence. Robert looked away from her, his face dark-red. He was bitterly ashamed, and angry too. This girl seemed bent on humiliating him.

Sally strove for lightness. "I suppose I could be taken up for doing a thing like that," she said quickly, "burglary or something, or being on the premises with felonious intent; but, you see, I had to. You are so much too good for that sort of thing. I can't believe that—that—" she paused, stammering a little, but her eyes asked a question.

"There are things—" he began with set teeth. "It's for forgetfulness."

"I was sure it was only that," she said, relieved.

"Yes, only that," he echoed in tones she did not like.

"Surely people can—can forget worthily, as well as unworthily."

He looked at her directly. "How, Miss Lunton?"

Sally had no answer. She simply did not know. She knew there must be ways and means, if only she could think of them. "It's only since—then?"

He nodded.

She drew a breath of relief. Oh, he could be easily saved, if she could find the way. "You don't like the—the stuff?"

He made a face of disgust. "I hate it!"

"But you realise? Hate it or not, after a time a craving for it will come; you will not be able to stop then, but you can stop now. Oh, Captain Kantyre, be worthy of what you were before disaster overtook you, and of what you still may be! Don't go under to such a mean, low enemy!"

He knit his brows. Here was the goddess-girl again! How low and bestial she made him feel, because she could not understand. "When I'm working I can stick it," he said rather sullenly, "and I love the horses; but when the work's done there isn't a soul to speak to, no sleep, and—and things crowd on one so."

"I know how they crowd," she said in a low voice, "but there must be something. It is the evening hours after work? Oh, couldn't you do something, go somewhere?"

"Where do pariahs go, Miss Lunton? There are only the public-houses. I have not come to them yet, but I shall do. There will be companionship of a sort there."

"I wish you'd come to the vicarage. You would like my guardian. I have spoken of you, and he's an understanding dear and a real man, not a bit like the average parson."

Robert's grey eyes flashed. "You have told him my history?"

"Oh no, no! How could I? The secret is not mine."

"I couldn't come to see him without his knowing," he said restlessly, "and I cannot endure the thought of anyone knowing. Besides, I am just a working-man now."

Sally considered for a moment, and then said slowly, "Do you know The Mountain?"

"Do you mean the hump behind the vicarage?"

Sally laughed. "The hump! Good gracious! If a really true Cramptonian could hear you! Why, even Lovey would exhibit the old Adam—his name is Adam," she explained, "and you would see most unclerical fire in his blue eyes. Yes, that's The Mountain, and the vicarage back gate opens on to the path that winds up it. From here you reach it by the other side, if you go through the cattle way, down the moor road, and turn into the lower moor road, the first turning on your left. I usually go to the top and have a look at the sea in the evening. Won't you come too? There must be heaps of things we could find to talk about, and we've saved each other's lives, and are both strays—"

He stared at her in astonishment. This beautiful, elegant girl a 'stray!'

"You mean we neither of us belong here. Well, that is so, of course."

"No," said Sally sombrely, "I did not mean that. I meant that the war has flung both of us on the rocks, and that we've got to hang on to our courage and help each other for all we're worth."

His eyes lightened. "Do you mean I can help you in any way?"

"Indeed you can, if you will be my friend. There is nobody here." She held out her hand. "Then that's a bargain?"

He took it in a firm clasp, noticing its slender beauty. "Thank you," he said, "it is a bargain—till you break it."

"Oh, I shan't do that," she exclaimed confidently; "it's about my only virtue—keeping my word. What a relief it will be to be myself, to throw away the mask now and then. It's been simply gummed to my face lately, and that's so uncomfortable, isn't it?"

Perhaps if she could interest Robert Kantyre in herself, gain his real liking, the battle would be half won. She was ready to make certain sacrifices. She knew the man was worth saving, and she did not stop to count the cost. That was not her way; when she gave, she gave generously.

He thought of the mask he would be henceforth compelled to wear. "It is horrible," he said. "Now I must go and see to the cattle. Thank you so much, Miss Lunton."

"For having my life saved?" she laughed.

"Yes," he said, "for that, and other things. And may I come on Monday? if it's fine, of course."

"You can depend upon finding me there," she replied. "There are bowlders on the top; I take a seat on the very topmost of them." Then she remembered that at Farleigh it might occur to him to replenish his store of brandy. She could not mention her fear, but she tried to make her voice confident as she turned with a gay farewell.

Robert had been about to replenish his stock, though not to use it for that night, at least; but he returned to The Hut without a parcel, and wrestled with the thing that sought to overturn his reason. If he could endure for to-night, and Sunday night, then on Monday she would be with him to help him, perhaps to make him forget for an hour or two, give him something to think of so that sleep might become possible.

Sally passed Miss Maggie, who wondered at her flushed cheeks, and when near Little Crampton started and frowned at sight of Mr. Bingley walking in the distance with a dove-coloured costume. Odd to think that she had actually forgotten Mr. Bingley and all that was his! She remembered him now as her one means of escape.

"I must get something more doveish still," she decided.

She turned into Red House Lane, and here, quite suddenly, she forgot the man of the moors, Mr. Bingley, and everything, for not far away someone was trying to whistle 'Tipperary.'

The colour drained slowly out of her face, and then flooded it again in a burning wave of scarlet. Her heart seemed to stop, and then to bound chokingly. Sheer joy flooded her being, and she stumbled blindly forward, her hands held out.

There was only one person in the world unable to achieve something a little like the tune of 'Tipperary' after its many months of ubiquity.

"Jimmy," she cried huskily, "oh, *Jimmy*. ..."

CHAPTER XI

"What on earth are you doing here?"

An ordinary left and a bandaged right hand grasped Sally's. "If it isn't Sally Lunn! What on earth are *you* doing here?" exclaimed a young man, shaking her hands up and down. He was little and lithe and full of vitality. He had eyebrows slanting upwards like the picture of Puck, and a mouth that was Puckish too. His other features simply did not count, though his eyes were nice enough. His nose turned up, and that did not matter, either; he possessed that nameless thing called charm.

"Me! It's what are *you* doing?" she got out.

So he had cared, after all, and now that at last he was free to do so he had sought her out, and would ask her to be his wife! They would go out into the world together, beggars, but happy. A camp in summer on life's highway, in the winter a garret, but a camp and garret shared with Jimmy!

"Me doing here?" he laughed boyishly. "Well, that's good, that is! Why, Sally Lunn, I'm simply swanking all round the place, a millionaire, not even a Thompkins any longer. I'm Wilmot-Randal of the Red House now. Luck devil, ain't I? But I was always that."

Sally pulled away her hands, and the colour came and went in her face. "So you are the lucky one!" she exclaimed at length. "How—how frightfully jolly!" She laughed shakily. She felt sick at heart and dazed.

Then a sharp anguish shook her, and a bitter sense of incongruity. It was so obvious that the man had forgotten the one mad month of their lives and remembered only their months of friendship, while she had forgotten neither, but thought only of that which had had so little to do with friendship, and which she had hugged so closely to her heart all these years—the blazing passion of her youth.

It was as if Paolo and Francesca had not been slain but only separated, and that years afterwards they had met, in town, perhaps, and while Francesca came forward to fling her life to him he had said:

"I say, this *is* a surprise, isn't it? What jolly weather we are having! Sorry I can't stop, but I've got to hop it into the Park and 'form fours' and rot like that."

He drew her towards a stile. "Sit down, Sally Lunn, and then we'll give our tongues a chance. Ladies first!"

She pulled herself together, laughed as she had laughed six years back, and, seating herself on the stile, swung her feet backwards and forwards.

"No, Jimmy, you are bursting with it. You shall have first go."

He had gone out of her life like a flash, and now, after six years, he had come back into it again—but with what a difference!

He had been a clerk in a British firm when she knew him, one who loathed clerking, but had no other chance of livelihood. His mother had been partly dependent upon him, for her income was only some sixty pounds a year. He had been twenty-two—he was three years her junior—and, as he owned frankly, barely worth the hundred pounds per annum his firm paid him. They had sent him over to a branch office in Paris for six months, and he had come across Sally, and practically lived at her studio. They had been chums, and the young man had not thought of her in any other light until her own passionate love for him had awakened some response, something not quite love, perhaps, but akin and easily mistaken, something young and reckless.

His work in Paris ended, he was given a month's holiday before returning to the occupation which meant his mother's livelihood as well as his own, and to the tiny cottage in the suburb where they lived together.

Friends were going on a tour in Italy, doing it cheaply, walking from place to place. It was arranged that Sally and Jimmy should go with them. Neither meant it to be more than that, though the girl hoped that the man she was so desperately in love with would come to love her before they had to say good-bye, and that they would part betrothed and with a mutual future before them.

It did not happen like that. First of all the friends decided on a route the others did not care about, and Sally and Jimmy left them to go their own way, not thinking much about it one way or the other. The man, who had come of conventional people and their ways, would have qualms now and then, and feel a little startled and a little uneasy. Sally had no such qualms; she was too happy.

The land of lovers and passion; love and passion and youth! Most could have foretold the end, kindly philosopher or cynic. The tour became no more and no less than a honeymoon.

Then the parting—kissing, clinging, tears, incoherent words. And then six years of silence. And now!

Jimmy had returned to find his mother very ill, and in the losing fight for her life he had forgotten Sally. When she did not hear from him she was too proud to write and ask him why. She tried to put him out of her life, but she never blamed him. Perhaps she knew too well who had been most to blame.

After his mother's death Jimmy remembered Sally; that is, Sally the friend, not Sally the lover. Somehow he had grown ashamed of that, and wished only to forget. He had met Dinah, a magnificent young creature whom he had loved magnificently at first sight and since.

Dinah had been worth his love and any sacrifice. She had come out of a crowded Cornish vicarage to do typewriting in the city. This freeborn daughter of English hedgerows had hated her job just as much as Jimmy hated his, but she had been no less conscientious. When the young man returned to the office after his mother's death he found her there, and at once hated the episode of Sally. He could find no excuse for his own conduct now, and called himself every hard name under the sun. Then the head of the firm, a rich and kindly man, had proposed to splendid Di, and the foolish girl had refused him and fallen in love with the clerk. The head of the firm very sensibly married someone else, and showed no resentment towards the rash young couple.

It was they who thought it kinder to seek another post, not he who dismissed them. Jimmy took the post of clerk at the same salary elsewhere, and Dinah took the post of clerk's wife. After all, that sixty pounds per annum private means made things seem a little less rash. Unfortunately, while expenses increased, for a small Jimmy and Di appeared on the scene, neither private means nor salary did, and though life was happiness it was none the less a struggle.

Then came the war to complicate matters. Jimmy's firm failed and he was without a berth. It so happened that his life had been insured for a thousand pounds when he was very young, on his mother's account, and the insurance company agreed to make out a new policy covering war risks. Consequently, if anything happened to him, Dinah would have about a hundred a year and a tiny pension, and would just be able to manage in a country cottage. The vicarage was not so crowded now, and her people could well do with a daughter at home.

Therefore Dinah and her husband made the sacrifice, nerving themselves up to the parting that might be for ever on this side. Neither guessed the extraordinary good turn it was to do them. Jimmy returned with a bad hand, and to riches beyond the dreams of avarice. The young couple almost went off their heads with delight, and rushed into a perfect orgy of shopping. They did not, however, forget others, and there were many who could already testify to thoughtful generosity.

Jimmy had told his wife the episode of Sally, though not her name. At the same time there had been something so vital about the personality of the girl he had almost loved that he had given rather a clear little portrait of her. Dinah was horribly sorry for the girl, but, knowing herself to reign alone in her husband's heart, was utterly above the littleness and insecurity of jealousy.

"Go on, Jimmy!" prompted Sally.

"It's all so rum. Well, I had an aunt, an awful old dragon," he began. "She came to see us once, said to my mother, 'No gentlewoman ever marries a man called Thompkins,' refused to see my father, asked for me, and observing, 'What an odd-looking child! Is he all right?' without waiting for an answer marched out of the house. We never saw her or heard of her again till the lawyer's letter came. Di and I—well, we went clean off it!"

"Dinah is your wife?"

"Dinah is an angel. Oh, I can't talk of Di!" There was a note she had never heard before in his voice, a look she did not know they could hold in his dark-brown eyes.

She kept steady under the stab. "You are happy?" she asked slowly.

"Happy! It's more than that."

"You have two children, I think?" She paused for a moment, and added, "What a lot has happened to you, Jimmy, and how little to me!"

"Little James is four, just like me—poor little fellow!—tea-pot nose and all. But Di is exactly like her mother; she's two, and rather decent. They're not so bad, you know, Sally, for kids." He tried to sound casual, but was not altogether successful.

Sally realised how far this man with his idols and his riches was from those old Italian days.

There was indeed nothing of that Jimmy left. He really had forgotten Italy, if not Paris. He was too happy and devoted with the one woman to remember what another had been to him for one casual month. Casual! That just expressed it, and now that the real thing had come the casual ones were as if they had never been. He had only really begun to live since he met Dinah.

Sally realised this, and tried to be glad that he was happy; but at his mention of the little boy so like himself a fierce pang of jealousy rent her. She was certain she would hate Dinah, who was, of course, an entirely commonplace person with a beautiful face, masquerading as the ideal.

"Yes, you're lucky, and no mistake," was all she said.

"Rather! You see, though Di is an angel, she's a human angel. Not the icy kind that freezes you a little and makes you feel all base clay, but the helping sort. Too good people hinder us earthly ones, instead of helping. They can't enter in. Di keeps the wings well out of sight, and the feathers are the soft, not the scratchy kind. Some angels scratch you, don't they? Oh, you will like her awfully!"

"I'm sure I shall," asserted the dispossessed, already heartily sick of Dinah and all her virtues.

"And she will take to you no end."

"That will be jolly."

"Yes, won't it? She wants a woman friend badly. In the meanwhile, where do you live? Tell me everything."

"I live with Lovey, *pro tem.* In other words, the Reverend Adam Lovelady. A sort of guardian of mine. You've met him."

"The parson? A ripping chap."

"Rather! Dear Lovey is a man first, a parson next, and a gentleman all the time." Then her eyes twinkled and she added, "He ought to be put in a glass case and labeled 'unique.'"

He laughed. "The same Sally, I see."

"Oh, exactly the same," she lied, "save that my skin and-bones livelihood has taken to itself wings and fled away."

"Then you aren't doing anything special now?"

"Aren't I!" she exclaimed recklessly, "that's all you know about it. I am very busy trying to marry a simply awful man called Bingley!"

CHAPTER XII

"Jimmy, that is the girl you told me about?"

Jimmy threw back his head and laughed. Then he gasped out, "Marry! You!" It was somehow difficult to associate Sally with marriage.

"Well, why not?" demanded the girl, perhaps a trifle sharply. "Have you forgotten that I am rather an elderly person? Thirty-one, and looking it."

"You look ripping," he returned, contemplating her. "I say, what's—what's happened to your hair?"

She explained briefly, adding, "It attracts the prize, but he isn't quite sure whether he approves of it or not. I had no idea marrying was such hard work. I advance, but I can never maintain my position for any length of time, let alone consolidate it. Oh, Jimmy, he would make you laugh! He plays at being the perfect gentleman all the time, and merely succeeds in being the imperfect lady. I hate the beast!"

"I thought you were joking," he exclaimed, relieved. "Bingley—what a name!"

"With Alfred before it, but an income with it. No, I am not joking. I can't afford to joke any longer. I'm in dead earnest, but unfortunately so is my rival, Mrs. Dalton." She explained the situation, and Jimmy laughed, but rather mirthlessly.

"Oh, Sally, you have changed, after all," he reproached her. "You would never have thought of a thing like that once. It—it sounds rather rotten, I think. Surely a man has a right to—"

He paused, for he did not quite know how to put it.

"What?" demanded Sally rather tensely.

Then he remembered, and went scarlet. He could find no words to say, only stand there the picture of agonised shame and embarrassment.

"Please go on," commanded the girl.

"To—to be m-m-married for himself, not for his m-m-money," he got out at length, stammering badly.

She turned for an instant and looked straight into his eyes, and he could not meet her glance. Jimmy was incapable of lying or deceit; when, for the sake of another, he forced himself to a lie, he made a sorry bungle of it. To the two women who loved him he was absolutely transparent. He was rather fatally so now.

"I thought you were going to say something else," said Sally in a hard voice; "what all men think, I suppose. There's only one virtue that really matters in a woman, is there, Jimmy, when it comes to marriage?" She longed to strike out like some tortured thing.

The young man went hot all over. He caught her hand. "Oh, hush, Sally, old girl," he implored her, "I was a scoundrel."

She snatched her hand away, bent on self-torture. "Even a Bingley thing is too good for me now? You would take his side against me."

"No, no! Don't, dear. It was all my fault."

"No, it wasn't," she contradicted flatly, "and you know it wasn't. You won't be able to introduce me to your wife now you remember, will you, Jimmy?" Her face twisted.

He flushed. "But she knows," he said, "of course I told her."

Sally stood very stiff. "Did you give her my name and address while you were about it?"

"No, not your name, just—just … she has no idea who it was."

"What did you tell her?"

"How we became friends, what a Bohemian lot we were—"

"Bohemians are more often respectable than not. Didn't you use the words 'sordid' or 'disreputable'? *Didn't* you, Jimmy?"

He stood first on one foot, then on the other. "I—I might have done."

"You could truthfully have done so. Well, what then?"

"How we went away quite—quite innocently, and drifted into—into—"

She set her teeth hard. What had he named the wonderful thing that had glorified her? "I suppose you used the word 'sin'?" she said. "Did you also add, 'The woman tempted me'?"

"Oh, Sally, never! How can you, dear! She knows I was alone to blame, that we mistook passion for love."

The girl laughed harshly. "So that was your explanation!"

"I felt so bad about it afterwards."

"When you remembered. But you didn't often remember, did you, Jimmy?"

"My mother was dying, and then I met Di."

"And only thought of her?"

"Yes."

"I just ceased to exist?"

"No, no, Sally. I forgot how I had wronged you, and remembered only our happy friendship days. They were so much the best, the—the finest."

"Oh, much!" she agreed, catching her breath.

"I knew you thought so too; that made me hate myself the more."

"How tiresome of me to remind you about it," she said coldly, "and now of all times! Do you consider such an—an episode in a woman's life and a man's on the same footing?"

He did not, and was silent.

"I see. As far as marriage is concerned, I am beyond the pale now, because I am the woman. If it had been your wife—"

Something in his face stopped her. "Hush," he said fiercely, "such a thing would be impossible."

"You mean you would not have loved her the same, trusted her, married her, if—just the little 'if,' Jimmy." She laughed rather drearily.

His eyes snapped. "We will not bring my wife into the discussion."

"Thank you, I am answered indeed!"

For a moment neither spoke, and the silence grew unbearable.

Then the man said huskily, "Oh, can you ever forgive me?"

"There is no question of that, only you are a little illogical, aren't you? You are to be permitted to forget, but never I. Yet you have paid no price. Your wife forgave you and married you just the same, as women, wise or foolish, do the whole world over. You look at the matter one way and I the other—the man's and the woman's way. You ran no real risk of losing your wife by confessing. I lose everything in this world; some think everything in the next. No, such things are not on the same footing, after all."

"I—"

"Mr. Bingley is the most outrageously virtuous man I have ever met; he is the first, and I hope he'll be the last. For him even to suspect would mean ruin, and you ask me to pay a further price. To go on paying and paying, I suppose. Oh, it is not fair, it is not reasonable."

"I do not—"

"You ask me to give up Mr. Bingley."

"Not that, only to be straight with him."

"The same thing! Oh, push me into the gutter, Jimmy; perhaps I haven't so very far to go."

"*Sally!*" He was deeply shocked.

"That's the alternative," she went on; "he's the other, not a nice one either, but the lesser evil, and—marry him I will!" She brought her hand down smartly on the stile and tightened her lips.

Randal said nothing.

"Of course, if you consider it your duty to tell him—"

He cried out at that.

"*He* would, if the positions were reversed."

He put his hand on her arm. "In the old days you always did the straight thing; you will do it now when the test comes."

"In the old days I hadn't learned that the straight thing doesn't always pay; I know better now. You would be surprised at what I have learned since, Jimmy."

"You haven't unlearned how to play the game," he said steadily. "You'll do that when the time comes."

"And lose fifteen hundred a year, and ease!" she exclaimed, staring at him. "Good Lord! Not much, Jimmy!"

"If he cares for you truly—"

"They never do—when it comes to facing a thing like this. In any case, he would think of me differently, be jealous always and exacting, and never trust me. You are all the same. Suppose it had been—"

His face set. "Sally, there are things one can't suppose," he said in a tone that closed the discussion.

"The Bingleys are a race apart. They never care for anybody but themselves and their own inflated dignity and importance. Their women must be like Caesar's wife. They wouldn't take off their hat to Venus or the Queen of Sheba unless they were sure they carried perfectly correct marriage-certificates. It's not hypocrisy; they aren't hypocrites; they carry out their own laws and limitations exactly and at any sacrifice. They are estimable in one way, and hateful in all others. And you ask me to put myself at the mercy of the unco guid! He would fly in horror, fearful lest he had been contaminated. He shall never, never guess. If he were a different sort of man, someone I cared for or could get to care for, or even to admire or respect, I would tell him, yes, whatever the cost! But I'd never tell the Bingley people anything. One can't afford to."

"Then let him go. He is unworthy. Wait till someone comes along that you *can* care for."

"That is impossible; and oh, you talk like a fool!"

"Why impossible?"

"There's nobody to come, for one thing; for another I can't afford to wait any longer, and finally I neither desire to care nor possess the capacity of doing so."

He was startled, shaken by a sudden fear. "What do you mean?" he asked quickly.

"My dear Jimmy, there are many of us like that. We're too selfish or too casual, too ambitious or too pleasure-loving. We don't do it, that's all. We try and get somebody with a comfortable income to care for us. It comes cheaper and, after all, lots of men never know the difference."

"They do if it's the real thing," he insisted.

"Then I'll play the game as men play it," she retorted. "It's always best to ask no questions and receive no lies. Present and future belong to husband or wife, but the past is ours, a dead thing they have no right to. Mr. Bingley is a caricature of all the worst virtues. Besides, he hasn't proposed yet. I have encountered heavy reverses lately; the enemy has taken up an impregnable position and is shelling me out of my trench. He has also brought up reinforcements in the shape of a nice plump widow and a jolly little girl."

"You were ever so different six years ago. You had ideals then."

"Doubtless I had many things then I haven't now. One sheds as one goes along. How bare we must get by fifty!"

"One gains, too."

"Not all of us," she said bitterly; "it's mostly the losing game we play, more kicks than halfpence that fall to our share, more breaks than mends. But I will not talk like this any more if you don't like it. I don't to others often."

"When you and Di become friends—"

"I'll drop being unworthy and pursuing Bingleys in the face of such an example? Oh no, I won't, Jimmy; that isn't this Sally's way. When she wants a thing she wants it badly, and fares forth to get it. She wants the Bingley, not for himself, but for what he represents. She won't confess either, ever. When a woman comes down to a man's level in this way he always considers her immeasurably below it. I don't expect to be soulfully happy, but I'd rather be uncomfortable with money than uncomfortable without. I have a very keen zest for life and fun and all the fleshpots. True, I can rejoice in a lark's song, but I can equally rejoice in a Bond Street shop-window—and I should miss the shop-window most. I'm not the type of which heroines and pioneers and Colonists are made; I leave that splendid work to others. You don't catch me going off to the wilds with my bundle on my back to make a home for some man, and tread the lone trail. Oh no, Jimmy, my dear, have no illusions! I've never known what it was to have what I am out to get now. I'm not going to become such another as Lydia Hopkins, either. Her life is a tragedy because she never wanted anything in the world but to get married—and she didn't. That reminds me: we must be careful of Miss Maggie Hopkins. She has a sort of evil genius for lighting on—on things."

"Why can't some nice man turn up for you? Why can't you be happy, as I am?" he exclaimed.

"Ask me another," she returned lightly. "Perhaps I don't deserve him, though it's the undeserving that carry off the various prizes in this world,

I think. Still, your 'nice man' might be a beggar, and really I couldn't face that. I'm a little beast, I know, but there it is, and it's too late to change now. So many nice men have a nasty way of being beggars. I don't want sentiment, it doesn't pay, and I don't even believe in it, but I want safety and all the things women hold dear."

"The best things, surely?"

"Oh, good gracious, now you are trying to preach at me! Everybody preaches at me sooner or later," she complained, "mostly sooner, dash it! It's such a superior world. I do envy the preachers. Such a nice soft, fat job; so full of unction. How delightful to be bung-up with virtue, and preach at those without! Or rolling in money and preaching at those with none on how to live on a farthing a day, and how wicked to descend to deceit to obtain something in an hour of desperate need! How delightful to be a richly-endowed British matron with an admirable husband, and to preach at spinsters with none. 'You really *should* get married, my dear; time doesn't stand still.'"

"Sally—"

"Young spinsters with shady pasts trying to marry silent, strong men with fifteen hundred a year and 'perks'! Shocking! As if they deserved any sort of husbands, the hussies! Just wait till I am Mrs. Alfred Bingley, one of the 'haves' instead of one of the despicable 'have-nots'! Won't I give it them, just! Won't I be the very devil of a preacher!" Her face was flaming.

Jimmy looked at her in distress. A new Sally had arisen from the ashes of the old, and he liked the old one best. "Don't get bitter, old girl," he said at length, "it takes the flavour out of everything. You were gay as a lark six years ago."

"I was twenty-five, and had a livelihood and a career of sorts. Now I have nothing. I am a failure and thirty-one. I suppose your wife is younger than you?"

"Three years younger; she's just twenty-five."

"Ah, the ideal age for everything and everybody, not too young, and not yet too old. Is this Mrs. Wilmot-Randal coming now? You were right; she is very beautiful."

The woman that came towards them was most nobly planned in every way, and her beauty was magnificent. Perfect features, an exquisite skin, the hair that artists love to paint, and yet warm perfection. Even more than beauty dwelt in her face, for a radiant happiness and something noble illumined it.

Jimmy gazed at her with all his heart in his eyes. "She is lovely all through," he said in a hushed voice. He went up to her, and drew her hand through his arm. "Dinah, this is my friend Sally Lunton. She lives with that jolly parson we met the other day, and she's an old chum of my Paris days."

Dinah Wilmot-Randal held out a friendly hand. "Oh, how nice!" she exclaimed. "All this is so new to us, money and things, that we simply ache to show them off, and we want to know about Little Crampton and the people and everything. The house is so lovely, and the garden is a dream. Will you come back with us now?"

Sally tried to hate, and failed. Dinah Randal was too frank, too simple to gather hatred as her portion. She stood far above rivalry and jealousy.

"I have to get back to Lovey," said Sally. It was easy for the possessor to be friendly; less easy for the dispossessed. She departed, promising to come and see them, and all their possessions, very soon.

Randal and his wife walked home arm-in-arm. At last she said slowly, "Jimmy, that is the girl you told me about?"

"Yes, darling, but how did you guess?"

"I just knew."

"I am sorry you guessed."

"She shall never know I know, Jimmy."

Silence fell again, a silence of complete understanding.

"After I had told you, and you forgave me, I forgot," he said. "I seemed to have no time to think of anybody but you."

"When you saw her again didn't you remember?"

"No, only about the friendship. Then something she said brought it all back. It was a bad moment, Di, as if a corpse long dead, long forgotten, had come out of its grave. I shall never cease to reproach myself; yet I think she had forgotten too, till something we were talking about led up to it."

Mrs. Wilmot-Randal said nothing. She knew that Sally had not forgotten, believed she never would forget, and she knew that she still cared for Jimmy, and that the girl had flung her all into the scale and lost. She did not despise her, far from it. She understood too well, and was too sorry.

She had everything that life could offer; the other had nothing. She was right in the heart of an earthly Paradise; Sally barred out. One had love and riches and children; the other had not even a home. She wondered if there was anything she could do to help the other, any possibility of becoming real friends. She felt a little guilty, as if she owed Sally something.

"She is most attractive," she said at length. "What a contrast between eyes and hair!"

Jimmy explained about the hair, and Dinah was interested and amused.

The children met them on the doorstep, a delightful pair, and the happy family went into the house. Jimmy caught up the little boy so ludicrously like himself, Dinah the little girl.

"Let's go and gloat over all the things that seem too good to be true," Randal suggested, "and see if there's anything else in the catalogues we can find to buy!"

They turned, laughing. They had already forgotten Sally.

CHAPTER XIII

"I might have known she would fail me"

On Monday afternoon Sally had tea with the Bolivers. As she came out of their gate she ran into Dinah Wilmot-Randal, and felt compelled to stop. She murmured some conventional greeting and looked down at the exquisite baby girl toddling by her mother's side. "What a picture!" she exclaimed.

Then the little boy ran from behind bis mother, and at sight of this miniature Jimmy, Puckish eyebrows, mouth and all, startled anguish gripped Sally, and she was not quick enough to hide it.

As she looked up she met Dinah's eyes, and knew that she knew—and pitied. She could have borne anything but the pity, and burst into rash speech.

"So you have heard of my wild oats?" she said jerkily.

Dinah did not know what to say, and murmured inadequately, "It was so long ago. I'm—I'm very sorry."

"How good of you!" Sally's voice was a little icy. "Are you sure you wish to continue the acquaintance? It's scarcely usual, is it?"

"I want to be your friend if you will let me." Dinah was horribly embarrassed, and wished she could think of the right thing to say.

"Then you don't insist on the 'gallery-picturesque' idea? The dim-lit cathedral, dim religious light, slow music, and kneeling penitent, voicing, 'God be merciful to me, a sinner'?" asked Sally with a sneer.

"Don't!" begged Dinah, shocked and startled.

"I'm pretty horrible, aren't I? It isn't Jimmy, you know," she looked with hard eyes at Jimmy's wife, "it's his ten thousand a year. Naturally that rankles. You have so much, haven't you?"

"Too much," said Dinah, "and I don't deserve any of it."

"And I have nothing, and can't even get that beastly Mr. Bingley," thought Sally, while aloud she said, "Oh, I expect you deserve it; but it's easy to be an angel on ten thousand a year."

"It is indeed!" agreed Mrs. Randal, trying to laugh naturally. Both made the most of the worldly question and ignored the other; and both knew that it was only the other that mattered.

Then they saw Jimmy coming, and flushed, avoiding each other's eyes. He greeted them gladly, and they went part of the way home in company, Sally her gay self again. The awkwardness passed, and Sally promised to be their first caller at the Red House and come for tea on the following day. Then, waving farewell, she ran into the vicarage. Dinah said nothing of her outburst.

"Well," thought Sally, "some get all the ups and others get all the downs, and we must just make the best of it, I suppose." Tears started behind her eyelids, but she swallowed them resolutely. "Now Sally, you silly ass, stop it!" she commanded. "Where's your grit? Besides, it's no use. I wish she wasn't such a good sort; it puts one at such a disadvantage. Anyway, it's always better to laugh than do the other thing, and one can at least *try* to laugh!"

It was, however, rather a shaky attempt.

"It's a nasty facer all ways," she told herself. "That lucky, lucky woman—and luckiest because she deserves it all! She's in the fold, I'm barred out, 'a little black sheep that's gone astray.'"

She remembered a text not long since chosen by the Reverend Adam for his sermon, 'Other sheep have I who are not of this fold.'

"Grey sheep, I suppose," thought Sally, "for I'm not even a nice glossy inky black, just a dingy grey. Ugh! The black sheep have no fold, and we all know the fold of the white sheep. I wonder what that of the grey is like, and if they ever find it? Perhaps it's just like walking to the sea; something at which one never arrives."

She entered the hall in no cheerful frame of mind, and found Mr.

Lovelady awaiting her. "Your new frock and hat have come," he said; "let's open the parcel, and see if we think Little Crampton will approve."

"One can only hope not," thought Sally, for Little Crampton, for the most part, wore coverings, not clothes. She forced herself to take an interest in her parcel. Yes, the scheme had been skilfully carried out.

"Well, what do you think of it, Lovey?"

"How wide the skirt looks, and how short!"

"The better to show one's ankles, my dear, as the wolf didn't say to Little Red Riding-hood."

"But I thought they had been doing that—er—quite enough," said the puzzled parson.

"Not *quite* enough, it seems. How do you like the colour? Love-birds, you know, doveish, only more so. So piquant with the right sort of legs. Now doesn't it remind you how love-birds look? I wish I could remember the right sort of noise to make. I must learn to coo softer than the dove in this, and seem less sinuous. My latest ambition is to cease to curl and learn to creak."

Mr. Lovelady looked bewildered at nonsense which to him was quite incomprehensible; then he put his hand on the girl's shoulder.

"Aren't you well, dear? You look very white, and your voice sounds odd. Is your throat sore?"

"I have been laughing with Jimmy and his wife," she returned, "and perhaps that has made my voice sound husky. It is all so awfully amusing. Of course I'm well. Fate has left me that asset, as yet. If Mr. Bingley were here he would make the 'bromide' remark that the world is a small place, after all."

"It certainly is an odd coincidence," agreed Mr. Lovelady, who had heard of the matter at once, "but very pleasant, my dear."

"Oh, very pleasant. It's so pleasant for Jimmy coming into ten thousand a year and the Red House property, but it makes even Mr. Bingley seem mighty small 'pertaters,' doesn't it? Well, I must go and try on the new creation."

She caught it up and ran upstairs, but she did not try it on. Till the gong sounded for supper she lay face downwards on her bed, and went up early to her room. It was proving a difficult and trying time, a very difficult time.

Meanwhile, on the top of The Mountain, Robert Kantyre waited feverishly for Sally to keep her appointment, to hold out the promised help. He was very close to desperation. For two nights he had not slept, but had lived over and over again those ghastly hours. He must sleep to-night or go mad; have something else to think of, some human hand to cling to. This girl who seemed so strong and sure must find a way.

When she did not come he grew impatient, but he never doubted her coming till the dusk crept up from the valley and covered his feet. Then he knew she would not come. Rage and bitterness seized him. So quick to promise, so casual about keeping the given word!

"I might have known she would fail me," he thought. "Well, I'll not make a fool of myself a second time. I have done with her, done with the losing fight."

He took a parcel back with him to The Hut. When midnight came he lay across his bed in a drunken stupor, his face dark-red, an uncomely sight. He was lower than the beasts that perish, but he had at least shut out those sights and sounds, and forgetfulness, if not peace, was with him. Henceforth it was to be the line of least resistance.

CHAPTER XIV

"What sort of an Italian tour?"

It was Maggie's undisputed privilege to make the first call on newcomers and issue her report in detail. Previous to this call she found out what she could, usually more than anyone would have believed possible.

She had been unable to find out anything against the Wilmot-Randals, so far. True, they had been very poor, and their name had previously been Thompkins, but that was not a thing a Hopkins could dwell on overmuch. They had been perfectly frank about the poverty and the Thompkins, too frank about everything. Miss Maggie liked people to be close; then she knew they had the more ta hide.

She always called between four-thirty and five, because then the victims were either engaged upon or just about to have tea, and could not hurry her off. Not that Miss Maggie was ever hurried off!

She did not, of course, expect to discover the family skeleton at the first visit. No skeleton worth counting was ever discovered so soon. There had to be clues, and thrills and difficulties, first: she did hope, however, to discover the cupboard in which the skeleton was kept. She also hoped that it would not be one of those cupboards that only yielded a bare bone when opened at last. Of course she always pointed out what a big bone it was, and what a smelly one, but that was nothing to the satisfaction of finding the grisly skeleton complete.

She had hardly greeted the Wilmot-Randals when Sally walked in, not noticing Miss Maggie in her little comer. The vicar's ward was attired in her new costume and looked very gay and pretty. She greeted Mrs. Randal pleasantly and then turned to the man.

"Well, Jimmy," she laughed, "what does it feel like to have a fairy princess and a castle? Princely?"

"Yes, that's about it, Sally," laughed the young man in return. "I have to pinch myself about ten times a day."

Miss Maggie pricked up her ears. 'Jimmy!' 'Sally!' What was this? She must look into it.

She fancied she saw slight dismay on the girl's face as she turned and saw the other visitor, but, before she could be certain, Sally was explaining.

"Isn't it jolly? We are old friends, you know."

"You and Mrs. Wilmot-Randal and her husband?"

"Mr. Randal and I. We met in Paris."

"People so often do, don't they?" gushed Miss Maggie. "Delightful! So you know Paris too, Mrs. Randal?"

"No, I have never been there."

"Oh, before your marriage, when you were engaged, perhaps?"

"I had not then met my husband," returned Dinah, a little surprised.

"Dear Sally and I are such old friends," explained the caller. "I always envied her her life in Paris—so free. It was free, wasn't it, Sally? Didn't you enjoy it too, Mr. Randal? Men do, they say." Her gimlet-eyes went from one face to another.

"It was a pleasant change," said the unconscious Jimmy.

"It must have been. What year were you there?"

He mentioned the year.

"That is very interesting. That happened to be the very time I almost made up my mind for a little visit myself with some friends, but it fell through, somehow. How different Little Crampton must seem after Paris! And haven't you met since those days?"

"No, it was a most delightful surprise."

"Fancy saying good-by in Paris six years ago, never expecting to meet again, and then finding your friend in Little Crampton. Quite a coincidence, I'm sure! Such a small place as the world is, isn't it? as dear Mr. Bingley would say. You *will* like Mr. Bingley, won't they, Sally? One of our most precious possessions, so to speak. What month did you leave Paris?"

He mentioned the month. What tiresome small-talk some women made! So pointless and futile, without either beginning or end.

Miss Maggie cast back her unerring memory, and her glittering eyes modestly studied the toes of her large, flat boots. "Dear me, so you and Sally said adieu or au revoir, or whatever they *do* say in Paris, in April?"

"Yes, I suppose so." He gave an uncomfortable little wriggle, which Miss Maggie saw in spite of her close attention to her religious-looking boots, as Sally termed them.

Miss Maggie looked up innocently. "Now that is very odd, Mr. Randal, for I remember it was then I had two of Sally's letters returned to me, and now I think of it, I remember her telling me later she had been on a sketching tour in Italy. Are you also an artist, Mr. Randal? Now that's another delightful coincidence! I always think artists and writers and those sort of people are so different to us common and garden folk, so much less stupid and conventional. They understand each other at once. I have often regretted not going in for the artistic world. So free!"

"Quite so," agreed the bored listener, "but you flatter me. I neither paint nor write nor—anything."

"But perhaps you have the artistic temperament, which does almost as well, doesn't it? Of course then the Italian tour wouldn't be the same sort of treat to you as to Sally?"

"No," said Jimmy, wriggling again, and turning rather red, "no."

Damn the woman! How she hammered at the subject in her tiresome, purposeless way!

"Still, I daresay you found plenty to amuse you, and it must have been quite a fresh experience for both of you."

"Oh—er—yes."

"What did you do with yourself while Sally was painting her naughty pictures?—for don't tell me they weren't naughty." She shook an arch forefinger at Sally. "Don't I know! Didn't I see a paper once with one of hers in? The more you looked at it the more you found things."

"Then I suppose you looked at it quite a lot?" suggested Sally.

Miss Maggie smiled at her and turned to her victim.

"These conducted tours are a delightful invention. So cheap, so comfortable. I suppose yours was personally conducted?"

Jimmy looked very ashamed and uncomfortable. As a liar he was worse than useless; besides, he was confused as to what he had, and had not, already admitted. His wife made a signal to him not to answer at all. He did not see it. Sally broke in with her seductive little laugh, and opened her lips to say something, but Miss Maggie was first. It was truly said of her that she had both the first and the last word.

"Are the lakes as blue as they are painted?" she asked Randal eagerly.

"Quite," he said, "a wonderful blue."

"We are going to see them," broke in Mrs. Randal. "Of course we must wait till after the war."

"You will go comfortably in your own car," returned Miss Maggie; "rather a different way of doing things, I fancy. I expect these conducted tours are rather mixed. What sort of people had you in yours? A bishop?"

"Yes," replied Sally carelessly, "the usual bishop. By the bye, Lovey is putting up our special bishop for the Confirmation. You must come to tea. What's your idea about the Mombaza affair?"

"It will be charming to come and discuss it with him," enthused Miss Maggie. "Bishops are so amusing. Was the tour one amusing, and where was he bishop of?"

"Some place in Australia, where the kangaroos come from," replied the girl. "He hopped just like them. We used to laugh, didn't we, Jimmy?"

"Yes, oh yes," he agreed, looking miserable and quite unamused, and speaking without conviction. "It was very funny."

"Did the bishop think it funny too?" asked Miss Maggie innocently.

"Think what funny?"

"The tour."

"I don't think so; why should he?"

"They often are, aren't they? Or are Italian tours different—I mean tours made up in Paris for Italy? I know a lady who was going to join, but of course she couldn't when she found out."

"Why not?" asked Sally. "And found out what?"

"She thought it was too much of a Noah and his Ark tour for her."

"Noah and his Ark! Do you mean obsolete?"

"Oh no, rather too much up-to-date, she thought. She called it that because people joined two by two, and she'd been religiously brought up. Besides, she hadn't one."

Jimmy stared. "Hadn't what, Miss Hopkins? An ark or an animal?"

"Oh, naughty, naughty!" exclaimed the highly-delighted spinster; "as if you don't know what I mean."

"I assure you I don't. It sounds an odd sort of tour."

"It *was*, Mr. Randal. What sort of an Italian tour was yours and Sally's?"

"Oh, just the usual sort," returned the girl; "it would have been pleasant if it hadn't been for some of the others, eh, Jimmy?"

Jimmy coloured uneasily; his laugh was a failure.

"You must tell me the hotels you stopped at, the places you saw," commanded the inquisitor, and changed the subject of her own accord, seeming to forget it. She imagined relief on the two faces concerned. Needless to say, she had not forgotten; she was merely preparing a few traps. She meant to have the whole skeleton while she was about it.

She waited till Sally rose to say good-bye, and said she would walk home with her. Mrs. Randal and Sally went on ahead through the drive, leaving the reluctant Jimmy to bring up the rear with Miss Maggie. He had taken rather a dislike to their first caller. He thought her inquisitive, and the worst type of futile woman. She dawdled, admiring this and that, her gimlet-eyes piercing, her cunning brain active.

"Mr. Lovelady's bishop is rather a nice man, for a bishop," she remarked vaguely.

"Indeed?"

"Not like your kangaroo one," she said archly. "Had he a kangaroo wife with him, too?"

Jimmy was quite incapable of inventing a wife; he heartily wished Sally had not taken upon herself the office of Creator in the matter of the bishop.

"Oh no," he said.

"Such a sacred privilege to be a bishop's wife, though I cannot say I should care for it myself."

Jimmy murmured something inaudible. It occurred to him that it was quite possible that the bishop might not care for it either.

"And you saw Lake Maggiore, you say?"

Jimmy had forgotten saying anything of the sort, but he nodded. They had seen it.

"Let me see, what's the name of that great hotel they have there?"

"There are so many, you know."

"Which one did the tour go to?"

He mentioned the one they had stayed at; he could not, just for the moment, remember the name of any other. Besides, what did it matter?

Miss Maggie gave an envious sigh. "Dear Sally! What a lot of travel and changes she has had in her life. What experiences! And I have had none, just lived on in Little Crampton. It's too bad. Don't you think it's too bad, Mr. Randal?"

"Certainly, certainly," he agreed. He would cheerfully have subscribed a handsome sum towards her living elsewhere. Tedious woman!

They came up to the others, and Sally and Miss Maggie went off together. Jimmy dismissed the thought of the tiresome caller, but Dinah was thoughtful. She could not tell her husband how bad an actor he had proved. She was too thankful to remember that no real harm was done. Miss Maggie could not possibly suspect the truth.

"Let's hope she's not a typical Little Cramptonian," she said.

"Awful female," returned Jimmy in disgust; "how she bored! A woman without one charm, a single interest, and with the brains of a rabbit. Did you hear how she meandered on and on? Rather awkward, too. Hullo, here's the young James!"

Meanwhile Miss Maggie had thrust a Judas arm through Sally's. "What a charming pair!" she began. "How beautiful she is, and quite a girl. How old it makes one feel, doesn't it, these young things with their husbands, and children! So the bishop is staying with you? How exciting it will be for you, Sally. A widower and getting doddery. Do you think you could be a bishop's wife? I couldn't. Such a religious position, most trying. 'My Lord,' and you only 'Mrs.'! So like a man, grabbing everything and leaving our poor sex nothing. Even bishops are men, I, suppose, in a sort of way. Still, easy enough to be a bishop's widow. Of course your Australian bishop was a gay bachelor and you flirted dreadfully—and it really *was* a Noah and his Ark affair?"

"Oh no," said Sally, determined to be respectable, "his wife was there." ("How prolific lies are," she thought.)

"How tiresome, dear! Did you go to that lake, Lake Maggiore?"

"No." ("There goes another," thought the speaker. "How many more, I wonder?")

"How clever of you to avoid the beaten track, so different to most girls!" gushed the delighted sleuth-hound. "And was Mr. Randal yours?"

"My what?"

"I mean your friend, of course, dear, for the tour. Everybody had one, hadn't they?—even the bishop, it seems, even if he called her his wife. So jolly for everybody, and doing away with all stupid stiffness. A most delightful young man—Mr. Randal, I mean. He must have been quite a boy; he's only twenty-eight now, I find."

"Yes, just a youth," agreed Sally in a very casual voice.

"One can go about two and two with a youth, can't one, when it might look different with an older man. Even the most spiteful person—and other women are so spiteful to one, aren't they?—can't say you are trying to marry them when they are years younger, and haven't any money. What a happy time you must have had together!"

"Oh, we all enjoyed ourselves, I think."

"I'm sure you did, and after all, one's only young once. You must be glad to have something to look back upon. And the man who conducted the tour did you well? Let me see, what was his name? Mr. Randal happened to mention it. Henri Rénard, I think?"

Sally nodded. She also 'confounded' Miss Maggie in her heart, and was a little uneasy. Not to answer simple questions, and they had all been so simple, was fatal; it made Miss Maggie think there was something to be found out, and set her to work to do so. The only thing that was ever any good was to answer quite frankly and throw her off the scent if possible. Sally thought she had done so.

"It was Rénard, not Bénard, yes. I remember thinking of a fox—which reminds me, Mr. Paton has sent his hunter to the Front, and his wife is getting better. I suppose he can't have done it right, or his nerve failed at the last moment. The Criminal Department is sharper than it used to be. After all, two dying like that might lead to questions."

"What do you mean?"

Miss Maggie was only too ready to explain, and Sally laughed incredulously. Miss Maggie lit on so many mares'-nests.

The spinster squeezed the girl's arm. "My dear, you little know what goes on even here—if you keep your eyes open. Oh, Sally, what a jolly life you've had, haven't you? so full of variety. No wonder you never stayed here long. I suppose you will go back to Paris after the war—unless—I mean, of course, one never knows, but to live in Little Crampton after Paris and Italy! Oh, it simply couldn't be done! Do tell me the places you saw."

Sally remembered one or two she thought might satisfy the questioner.

"Let me see, you would be there by the middle of the month?"

"I daresay. One forgets."

"Of course one forgets," agreed Miss Maggie. "I'm sure I should have forgotten *everything*. I wonder if you will ever go on another personally conducted tour, and who will conduct it? Perhaps," she pointed with sly meaning to an advancing figure, "Mr. Bingley. My dear, I am positive that he adores you." She squeezed the arm she held again. "How glad I am I gave you the tip, dear child, as that horrid Mr. Paton would say!"

She waved archly to Mr. Bingley, who advanced upon them with all flags flying, so to speak.

CHAPTER XV

"Won't you give me another chance?"

Mr. Bingley's eyes fell on Sally's imitation of a love-bird, and his heart stirred pleasantly. How exquisite, how modest, and yet not puritanical, for there was a long length of slim, silk-clad ankle. He was glad to remember a text out of his mother's book that he had read only the previous evening:

"*Don't marry the over-dressed; your money will fly. Or the under-dressed—in either of the two senses of the word. One may mean a dowdy mind, the other a too-rapid one.*"

Here was surely the perfect mean, and the maternal guide pointing to Sally!

"You've been calling," he said accusingly, as he greeted them; "the Red House, of course. Well, what's the verdict?" He had already given his without seeing them. The money was in the bank.

"Such delightful people," responded Miss Maggie. "You must get to know them at once; and so rich! She's lovely, and such a figure; they say shapes are coming in again. Poor Sally and I felt such awful scrags, didn't we, dear? Do you know, Mr. Bingley, I can sometimes imagine I can feel my bones knocking up against each other when I walk. You wait a year or two, Sally, and you'll know how horrid it feels. But about the Randals—isn't it exciting?—Sally knows them quite well. They are old and dear friends, at least Mr. Randal is, Jimmy as she calls him. I don't think you had met Mrs. Randal before, had you, dear?"

Sally shook her head. She was hearing quite enough of her friendship with Jimmy. What a mercy Miss Maggie could not suspect it had been more than friendship!

"They met in Paris," went on the 'babbler,' "and went together on one of those tours, personally conducted, with bishops and things. Makes one feel quite envious. Would you like to go on a personally conducted tour, Mr. Bingley?"

"I think not," he returned with some hauteur; "I have heard they are very mixed."

"But so free, aren't they, Sally? No silly conventional notions, you know, nothing *stiff* about them—the Paris ones I mean, of course. Ours are almost *too* proper, perhaps, clergymen and their things, and people from suburbs. Still, Italy is so romantic. Francesca and Paolo, Dante and Beatrix, and all those sort of people. Not that Beatrix ever had what you could call a lively time of it, married to a worthy citizen, and with twelve children, and Dante always so dreadfully distant and respectful—for the times, of course," she added hurriedly, for Mr. Bingley was looking shocked. He wondered if Miss Maggie guessed what she was implying; he could only trust not.

Sally's mouth twitched.

"You really should go on your very next holidays, Mr. Bingley," persisted Miss Maggie. "Sally and Mr. Randal went in April, an ideal month."

The bank-manager frowned. He did not care for the combination of names; neither did he approve of conducted tours, they sounded vulgar. He had seen them advertised beginning at five pounds. All sorts of people would go upon them.

"I do not care to rub shoulders with Tom, Dick, and Harry, and their Harriets," he said haughtily.

Miss Maggie used her arch forefinger. "Naughty, Mr. Bingley! When you wouldn't have rubbed shoulders with Tom, Dick, and Harry, but only with Sally and her Mr. Randal, and their dear Australian bishop who hopped all the time to make the thing go off pleasantly."

A man came down the road seated on a young horse. He was trying to make it pass first a car and then a heap of stones; no easy matter.

"Who is that man? How well he rides!" exclaimed Miss Maggie. "He might be part of the horse. Good-looking, and slim too."

Mr. Bingley frowned. What vapid talkers women were!

Sally looked, and her face quickened with interest. She recognised Robert Kantyre, and concluded he was breaking in one of the colts. Yes, he could ride. He was a fine specimen of manhood, with a frame that seemed all steel, and brown, finely-featured face. She liked the very close military cut of his hair, the way his head was set on, and his dark grey eyes. What a contrast to Mr. Bingley!

"It's Gillet's new man," she said.

"Oh," said Miss Maggie, who had heard much of him, "so that is the mysterious stranger! Didn't you find him in a dead faint or something, or was he drunk?"

"He was ill," said Sally quietly.

"He looks superior, for all his rough clothes," went on Miss Maggie, "not just like a labouring man; and he certainly *is* handsome, isn't he, Mr. Bingley? Is it true that he's a gentleman in disguise, and awfully romantic, and so on?"

She remembered how often Sally had been to the moors lately, and the flush on her cheeks, and decided to keep her eyes open. She believed Sally quite capable of running a flirtation for amusement, as well as a man for matrimony; in fact, there was nothing she could not believe of Sally now.

"Not quite that, I think," the girl answered easily. "I imagine he had a farm somewhere in Canada till things went wrong in some way."

"Why isn't he at the Front?" demanded the bank-manager. "He's no right to be skulking round here at such a time."

"Everybody can't go to the Front, can they, Mr. Bingley?" she returned. "It would dislocate the country's trade too much."

"Have you spoken to him since you found him?" asked Miss Maggie.

"Yes, as a matter of fact he saved my life." She explained the circumstances.

Mr. Bingley frowned again. He felt it was hardly the thing for the future Mrs. Bingley to put herself in the position of having her life saved by any chance comer. Something akin to jealousy stirred in him. The fellow did not look like a working-man at all, and he had those 'barber-block' attractions that took in the foolish, superficial sex. Women were so incurably romantic! This good Christian did not realise that he was a Turk at heart and believed that women should be more or less shut away from the eyes of other males.

Kantyre came up to them. His eyes fell on Sally, attired with a frivolity and extravagance that he thought must show an extravagant and frivolous nature at such a time. He was aware of 'the rich Mr. Bingley' bending over her with a sort of fussy, protecting possession.

So this was one of the reasons why she had not come!

His eyes became steel, his face hard, and he acknowledged the girl's friendly nod and smile with the barest courtesy.

Sally had looked for interest and perhaps a little admiration, certainly for a greeting as friendly as her own, and she was startled. Then in a flash she remembered. She had broken her appointment; he had waited in vain, and perhaps he had needed her.

She was overwhelmed with remorse, and did a very foolish thing, seeing that she had Miss Maggie on one side of her and Mr. Bingley on the other.

"I never thanked him for saving my life. How horrid!" she exclaimed, and at once ran down the road after the horseman, calling upon him to stop.

Of course he stopped, but he did not look very pleased to do so.

"Please be careful, don't come so near," he warned her sharply; "he kicks."

"Oh, I'll look out. Mr. Kantyre, what must you be thinking of me?"

"Why should I think of you, Miss Lunton?" he returned rather icily.

"You know what I mean. I never went."

He made no reply.

"No wonder you are disgusted. Oh, it was hateful!"

"Doubtless you had a pleasanter engagement, Miss Lunton. What else could I think?"

"Then you waited? Oh, if only I had remembered!"

His mouth closed tightly. "Then you had no other engagement? You merely forgot, Miss Lunton?" He could have forgiven anything but that; it humiliated him afresh. It had seemed to mean everything in the world to him; it had been less than nothing to her, so little that it had slipped her memory. He looked down upon her in her charming attire, into the face flushed with beauty, and his eyes narrowed with contempt. A beautiful clothes-horse, a soulless thing, a trap for the desire of the eye. In the distance he could see stout, pompous Mr. Bingley waiting the return of his property.

Sally hung her head. "Yes," she owned abjectly, "there is no excuse for me, none. I—I got—got thinking about something, and I forgot."

Again he looked at the bank-manager. This was the man who occupied her thoughts, he or his possessions. He remembered Mrs. Gillet's idle talk and conjectures now.

"It is of no moment," he returned. He raised his cap and made to go.

"Oh, Mr. Kantyre, forgive me just this once! I will never, never fail you again in *any* way. Won't you meet me there to-night or to-morrow? Won't you give me another chance?"

"You make too much of a trifling matter, Miss Lunton," he returned, smiling coldly. "I assure you I have also forgotten the whole incident. Pray do not apologise to me, it is rather I who should apologise for making a nuisance of myself. Good afternoon; do not let me keep you from your friends." And he was gone.

Sally walked back with a crestfallen face. What had she done? And all through one little omission! He would not give her a chance again; he was far too proud. She would have to make one and take it herself, but, thanks to her first failure, her fight for Robert Kantyre's body and soul was not likely to prove easily victorious, if it ever proved victorious. Defeat, because she had missed the one little golden opportunity!

Miss Maggie looked at her sharply. "He didn't seem to accept your thanks very gratefully," she said. "Oh dear, here's Mrs. Hill running about like a rabbit without cover. How excited she looks!"

Mrs. Hill rushed up to them, her eyes shining. "Douglas has won the V.C.!" she got out breathlessly.

Sally congratulated the proud mother warmly; the others murmured something conventional. Mr. Bingley was not stirred; he was aggrieved. He had never seen that light in Sally's eyes before, it had not shone for him. What was the V.C.? Just a bit of luck.

"Won't he think a lot of himself when he comes home!" said Miss Maggie. "Such a handsome lad, so tall and broad. No wonder the girls run after him. It will be worse now. He will be a hero, and when he returns nobody else will get a look-in, will they, Mr. Bingley?"

"I don't know that I altogether approve of giving the V.C. to mere lads," began Mr. Bingley portentously.

Sally interrupted him, rather crudely he thought. "Not even when they've done men's work, hero's work?"

"The heads of the older men are not so easily turned," he went on, not heeding. "But a mere school-boy! They think so much of themselves as it is; this sort of thing is a direct encouragement to think more. I—"

He paused. Sally was looking at him with an expression he did not like. More candid opinions crudely expressed! Oh, these modern women!

"*Don't marry a woman who knows too much, or talks too much,*" said that priceless classic of the late Mrs. Bingley. "*She'll take care you both talk, and know, too little.*"

Yet how lovely she was! How smart, how piquant! Piquant. Yes, that was the word, a word with a thrill in it. Doves were all very well in their place, but who had ever heard of a piquant dove? A thing could be too tame. There was more credit in training the wild bird to eat out of one's hand than in the feeding of a dove who would alight on almost anybody's shoulder.

In no sense of the word was Mr. Bingley a sportsman, but he felt the stir of the chase in his veins that moment—and the stir of spring, for he decided to order rather a smart new waistcoat.

Miss Maggie ran after Mrs. Hill. She remembered that she might know the truth about a certain mysterious illness of a friend; she would pretend not to, of course, but one might get 'warm' by some judicious questioning.

"What a woman!" said Mr. Bingley.

"Oh, she's not so black as she's painted," returned Sally; "she's been a good enough friend to me." She smiled to herself. "Isn't it a gorgeous day? I could walk miles. I'm glad I'm strong. So were my parents; my mother was really wonderful."

Mr. Bingley's figure became extra stiff, and Sally realised he knew her family history.

She thought it wiser to be frank. "Isn't it absurd to think," she remarked confidentially, "that there are still people who consider a chorus girl in the family worse than gout, more incalculable, and less respectable."

"Indeed!" said the man who infinitely preferred gout as the lesser evil.

"She worked very hard, and tried hard too, my poor mother," mused Sally, half to herself. "I did not understand then, but I do now. I wish they hadn't christened me Salome, though. You see, they were young and romantic and very much in love—"

She paused abruptly, remembering how sordidly the romance had ended. So many beginnings to love, and yet, so it seemed to her, always the one inevitable end.

"Salome! I must be thankful nobody called me Sal!"

"They called *me* Alfred," said Mr. Bingley resentfully.

"How you must have hated them for it!" said Sally heedlessly; "but how suitable!" She pulled herself out of the morass. "So kingly," she explained; "the good King Alfred. A noble tradition."

"Yes, still—" On a spring day, and with a piquant vision of beauty, such a name seemed hardly worthy of his true self. There was a finality about it he did not like.

"You would rather have had something a little lighter? Something more romantic, perhaps?"

Mr. Bingley's eyes gleamed. He felt ready to bear some knightly name.

"Lancelot? Oh, I beg your pardon, I'd forgotten about the queen." She saw Mr. Bingley had not, and that he had been jarred. She made haste to suggest something more respectable, for, after all, romance can be respectable as well as the other thing.

"Galahad," she burst out, "Galahad Bingley?" Then she bit her lips and smothered her inward mirth. She had gone too far. After all, though vain and pompous and without a sense of humour, the man was not a fool. He was indeed, as she thought regretfully, very far from being a fool. He must see that she was poking fun at him, talking lightly of that which was sacred, namely, Mr. Bingley.

Certainly he gave her a suspicious look. "I hardly feel myself worthy of a name like that," he said humbly. "I do not think I should feel it right to leave the bank to go questing for the Holy Grail." (He did not put into words the thought that shocked himself: "Besides, there is no money in it.")

"I beg your pardon," said Sally, very low; "it is the way you read the lessons in church that made me think of it."

"I am all unworthy," he said loftily.

"You are very modest," she said, "so rare in a man." She considered she had filled the creature's maw for the time being.

He left her with reluctance, but he dined at seven-fifteen sharp; the fate of empires could not put that time back or forward. He knew it was not a fashionable hour, but it suited his digestion. He could spend an hour over his dinner, and, by the time he was in bed, consider his meal sufficiently digested for health's sake and to leave him an excellent appetite for breakfast.

He looked up his mother's book as usual, and was rather pleased by the first gem he lit upon:

"*The strong man may not be able to help falling in love, but he can always see to it that he falls out the instant it becomes necessary.*"

What could be more delightfully simple? He considered that, seeing he would be able to put a stop to it the moment he thought fit, there would be no harm in falling in love with Sally sufficiently to be pleasant, but not enough to be uncomfortable. In fact, sure of being able to adjust matters for the best, he decided that he would really let himself go as far as his feelings were concerned—though not where words were, or anything committal.

Meanwhile the 'love-bird' had passed the 'dove,' and, if disturbed, both had smiled. The thing had its funny side. '

As Sally put her investment carefully away in tissue paper she wondered if she dare seek out Robert Kantyre on the moors and risk another snub. How he had snubbed her! No man had ever done that before, but the stranger was different from anyone she had ever known. She wondered what it was. She was still asking herself that question when she fell asleep.

She awoke strong in the resolution to seek him out that very day.

CHAPTER XVI

"You are hateful! I wish I hadn't saved you"

One thing after another kept cropping up to prevent Sally going to the moors either in the morning or the afternoon of the next day. It was evening before she found herself free, and then she hesitated. True, it was a beautiful evening and very light, but it would mean rather a rush to get there and back before dark. Because she would so much rather have waited till the next day, she decided that, under the circumstances, she must go. She would dare the cattle way, seeing that she was on the right side of Wednesday, and it was unlikely the same contretemps would happen twice.

It would have to be rather a rushed visit, but that would be better than nothing. Perhaps she could persuade him to give her another trial. Whatever came or went, she would prove staunch to the test now.

She found Gillet, but she could not catch a glimpse of the man she sought anywhere about. She had not wanted to ask the farmer, but there was no help for it.

"Where's White?" she asked directly.

"Drinking hisself silly in The Hut, I expect," the man answered dourly. "We knocked off a bit earlier to-day, and he went off directly after supper. He was all right for two days, and I had hopes, but he's been a deal sight worse since."

"Perhaps my fault," thought the dismayed girl as she hurried to The Hut. She was not going back without seeing him now she had come so far. She hoped he would not already have started drinking; anyway, she felt she had to face it, though it happened to be one of the things she shrank especially from.

The door was closed, but through the window she could see him sitting in the chair by the cupboard. He had a glass and bottle on a table beside him, and his face was flushed, his eyes unnaturally bright.

Sally's heart beat fast with fear, but she nerved herself for the ordeal. She could see he had had too much, but he did not look drunk or stupid. She tapped on the door.

He started, and then came slowly forward and opened it. "Who's there? What do you want?" he demanded sharply. His eyes fell on Sally, and his voice changed, grew hard. "Oh, it's you, is it? You've come to see for yourself, have you? Honoured, I'm sure." He ran his words together a little.

"I came to apologise," she began.

He pointed to the table and its contents, and laughed unpleasantly. "You came to look for that," he contradicted. "Well, you have found it, Miss Lunton. What next?"

"It's all my fault," she said rather desperately, for his attitude was not encouraging. "Oh, Mr. Kantyre, don't punish me too severely for one mistake! Don't make me feel that I am responsible for that!"

"Nobody's responsible but myself," he returned, manipulating 'responsible' with some difficulty. He was much more affected by the drink he had taken than he appeared to be. He felt as if he were struggling to get out of a dim pit, while all the time something seemed striving to pull him down. "Please go, Miss—Miss—" Odd that he could not remember her name for the moment, and such a pretty girl, too!

"Not like this," she returned; "you must forgive me first, and promise to let me try and undo what I have done. You've got to tell me how I can help you, and accept that help."

He smiled foolishly, rocking a little on his feet. "You think I don't see through you? You are after that," he pointed again to the brandy. "You got it once, but not this time, my dear!"

Sally winced at his tone and the insolence of that 'my dear.' At the same time, she was determined not to take offence. Until he put it into her head it had not occurred to her to make a second assault upon the brandy, but the idea appealed to her now. She considered that he was not in the least drunk, and only a little affected by what he had taken. If she could destroy it he might have to go without for one night, and that would be something gained.

Though the door was open, he had an arm across the threshold, barring her ingress. She made a sudden dart, slipping through underneath it.

She had reached the table, had seized the glass in one hand and the bottle in the other, before his bemused faculties grasped her object. She ran towards the little scullery.

Then Robert turned in hot pursuit of her, the drink he had taken steadily mounting to his brain. He made a dive at her, but again she eluded him, and something savage awoke in him. This girl … always this girl … making a fool of him … mocking, laughing, treating him as if he were a child!

Sally flung the stuff in the glass into the sink, and dashed the bottle violently down on the stone of it. It broke, and the contents rushed out.

She turned to face Robert Kantyre—and something in his eyes which made her afraid. He seemed to have forgotten all about the brandy, but he had not forgotten her, as she realised when she sought to pass him.

"No, you don't," he said, laughing wildly, and catching her in his arms. "You're a pretty girl. … Give me a kiss before you go."

Sally struggled vainly in an iron grip. "Let me go at once!" she commanded.

His grasp tightened, and he laughed again. "No, no, my lady; pay toll! Give me a kiss, then perhaps I'll let you go."

She realised that he was no longer responsible for his actions.

"Mr. Kantyre," she tried to say calmly, "you are not the type of man who insults women—when you are sober. Let me go."

For answer he dragged her face against his. She was conscious of a reek of brandy that sickened her, of a violent kiss upon her lips.

She got an arm free, and with her all strength struck him across the mouth.

He let her go abruptly. She nearly fell, and he, staggering, subsided into a chair, his hand to his smarting mouth. Clarity was growing out of confusion; the blow had sobered him.

"You are hateful!" gasped Sally, turning on him with flaming eyes. "I wish I hadn't saved you!"

Her words reached him through a mist of shame. He dropped his face in his hands. He was sickened at himself and his own incredible conduct. He saw the pit yawning at his feet. Already drink had brought him to this; to what might it not bring him ere the end came?

"Miss Lunton—" came from him at last, as he lifted his face from his hands; but Miss Lunton had gone.

Robert groaned aloud. Too late! She would never forgive him now. No decent woman could ever forgive him. And she had come to help him, to try and make up. He might have had her help and her friendship; instead he had her loathing and contempt.

He rose and straightened himself, and cleared up the mess in the scullery. As he removed all traces of his weakness he swore that never again, come what might, would he give way to drink even for forgetfulness. Sally had saved him indirectly by revealing the brutal possibilities of the most decent nature in the grip of the drink fiend.

He would have to fight alone, but fight he would to the very bitter end.

That night he thought only of Sally and the incident in The Hut; not happy thoughts, but more bearable than the others. She would never offer to be his friend again, but he could make himself more worthy of the friendship that might have been. He could fling cowardice from him and cling fast to the courage which was his heritage. He remembered what she had said to him at their first meeting: "Wealth lost, something lost; honour lost, much lost; courage lost, all lost!" He would not lose all; he would be strong, quit himself like a man, *face* it.

Gillet was delighted with the results. "Miss Sally must have got round him somehows," he thought. "She's a way with her, parson's Sally."

Sally went home angry and humiliated. She felt she hated the man of the moors, and would have nothing more to do with him. He was deliberately drinking himself to utter degradation and to death. He was a coward; he'd have to go. She had done her best and could do no more. She could not risk another insult.

"You are very late," said Mr. Lovelady. He went himself and fetched the supper Elizabeth had kept hot for her.

She smiled and thanked him, but she only toyed with the food, and the anxious parson scolded her. He was worried; she had not seemed herself lately.

She listened absently. She was still thinking about Robert Kantyre. If he wrote and apologised when he was sober, and that seemed to her the very least he could do, she would reply to his letter and formally forgive him; but till he definitely expressed an intention of giving up this corroding vice she could not see him again.

The days went by, but Robert never wrote, and Sally hardened her heart against him. It never occurred to her that he did not write because he felt that his offence was beyond forgiveness, and that his horror of himself was greater than she could even imagine.

Then something happened to put Robert Kantyre out of her thoughts.

She ran into the ubiquitous Miss Maggie in High Street and the spinster rushed excitedly at her.

"Oh, Sally, have you heard about Mr. Bingley?" she began breathlessly.

Sally nerved herself for the worst, her heart sinking. Mrs. Dalton had won, and she had lost the last throw. The horror of the future seemed to press down upon her, a great black, suffocating cloud, like the shadow of death.

She managed to laugh and ask lightly, "What has that bold, bad man been doing? Running away with anybody's wife? How frightfully exciting—except for the wife!" She thought that Mr. Bingley would make even such an elopement boring and respectable, somehow or other. "Is he married, or only engaged?"

What would happen to her now? What could she do? Where must she go? She could not stay in Little Crampton in the vicinity of Jimmy and his happy wife. "It's come sooner than I expected, the alternative," she thought, turning sick. She realised now how absolutely she had counted upon Mr. Bingley to play Perseus to her Andromeda. Even at such a moment she could smile at thought of Mr. Bingley's romantic, winged flight. "He is really not the shape for it, poor dear," she murmured to herself, "and according to history and the pictures, Andromeda was slightly under-dressed. He would fly back quicker than he came, a very shocked Perseus-Bingley!"

Miss Maggie was astonished that Sally should burst out laughing and appear really amused if she supposed anything of the sort in the matter of Mr. Bingley's engagement or marriage. Was she calculating on getting the rich Mr. Randal from his wife? How exciting Little Crampton was!

"Neither," she returned, intending that the prize should remain the centre of strenuous endeavour for many a long day to come, "neither engaged nor going to be married—that he *knows* of." She broke off with a titter.

Sally almost reeled with the sense of relief. He was not lost; indeed, unless she was very much mistaken, he was far from lost. He was struggling to escape, oh yes, she saw that very plainly, but there was a traitor citadel within the gates that longed to capitulate.

"Much more exciting than that, for Mr. Bingley," went on Miss Maggie. "He's always been one of the lucky ones, relations simply dying off like flies! All adding to the 'collection,' too," she added, highly amused at her own way of putting it. "I'm sure his motto is 'all contributions thankfully received.' He's lost a relation—so trying!—but he's been left that relation's fortune, about thirty thousand pounds. What do you think of that?"

Sally could hardly think. She realised that Mr. Bingley was doubly a prize, and had a feverish longing to proceed upon the quest without loss of time. How terrible if she lost him now! To lose Mr. Bingley was literally to lose everything. She must not waste a minute, not a minute.

Miss Maggie looked into her excited, dilated eyes and smiled. "I thought you'd be interested," she purred; "so was Mrs. Dalton. When I left her she was looking in the motor-window at that new Rolls-Royce."

"Oh," said Sally blankly.

"It was left to Mr. Bingley because the other relations had wives and children, and were poor and really needed it, so that Mr. Bingley could afford to be careful with it. That's the sort of people they all are. He's to come back to-day, after the funeral."

Sally wondered by what train the fortunate man would return.

If Miss Maggie knew she did not say. "Such an ordeal, a relation's funeral," she went on. "Still, Mr. Bingley has great tact. He would imply how certain he was of the corpse's salvation, and how much better off he was 'There'; religion is such a comfort at such a time. He will be quite a *parti* now, won't he? About three thousand pounds a year, I suppose, with a big bank and salary to come any day. What a lot of sympathy he will get! Such a sad loss! but I suppose somebody's gain in the end. That's the way the world wags, isn't it? Look at Mrs. Wilmot-Randal. I daresay more than one would like to be in her shoes; and such a charming man, so different from Mr. Bingley, though rather young, of course. My dear, I thought you'd like to know at once."

She rushed away to spread the tidings elsewhere. What a lot of tea-invitations she would get! She would be able to tell everybody exactly what Sally and Mrs. Dalton looked and said and felt.

Finally she decided to favour the Patons. She hated Mr. Paton, but their teas were a dream. "My dear," she gushed to the recovered Mrs. Paton, "how well you are looking! How splendidly Mr. Paton looks after you, giving you stuff and things to make you better—what's the name of it? Not many husbands like that, unfortunately." Then she plunged into her news, and added, "I assure you if ever I saw determination in two women's faces I saw it then. They just set their teeth with that 'I *will!*' look."

She was not far out. Sally walked up High Street 'willing' very hard indeed. At the motor agency she ran into Mrs. Dalton. That lady still had her nose glued to the window.

"Isn't it a beauty?" she cried longingly.

It was Nina, bored to death, who first hailed Sally. "Mummy won't come away," she complained, "and I'd rather go to the confectioner's. Poor Mr. Bingley's gone to a funeral; isn't it sad? I wonder if there'll be those funny nodding things. Miss Maggie said he'd borned up well and been awfully brave. I like weddings better than funerals. Who will you marry, Miss Lunton?"

Mrs. Dalton glanced at her rival with anxious eyes. Then she turned again to the window. Would it ever be hers? She sighed.

"Mummy, you are creaking. Why do you and Mr. Bingley creak? Miss Lunton never creaks. Who will you marry, Miss Lunton?"

"Mr. Nobody. I'm thinking of being a nice old maid with cats."

"Like mother making up her mind to be a widow," said the child in all innocence; "but you haven't an old-maidy look in your eyes. They are all sparkles. I wish mine were all sparkles. I wish I had yellow hair like yours. I want to stroke it. Don't people always ask to stroke it? Do you let them? Mummy has tweezers to pull out the whitey bits. Do you pull out the whitey bits?"

"No, Miss Chatterbox," said Sally, suiting the action to the word; "I only pull out sixpences. Now run away and spend it."

The child needed no second bidding.

Mrs. Dalton moved to where she could get another view of the car.

While she coveted that, the homeless vagabond by her side furnished her drawing-room with an artistic taste that Mr. Bingley, who clung to the Early Victorian in everything, would have thought almost wanton.

"I *am* lucky," she thought, counting her chickens; "he is manageable up to a certain extent by flattery. He isn't the amorous sort, and he's honourable, self-respecting, truthful, and yes, kind too, in his way. He is really human with children, and a better Mr. Bingley could be reached through them. Only—would they be Bingleyish children?"

She gave a sharp sigh, and Mrs. Dalton echoed it. The two women looked into each other's eyes, hesitated, and laughed.

"We may as well see what humour there is," said Sally, "for it's pretty beastly on the whole, isn't it? We are not playing it low-down because we like it, but because we must. Let's be friends," she added impulsively, "as far as it's possible."

"Why should we hate each other?" asked the widow. "It isn't the—the person, only his things."

"Three thousand 'things'!" laughed Sally. "It has made me—well, determined."

Mrs. Dalton thrust out a dogged jaw. "And me!" She looked towards the car. "I've simply *ached* for one all my life," she confessed.

"And I for a home and ease," said Sally.

"Isn't it sickening to think how easily men can earn such things, and that we can earn nothing, hardly bread?"

"Rotten!"

"It leads to so much; it's bad for us. You know how a stray dog goes about looking up into each face, seeking to find a master, anyone who will be kind, mean warmth and food. We get like that, some of us." She felt compelled to speak out to Sally; she knew she would understand, and it was a relief to drop pretence. "I was like that once. I had a miserable life in a miserable home. I was like a stray dog … and he wasn't kind. I got Nina; but for that … and now it's the same thing all over again, but none the less hateful. A car would make it so much easier. One could get away from—from things more."

"One could," agreed Sally. "I shall do my best to win the car, but of course I shall play fair."

"I know that. So shall I to you. Not to others, though. You are better off than I, elegant, beautiful, younger—I'm thirty-five—with a career and independence."

"I'm much worse off, as a matter of fact," returned Sally, "but we need not go into that." Then an idea struck her, and she smiled. "Suppose, just as you had acquired a cheap two-seater, perhaps second-hand, you were offered a Rolls-Royce? What would you do?"

"Palm off the two-seater on somebody who hadn't got a car at all," returned Mrs. Dalton promptly, "and run the Rolls-Royce into the garage. Wouldn't you?"

"If I had any sense."

"Business is business. The other is quite a different thing; it never came my way."

Sally was silent.

"How have you been getting on?" asked Mrs. Dalton. "He does zigzag so."

"He does indeed! Whoever wins deserves it, and will probably need a rest-cure, and go on needing one. It's hateful that we have to do it at all, and yet I mean to go on to the bitter end and get the beast."

"So do I. There's Nina."

"Bring Nina up differently. You have, at least, that in your power. See that she has the right sort of education, pride, independence."

"I must first find something to bring her upon."

"Will the girl of to-morrow do this sort of thing?" asked Sally sombrely. "And yet I suppose some always will—those that hate work, or can't find it, or haven't ability. After all, it's the shortest cut to many things, and as long as the marriageable women outnumber the marriageable men it will always be done. Yet our Colonies are being starved for want of women. War will not wrest them from us, but a dropping birth-rate of the best type of colonists must in the end. Still, you and I aren't out for slavery and cutting off all ease, are we?"

"It's such a sacrifice. I can't imagine a man being worth it," said Mrs. Dalton rather grimly. "In some of the parts in the North-West Territory the lives of the women must be ghastly. They are cut off from everything."

"Yes, but what a lot they are doing, how splendid they must be! However, I don't belong to such high types, but to a low one. I want the soft job if it's to be got by hook or crook."

"I don't belong to the noble type either," said Mrs. Dalton. "Why pretend?"

"I'd like to be able to afford it, though," answered Sally, thinking of Dinah Randal; "after all, there's only disgrace in failure. It's the sorry success, or the scrap-heap. Nina is no end of an asset to you. He is really fond of her, quite paternal."

"Black eyes and yellow hair are assets too, and slim figure and ankles and feet. That X-ray idea was wonderful, but isn't it beginning to show a *little* dark at the roots here and there?" Perhaps the wish was father to the thought.

Sally's eyes twinkled. "Oh, it will hang out," she said. "I've just thought of such an awful thing! Suppose, while we fought like two dogs over a bone, a third one carried it away from under our very noses!"

"Oh, Miss Lunton, *don't*!"

"Such a valuable bone, isn't it? I wish there was more bone and less meat!"

Mrs. Dalton chuckled. "I can't afford to mind that," she said, "I'm a trifle on the 'meaty' side myself. It will be a close thing. You have the wit and beauty, but I am safe and domestic and have been through the mill, nicely broken in. You look as if nothing could either bend or break you, Miss Lunton."

The laughter and sparkle died out of Sally's face. "You are mistaken," she said, "life itself has broken me in more ways than one. Here's Nina," she added abruptly.

CHAPTER XVII

"Here's luck to my husband's wife!"

It was later in the day, and Sally had started for a climb. She was trying to feel absolutely certain that everything would turn out for the best and she would still know security and success. Happiness? Well, happiness was far to seek, and lay behind her. There had only been one thing to matter in her life, and that was over and done with years ago. It was a dead thing; let the dead past bury its dead. To let what had been spoil what might be was against her whole philosophy of logic and life. It meant walking in the shadows instead of the sunshine; clinging to the dead hands instead of the living.

She would forget. Only it was awkward when the past became the present, as it had a way of doing, and came hurtling into the life that sought to thrust it back. Here was Jimmy at her very doors, making the thing alive; just the same Jimmy—save that another woman owned him.

She climbed The Mountain, and looked at the sea lying in the light like a sword. So was Jimmy and the best part of life set for ever beyond her reach.

She came down and turned towards the moor road. A strong, keen wind blew from the east, ruffling the hair on her brow. It ran like wine and fire through her veins; she thrilled to the mere pagan love of life.

"What is money, after all?" she thought. "What can it buy really worth having? Love? Peace of soul? Happiness? One inch of the sky? What is its purchasing power? Just a cage to live in. Here I am free. The earth, the sky, the very wind is mine. Money could neither give me that nor lack of money take it from me."

She stood drawing in deep breaths. How mean and low was her ambition! How fatal in its consequences, a selfish ambition. One sought world-dominion, but Death was still overlord, his power omnipotent, his throne unshakable; to him went the victory.

"Selfishness is the root of all evil," she told herself. "I can realise it, but I won't alter it." She thought how selfish she had been all her life, how self-seeking. "I'm a true Lunton, there's no doubt about that."

She put herself by Mr. Lovelady and his thought and life lived for others, and did not like the contrast. She almost forgot Jimmy; she quite forgot Mr. Bingley.

Yet Mr. Bingley had not forgotten her. All the way back in the train he thought of her. Should he, should he not? At home, as he changed into a grey suit that seemed to him just the correct sort of mourning for a relation who had made him his heir—it was a pleasing grey, smartly cut, but not frivolous—he thought of Sally. Did grey make him look less slim than blue? To be, or not to be?

He decided to go for a walk till dinner-time and think it over. His luncheon had been most unsatisfactory. No man of feeling would eat heartily at the funeral luncheon of a relation, even though the will had been read, and he knew exactly where he was. Besides, the cook had been upset about something; she had been there twenty-five years and possibly expected a legacy, as those greedy parasites did, and the meal was rather bad.

On his way to the station he had telegraphed directions to his own cook on the matter of dinner. She was to spare neither trouble nor expense. Fortunately he had a suitcase with him, and there was a good wine-merchant's close to his cousin's house, so that he was able to slip out and get some excellent port, champagne he considered unsuitable under the circumstances, and put it in his bag without a soul being any the wiser. It was not that he was in any way ashamed of his action—everyone knew he had never exceeded by as much as half a glass in his life—but he was afraid of being misunderstood and thought heartless. It was a censorious world!

He decided he would go on the moors. The wind there gave one such an appetite. Vanner had told him to what he might look forward, and he would please the decent woman by doing her cooking full justice. His face was solemn, as befitted the occasion, but his step was buoyant. He had lost a relation and gained a fortune. Debit a relation: credit a fortune. Well, well, such was life! He looked round him with a genial smile. Undoubtedly there was no season like spring!

His strong sense of religion had supported him throughout the whole trying ordeal. The relation was so obviously much better off; he would not wish anything different himself. Dear fellow, he had gone to his happy home. He had proved himself a true Bingley, and what higher standard could there be? For instance, he had many beggarly, and consequently worthless, nearer relations, but they would have used the money for spending, for pleasure; they would not have been able to afford to be its sacred treasurer. In a word, they would not have *cherished* it. Yes, his cousin had acted with far-seeing good sense; it was always a pity to split up one good thing into a lot of poor things.

"Three thousand per annum," cooed Mr. Bingley, "and increasing all the time. It makes one feel quite a man of substance."

It certainly made him look it.

"I could marry almost anybody," he thought. Was it fair to other women to restrict his choice to Little Crampton? He might marry a society girl. 'Lady Clare Bingley' sounded very well, he thought. Yet these people were so often frivolous and extravagant. He had heard of them as regarding home and husband as merely something to keep away from as much as possible. A shocking idea, most pernicious!

Then he remembered a maxim of that wonderful woman, his mother:

"*Never marry your social superior; she will look down on you. Never marry your social inferior; you will look down on her.*"

Mr. Bingley could not imagine even a duke's daughter looking down on Mr. Bingley, once he was her lord. After all, it was sufficient for any woman to be Mrs. Alfred Bingley; that was title enough. He would not be the minnow in a great family; rather would he be his own great family.

Yes, but would Sally be an absolutely *safe* investment? A solid five per cent? What about these bubble things that seemed to promise twenty, and, as soon as they had you, burst?

It was hard that duty could not always go hand in hand with pleasure. Still, there was no harm in seeing her, in being decently civil. He would probably do that to-morrow. No harm in showing a little gallantry towards both the ladies; there was safety in numbers.

What a prize he was! a man who was bound to get to the top. Of high moral rectitude and great mental ability, with easy manners that women found so charming, and a sense of humour they seldom appreciated. Of a pleasing exterior, too. He did not call himself actually handsome, did not wish to be. Handsome men were apt to be like barbers'-blocks, and effeminate and conceited. No one could ever accuse him of being either.

A man should not be beautiful to look upon; that was the woman's part. He should be strong, able, responsible in all matters. If he had had any vanity he might almost have suspected himself of being the ideal man, but vanity he left to the weaker sex. It was their prerogative.

How delightful the moor road was! He liked Little Crampton. The place absolutely revolved round him and his bank; he reigned undisputed king. Even Wilmot-Randal could not dispute his sway. Wilmot-Randal was married. When he married would the sceptre fall from his hands, and some mere nobody pick it up? A disturbing thought. But no, his position was so important. Even Mr. Lovelady was simply nowhere without him.

Mr. Lovelady was jealous of Sally; anybody could see it. A most lamentable fault in a clergyman! He would put a stop to Sally's great chances if he could, deprive the poor girl of her happiness. Oh, too bad, too bad!

Then just ahead of him he saw the subject of his thoughts, and his pulses and footsteps quickened. This was really a remarkable coincidence! They would be able to have quite a nice little walk before he must turn back for dinner.

Sally turned as he came up to her, and her pulses also quickened. Her chance at last! Her dark mood was past, and she looked very pretty with her wind-flushed cheeks.

"Well, here's luck to my husband's wife!" she inwardly toasted. "It's now or never; I can feel it in my bones!"

They had paused outside the Hopkins' house, and Miss Maggie, looking through the window, shivered with excitement. Would Sally get him? That she was going to try she felt certain. Well, she would watch for their return, and the girl's face would tell her all she wanted to know.

Mr. Bingley greeted Sally with impressive pleasure. He thought he had never seen her look so lovely. Her eyes were sparkling, her cheeks carmine, the corners of her mouth curling demurely at sight of him. It was well to have it in one's power to bring this look to a woman's face!

He liked her half-shy welcome. It suited her; it suited his mood. He had buried a rich relation. He was dying to discuss the great happening, and there was something especially alluring at thought of discussing it with Sally.

"I may accompany you?" he asked with that elaborate courtesy he kept for the favoured few. "I have only just returned to Little Crampton."

"Miss Maggie was telling us of your loss," she returned soberly. "Believe me, I feel for you in every way." Her lips did not twitch; she believed Mr. Bingley would consider she had expressed herself with perfect tact.

He did.

"Ah—Miss Maggie," he said as lightly as he thought suitable under the circumstances; "the tongue is an unruly member, in a woman." He did not foresee it becoming more unruly yet, and at his expense. "It has been a great ordeal, a very great ordeal—"

"It must have been," she agreed, "yet I feel sure your courage would always be equal to such ordeals." She wondered if she had ventured too much.

But no, he had swallowed it with avidity. "One does one's best," he said modestly.

"But *your* best, Mr. Bingley!" she murmured expressively, wondering to herself, "Will the creature's maw never be filled?"

"Poor fellow, it would not be right to wish that he should linger on, perhaps suffer. One knows he is so much better off, Miss Lunton."

"They always are under such circumstances," thought Sally cynically, as she said aloud, "Of course." She tried to look as if she were in church, and saw that Mr. Bingley was both pleased and impressed.

Mr. Bingley began to feel as if he were in church too, reading the

Scriptures at a large congregation. "What a libel to imply she is frivolous, flirtatious, unsuitable!" he thought indignantly. He always felt this disadvantage, and more, when Miss Maggie talked of Sally. He now felt certain she was a true woman, and modest and religious.

"In the midst of life we are in death," he said, and blew his nose.

Sally was not affected, save unpleasantly. She was jarred, and winced for a moment. Mr. Bingley's heavy touch, his platitudes, seemed to take all the beauty out of the world. She rebelled.

"Sometimes I think," she said, "it is equally true to say that in the midst of death we are in life. We see it every day. Someone drops in his traces, and yet everything goes on just the same. The greatest man, even The Man, did not hold back the beating pulse of the world for an instant. Thousands are dying only a few hours' journey away, and nothing seems to mark it. 'In the midst of life we are in death' has a terrible, almost a morbid sound; but if we remember that in the midst of death we are in life, then we can still march forward, keep our courage up, the flag flying. We can leave the dead and the past behind, and go on and on—"

Mr. Bingley stared at her with surprise and disapproval. Apart from the fact that she was talking nonsense, and irreverently, she was talking far too much. Besides, one did not talk like that at all on a week-day, though, of course, a funeral made a difference.

Still, he was aching to discuss his fortune. But would that seem a little callous, or wanting in good taste? It was obvious she had placed him on a very high pedestal indeed, perhaps too high for mere mortal man to occupy; after all, he was but human. It would be more restful to come down, but it was more dignified to stay up.

"You must not puzzle your charming little head with such thoughts, Miss Lunton," he said at length. "Leave that to your elders, and the wiser. Remain free of care, free of responsibility, while you can."

"Yes," she agreed obediently. "Was your cousin quite old?"

"Close on fifty." He spoke a little reluctantly.

"Oh, still in the prime of life!" she exclaimed, astonished. "That was hard."

His glance was reproving as he said, "He is at rest, dear fellow."

"Oh yes."

"In my Father's house are many mansions."

Again the girl winced; again she felt moved to protest. "Yes, I know, but sometimes I wonder. Suppose you got the finest mansion, and the other did not get one at all, or inhabited one with someone else? How be happy then?"

"*What* other?" asked Mr. Bingley, staring. He was pleased that she should bring her religious difficulties to him. Who more fitted to relieve them than the valuable lay-reader?

"The one that mattered," and she looked tragic for a moment. "You in your mansion, and he, or she, in another, or perhaps cast out altogether, between you the Great Gulf set."

Mr. Bingley felt a little irritated. As if any nice person would commit the *bêtise* of setting his or her affections on an individual who went to the Wrong Place.

"If thy right hand offend thee, cut it off," he murmured firmly, feeling himself strong enough to make the necessary amputation. "If this person will not come up to your level you cannot go down to his, or hers."

"You must just save yourself?" asked Sally, looking at him oddly. "There is no redemption through a great love?"

"You must do what is right," said the man of three p's—principles, prejudices, and platitudes. "One cannot touch pitch without being defiled."

"Or if a sinner burns, endeavour to put out the flames lest one get a little scorched? Love cannot count, sacrifice cannot count; neither can buy an ounce of redemption for the lost one? How sensible you are, Mr. Bingley."

"One has to be, in a bank." Then he remembered the part of lay-reader. "Strait and narrow is the way," he said.

"Very narrow, seemingly."

"It has to be."

"Of course there's nothing like keeping it select," she retorted recklessly, "but it makes one feel sorry for the very fat. Think of poor Mr. Boliver being taken up for causing an obstruction."

"There, I've done it now," she thought, "and I don't care, I don't care! He's utterly contemptible—almost as contemptible as I am! Everything was going splendidly, and then I began to think of other things, things that hurt, and now, matrimonially speaking, I'm in the cart! Oh, Sally, you silly ass! Do you *want* to face the alternative?"

"I beg your pardon!" gasped Mr. Bingley, thinking he could not have heard aright. "*What* did you say?"

Sally pulled herself together. Perhaps all was not lost yet. When they were married they would not be going walks together like this. One could mostly be out when he was in, and in when he was out.

"How silly of me!" she said. "I was just thinking of ordinary narrow paths, like the one leading to The Mountain stile, and wondering how Mr. Boliver would manage if there was a crowd. No one would be able to pass."

"Oh," said Mr. Bingley, relieved, and not objecting to have stones thrown at 'that fat fool, Boliver.' "I hardly suppose he would go at all in such a case." What a monstrosity the fellow was, and so oblivious of it! Why, the very name Boliver exuded fatness! Imagine being cursed with a name that designated a shape—and such a shape!

"Poor Mr. Boliver," sighed Sally, "and such a big, warm heart! Hearts don't count enough, I am afraid. Sometimes I am afraid we women admire brains too much. What do you think, Mr. Bingley?"

Mr. Bingley didn't think; he knew. His innate modesty made him seem a trifle self-conscious as he said, "Oh, I don't know about that, Miss Sally. So hard on the others, don't you know!"

"Ha!" thought the schemer, "the right bait, and swallowed in one gulp. If I can only keep my head I'll do it yet. What a triumph to return home engaged! Poor Mrs. Dalton! But Miss Maggie would be pleased that her plan had come off. What a relief to sit on velvet instead of rocks!"

"The others must take their chance," she said; "what have they to do with us? Do you know the sort of man *I* admire?"

Mr. Bingley blushed. "How should I?" he asked, all confusion.

"I wish I knew how one laughed inside," thought Sally wildly, as she tried to prevent the comers of her mouth from twitching. "To laugh is to lose. Oh, I mustn't, I won't!" Her face was contorted for a moment, and she felt his eyes upon it.

"Such a twinge—neuralgia," she explained, "but it's gone now." Then she baited her hook and offered it. "Well, Mr. Bingley, if you *must* know," she looked down in maidenly confusion, "it's the silent, strong man."

"Odd," she thought cynically, "how in real life the 'silent, strong man' is seldom strong, and *never* silent!"

"Oh, Miss Sally," said the fluttered Mr. Bingley, "aw—really!"

"Yes, really. If only they weren't so rare! Yet now and then an ideal materialises." She looked away as one who had said too much.

"Yet I can't act on the stage," she thought. "Now if I can stop thinking of inconvenient things it's as good as done. Will he kiss me? Hold me against his heart? Such a pulpy body, and I shall have to seem as if I liked it!"

She felt rather like someone who had screwed up courage to go and have a tooth out, and longed for it to be over. In the meanwhile she was being kept waiting on the dentist's doorstep.

Mr. Bingley almost purred as he moved a little closer. "It's strange how people come across people—" he began.

Sally kept her gravity. "Perhaps it's meant," she said in a hushed voice.

"Yes, perhaps it is—who knows?" He was busy thinking; he must keep his head, he must remember his mother's Guide, he must not act like an impetuous boy. And yet—and yet—he did so want to!

"Did you hear about a little money coming to me?" he asked abruptly. "It worries me rather."

"*Worries* you!" she gasped. He had not given her that impression.

"Such a very grave responsibility," he said with slight reproof. "I assure you, Miss Sally, I feel it deeply. The careless, shallow natures seem to think we are put into the world for the thoughtless enjoyment of money, the mere spending, the selfish scattering. To me it is a trust; something to be guarded."

"What a beautiful idea!" cried Sally, mentally spending a considerable portion of this 'trust' upon herself and some of life's luckless.

"A worthy treasurer, that is my ideal. You remember the ten talents, the lesson of increasing, so clearly expressed?"

"The devil can always quote Scripture to his ends, and the 'unco guid' likewise, it seems," thought Sally as she nodded, fixing admiring eyes upon his face.

Mr. Bingley would 'guard' indeed; he would not squander on that illusive, thankless thing called 'doing good'—in other words, doing harm by pauperising. When one had a rare specimen, one did not go throwing it about the world to get its priceless edges knocked off; one put it in a glass case, and locked it up out of harm's way. Now and then one took it out and looked at it, perhaps measured it to see how much it had grown, for if a rolling stone gathers no moss the guarded treasure does. He had already decided upon the special glass case which should contain this hoard.

Women got such fly-away notions into their shallow little heads. He was glad Sally did not possess them, that she saw the thing with his eyes, seemed indeed prepared to see everything through the wider, wiser vision.

"At first I did not know why I had thus been honoured above the rest," he said modestly, "and then I realised what it all meant. My dear cousin knew it would be safe in my hands."

"Yes," said Sally, adding to herself, "worse luck!" She would have to get him to make a settlement somehow or other.

"Let us go this way," he suggested, turning on to the moors.

She followed his lead, even though she saw it would take them past The Hut, which she would rather have avoided. This was no time to cross Mr. Bingley in the slightest of his desires. She trod obediently along the rough track by his side.

She shrank a little as she saw a figure come out of the miserable dwelling and lean listlessly against the portals.

She had to remember his insult to her, and harden her heart, otherwise she must have felt sorry for him, so dejected was his attitude. She stole another glance at him. He was looking ill, she thought, his face very strained. It still retained its Indian bronze, but it was thin and haggard, his mouth painfully compressed.

"Drink showing at last," she told herself. Then she looked at him again. It was difficult to associate such a weakness with this man's clear-cut, refined face, more difficult than ever just then.

He turned and saw her, starting violently. His face flushed scarlet, and for an instant his eyes met hers. There was shame in them and apology, and a desperate moving appeal as well.

Sally could not be ungenerous. She moved forward impulsively to meet it, to say she would forgive and forget if he would conquer even at the eleventh hour. She would once more offer her help and friendship, and they would start afresh.

And then … she caught sight of the disapproving frown on Mr. Bingley's face. Was this a time to offend Mr. Bingley? To offend him was to lose him for ever. She was sorry for Robert Kantyre, but she was sorrier for herself; oneself naturally came first.

She passed the man of The Hut with a casual little nod. When she was Mrs. Alfred Bingley it would be easier. She would be able to afford to help others then. To descend into the gutter was to be helpful to none, and economically a crime when it could be avoided. She must avoid it at all costs. She was pleased with her own sensible arguments as they walked along, and waited for the momentous words to be spoken, and she was annoyed that a pair of desperate grey eyes went with her.

"Really, I have no patience with the working-class," exclaimed Mr. Bingley, who felt extremely put out, why he could not have said. "You never see them doing anything useful in their spare time, always just lounging, and usually round the public-houses."

"Perhaps a man who has laboured hard for eight hours a day, week in and week out, requires to lounge somewhere," said Sally. "It's a pity we haven't the continental café system, with a sort of combined club arrangement. We not only ask them to drink, but ask them to drink poor stuff and as uncomfortably and expensively as possible."

Mr. Bingley looked his opinion of such nonsense, and Sally hurriedly changed the subject. She must remember one thing, and one thing only.

CHAPTER XVIII

"I'm afraid we are lost, my very dear Miss Sally"

Mr. Bingley took out his watch. He must not be late for the sacred function of the day. He had never been late in his life. Ought he to turn now, or could he venture another ten minutes? Miss Lunton was evidently out for a long walk.

Would it be too pointed if he asked her to turn with him? It was a perfect evening, and it would be pleasant to go back with an increased appetite. Yes, he could afford those extra ten minutes. They could walk back at a slightly quicker pace; she was an excellent walker. He would get in, he calculated, by seven-fifteen to the minute.

Sally noticed his action and her heart sank. "Oh dear," she thought, "I'd forgotten the creature's dinner! I had a vision of walking on and on till he did it. Once back in Little Crampton all is lost."

She caught sight of a small compass dangling from the watch-chain. "How clever!" she said admiringly; "now a woman could never learn to find her way about by a compass." She knew two who could.

Mr. Bingley did not like to spoil her pleasure by owning that he doubted being able to make use of the compass. He shook it and looked very wise; then he put his watch back, and said:

"Where does that funny, crooked little path lead to? I have never been down it; have you?"

"No," returned Sally, who knew it led to getting hopelessly lost. "I should be afraid to go down it alone." She moved timidly nearer her protector.

"And you *shan't* go down it alone," said the gallant Mr. Bingley; "*I* am with you, Miss Sally. We will just go down it for ten minutes, and then turn."

"Excellent!" thought the girl exultantly. "I do hope there will be a moon. He's just got to the stage when moonlight is the sure push-off. There was a lovely one last night—when I had no special use for it!"

The crooked little path merged into other crooked little paths; the same, yet not quite the same, as Sally knew. She followed her guide with a trusting faith he thought very beautiful. She would lean. She would be the ivy to his oak. Never, never would she dispute his wise decision, his will, his way.

She began to hum softly, "It's a long, long way to Tipperary!"

"Quite a pleasant tune," said Mr. Bingley, "keeps one going, you know." It was certainly keeping them going. The bank-manager made quite a good imitation of quick-marching to it.

More crooked little paths, the same, yet not quite the same, and Mr. Bingley ever confident! The ten minutes were not up.

"'The Girl Who Took the Wrong Turning'!" quoted Sally to herself, as she looked trustfully up at him. "We've got a bit mixed, for here's little Mary following the lamb!"

Mr. Bingley looked into the soft black eyes. How sad they were! They did not sparkle now, but they were infinitely sweeter so. He looked long into them, and Sally whistled 'Tipperary' again, a little plaintively, perhaps, and now it was Mr. Bingley who followed, blindly, besottedly.

"And everywhere that Mary went, the lamb went too—you bet!" thought pleased Sally. "I am almost Mrs. Alfred Bingley! Ugh! he is sure to kiss me. Oh, our poor shrinking flesh, how cowardly it is! Perhaps, if I keep my eyes shut, I shall be able to bear it. Anyway I must. I'm about in the dentist's chair by now, I suppose. I wish I could have gas. Hurry up, man, and get it over! What a wrench it's going to be, but how comfortable afterwards!"

She looked at him, smiling shyly.

"Miss Sally—" began Mr. Bingley huskily. He made a step forward, his hand outstretched to seize hers.

She set her teeth and waited. "It's going to be a wisdom tooth—oh! oh!" she cried to herself. "Now for it!"

Then a strange, illogical thing happened. If the face of Jimmy and the dead past had risen to appal, to bid her pause, she could have understood, have conquered them; but it was instead the desperate appeal in Robert Kantyre's grey eyes she saw, and that so astonished and disconcerted her that she could not recover herself all at once.

"I—" went on the lay-reader, and then something about the girl, perhaps the tenseness of her figure, the stiff smile on her lips, brought him sharply to himself. What had he been about to do, or say? Once spoken he could not have taken the words back. He was most strictly honourable; his word his bond. He had saved himself, though only on the brink. What a mercy she had noticed nothing!

"Miss Sally," he said abruptly, "we must turn back. I shall be late for dinner."

Sally bit off a naughty word in time, and turned, smiling. "Oh, that would never do!" she said. After all, since they happened to be going in the wrong direction, things were not yet lost. The moon, the blessed moon, friend of lovers and the designing, would come out and save her yet. What a fool she had been to look like that, feel like that! And all because of a stranger's unhappy eyes! Did she want to remain Sally on the rocks to the end? Next time she would manage better, be a little helpful. That thrust-out hand should find hers; the irrevocable words should be spoken; the kiss not only received, but returned. "Though that will take some doing!" she told herself.

In his relief Mr. Bingley was hardly aware of where he was going. He had been almost over the precipice. How providential to find his feet on firm earth again.

He broke into a quicker walk. The sooner they got home the better. He began to feel the need of his dinner. Funeral luncheons were most unsatisfactory. Even if the repast had been all it might have been, he would scarcely have cared to let himself really go.

"Mary continues to follow the lamb, which is losing Mary," thought Sally, highly amused. "Lost, stolen, or strayed, a Bingley answering to the name of Alfred!"

Once more Mr. Bingley took out his watch, but Sally did not mind this time. It would need more than a watch to spoil her plans now. There was horror on his face.

"Really, it's most peculiar, most peculiar!" he muttered.

"What?" asked Sally, all innocence.

"This path, or paths—I had not noticed what a lot of them there are, and all exactly alike. The County Council ought to put up signboards. Disgraceful! I gave ten minutes to going, and ten to getting back where we started from, and though it's eleven minutes, and we've been walking faster, I don't see the path, do you?"

Sally had not expected to, but she affected great surprise. "No, wherever can it be?"

"It almost looks as if we might have come a little out of the right direction. Now which way is it, I wonder?"

Sally left it entirely to him. She knew he could be trusted to do as she wished. He would never own himself at fault, never ask a woman's help. He would be the silent, strong man at any cost.

"How thankful I am to be in your care," she exclaimed; "how awful if I had been alone!" She certainly would not have been lost in that case.

Mr. Bingley looked at his watch again, and then at the maze of paths.

Sally clapped her hands. "Oh, Mr. Bingley, how like you, and how clever to think of it! Now we shall be all right!"

He stared.

"The compass, you know."

Mr. Bingley took the compass in his hand and shook it; then he stared at it hard, then at the sky. The wretched needle seemed to him to dance about in the most ridiculous fashion.

"So few men—civilians, I mean, of course—can manage a compass," cooed Sally admiringly.

He shook it again; again the needle' danced round. Then it stopped and pointed to the north. Did that mean they ought to go north? And which *was* north? Why couldn't the inventors make a thing that would work properly? He turned slowly round, revolving on a pivot.

"Are we going to play at Blind Man's Buff, or getting giddy, or what?" thought Sally, interested. "I wonder what time the moon is due."

Mr. Bingley counted the paths. One, two, three, four, five. Odd he had never noticed that there were five; he thought there had only been three. He decided that the middle one looked the most familiar.

He marched down it with an air of confidence he was far from feeling. After walking another ten minutes he came to a branch of seven paths. He began to be a little alarmed. Impossible that they should be lost, and such a short way from the big, broad path he knew so well; but tiresome, very tiresome. He was certain he had not noticed a branch of seven paths.

He took the third.

At the end of fifteen minutes they faced a tangle of eleven paths. Then he grew really alarmed. It was like a nightmare. Next he supposed there would be twenty. He was prepared for anything—except to own up. He took the path to the right. It had a shrub he thought he remembered. They came to a branch of three paths.

He drew a breath of relief. This was better. Nothing like keeping one's head. Women never kept their heads in an emergency; they only made it the more emergent. Only another ten minutes. It had been the middle one, he remembered that distinctly. Why, it was the very spot where he had nearly met with such fatal disaster!

"We are all right now," he said kindly to Sally; "don't you worry."

"I'm not worrying," she said, truthfully enough. She looked at the remains of the sunset. Oh, excellent young man!

They walked a little way, and then Mr. Bingley had again recourse to his watch. His face was very grave as he consulted it. Then he made the needle of the compass dance again.

"I think we will turn to the right."

"Which happens to be the wrong, I fancy," thought Sally, turning. The more hopelessly she felt he was losing her, the more confiding grew her manner. "At this rate we shall land in the sea in six months or so. How jolly for the mermaids to have Mr. Bingley to play with—that is, if Mr.

Bingley permits the liberty!" She looked up at him—she had not very far to look—like a dog following its master. As soon question the wisdom of the Almighty as Mr. Bingley's!

He looked down at her—a long way down it seemed to him—and his heart grew dangerously soft. How enthralling when grave and sombre, how fascinating when bubbling over with laughter! How beautifully she followed his lead; what a valuable quality in a woman! The silent, strong man; the weak, trusting woman. His chivalry was stirred.

"The dentist's chair again," thought Sally. "We shall walk home by the roseate hues of early dawn—engaged. The moon will have pushed off our matrimonial craft!"

A peevish sound came from Mr. Bingley. "Look! We ought to have got to the big path, and just look what we *have* got to!" The County Council deserved shooting. He would have to go on it himself, he supposed, if any work was to be done. Losing people like this!

Sally was amused to discover they had got to a tangle of nineteen paths, crossing and recrossing, blending, and branching off again. The maze at Hampton Court was nothing to it. But while he had expected something different, Sally had entered it with her eyes open.

"It does seem funny, certainly," she agreed.

"*Funny!*" He checked himself abruptly. An awful realisation was coming surely and slowly upon him. They were lost! First the infernal compass and then the County Council had lost them. He remembered, with horror, what getting lost on the moors meant. Sally must not guess the nature of the disaster that had come upon them. Women get so hysterical. Suppose she cried? The womanly woman always cried. He would find the way back to Little Crampton and his dinner somehow. The inner man was crying out for that dinner. He was annoyed that he had saved himself up for it so carefully. He might have risked a little more of that funeral luncheon, after all. The beef-steak pie had not looked so bad. He could have left the pastry and the beef-steak—it would look more feeling to leave something—and have eaten the kidneys with potatoes and plenty of gravy. It would be more like eight-thirty than seven-fifteen by the time he got back, and he would have had nothing, simply nothing, to go upon.

It was well to be a woman at such a time. They never seemed to bother about meals or be really hungry, at least, refined gentlewomen didn't, and could eat anything, and at any time. Possibly Miss Lunton would just as soon have her supper at nine as at eight, her usual hour. She would only be a quarter of an hour or so late, and he an hour; and *his* meal might be spoiled.

"Confound this compass!" he exclaimed with asperity. "What right have people to sell a thing that isn't in working order?"

"They *will* do it," returned Sally sympathetically. She peered at the compass. "It *looks* as if it's gone wrong," she remarked; "I'm sure the needle should not go on like that all the time, just contradicting itself. I should take it back if I were you."

"I certainly shall, and get my money back too, and tell the man what I think of him!" he exclaimed. "It might have lost us!" He gave a nervous little laugh. "That would have been a nasty game to play on us, eh, Miss Sally?"

It was clever of her to find out that the compass had gone wrong. Some women—women were so unreasonable—might have blamed him.

Sally managed to shudder realistically at the mere thought of being lost. She wondered what her rôle had better be when the facts could no longer be concealed. Perhaps she had better wait for a clue. Her natural one was the helpful comrade, but Mr. Bingley might prefer a few womanly tears, and a state of almost abject dependence. She must not make a second mistake. "I wonder what time the moon is due?" she thought.

Mr. Bingley pulled himself together. "We will try the next curve," he said; "we *must* find ourselves somewhere familiar soon." He looked at the sky; it was growing dusk. Dusk—and then dark! Good Heavens! the way must be found at once, or—

He refused to follow that 'or' any further. Would Vanner be able to keep dinner back without spoiling or wasting, or would she, shaken to the foundations, womanlike, lose her head?

He hurried round curve after curve, now and then breaking into a little trot.

"Just like a rabbit seeking cover!" thought Sally, inwardly convulsed.

They arrived at four paths.

"Another junction," murmured the girl; "change here for Manchester, Birmingham, and Crewe!" Aloud she said, "I think you could claim damages against the man for selling a compass like that. I'm afraid you will be a little late for your dinner."

"How understanding she is!" thought Mr. Bingley, sighing dolorously. "I'm afraid so too, Miss Lunton," he said aloud. "How good of you to take it like this."

"Oh, but I do not mind at all. You look after me so nicely. Suppose I had been lost alone, or with the average man?"

"I could not bear to think of that!" he exclaimed truthfully. "You are safe with me whatever comes or goes."

"I hope a mad bull won't come," she thought, "because then I am afraid Mr. Bingley might go in earnest."

She did her escort an injustice. Even in such an hour he would not have forgotten to play the gentleman. He would not have left Sally to the bull; he would probably have seized her hand and saved her by his dodging and running.

"It's not as if we are really lost yet," he murmured reassuringly.

"Oh no!"

They went on, only to discover another junction. Then Mr. Bingley's proud spirit crumpled up, and he prepared to break the news to the unconscious Miss Lunton.

"Bear up, I beg of you," he began bravely. "The fact is, I really am afraid we are lost, my very dear Miss Sally."

CHAPTER XIX

"But perhaps bank-managers don't curl?"

"Oh dear, what's the cue?" thought Sally.

"Will it help or hinder if I drop into his arms and cling timidly?" She looked at him, and decided it would hinder. "I must just be very unselfish," she decided, "and of course surprised."

"Really lost! Oh, you cannot mean it!" she gasped.

"Thanks to the County Council and the compass. Disgraceful!"

"How trying for you! Why, your dinner will be quite cold. It does not matter to me; I can take a scratch meal any time and not notice the difference." As a matter of fact, she was quite as hungry as Mr. Bingley.

He warmed to her. "Yes, it is trying," he owned, "but I am fortunate in my charming company, Miss Sally. I am sure Vanner will keep her head and hold it back. It's the first emergency she's been faced with since she entered my household, and it would be deplorable if she did not rise to it, simply deplorable."

Sally fought with a desire to laugh, and conquered, making a 'doveish' sound, as she described it to herself. Mr. Bingley took it to mean what he wished.

"You think Vanner will keep her head?" he asked eagerly.

"Yes, oh yes," she assented, but could not resist the malicious query, "And which way do we go *now*, Mr. Bingley?"

Mr. Bingley determined to go dinnerwards or die in the attempt. It was all very well taking exercise to get up an appetite, but it was rather awkward, having taken so much exercise and having got the sharp appetite, to have so little prospect of getting the dinner.

He took Sally's hand, pulling it through his arm. "You must be tired," he said sympathetically; "just lean on me, my dear Miss Sally. I will see to everything."

"I feel sure you will," she returned, looking up at him under lowered black lashes; "somehow I hardly mind being lost with you at all, Mr. Bingley."

He patted her hand. "My dear child, don't you worry. If we are a *little* out of our way you can trust me to find it."

"Dear old moon! Come quickly and let's get it over!" begged Sally. "I'm sure I could bear it better by moonlight. If one might only shut one's eyes, and hold one's nose, as one used to do when swallowing something especially awful, I might be able to bear up really well."

"Need you ask me to trust you? Cannot you *see*?" she asked reproachfully.

He looked down into the piquant, sparkling face, and forgot his crying need of dinner, as it occurred to him that Sally had even more than a beautiful face—a beautiful soul. He placed his hand over hers.

"You are a true woman," he said emotionally.

Sally wondered how long he was going to 'hedge'; when, if ever, he would come to the point. He was keeping her such a long time on the dentist's doorstep. Besides, she wanted to laugh, and she knew she had got to look soulful.

She was sure Mr. Bingley did not yet recognise the gravity of the situation. He was aware that they were lost, temporarily, but not that it would be dark before he found the right path, which she believed to be absolutely in the opposite direction. When it became dark they would have to stay where they were till the moon rose. If the moon did not rise they would have to stay there till the dawn broke. When a romantic veil of moonlight shone over the moors he would probably propose, if he had not already done so, but he would certainly insist on losing her still more in his efforts to get back at a respectable hour.

She thought of the sensation in Little Crampton, when Mr. Bingley, by whom people set their clocks, did not return for dinner, and when Miss Lunton did not return either!

Bedtime, but no Miss Lunton or Mr. Bingley. Was it possible they had fled together to the nearest registry office? Had Miss Lunton abducted Mr. Bingley on hearing of his fresh fortune, bent on compromising the poor dear man?

And then—Mr. Bingley and Miss Lunton and the milk all turning up together! Are such things possible in Little Crampton? What a thrill! Why, he'd almost have to marry her for the sake of the bank!

She choked into her handkerchief.

"Don't, don't," he implored, "be brave, Miss Sally!" He pressed her hand. "The average woman would be crying or making a fuss, or saying she could not walk another step, but you are different."

Sally forced herself to return the pressure of his hand, looking down, and seeming to blush. "He's taking his time, but he's getting there," she thought. "Oh, poor Mrs. Dalton! But that's the way the world wags, one's gain is another's loss. When he gets a bank elsewhere she must come and stay and I will find someone for her."

Mr. Bingley took away his hand abruptly. Good gracious! what had he been about to say? And his dinner spoiling while the inner man raised a loud clamour for it! How gross only to be able to think of his appetite. He must be careful never to find himself in such a coarse situation again. By having an excellent dinner before he got too hungry he had been able to go through life unconscious of what he called, in others, a carnal appetite.

"We must bustle along a bit, we must really!" he exclaimed. "I'm afraid I am making it uncomfortable for you." He took away his arm.

"Oh dear, he thinks me too bold. Good Lord! is it all to go through again?" thought Sally, beginning to feel exhausted. "Husband-hunting, or getting a man to propose, is the strenuous life, and no mistake!"

"Are you very tired?" he asked anxiously. "You can go on a bit, can't you?"

"Oh yes. I'm a splendid walker. I went on a tour once, and we lost ourselves, and had to walk hours after the moon rose, and then sleep out under the stars. It was heavenly!" Her face flushed and her eyes shone. Then she remembered Mr. Bingley. "I hope there will be a moon to-night."

"Oh, we'll be home long before that!" he gasped. "What a strong girl your friend must have been!"

"Oh yes, very strong."

"As strong as a man almost."

"Quite as strong as a man," agreed Sally. "He—she—was even stronger than I. Oh, Mr. Bingley, here we are at the seven-junction again! Is it the *same* seven? I don't remember those trees."

Mr. Bingley did not remember them either. He pointed vaguely. "Surely Little Crampton lies in that direction?"

Sally nodded. "It's wonderful how men always know best." Oh, they would be there for the moonlight all right!

"I wish I could have known a little better on this occasion," he returned ruefully. Still, he had every hope of getting home by, say, nine. Nine was quite a respectable hour to come home with a lady. Even Miss Maggie if she happened to hear of it—and why need anybody hear of it?—could not say very much. Of course if it were ten she might find a theme for foolish gossip, which would be painful and unpleasant to a man in his position; but nobody could make a *scandal* out of ten o'clock, even in Little Crampton. Beyond ten his imagination simply did not go. His dinner might be still eatable by then if Vanner kept her head.

What a pity Miss Lunton's feminine intuition had served her so badly! If only she had thought fit to suggest earlier, before it was too late, that the compass had gone wrong! As far as that went, she was mainly responsible for the mishap. She had lured him on, as it were, not deliberately, but still lured. She had even *suggested* the use of the compass; it was she who seemed so eager to set forth upon the adventure of the untried path. Oh, reckless, unthinking womanhood! Finally, if he had not met her at all he wouldn't have been lost. He would be comfortably at home, seated at his dining-table, his appetite being appeased, his dinner unwasted. Instead here he was, landed, absolutely landed! It was growing very dusk, not to say dark. Suppose they got seriously lost, suppose—

Sally met his rather antagonistic eyes, and her spirit failed.

"Am I to lose, after all?" she asked herself. "Shall I have once more to abandon my hard-won position, and consider from what vantage I will issue the next attack? If only there were some biscuits to nibble! If only all this horror were not necessary, and I could get him to do it, and be able to tell him quite frankly to—go to the devil! What a priceless moment! Still, the moon will help; even Bingleys look better by moonlight, you see less of them! After I am settled down to being Mrs. B. it will be all right."

"What time is it?" she asked meekly. What time had that unappreciated moon of the previous evening risen?

Mr. Bingley looked at his watch and gave a jump. "Almost nine!" he gasped.

Would they do it by ten? They must; that was all there was about it. If he had tried that pie, after all, crust, beef-steak, everything! Distance lent a distinct enchantment. He thought of the wasted opportunity as one might think of ambrosia foolishly foregone.

By nine-thirty they were no nearer. In fact, they were much further, and it was a case of groping now. The moors stood high, and it had been a light evening, but the sky was beginning to hang like an inky pall above their heads.

Sally had had enough of it. "Let's sit down and wait for the moon," she said cheerfully. "We mustn't risk getting lost too far."

Mr. Bingley sank down upon the ground, the spirit out of him. Then he got up again and spread his handkerchief beneath him. It felt dry enough, but one never knew whether that insidious damp he feared might not be rising all the time. He was too tired and hungry to care about anything; too tired to think. He leant against a tree and hoped there were no insects about, or that there would not be any dew. To return with a cold would really be too much! If only he had guessed what might happen, and brought those cherished possessions, his goloshes!

To think they would have to wait for moonlight to get back! There was something so compromising about a moon! On the moonlit moors alone with Miss Lunton at goodness knows what time! There was something rather compromising about Miss Lunton!

"What time *does* the moon rise?" he inquired peevishly.

Sally yawned; she could not help it. "I don't know, I suppose it depends upon how it feels about it. Doubtless it oversleeps itself at times."

Mr. Bingley was jarred by the foolish frivolity of this answer.

Sally looked round. "I say," she exclaimed, "somebody has been gathering stuff for a fire, and then not used it! Let's take some of it and light one! It would be more cheerful, and someone might see us then, perhaps. It's getting pitch dark."

Mr. Bingley thought it a good idea. He collected some of the stuff; it would at least ward off the dreaded chill.

Sally watched his efforts with impatient amusement. How futile he was! "That's not the way," she exclaimed, showing him how to do it; "it's plain *you* have never been lost before, or played at being gypsies!"

"I am glad to remember I have done neither, Miss Lunton," he returned with dignity.

"Well, you have done both now. I think you had better give me the matches."

In a very short time she had the fire crackling and burning pleasantly between them. She remembered another such fire, and another couple. How Jimmy and she had laughed at each other across it! How they had enjoyed the vagrancy and the freedom! And now—

She sighed. "Quite an adventure, isn't it?" she asked listlessly. "We ought to have a pot to swing in the middle with a poached rabbit in it."

The idea did not appeal to Mr. Bingley, and he let her see it. He never ate rabbits; as for a poached one …

"I am wasting my cheerfulness," she thought; "he can think of nothing but his dinner and the awful impropriety of the situation. He is annoyed with me for getting lost with him. Soon it will be 'Miss Lunton'—not 'my very dear Miss Sally'—who has lost Mr. Bingley!"

She decided she would forget his existence. She flung aside her hat and lay back with her hands clasped under her head staring up into the sky. She began to dream and muse … further and further away she drifted from Mr. Bingley. Soon he had ceased to count.

He looked at her careless attitude with disapproval; he thought she was looking for the moon, but considered women should never lounge off chairs or sofas.

"There's a star," she murmured drowsily at length, "with such a naughty little twinkle in its eye. Looks as if it's going to have a night out without its mother knowing."

Mr. Bingley preserved a disapproving silence; he was jarred.

"Of course it may be genuinely lost, just as we are," she went on. "I hope it's found somebody nice to be lost with—poor dear!"

"I'm afraid you are talking rather foolishly, Miss Lunton," reproved the bank-manager in his very stiffest tones. "I am not interested in the stars. The moon would be more to the point, I think."

He wanted the moon desperately—and his dinner.

"Suppose the moon runs away, as I feel sure that naughty star has done?" demanded Sally, irrepressible now. "Where should *we* be, Mr. Bingley? Where was Moses when the light went out?"

"I fail to understand you," he returned frigidly. Had he once admired this flippant young woman?

"It was a silly question to ask. Of course we shall still be here. We will have to sleep on the hard, hard ground, and make the best of our aches to-morrow."

"We will do nothing of the sort," gasped the utterly horrified lay-reader. "It is essential, absolutely essential that we get back to-night."

"But if we can't?"

"We must. What would people say?"

"Fools say—*let* them say!" she quoted.

"You seem to forget the position I occupy in Little Crampton, Miss Lupton."

"Alas! The fierce white light that beats upon a throne! It's like the limelight, isn't it?" she went on; "it will follow the popular star about everywhere. It must annoy him dreadfully. How fortunate for me that I am of no importance save to myself."

"It makes the situation very difficult, very difficult indeed," said Mr. Bingley fussily. "I insist upon getting back to-night, simply insist."

"Insist by all means," retorted Sally, losing patience.

What a tedious, insistent little mind it had! What a Bingleyish person he was! She could imagine the real trend of his prayers. "Dear God, don't let me ever be seen doing anything unconventional, or let me feel anything uncomfortable!"

Well, his prayer did not look like being answered this time. Oh, bother Mr. Bingley and all that was his!

She gazed up into the sky. How magnificent and how austere was the shadowland over her head! How small and petty and contemptible it made her feel. "What are we? A couple of insects, no more," she thought. Were the very heavens to burst open and pretence and pettiness fly away, Mr. Bingley would still be Mr. Bingley of the Bank, a Somebody in his tiny world, because it was so tiny, and because he was unmarried, and—as the Cramptonians went—rich. He would persist in Bingleyism in the face of highest Heaven, for he was of those who have no sense of proportion.

"I know Vanner will lose her head, I know it!" burst out Mr. Bingley in a wail. "Goodness knows if there will be anything eatable left!"

Sally sat up and looked at him, and he thought her eyes very odd. "What awful risks we are running, you and I, aren't we?" she asked, as she thought of other risks not so far away.

"What do you mean?" he asked anxiously. "It will be all right when the moon rises. It can't be so very long now." He felt that the least it could do was to be punctual. "It's the sort of thing that might happen to anybody with a bad compass. Most of the dinner will be spoiled, of course."

"More than that is being spoiled," said Sally sharply. "What does it matter what happens to us, after all? We're not of any use. We have got to leave the big struggle to others, to play the looker-on at the greatest of life's games—just a couple of miserable atoms!"

Mr. Bingley hated Sally for a moment, almost as much as she was growing to hate him. To be called a 'miserable atom!' Mr. Bingley of the Bank, and three thousand pounds a year! The girl must be mad!

"You are ill," he said, "the walk has been too much for you. You cannot know what you are saying!"

"I am saying I wish I had never been born!" she burst out.

"Very morbid and irreligious," reproved Mr. Bingley, his mouth tightly buttoned. "The fact is, you want your dinner. It does make one feel rather desperate; still, one must not give way. I beg you not to become hysterical.

We will get back the moment the moon rises. No one need be any the wiser."

"To whom would it matter if we never got back at all?" she demanded. "Oh, Lovey would be sorry, I know, and I suppose your directors would have to appoint another bank-manager, but there are always plenty of them about, aren't there, and I don't suppose anybody would notice the difference. People would get their money just the same, and after all, that's the only thing that matters about a bank."

Mr. Bingley gasped. "Miss Lunton, you are lightheaded. Keep calm, I beg of you!"

She was going to have an hysterical attack. He knew it, he felt it. What on earth was to be done now? Was he to return through Little Crampton with a crying, hysterical woman calling attention to the situation? If only women had a little more ballast, a little logic, more courage! Here was he, rent with the pangs of hunger, yes, absolutely rent, and yet bearing it like a man. *He* did not cry and look like that. He felt sure she was going to cry; the tears were there, her eyes burning. Such wicked, unwomanly black eyes!

"You cannot have hysterics here and at this time of night," he said firmly; "you *must* command yourself."

Sally burst out laughing, and laughed, and laughed.

Mr. Bingley went as near cursing as a lay-reader may. She'd started! Good Heavens! and there was no water to throw at her! Next tears and drumming of heels and perhaps clutchings.

He hated to think of clutchings, and at that time of night! He stood up, and, taking his handkerchief from the ground, shook it out and wiped his face. What a situation! Never, never again! To think he had, at one time, almost been a little attracted by this dreadful woman!

Mr. Bingley of the bank clutched! …

He took out his watch with a shaking hand, and prepared to dodge Sally the moment she began, almost sooner if necessary. "*Don't*," he implored piteously; "wait—wait till you can do it comfortably at home, with Elizabeth and a cup of tea, or at least till the moon rises."

"I'm not going to do it at all!" gasped Sally, rocking with laughter. Oh, these Bingley-things!

"But you *are* doing it! They always start with laughing. Do, do wait till the moon—"

"There isn't going to *be* any moon!" spluttered the convulsed Sally. "It's too late now. Oh dear, oh dear!"

"Not be a moon?" gulped Mr. Bingley, looking tragic; "not *be* a moon!" No wonder she felt hysterical. He felt rather queer himself. If there wasn't a moon, what about his dinner, and getting home in decent time? What about his reputation? It did not occur to him to think of Sally's; she hardly seemed to have one, somehow.

"No," said the girl, "it hasn't risen to the occasion. But *you* have, Mr. Bingley, you have!" She rolled in mirth.

"A man does," he replied, "his life and training teach him that from the first, and self-control. Oh, won't you *try* and stop! There's no water, nothing! No burnt feathers! You will make yourself ill, you won't be able to walk home, and then … and as it is—"

Sally sat up, wiping her eyes. "We won't go home till morning!" she broke out with vulgar gusto. She was enjoying herself now; she could not help it. Mr. Bingley was delicious.

He shuddered. "There must be some alternative," he faltered. "We cannot stay here, like this, all night. *Impossible!*"

Sally began to bubble again. "It'll be all right," she said; "we've only got to wait till dawn, and arrive home with the milk. I don't suppose we shall miss our breakfasts as well. One of the shepherds is sure to come across us."

"'Arrive home with the milk,'" repeated Mr. Bingley to himself; "arrive home with the milk; arrive home with the milk; arrive—"

"Little Crampton lies due east. We must just walk into 'the roseate hues of early dawn' and see what happens. We won't look at the paths, only the sky, and trust to luck."

Mr. Bingley shuddered. What a terrible disaster had overtaken him! What would people say? What would they expect of him? Would public opinion marry him to this flippant, hysterical woman? No, he was hanged if it should! Marry a woman who had got herself talked about! Never. A sentence in *The Book* came to mock and madden:

"*Never compromise an unmarried woman,*" commanded the old dame, with conscious, or unconscious, cynicism; "*there is nothing to prevent her marrying you.*"

Had he compromised Miss Lunton? Had she not rather compromised him? Must he marry her either for his reputation or hers? What a problem to be faced with!

After all, men could be thought a 'little wild,' even in Little Crampton, and still be asked out to dinner, and treated as admiringly as ever, perhaps more so—when they were unmarried. On the other hand, neither bank-manager nor lay-reader could afford to be thought a 'gay dog.' To come from burying a relation and inheriting some thirty thousand pounds to this! What a cruel irony of Fate!

"And till then?" he inquired icily.

"Oh, I shall just curl up and go to sleep," she said casually. "I advise you to do the same."

He gave her a look which spoke volumes. Mr. Bingley of the Bank *curl*!

Sally took the offensive. "But perhaps lay-readers and bank-managers don't curl!" she drawled.

Mr. Bingley vouchsafed no reply. His attitude, however, very plainly expressed the fact that, as far as he was concerned, they most certainly did not.

Sally suited her action to her word, in the matter of curling up. "If you're waking, call me early," she said lightly, adding to herself, "Bingley dear!"

Mr. Bingley made no response whatever. His eyes were stony, his mouth a tight little button. He was not only shocked, but grieved.

"Mind you don't let the fire out," she commanded. She was really very tired and sleepy, and her eyes closed thankfully. She was snug and warm in her little hollow with the firelight playing on her. The silence seemed to wrap her round like a magic cloak. Soon she was fast asleep.

Mr. Bingley did not sleep. To have done so would have added to the impropriety of the proceeding, he considered. He stared straight in front of him, once more seated on his handkerchief, and longing for his dinner and his goloshes. "What will Little Crampton say?" whirled round and round in his brain. Then he thought of that wasted opportunity at the funeral luncheon—the pie had become delicious in retrospect; of scandals, of Sally's impertinent, "But perhaps bank-managers don't curl?" She had dared to make fun of him. She had gone against *The Book* unto seventy times seven.

"*Never marry a woman who makes fun of sacred things; she may come to make fun of you.*"

And Sally had done little else than make fun of sacred things! How his dead mother always *knew*!

She looked very pretty lying asleep by the firelight. Her wicked black eyes were closed, her lashes made a soft shadow on her cheeks; the firelight gave a rosy glow to her face, and gleamed on her yellow hair. Her lips were a little parted; he caught the whiteness of perfect, and natural, teeth. She looked years younger, almost a child; very desirable, very gentle. A sharp revulsion of feeling shook him.

Yet she had said that about 'curl,' implying that he was scarcely the shape that could! She threatened his liberty and his reputation, and she slept heedless of it all. How like a woman!

Of course she might not have meant it. She might have been joking, not thinking of what she was saying. Very bad taste, of course, but still, a joke is no more than a joke. She recognised his keen sense of humour. Her admiration of him was almost obvious; try as she would, she could not hide it. She had understood him, appreciated him from the first.

What long lashes she had! What a pretty pointed little chin—no obstinacy there! What a perfect nose; she had inherited that from her ancestors, the Luntons of Castle Lunton. Really she looked like a fairy princess lying there in the flickering, rosy light! It made him forget his dinner for the moment, feel almost romantic. Of course he was still a young man, though not a raw boy, thank goodness. He felt like the prince watching over the sleeping beauty, or like some gallant knight in armour. Would she sleep on for ever unless the prince—

He stopped these traitor thoughts in horror, blushing hotly. What had bank-manager and lay-reader to do with the fairy legends of childhood? How did he come to remember that ridiculous, fantastic fairy-tale now? He had better think of his dinner.

He leaned against his tree and began to doze uncomfortably. He felt very stiff and cold and wretched. Impossible to close one's eyes!

He must have closed them in earnest, for when he opened them a cold grey dawn was peering at him, and the fire was out. He looked at Sally and gave a little gasp. What a transformation scene! What a sight! So *this* was how she looked in the early morning!

Her hair was pushed from her too-high forehead, revealing its ugliness; it clung dankly to her head, a hideous, untidy, tangled mass. Her face was grey and pinched and haggard. She looked a hundred. She was tossing restlessly to and fro and moaning in her sleep, now and then making a sound between a snore and a snort.

Marry her? Never! Not to save a thousand reputations! Not to stop the tongue of Miss Maggie herself if she happened to find out. No, they could say what they liked of him, the directors could ask for an explanation, but he would bite on the bullet—the silent, strong man to the end.

Sally started and sat up, pushing the hair further from her face, staring at him, puzzled. What an awful dream! She shook all over.

"Then I've married him!"

So this was how he looked first thing! The carefully-brushed hair was disordered, the little bald spots showing here and there.

"What a moth-eaten husband!" she shuddered, still half-dreaming. His face was yellow and flaccid, both his chins sagging, and peevish disgust was written all over him.

Then she shook the dream from her, giving a thankful sigh. It had not come to that yet.

Mr. Bingley was the first to speak. "We can get back now, I hope," he said. "I daresay you would like to tidy yourself. I will await you there." He pointed to a small clump of trees.

"She looks like a tramp, a disreputable tramp," he thought in horror. "How can I be seen in her company?"

When he returned he was more than exasperated to discover Sally once more curled up in a tight little ball, and sound asleep. As he stooped over her and shook her arm no thought of princess and prince came to him, or even knights in shining armour guarding their ladye's sleep.

"Wake up! oh, *dash* it, wake up!" he commanded.

Sally shivered, her eyes tightly closed. "Oh, Elizabeth, it can't be time yet," she objected; "where's my cup of tea?"

The question further infuriated Mr. Bingley, who wanted his own cup of tea.

Sleeping on as if it did not matter, and looking like a vagabond who hadn't had her clothes off for a week! It was plain to be seen that reputations were nothing to her. She probably regarded them like eggs—as something carefully laid to be broken. It simply did not occur to her shallow little brain that bank-managers in Little Crampton had to be *sans peur et sans reproche*, or Miss Maggie Hopkins got the directors to remove them. That was a nice sort of thing to contemplate. The ruin of a Great Career, and through a woman!

The highly-respected, much-talked-of Mr. Bingley in such a hideous position! Well, he'd be the most-talked-of personage now, no doubt of that! It would take him all he knew to steer clear of the rocks. He was between Scylla and Charybdis, matrimony on the one hand, scandal on the other.

Goodness only knew where he would find himself before he had finished! And all through Miss Lunton, who never gave a thought to the hideousness of his position. That was women all over; egotistical, eaten up with selfishness.

"Sorry to remind you of my awful predicament," he said sharply; "but we are on the moors, and lost. I've been awake all night," he added bitterly.

"How silly!" yawned Sally. "Though I only got a frightful nightmare by sleeping on the ground." She got to her feet, rubbing her eyes. "Well, we'd better start, I suppose. There's the sun rising, isn't it? Let's go bang into it."

"Aren't you going to tidy yourself?"

"Unfortunately I didn't bring my dressing-case," she replied, as she gave a casual tug to her hair; "and you haven't brought me my hot water. I don't even see any cold anywhere about. Won't it be lovely to get into Little Crampton? I shall get into bed and stay there till tea-time. Won't you?"

"*I* shall have to attend to the bank," returned Mr. Bingley, quailing. To be short-handed at such a time. For him there was no escape. "We men have to carry the burden, whatever happens," he added gloomily.

Sally felt herself all over, not attending. "I had forgotten what a crowd of bones I had—ugh!"

"I got no sleep at all. I never closed my eyes."

"Then why did you let the fire go out? I don't call that acting sentinel nicely. You would get 'cells' for that even in peace time, and during warfare you'd have to be shot at dawn, and it's dawn now. Isn't it gorgeous! What a sin to go through life missing dawns!"

Mr. Bingley considered it more sinful not to miss them, but he was too angry to answer.

"How quickly the glow goes," she sighed. "Is life shorter at its morn, and only long at its close? We don't take the glow very far with us, do we? That is for first youth, 'radiant as the morn.'"

"Do you see anybody likely to direct us?" inquired Mr. Bingley sharply. "I thought I saw a man beyond that rise, but I am a trifle short-sighted."

"There *is* a man—a shepherd, too. They know the moors from A to Z. We are all right now."

She put two lingers in her mouth, and a loud, piercing whistle made the man turn and come quickly towards them.

"Not a ladylike accomplishment," she said, "but useful, and one of mine. Douglas Hill taught me six years back."

The shepherd came up to them. He gave a rather knowing smile, but he took them to a familiar path. They had merely gone round and round in a circle, and were quite close to it.

Mr. Bingley gave him a shilling. It was a moment when even the Bingleys become recklessly prodigal.

"Well, we are out of the wood now!" said Sally cheerfully.

But Mr. Bingley, quaking in trepidation, wondered. … There were still the consequences to be faced.

CHAPTER XX

"Oh, Mr. Bingley, what a mercy you are safe!"

As they came in sight of the Hopkins' house Mr. Bingley was disagreeably conscious of one or two factors which, small things in themselves, made a well-nigh unbearable total.

To begin with, in the room he knew for Miss Maggie's was the vague outline of a dressing-gowned figure hiding behind the curtains; but, only too plainly visible, was a long, thin, pointed nose pressed against the pane. Add to this the fact that the milkman was even then entering the gate, and that, slinking shamefacedly behind him, was a dissipated cat, and you get the sum total.

As they got exactly opposite the house Miss Maggie, wrapping herself chastely in the curtains, waved gayly.

Sally waved back, laughing.

"Don't do that!" commanded Mr. Bingley sharply. "She's an awful woman, an *awful* woman."

"Oh, she's quite a friend of mine," returned Sally, "and not so bad when you really come to know her. I'm afraid she will talk about this, though."

Even then Mr. Bingley did not say anything a lay-reader may not, but he let his thoughts run a little wild.

He wondered why it should be necessary that they should encounter the whole working population of Little Crampton setting forth to its labours—and such an interested population! They touched their caps, of course, but they looked. Those sort of people had such minds!

Finally they met Mr. Lovelady, who looked with most unclerical anger at Mr. Bingley, and caught Sally's hand.

"My darling child, where have you been? What has happened?" He ignored her escort.

Sally explained, then she nodded a casual dismissal to Mr. Bingley, and slipped her hand through her guardian's arm.

"Oh, Lovey, never get lost with Bingley people; it's dull!"

"I wish—"

"Or calculate on the moon rising."

"I wish you hadn't got lost with that fellow," exclaimed Mr. Lovelady; "there may be some foolish gossip now."

"There may," agreed Sally indifferently.

Later in the day she ran into Mrs. Dalton. That lady sighed enviously. "Oh dear! I could never have thought of anything so clever. Besides, I couldn't have walked far enough to lose him. How did things go off?"

"Things *didn't* go off," said Sally ruefully, albeit with a twinkle; "almost, but not quite. It's weary work, though I cannot deny I feel the thrill of the chase at times. It's fun fishing, and awfully exciting when at last you strike the right bait, but a bore when he gobbles it up, and, just as you are playing him skilfully, the line breaks and he's secure in his 'funk-hole' again."

Mrs. Dalton cheered up. "Then in spite of all the opportunities—"

"I wasn't quick enough in saying 'snip' to his 'snap.' You know how it used to be when you were a child, and they gave you a pill to swallow. The pill seemed so big and beastly and impossible. Your throat simply closed up and would not have it. Well, my throat closed up when it came to the psychological moment. Of course I shall not bungle the opportunity another time."

"If it comes?"

Sally accepted the correction, laughing. "One must make one's opportunities sometimes. He was rather Bingleyish, which was bad, but I was really Sallyish, which was far worse—a fatal combination, at any rate."

"Do you know there's a serious run on the bank?" asked Mrs. Dalton, beginning to laugh violently; "and, owing to the recent enlistments, Mr. Bingley has to face it all by himself. Miss Maggie has just gone to save her money in time. How pleased he will be; he does so love being the centre of the stage, and he's got that all right now. Nobody has even mentioned the war to-day."

For once, however, Mr. Bingley did not care for the blaze of publicity. The 'fierce white light' could be positively too glaring.

The 'boy,' however, enjoyed himself hugely. When he saw the steady onrush of customers a thrilling solution occurred to him. Mr. Bingley had been tampering with the till, and people had found out!

Contrary to the usual custom, he opened both the doors.

"What are you doing?" asked the bank-manager angrily.

"It looks like a run, sir," said the boy respectfully, "and I thought there would be too much of a crush, sir, for the one side of the door."

He wondered if Mr. Bingley would get away to America.

"Shut the door at once!" commanded Mr. Bingley, turning yellow.

"Both sides, sir? To keep them out altogether, sir?"

"No, you fool!" barked the bank-manager; "as usual, of course."

"Ratty!" thought the boy, and had no longer any doubt of his manager's guilt. He supposed that, when the cash fell short, Mr. Bingley would make a bolt to the back and try and get to the station, *en route* for America. He had a delightful vision of 'the fat old buster sprinting for all he was worth' stationwards, pursued by the portly police of Little Crampton.

He feared that the police were too Cramptonian to overtake a gentleman with an income. On the other hand, Mr. Paton and fat Mr. Boliver were special constables, and if Mr. Boliver only had the presence of mind to stand in the narrow entry leading to the station it would be all up with Mr. Bingley.

The boy had not decided what part he would take himself in the hue and cry. Suppose Mr. Bingley paid to be let off, or not to be taken up—he had an idea justice for the rich was tempered with mercy—and came back to the bank? He had too good a post to lose, and a good enough master. He decided to lie low till he saw how things went. He had heard of Mr.

Bingley being lost all night with 'parson's Sally,' but he thought nothing of that. It was the scandal of embezzlement he had in his mind's eye.

"They are all coming, sir," he announced about eleven o'clock, trying to make his voice sound calm.

Mr. Bingley did not vulgarly say, "Let 'em all come!" Neither did he think it. Sally comfortably in bed, he bearing the brunt! That was life. He stood very erectly behind the counter, keeping a stiff upper lip. He felt like Daniel in the lion's den, but trusted rather to his own abilities to bring him safely through than to a miracle.

A crowd of his acquaintances came hurrying in; then Mr. Boliver rolled up, blocking the way.

"Don't stand there, Boliver, please," commanded Mr. Bingley sharply; "nobody can pass." The fat fool!

Nobody mentioned the moors. They talked of everything save Mr. Bingley's adventure, but how they looked!

When the bank was absolutely crowded Miss Maggie entered, having waited her moment. Interest quickened, and all made room for her. People who had been served examined their money again, or could not get the clasp of their purse fastened, or find this or that. Mr. Paton stood in a corner folding and unfolding a cheque he had not yet presented. He had known Miss Maggie would come.

She knew she had the ball at her feet, or rather Mr. Bingley. People would leave him to her gladly. She came to the counter.

"Oh, Mr. Bingley, what a mercy you are *safe!*" she exclaimed thankfully. "You little guess what I suffered on your account."

"Very good of you," said Mr. Bingley stonily, "but quite unnecessary. I fancy I am not the first Little Cramptonian to be lost on the moors. Many have done that, I believe."

"Oh yes, Mr. Bingley, but they did it differently. Your circumstances were quite unique. I cannot tell you how upset I was!"

"I trust you had a little sympathy to spare for Miss Lunton," said Mr. Bingley suavely. "I am so afraid she may catch a chill."

"Oh, Sally never catches chills, and she can look after herself. I daresay she's been lost before."

"Yes, so she told me."

"With whom?" asked Miss Maggie, pouncing.

"Her friend was another girl; they were on a tour."

"Another girl? How unlike Sally! In Italy, I suppose? She is so very fond of Italy. What a varied career the dear girl has had, has she not?"

Mr. Bingley reached out his hand for her cheque. "And how will you take it?"

Miss Maggie tightened her grasp on the cheque. "Oh, I haven't signed it; how silly! I must see to it when the pen and ink are vacant."

She knew they were not going to be vacant just yet. People's eyes were anywhere but on the two conversing, but their ears had a sort of tense look, and one could certainly have heard a pin drop.

"What was the name of the other man she got lost with in Italy?" she asked.

"I don't understand you," returned Mr. Bingley; "her friend was a girl, of course. She did not mention her name. Haven't you done with the ink, Boliver?"

"I have *not*, Bingley," returned Mr. Boliver firmly.

"Poor Sally must have been surprised to find herself lost on the moors she knows so well, and such a dark night, too!"

"Yes," agreed the tortured Mr. Bingley. "We hoped for the moon—"

She did not let him finish. "Oh, Mr. Bingley, what a romantic confession!" she cried archly.

"—to find our way back by."

"What a waste of a moon! Oh, forgive me, but you know we women, especially we old maids, are so romantic. We always associate the moon with—well, *you* know—" She looked down coyly, and somebody tittered and then tried to turn it into a cough.

"Not being a single lady—"

"But you are a single man—at least we *suppose* so?"

There was another badly-managed cough.

"We wished to get back as soon as possible. It was very chilly and uncomfortable."

"But what a lot you must have found to talk of in all that time—a whole night!"

"We lit a fire, and Miss Lunton went to sleep. I, of course, kept the fire up."

"How romantic you must have felt! Like a knight in armour, or a sentry, or one of those sort of things!"

"Not at all," he frowned, "I was very hungry and chilled—chilled to the bone."

"Still, it was exactly like the hero and heroine in a novel, where they marry and live happy ever afterwards. You can't think how it moves me to think of you sitting there all night, just like a guardian angel. I wonder if the other one she got lost with did—the girl, I mean. Oh, Mr. Bingley, forgive me, I know you will understand, but didn't it make you feel—well, just a *leetle* bit *risqué*?"

"It did not!" barked Mr. Bingley, flushing darkly. Oh, dash the woman!

"Perhaps I can have the ink at last?" demanded Miss Maggie. "Thank you so much." She took out her cheque slowly. "You know I happened to see you pass, such a coincidence, and of course I expected to see you return. When you didn't ... *Oh*, Mr. Bingley!"

"The blotting-paper is to your right, Miss Maggie."

"Thank you—oh, could I have a cleaner piece? You little know what a night I spent, wondering and wondering, so very worrying! If only I had known what to do for the best. You see, the farm boy knows the moors well, and I thought of sending him with a lantern, and then again I didn't *quite* like to. People don't always *want* to be found."

"It would have been a great help if you had sent the boy."

"I did so want to act for the best. As you would wish, you and dear Sally."

"A boy with a lantern would have been a godsend. I'm afraid Miss Lunton may have caught cold; I know I have. What you could have saved us!"

"How very unfortunate! But as an elderly spinster one does so hate to meddle. But next time! ... I happened to be looking out of my window early, and such a coincidence! There was the milk coming, and poor Tom slinking home—such a dissipated cat!—and you and dear Sally; poor girl, her hair was half down, and her hat anyhow—in the road, too! Oh, is that the clean blotting-paper? Thank you so much. I will trouble you, Mr. Boliver."

She took her money and left with a beaming smile. Others followed her. She was the heroine of the hour, and overwhelmed with tea invitations. She accepted one for four and one for five. She would do full justice to both.

Mr. Paton rushed to the club; Mr. Boliver bounded after him.

Gradually the crowd thinned, and the boy realised that nothing had happened, that nothing was going to happen. Probably Mr. Bingley had got alarmed and replaced the money.

To Mr. Bingley himself it did not seem as if nothing had happened. He went home a nervous wreck. For some days he did without exercise, as he did not wish to meet anyone, but he ate just the same meals. The results were unfortunate. He felt he had Sally to blame for a severe attack of indigestion.

He was glad to remember there was a war going on. Surely one of the generals would do something to get talked about—advance or retreat—and Mr. Bingley's unhappy adventure would pass as nine-days' wonders always do!

His mother's *Book* was less helpful than usual:

"*Don't marry the woman you intrigue with. Intrigue if you must—and then don't marry her.*"

Well, he hadn't intrigued, and he was not going to. Bingleys didn't.

"*Don't marry a woman who runs after you before; she will either run after somebody else once she has got you, or from you.*"

Had Sally run after him? On the contrary, had she not been almost rude?

"*The determined woman dares all.*"

Was Sally determined, or was *The Book* warning him against Mrs. Dalton?

This traitor citadel that longed to surrender unconditionally! That was why he fought so hard, refused to be thrust into marriage to stop idle tongues. He wanted to marry Sally for himself, even though he could not feel as certain as he would like about the absolute correctness of the future bank-manager; but he also wanted to marry her because he knew it to be the absolutely right, sensible, and profitable thing, and because his genius mother would have approved.

He had decided he might fall in love enough to be pleasant, but not enough to be uncomfortable, and that he would fall out the moment it seemed expedient to do so. Instead he found things much more uncomfortable than pleasant; and also that, once in, one could not climb out all at once. Some driving force was literally pushing him into Sally's arms.

Night after night he dreamed of her, the Sally of the rosy firelight, never of the grey dawn. In his dreams he loved more than was reasonable or quite seemly in one of his age and position, and was ever the Prince Charming watching over the slumbers of the Sleeping Beauty, and waiting breathlessly, thrillingly, for the magic moment when he should wake her with a kiss. He invariably awoke just before the vision materialised, and thought a little peevishly that he had not much luck in his dreams. He always awoke just a second too soon!

Once out of his dream, or lying awake in the early morning, he became more or less sensible again; and if it was a losing battle he fought, and in his heart of hearts he knew it, he still fought on.

He must have Sally, he *would* have Sally, cried the old Adam, to be amended by the wiser self, who said that certainly he should have Sally—not because others thought he ought to, but because he wished it, and it was right that he should.

He refused to be rushed or do anything in a hurry, and yet a burning impatience filled him. He sought safety in flight, but he could not fly from that surging insistent thing striving for life and utterance within him.

The toils were closing round Mr. Alfred Bingley.

CHAPTER XXI

"I think he's set on not getting better–dying belike, Miss Sally"

Mr. Lovelady was preaching, and his congregation was, for the most part, doing everything but listen. Church was the sort of place in which you thought things well out.

He preached from the text, 'They that go down to the sea in ships, and have their business in deep waters,' and pointed out what a new and terrible significance these words had come to mean. It was a moving little sermon, almost eloquent. It moved Mr. Bingley, for before he sat down to his luxurious repast he posted a cheque for five pounds to a sailors' orphanage. He had a heart for the child victims of the war.

He had not spoken to Sally since the moor adventure, and it was a little difficult to greet her as if nothing had happened, with so many looking on, but he managed it well enough.

"Quite a good sermon," he was pleased to say.

"Oh, I like the one about Lot's wife best," said Miss Maggie, coming up to them; "so original. One can hear it several times and still find it that. I thought it was the turn for it to-day. So unusual for a man to own a wife is *bound* to look back!"

Mr. Bingley shook Miss Maggie from him, so to speak, and fled. He had unfortunately to shake Sally from him also, for Miss Maggie had her in her clutches.

"How charming you look!" gushed the spinster, "so different from the other morning! How bored you must have got with his conversation."

"Mr. Bingley can be quite amusing."

"Really! And was the other one you got lost with amusing? How bilious he looked! I always think that the wife suffers most from her husband's indigestion, don't you?"

"I don't happen to have a husband."

"Oh, my dear, don't give in so soon! A man like that, too—always having dead relations. He must have been born under a lucky star, as the saying is. With us, just as you think it's about time you got an invitation to a funeral, you get one to a wedding, which simply means more of them."

Miss Lydia came listlessly up to them.

"If the worst comes to the worst, there's Canada, where husbands grow on every bush, they say. Oh, that's the place for women getting on!"

Lydia wondered why it had not occurred to her to go to Canada some years back. Why must she think of everything too late, be for ever viewing the might-have-beens?

"Canada!" gasped Sally. "I had a friend who married a rancher, and I happen to know what it means. Good Lord, that's the last thing I would do!"

"It would be your own home and your own husband," said Miss Lydia, "and think what it would mean to him! You'd be building the Empire through your work and children—"

"Yes, and be working like a slave! Give me civilisation every time!"

"And a good income," giggled Miss Maggie, "and someone to pay the piper. Well, after a night on the moors—"

"You can get lost with anybody—"

"So it seems," agreed the spinster, "so it seems!"

Mr. Lovelady came out of church, and Sally went off with him. He was looking very tired.

She slipped her arm through his, and began in her energetic fashion to post up the hill.

"My dear," said Mr. Lovelady, a little breathlessly, "there is no great hurry."

"Sorry, dear. Why, it seems only the other day you used to race me up this hill, and win!"

"Rather a long day, I think," he sighed. He knew he would never race up a hill again. Each time he felt walking up it more. "My dearest, I'm so thankful that absurd gossip has died down about you and Bingley, and that you are not encouraging his attentions any more. He's not worthy of my Sally."

She squeezed his arm. "Oh, blind Lovey! Ducky darling, do you think I could have a pair of shot silk stockings, and those new high boots? Something chaste and striking. They strike you first, and you think how chaste afterwards. If you *really* can afford them?"

He afforded them, though they seemed to him very small and trifling details to cost so much. "It will be awkward if you marry a poor man," he said thoughtfully.

Sally's mouth closed tightly. She had no intention of doing anything of the sort. Three thousand pounds per annum, with more to come, was not poverty.

"You're not out for romance at thirty-one; it's business," she thought. She made an impatient sound. That wretched man again! Why should his eyes haunt her so? What was it they asked of her all the time?

She went off to the moors to see.

On the way she ran into Miss Maggie, who had a sheaf of letters for the post, and thrust them hastily into the slit as Sally appeared.

"What a coincidence, meeting you again!" she said. "We always seem to be coming across each other, don't we? You off to the moors, and I posting letters!" She seemed very amused.

Ever since she had chanced upon her 'clue' she had been extremely busy running the scent to earth. She wrote to the managers of certain Italian hotels, explaining how she had lost sight of some very dear friends for years, but had last heard of them at such a place on such a date. Their name was Thompkins, a honeymoon couple, and their description so and so. She inclosed an International coupon and addressed envelope with each letter, and begged to be favoured with a reply.

The replies were slow in coming, and some of them were disappointing.

It was taking time, but on the whole she was satisfied. She considered she was getting enough evidence for a divorce case, if necessary. She wanted it all in black and white. Poor Mrs. Randal, what a shock, but kinder that she should be told!

In the meanwhile she was very friendly to Sally, and encouraged her in the pursuit of Mr. Bingley. That also fitted in with her plans. She liked to see her victims crashing down from a great height.

"What a lot of letters you write, and such long ones!" said Sally unsuspiciously. "It bores me."

"We poor spinsters have to do something," said Miss Maggie deprecatingly, "even Lydia is knitting. She is knitting something for a soldier, poor fellow!—one of those sort of things one can't get in or out of. She says they are not fussy in the trenches, and that it will keep him warm. It will certainly keep him busy. Talking about being busy, how Mrs. Dalton has launched out in clothes lately! Do you know, she has practically no money at all, but is putting it all into Mr. Bingley. It's to be hoped that he won't prove one of those bubble speculations that blow up when you least expect it. My dear, why don't you accept the poor man?"

Sally made the obvious answer, "It's usual to wait to be asked."

"He's walking about like a cat on hot bricks. One knows what that means. He gave Nina a box of chocolates with a dove on the box the other day. So touching!"

"Were they good chocolates?" asked Sally. "So often the picture is the best part."

"The very best; the dear child was dreadfully sick twice. The devotion between them is really most touching. Such a pity you haven't something like that—a dear little brother, say."

Sally laughed.

"How gay you always are, whatever comes or goes. Such a light heart! After all, it is better for a woman to be too light than too heavy—better for having a good time, I mean. How you must miss Paris and Italy and your naughty, naughty pictures! Well, if you are going on the moors, we may as well go as far as the house together. Won't you come in and have tea?"

"No, thank you."

Miss Maggie gave her arm a playful pinch. "You do love the moors, don't you? So many attractions! Naughty girl!"

Then she went into the house, and had a long gossip with Mrs. Gillet's daughter, who acted as their maid-of all-work, and preferred Miss Maggie to the others. She was always ready to come into the kitchen for a talk, and made very little work in the house. Give her hot cakes for tea, and plenty of them, and Miss Maggie stood up for you through thick and thin!

Meanwhile Sally hurried on her errand, feeling very nervous and anxious about it, but hopeful of finding Robert Kantyre at home, as it was Sunday, and coming to some explanation. If there were any signs of insobriety she would return at once, and never seek him out again. It was horrible to think she should be haunted like this by a man who not only drank, but who had insulted her.

As she passed Moor-end Farm, Gillet came out of the door and ran after her. "Oh, Miss Sally, I'm rare glad you've come up," he exclaimed thankfully; "I didn't know what to do or nothink. Pore chap!"

Sally felt herself turn white and sick. She was too late, he had passed through the ever-open door this time. Now, too late, she realised what she had seen in his eyes; he was asking her to help him, to save him, and she had left him to his fate.

Gillet caught her by the arm. "Oh, Miss Sally, you be took queer!"

"No, no, I'm all right now. You mean Mr.—you mean White? He's dead?" Her stiff lips could hardly frame the words.

"Not dead yet, miss, but going that way. He won't help hisself."

"How did it happen?"

"Oh, I didn't notice naught at first. Then one day when he was working he crumpled up like with pain; but he come next day, and said it was naught. But he was took worse, and yesterday we had to carry him to The Hut, and there he lies, miss, not saying anything, but looking awful."

"Poison?" she got out.

"Oh no, some of his innards gone wrong-like. Maybe this here appendicitus, but he won't see no doctor."

"He must."

"You talk to him, Miss Sally. It's wonderful the power you have over him. You mind the last time you come up to talk to him about the drink? I thought he was set in it, that nothink would save him, but arter you spoke to him, not a drop did he touch."

Sally stood very still for a moment, her face whiter than ever. "Are you sure?" she got out at last.

"I could take my oath upon it in a court of law. Don't look so upset, missie, maybe you can help him again and make him see the doctor, and put some heart in him."

"Yes, yes, he must see Dr. Hill."

"You see, it's like this. I think he's set on not getting better—dying belike, Miss Sally."

Sally ran to The Hut.

CHAPTER XXII

"Will you stay with me to the end?"

She was almost as panic-stricken as when she had run from the cattle. On each occasion it seemed like running a race with death—and losing.

She looked in at the cracked window-pane, fearing she knew not what; perhaps a still form lying under a sheet, and the last long silence; but it had not come to that yet. The door into the inner room was open, and a pale face lay on a pillow with closed eyes. Robert Kantyre certainly looked ill, but he did not seem to be in pain.

He seemed to know by instinct that she had noiselessly entered The Hut, for his eyes opened instantly. There was the same haunting appeal in them.

"I never thought to see you again," he said weakly.

Sally sat down on a chair by the bed, and took his hand in both hers. "That was a very silly thing to think," she said reproachfully.

His hand trembled. "I offended beyond forgiveness."

"*You* did not offend at all," she retorted, "that was somebody else, a somebody you have conquered and overthrown. Gillet told me. I think you are splendid; I wish I could be fine like that. I can only dimly guess what the struggle must have meant. And now, poor dear, you have the last heroic fight before you—to get well and strong."

Robert's face had lightened at her first words, but now the light died out of it, and an intense weariness took its place.

"I would not take the other way out now," he said, "but this makes everything so simple."

"It will be cowardice again, all the same," she scolded; "the line of least resistance, suicide to all intents and purposes. Of course you are ill, but think how strong you are. We are going to pull you through whether you like it or not, but don't throw *all* the work on us. Gillet is waiting outside, and I am going to send him for Dr. Hill."

Robert half raised himself. "I won't see him!" he cried angrily.

"Oh yes, you will, and you'll like him too." She went outside and gave Gillet the message.

"You don't allow a fellow body or soul of his own," burst out the patient when she returned. "It's been like that from the moment I saw you."

"And it's going on like that, or till you are out of the wood," she returned, "and there's a sound mind in a sound body. Have you any idea what is wrong?"

"It feels like an old bullet broken loose, or something. The pain is very sudden, both going and coming, and seems to move about. When I got it fifteen years ago I was warned drink might set up mischief."

"You will tell Dr. Hill? You need not tell him anything else. People do not guess the truth, but they do suspect you are not a real working-man. You are free from pain now?"

"Yes, just numb after the last attack."

"Is it bad?"

He did not answer for a moment; then he said, "It isn't pleasant."

It was indeed excruciating. He had never been ill in his life, and this, his first experience of weakness, seemed to him extreme. A young giant with the strength of an ox now unable to raise his head. That could mean only one thing—death. The fainting weariness too, that was its preliminary. He wished it were over. He felt he had only to 'let go' to be done with life. Yet Sally's black eyes, so soft, so vital, seemed as if they sought to drag him back. Back to what? To horrible memories, outlawry, a shameful and intolerable existence. He would not look in Sally's eyes any longer. To be quite on the safe side he closed his own. At the same time his grasp tightened on the girl's hand.

"You are going to do your best?" she said insistently.

"That's not much use if one's hour has struck, Sally," the named slipped out unconsciously, "you will stay with me to the end?"

Sally turned white and sick, and was horribly afraid. Then she flicked his hand lightly, and said, "End—what end? I never heard such rubbish! I will go away and stay away if you are going to play the coward." She got up as if to go. "Now I name my price. I'll stay with you as much as you like if you'll play the game like a soldier and fight and fight."

"Oh, very well," he grumbled crossly. His hand felt for hers.

She sat down again and took it in her own. "You must keep quiet and not talk any more till Dr. Hill comes."

He seemed ready enough to obey. He sank into a doze of exhaustion, and Sally looked down, a little ache stealing into her heart. She did not want Robert Kantyre to die; there would be another blank in her life if he died. She liked him, liked him very much. He was something that, in a sort of way, belonged to her. Just then she wanted him to live more than she wanted anything in the world, and would have purchased his life at any cost.

Dr. Hill was puzzled with the case. He did not think the theory of the bullet breaking away likely, but he did not say it was impossible. There was undoubtedly severe inflammation.

Sally took him into the other room, closing the door. "Will he live?"

"If we can get the inflammation down before it spreads or strikes deeper."

"And if not?"

"A bad case," he said briefly. "He must go to the hospital at once. There may have to be an operation."

Robert refused to be taken to the hospital. Once there he would lie in a ward with others, see Sally on visiting days, and then in the midst of a crowd. When he was discharged cured she would take no further interest in him; just one of the hospital patients she had gone to see out of good-nature. In The Hut they would be alone, and she had promised to come often.

The doctor was angry. "You are not giving yourself a fair chance," he objected.

Robert set a square jaw. "I shan't go," he said. To him it was nothing whether he lived or died, but everything that he should have Sally by him.

Sally tried in vain to shake his resolution.

"I don't want much," he said; "Mrs. Gillet will do it."

Dr. Hill turned with an exasperated expression to Sally. "Mrs. Gillet is clean and tidy," he admitted, "she can keep the place in order, though she is heavy-handed and heavy-footed; but she would chatter to the dying and gossip with the Angel of Death. I can send the nurse from Farleigh to-morrow, but there is to-night, and she can't stay long. It's out of her way, and not actually her district, and Farleigh is heavy with cases just now."

A groan from the inner room reached them. Robert was in agony, agony most heroically borne, but terrible. The attack passed as suddenly as it came, leaving the patient livid and gasping and dangerously weak.

Sally, powerless to aid, had watched with an anguished heart.

"You see!" exclaimed Dr. Hill. "How can he be left to that? He must have opiates, restoratives. He's pretty far gone."

"I will stay," said Sally instantly. "Of course I've never done any nursing, but I'm sure I shall be all right if it is nothing to do with—with blood. I can at least follow your instructions minutely."

He patted her on the shoulder. "My dear Sally, I have every confidence in you. You are a little brick. What about letting Lovelady know?"

"The Gillet girls always spend their evenings out at the farm," she returned; "I'll send a note by Kate, and she will leave it for me on her return."

She spent the night in The Hut and did what she could for Robert Kantyre. He had another attack of pain, but it was not so violent, and the means of relief were at hand.

All the night through, even when barely conscious, he clung to Sally's hand as a drowning man clings to a straw.

CHAPTER XXIII

"Parson's Sally is to marry Mr. Bingley of the bank"

When the nurse came up from Farleigh Sally went home and got some sleep. As she expected, the nurse was unable to stay for any length of time, and Sally spent another night with the sick man. For the greater part of three days, and all of the three nights, she fought for his life, and won—at least Dr. Hill insisted it was her doing, but then he happened to be very fond of Sally. The pain and inflammation disappeared as suddenly as it came. It became merely a question of recovering strength and taking a considerable amount of nourishing food.

Sally was not a useful person for choice, though capable when forced to be, but she had one domestic accomplishment. In her Paris studio days she had done her own cooking and done it well, and now she cooked for Robert Kantyre, and stood over him till he had eaten. After the first time he did not resist; it was useless for one thing; for another, everything that Sally did had a way of tasting delicious. Perhaps there was also the fact to be taken into account that his appetite was returning with his strength.

Mrs. Gillet came in to scrub and tidy twice a day, but it was Sally upon whom the patient depended. When he was allowed to sit up she still spent the greater portion of the day with him, and they found themselves with many subjects and interests in common. They learned more of each other also, or Robert learned much about Sally, but Sally soon learned all there was to know about Robert.

He worried continually about his uncle and godfather, the old man in Canada who had never written.

"We were such pals," he would say over and over again, "and somehow I felt there would be one person in the world whose verdict would be merciful; but I suppose it is the one crime no true Kantyre could ever forgive. Could I have forgiven it in another? God knows!" He was thoughtful.

"Yes, you would have forgiven anything but cowardice," she answered, "and I feel it is the same with your uncle. The letter must have miscarried."

"That is possible, but not likely. My sisters send everything on to me." He did not add that they never wrote themselves, but Sally felt it, and her mouth hardened. She hated those sisters.

"Uncle Robert hoped I would come across his grandson at the Front," went on Kantyre. "Cecil was my nephew, of course, but I have not seen him since he was a fine little fellow of ten. He's just twenty-one, and was one of the first to get out with the Canadians. He and I are the last now. I hope he will come out all right. What my uncle would do without him I can't think. They have a huge ranch out in Alberta, and were doing very well, but of course Uncle Robert is old now. To tell you the truth, I have been hoping and praying he would send for me. I should like the life, and think I could do well at it."

"Indeed you could; but how lonely!"

"Yes," he said slowly, "but a man's life, building, carving something out. There's freedom and space in it, and perhaps redemption and forgetfulness."

"He may write yet."

"No, he would write the moment he got my letter or not at all. It would only be not at all if he thought I had put myself beyond the pale. Well, I'll stay on with Gillet for a bit, that's only fair, and then I'll take a ticket to Canada and chance my luck. It will be a new life, like being born anew in a new land."

"New lands have not much attraction for me," owned Sally frankly. "I find Paris and London good enough, and Little Crampton in between—though it is spoiled by the Little Cramptonians. Isn't Lovey a dear, though?"

Mr. Lovelady had been up several times, and the two men had taken greatly to each other. They talked a lot of Sally, laughed with her and at her, laughter with a note of tenderness in it. Sally in turn teased both and tyrannised over them unmercifully. She was thoroughly in her element mothering the outcast.

"I'm getting quite fond of White," she informed her guardian as he came to fetch her home one evening; "he is brave and simple, and rather fine."

Mr. Lovelady nodded. He had found Kantyre this, and more. "He is also a very handsome specimen of manhood," he added slowly, "and well bred. There's been something, of course, and I fancy you know it, but it's nothing vile. He's hasty, proud, a little hot. Is he, staying on here?"

"He talks of going to Canada soon."

"He'll do well there, I should not wonder; but dear me, dear me! all the fine young fellows going, the fine girls staying. That's not the right way of it." He turned, looking hard at Sally.

She met his eyes squarely enough, though her colour rose. "Oh, well, Canada is scarcely an Eldorado," she objected.

"No, but it's Empire-building, my dear, and the lion cubs are proving pretty useful to the old lion in more ways than one. If—if my girl had lived, I should have been glad and proud to think of her making a home for some fine young fellow out there, helping the desert to blossom like a rose."

Sally wriggled. "Oh, Lovey, don't be poetical just before supper; wait till afterwards."

"I should have trusted her with a fellow like Kantyre," went on the Reverend Adam, determined to have his say. "He's true blue; he would not fail a woman. He'd be unselfish and devoted, and she'd be a very lucky, lucky woman."

"I daresay, darling, but I expect the lucky woman's nose would be bright red all the winter, and her hands blue."

He half smiled. "My dear, a woman goes with her man to the uttermost ends of the world, and gladly, as a man with his woman."

"They'd need to be good sailors," was all she said.

"Oh, Sally, ease and money and place go far in this little island, too far, God knows, but they are not the things that count in the end; bound with their shackles one cannot reach the mountain-top."

"Mountain-tops are drafty," objected Sally.

"It is character which counts, the high ideal," he persisted, "the reaching up to the higher. It is character which has built the Empire, and character and grit and sacrifice which are going to bring it through during this time of bitter stress. We have the money and power, we cannot fail for want of them, but we can fail, and only fail, when character and grit and sacrifice do. Sacrifice in great or little things is the reaching up to the higher and to happiness."

"Oh, Lovey, it is not like you to preach at me!" she cried, vexed.

He sighed, then pinched her cheek. "You don't let me, my dear. You head me off with flippancies which mean nothing; I know my Sally too well to be distressed by them. I suppose you guess what I am aiming at?"

"A cow would guess," she retorted crossly. "You are aiming at making me as uncomfortable as possible, instead of exhorting me to be sensible and comfortable as a wise guardian should. You can't 'guardian' for nuts, you silly old thing!"

"The young man with great possessions who turned sorrowfully away was doubtless sensible," said the Reverend Adam, "but I doubt if he was comfortable."

"Well, the young man's wife—if he had one—would be comfortable all right," she retorted, "and very thankful, and that's always something. Parsons have such rum ideas! Oh, here's Mr. Bingley! Isn't that a new suit I see before me? How chaste, and positively becoming!"

She smiled pleasantly on the bank-manager, who passed them a little stiffly.

Mr. Bingley knew all about Sally's latest proceeding. The whole of Little Crampton knew and discussed it with some gusto. Such a handsome young man, and so mysterious! Quite the gentleman, it was said.

Of course Mr. Bingley disapproved. How could he do otherwise? He would have disapproved if the patient had been the most unprepossessing of rough labourers. There were institutions and nurses and so on for those sort of people. Was he not taxed to support them, and taxed most heavily? But the patient was not old or unprepossessing or rough. A woman, romantic, foolish, might suppose him far otherwise, and there was a mystery attached to him. To the sensible sex mystery spelt discredit; to women, alas! it meant glamour only too often.

He was glad to find the too-easy guardian taking Sally home, and evidently giving her a good talking to. He would bring her to her senses; no guardian would encourage such conduct. He would have business at the vicarage that very evening, if only to see that everything was as it should be.

It seemed to him that it was. He found Sally in a mood that charmed and dazzled him, and he went home confident that all was well.

"*Don't marry a woman who has a male interest previous to marriage,*" advised the seer; "*she will have a multiple of male interests afterwards, and her husband will not even be one of the crowd.*"

Wonderful genius, foreseeing even the man of the moors! Mr. Bingley was most decidedly not going to marry a woman with another male interest—at least not till she showed her readiness to give up that interest.

Sally went up to bed three stairs at a time. Yes, Mr. Bingley was getting nearer every day, whether he knew it or not.

"I must be very, very careful," she warned herself; "he's only just on the verge; the least fright would cause him to retreat once more."

She decided to spare the bank-manager that fright. Then she forgot Mr. Bingley, but she did not forget Mr. Bingley's possessions. She wasted his money in riotous living, clothes, furniture, and other oddments. "I feel like an outcast cat that's got itself adopted at last," she thought.

Then—inconsequent Sally—she suddenly remembered that she had forgotten to tell Mrs. Gillet what Robert was to have for supper and breakfast. Could she trust that well-meaning gossip? She tossed from side to side. "What a silly, potty little thing to keep me awake!" she thought indignantly.

She was at The Hut earlier than ever the next day, and asked quite breathlessly about the patient's breakfast. Mrs. Gillet, however, had not failed her, and Robert seemed ever so much better, and in good spirits.

Sally was surprised when she glanced at her watch. How quickly time flew in The Hut! Odd how much they always had to discuss together! She got up with an exclamation, "Who would have thought it was so late!" and held out her wrist.

Robert's fingers closed tightly round it as he affected to be examining the time and suddenly afflicted with short sight. He had indeed turned so that for a moment his lips rested against the little hollow of the rounded wrist. How his fingers throbbed; it was as if she could feel the beat of his heart in hers.

"You have lovely hands," he said, very low; "all the time I was ill I thought of them. They seemed to bring me healing."

She coloured, and her eyes avoided his, as she said lightly, "Oh, you sick people get strange fancies!" Then she withdrew her hand, and, promising to come next day, went rather quickly out of The Hut.

Robert's eyes followed her wistfully, a great longing in them. "There she goes, the only one, the only one in all the world for me," he thought, "never, never to be mine!"

"Just a sick man's fancy!" Sally told herself, walking very fast. "Don't be a silly fool and get ideas into your head now, for goodness' sake. Remember Mr. Bingley! What would *he* think of ideas?" She gave a little laugh, but it was startled rather than mirthful. "Between two stools ..." Well she knew that. She was the last person in the world to come such a cropper. She happened to know what croppers meant—bruises that lasted. She had had enough bruises to last a lifetime, and was seeking rather the panacea to destroy even their memory. "And I've almost got it, almost, almost!" she thought feverishly. She became conscious that she was trembling, and rage mastered her. "Nerves, nerves!" she cried. "How perfectly ridiculous! ... He'll forget all about it when he's up and well again. One can't be *too* snubby with a sick man."

She was conscious that it would hurt her to snub Robert Kantyre almost as much as it would hurt him. There was something about him that appealed to her, appealed most strongly. She had loved Jimmy—she did not notice she was putting it in the past tense—but Robert she admired, respected. He was a man one could lean on; he gave one rest. Jimmy had leant on her. She had not loved him for greatness or for goodness, though he was good, but just because he was Jimmy. As for admiring and respecting him—well, that was quite a different thing, but it was a thing that brought its own peace with it.

How heroically Robert had borne those moments of cruel anguish; how thoughtful and unselfish he had invariably been; how courteous to the rather tiresome Mrs. Gillet; how patient, how strong. Yes, he appealed to her, for strength was rare, just as the great, noble simplicity was rare. Then he had the faults which made him human, she nearly said lovable. A touch of pride and haste and temper.

During his times of weakness he had seemed so much like a child, a little willful, but never peevish. He had appealed to her most strongly then; she had felt all mother-woman, a thing she had never felt before. He had brought her new sensations, new interests, and she supposed that was why he was seldom out of her thoughts.

His future certainly was a problem, but she had every confidence in his ability to face it. She would be sorry when he sailed for Canada, very sorry, but perhaps it would be a good thing. There was Mr. Bingley.

After Sally had gone Mrs. Gillet bustled in, and thumped about tidying up, her tongue going very fast all the time. She brought his supper, setting it down with a bang on the table by his side.

"There! Miss Sally has been here. She arranges flowers that beautiful, don't she, Mr. White? Well, she's a nice young lady, and always was, though one for the men, they say, and consequent the ladies have their knives into her somethink cruel at times; but I never took no heed on it. Handsome wins, *I* says, and win she has, right enough. I don't grudge her her luck. It must have taken some doing, but she done it, an' earnt it. Quite a handsome young gent, too, considering, and worth his millions, they say."

"What do you mean?" asked Kantyre, catching his breath.

Mrs. Gillet proceeded to thump about. She did not turn. "What! Haven't you heard? Why, it's all over the place. My girl Kate, what works there, says it's true as death."

"What is?"

"That parson's Sally is to marry Mr. Bingley of the bank. A very grand gent, I'm sure, and pleasant enough in the house, Kate says, once you get to know his little ways. Aye, she's rare luck, but I wish her all she can get, I'm sure, and a dartar with them fetching black eyes and yeller hair—not that hers ever grew that colour, and what *he* has is muddy-like. Why, you ain't never touched your supper! Ain't it cooked right?" She had turned round. "Are you going to have one of them attacks again? Are you took queer-like, Mr. White? My husband's brother went off just like that—all'n a suddent."

Robert Kantyre made no answer; he had turned his face to the wall.

"Oh, just whimsies!" said the good woman indignantly. "You'll catch it when I tell on you. She'll give it you proper, Miss Sally will!"

CHAPTER XXIV

"How fond you are of The Mountain!"

"There, Miss Sally," pointed out Mrs. Gillet next day, "I said as I'd tell on him, wasting good stuff shameful. No supper last night, and scarce tasted his breakfast this morning!"

Sally thought the patient looked paler than usual. "Don't you feel so well?" she asked anxiously.

He avoided her eyes. "I am quite well, thank you."

"Then why didn't you eat your meals?"

"Because I get sick of being stuffed like—a capon," he said ungraciously. "It's eat, eat all day and half the night. A fellow has got to put his foot down somewhere."

"Never mind your foot," retorted Sally, "it's the food you've got to put down. Now you are going to have a bowl of bread-and-milk for being so tiresome."

If there was one thing he abhorred it was bread-and-milk, but his tyrant stood over him till it had all disappeared.

"Now own you feel better," she said, laughing, and smoothing the bed-clothes.

But Robert showed more than a hint of temper. "I feel a jolly sight worse," he growled; "everything is beastly, and, please, I would like to be left alone."

Sally opened her eyes very wide, and started with amazement. "Do you mean you want *me* to leave you alone, to go? Not to come?"

She felt sore and angry. Here was gratitude! Here was logic! One day hating her out of his sight, the next unable to bear her within it! Of course it was the sick, irresponsible child who spoke, and it was obvious from the tumbled condition of the clothes that he had had a bad night; but she had never expected him to turn on her like this. Indeed, it gave her almost a shock. Could one never count on a man?

He turned his face from her, staring at the whitewashed wall. "I don't want anybody to make a martyr of themselves out of good-nature and charity," he said stiffly. "I have no right to take you away from—from more congenial company."

He remembered with a sick, jealous heart that Mr. Bingley was occupied from nine to four, and that it was between these hours he saw most of Sally. Very kind of her to kill time with him like that!

"Oh, the other company can wait," said Sally, puzzled. She had not been able to spend much of the previous day with him, and patients got a little exacting.

"Very good of it, I'm sure," snorted Robert, "but I am the last person in the world to deprive another man of his rights."

He looked at her left hand. The engagement finger was ringless. Did that mean that Mr. Bingley had not yet had time to get a ring? He would probably send to town.

"Another man!" echoed Sally; "what other man?"

He had been about to say "that Bingley fellow," but said instead, in a sulky voice, "I mean Mr. Bingley of the bank, of course. I am sure I congratulate you both and wish you every happiness."

Sally was taken aback. "You don't sound very congratulatory," she managed to say lightly, "but as there happens to be some mistake, that does not matter."

His eyes grew eager and hopeful. "Do you mean you are not engaged to the fellow?"

"Certainly not," said Sally, with the more emphasis that she had every hope of being so very shortly. Mr. Bingley was advancing very close to the flame these days; he was already more than a trifle scorched.

"I'm glad," said Robert at last; "I could not have borne that." Then he remembered, and flushing, added quickly, "I mean, of course, he's not half good enough for you. Pompous ass!"

"A kind ass," Sally felt compelled to say of her future husband.

"Oh, then I am merely being premature?"

"Don't be ridiculous!"

He lay very still, and then he changed the subject of his own accord. "You have the paper, I see. Any news?"

Sally started, and her face grew very grave. She laid her hand on his for a moment, then she said:

"Bad news—for you."

"The boy—Cecil is in the casualty list?"

"Second Lieutenant C. K. Kantyre, Canadian Forces, killed."

"Invaluable, wanted, and so taken," he said rather bitterly, "while I lie here a useless log, and an outcast. His is the luck. Asphyxiated—my God!"

He was reading with horror of the damnable gases employed.

"But the road to Calais held," said Sally, "and the world is ringing with the undying fame of our grand Canadian Force."

"My poor uncle! This will about finish him. First son, and then grandson; they worthily lost in battle, and a disgraced man the sole Kantyre left to carry on the family tradition. Oh, to have fought again! He may burn the letter, but I must write just the same. Might I have those things off the shelf?"

The letter was written with some difficulty, and Sally promised to post it. She was glad he did not return to the matter of Mr. Bingley. She did not care for lying for its own sake, and he pushed her rather close to falsehood.

By the time she was engaged to Mr. Bingley, and her future happily secured, Robert Kantyre would be up and about, quite strong and well again, and she would have him off her mind. At present he was very much on it.

"War nerves, that's what's the matter with me," she decided. "After all, the war is bound to come into our lives directly or indirectly. Robert Kantyre the last Kantyre, I the last Lunton, but with what different traditions behind us! He must be noble for the sake of them, but I have nothing to make myself uncomfortable for, thank goodness!"

The next time she saw Robert he was much better. Soon he was allowed up, and then out. In an incredibly short time he returned to work of his own accord, and seemed none the worse for it. It was difficult to believe he had been ill. He had changed though, in other ways, become a little shy of Sally, sometimes even brusque, though his eyes held their welcome.

In the evenings he would climb The Mountain, and he usually found Sally there. They would sit on the boulders and stare down at the sea. Sometimes they would talk a great deal, at other times they would sit there in complete silence. At all times the name of Mr. Bingley was most carefully avoided between them.

He had decided to go out to Canada before long. He did not say why he still remained in Little Crampton, or mention why he had come to love The Mountain he had once thought so ridiculous, and the sea lying like a distant mirage at their feet. He remembered he was outcast and penniless, and that some things must be for ever set beyond his reach. He would reach his heart's desire when he reached that sea.

"I wish I wasn't the last Kantyre," he burst out one evening.

"Let's hope you are not the last," she returned; "that would be a misfortune indeed. I like to think of you building up your life afresh in the Colonies, making good, and of some splendid woman, such as there are out there, helping you, and of sons to consolidate what you have begun."

The picture did not seem to appeal to Robert. He plucked at the short grass, his eyes very intent on his task.

"I shall never marry now," he said with finality in his tones.

Sally laughed. "Oh, thirty-five is not the end of everything," she said. "When you have the home ready I feel sure Fate will see to it that the woman will be ready too. Of course you must marry, that is absolutely the duty of the last, and a big responsibility. You must carry on worthily so that the Kantyre family goes on. Your mistake will be quickly forgotten, and the country will have reason to be proud of the next generation."

"No," he said with determination, "that is absolutely finished."

Sally felt a tide of anger and regret sweep over her as she looked down on the magnificent specimen lying at her feet.

"Ridiculous! It would be absurd, wrong! I am the last Lunton, but I should be sorry to think there would be no more of the race, in blood if not in name."

She broke off abruptly, her face flooded with scarlet. She could have cut out her tongue for her rash speech. That race! Bingley-Luntons! The Luntons had been bad, but the Bingleys would be ridiculous. The Luntons had been wicked but handsome; the Bingleys would be frightful. No, hers would be no fine progeny to do fine things, useful things, to make her proud. Her sense of humour told her she was being ridiculous, but some other sense made her loathe this unborn generation.

"How much one forgets; how serious it all is, after all," she thought, and groaned. "Fat, bald, pasty!"

She conjured up an awful mental vision. She saw little girls with pigtails so tight that their tiny eyes were always watering; little boys filling their suits so fully that the buttons wore a weary look. They stood in rows gazing awestruck at the sacred bank.

She knew this was absurd, really funny, but somehow she could not laugh.

Robert did not look at her, but his figure had stiffened a little. She wondered if his thoughts had travelled the same road as hers, and hoped not. It made her feel ashamed. She jumped suddenly to her feet and shook out her skirts.

"Well, I must be going, or Lovey will be cross, or at least as cross as an angel can be. Good night, Mr. Kantyre. By the bye, I shan't be able to come here tomorrow."

"No," he said slowly, "I suppose not. I quite understand." He knew there was a small dinner-party to be given in honour of the return of a wounded Little Cramptonian from the Front, and that Sally and Mr. Bingley were among the guests. "It is very good of you to come at all, Miss Lunton."

"Oh, what rot!" said Sally brusquely.

"I want to thank you," he went on with some difficulty, "for all you have done for me. I did not know a girl could do so much for a man. It has—it has been wonderful, more than one can talk of. I shall never forget it, wherever I may be, or whatever happens. I know our paths lie far apart, but indeed, if I may, I say—God bless you and make you happy always." He pressed his lips to her hand.

"Oh, *don't!*" she cried, and ran with all her might homewards.

Mr. Lovelady, who was in the garden, watched her flight and reproved her. "You might break your neck."

"Serve me right if I did!" was her snappish reply.

"How fond you are of The Mountain!" he said unsuspiciously. He guessed nothing of the man who climbed up from the other side, and of what the boulders hid. "But what a cross Sally! Does your head ache?"

"It aches like the very devil!" she said curtly.

Mr. Lovelady did not reprove her. "Well, Sally," he said, smiling, "the Scriptures say nothing of the devil aching, so I can't refute you by text, but won't you go and lie down?" He wondered if she was going to have influenza; her eyes looked very wild.

"Lie down be—be bothered!" was all he got for that suggestion. She seized his spade and began to dig like a fury.

The poor man pointed piteously to the devastating effect upon his bulbs. "Oh, Sally, you are digging them all up!"

She banged them down again, face downwards, most of them. "Well, I always do the wrong thing, and always shall," she asserted; "it's in my blood. Anyway, I *hate* the nasty, fat, pasty, bulgy, bulby things! So there! I shan't have any bulbs in my garden—or roses either. I shall just grow sensible things to eat. Oh, dash everything! There—now I've gone through that rose-tree root! What a nuisance things are, all over the place!"

Mr. Lovelady wrested the spade from her by main force. "Oh, Sally, what an element of destruction in those slim white hands of yours!"

CHAPTER XXV

"After all, what could mother really know? She wasn't a man"

Mr. Bingley enjoyed the dinner-party, but he did not think much of the man from the Front, a short, ugly little man devoid of charm or conversation, and considered rather an absurd fuss was being made about him. He did full justice to the excellent dinner and the conversation of Sally, whom he took in. She not only shone, but saw to it that he shone as well. Looking round him, Mr. Bingley was quite aware that they were the only two people in the room who counted at all.

Miss Maggie was there. She had to be asked to social entertainments, otherwise they would be labelled 'failures,' and any trifling catastrophe would grow into a disaster. Mr. Bingley looked at her. That woman! She did not count in the least. What was she? Just a gossiping old maid of appalling plainness. When she exhibited her own particular skeleton in her one evening gown she was enough to destroy the appetites of the unaccustomed, but everyone there had got hardened by time. They knew the very number of her bones.

The conversation was scarcely brilliant, or in any way interesting. There was, however, no stiffness; all were intimates.

"Such a bridal month, May, the blossom all out!" murmured a rather sentimental person present.

"But it's unlucky to be married in May, you know," some one objected.

It was here that Miss Maggie came in, though the conversation was not addressed to her. "Not as unlucky as not getting married at all," was her contribution.

Her partner was an old bachelor by the name of Joicy. "Or being married any time," he retorted. After dinner, in the smoking-room, he told the other men he had seen *one* skeleton coming out of the cupboard.

Miss Maggie was equal to him. "Ah," she said, "but you old bachelors are always so cynical." She glanced across at Mr. Bingley and caught his eye. "Aren't you, Mr. Bingley? Personally I always think the valuable ones get snapped up early."

She looked round her triumphantly. Her elderly partner disappeared into his collar, and Mr. Bingley frowned.

"Do you still go up The Mountain every evening?" she asked Sally. "Such a delightful view. I suppose you know it too, Mr. Bingley? You really should go and see for yourself some evening, shouldn't he, Sally? You'll be quite surprised, I'm sure."

"I'm sure I shall," said the unconscious bank-manager, glancing down at the girl by his side with an expression that gave him away to more than one present.

Ha, ha! Miss Sally up to her old tricks! But this would be a good provision.

Sally gave a nervous little laugh. She was not enjoying herself. It seemed a long time since she had enjoyed anything. What a lot of money to spend on mere food! How dull the 'hero' was, though none the less a hero! The whole world seemed out of joint. Why must Miss Maggie remind her of The Mountain and all that it stood for? It frightened her a little. How complicated life was! Of course, if Mr. Bingley took to visiting it, Robert would have to cease to do so.

She gave a sharp little sigh.

"Yes, the war has spoiled everything, everything," she heard herself saying mechanically as they all rose from the table.

Mr. Bingley frowned. Were there not other things to talk of in Little Crampton save the war?

He saw Sally home, pressed her hand at parting, and went down the road humming a little tune in a pleasant enough and musical voice. He felt very young. That woman and her 'old bachelors'! Of course poor Joicy was an elderly bore—never been any competition for *him*. He ought to have got married while there was a chance of getting a presentable wife; now it was too late. Serve the old buffer right.

Mr. Bingley was not going to be a selfish uncared-for bachelor. No, no, he was quite ready to do the right and noble thing. How the others would stare at his dinner-parties and his brilliant hostess-wife! Some day at the board there would sit one fair and correct Bingley daughter, tall and slim, and three worthy Bingley sons. That was a good solid British family; neither extravagant nor parsimonious. Old Joicy was without a stake in the country, a being of no account, and no value. Up to a certain age, say forty, it was tempting and pleasant to be a bachelor, but after a certain age one merely became ridiculous or pitiable. Now the reign of the desirable bachelor should be changed for that of enviable young husband and father. Now to make the right and wise choice, and stick to it!

He opened *The Book*.

"*Don't marry a woman with a big chin, a big nose, or a big mouth; she won't be malleable.*"

Mr. Bingley was jarred; his dream struggled in his grasp. Mrs. Dalton had a big chin and rather a big nose, but it was Sally who had the big mouth. Finely-cut and expressive, oh yes, but still very wide, many times the size of Mr. Bingley's own very neat little affair which was now buttoned up in consternation. Of course it was obviously better to marry a woman with one disability than a woman with two; still, he knew very well that he owed it to himself to marry a wife without any disability whatsoever. And—would Sally be malleable? Had she not expressed opinions, the wrong sort of opinions, more than once, and stuck to them?

"*Don't marry a plain woman in the hope of plain virtues. She may be just as selfish and conceited as a pretty woman without her saving grace.*"

That was all right. Mr. Bingley was not going to marry a plain woman; it was the last thing he would do. He really had no use for plain people; they annoyed him. He knew it was wrong, for they were to be pitied, not blamed, but there it was—they just got on his nerves. That fat fool Boliver! Mr. Bingley credited himself with enough of the artistic temperament to be interesting, though not, of course, with enough to be in the least disreputable. No, a plain woman could not hope for a Bingley.

"Don't ask a woman to marry you more than once. She will be sure to remind you of it at those times when you are filled with amazement inasmuch as you asked her at all."

There was nothing to object to in that. He absolutely agreed. He preened himself a little. How could that advice apply to him? Mr. Bingley of the bank asking anyone twice! But then came the pull!

"Don't marry a woman just because you are wildly in love with her. You'll have to spend your life with her when you are no longer in love."

Mr. Bingley was resentfully conscious of the fact that he was 'wildly' in love. Where was that merely decent attraction as of a rabbit for parsley? He had never expected the thing to happen to him, did not indeed approve of it, but it was there, deep, deep in him, and his very pulses bounded at the sound of Sally's name. Quite an ordinary name, not even refined, but the sweetest sound in the world! Cold, calm reason pointed out the folly, the risk—and he went on being in love just the same!

Instead of walking in, keeping his feet and his head, he had tumbled into this delectable place called Love, head first, anyhow. Now he could not tumble out. He was just stuck, for life, he suspected, or at least till he was married. Sometimes it even came to this: he did not care a damn whether Sally was suitable or not. He wanted her; he meant to marry her. That was all that mattered. He was shocked at his thought, but a little thrilled. There was something magnificent, exultant, in such a state of mind.

In spite of his artistic temperament, within limits, he had little imagination or sense of imagery. He did not see himself as a ship, rudderless, driven before the wind, at the mercy of the storm, the gulls screaming in her wake, shaken in every nerve, plunging on and on. Delirium, destruction—and yet life!

He would merely have described his state to himself as being 'rather in a fuss.' He was horrified at being dominated by such a turbulent passion. It hardly seemed proper. A wife was a commodity to be chosen carefully, thought of calmly, and he knew in his heart of hearts that choice had been taken from him. The tempest was behind him driving him on. It was indeed difficult to please the new Mr. Bingley and the old—and his mother!

He gave the late Mrs. Bingley another chance, almost imploring her aloud to be kind to it, to give the thing he sought to do her warm approval. And how did she meet it? Oh, the ingratitude of mothers!

"*Don't marry a woman who has lived God knows how or where,*" she commanded, "*for only God knows what your living may be.*"

Mr. Bingley flushed darkly, then suddenly he rebelled. The new love drove out the old, and he flung *The Book* aside, a revolting son!

"After all, what could mother *really* know?" he asked himself. "She wasn't a man."

Mr. Bingley had suddenly made the discovery of his life, and a very startling discovery it was. His mother had only been a woman, after all! He was shocked at this irreverent thought, but it persisted.

He had made up his mind. He would wait no longer. He would propose to Sally, sensibly, neatly, and get the matter settled. He could not endure to wait any longer. She would forgive him the impetuosity of a lover. He had heard that a woman liked being taken by surprise, swept off her feet. With her happy eyes looking shyly into his he would not care a—a button what anybody said, Miss Maggie included. *Let* them say! He would have Sally.

This time the dream should prove more satisfactory. He would not wake an instant too soon. He would hold that long, slim form in his arms, kiss the mouth that haunted him, in spite of its wideness.

He drew a deep breath and his hands shook. How happy he would be, how happy they would both be! His to have and to hold for always. He would teach her to adore him even more, as he was ready to adore her, unseemly as it might be for a man to adore his wife. She should not be boxed up in Little Crampton; he would take her about, show her off, spoil her. She should have wonderful clothes, and a car too, yes, even a car, though it was awful the way they simply *ate* up money. She should refurnish too, if she liked; only he would ask her to keep his mother's antimacassars; they preserved the backs of the chairs. If she coaxed him very nicely to put *The Book* on the top shelf he would put it there. The young wife should have no rival, till that happy, sacred day came when a small king should reign in his stead.

Mr. Bingley felt his eyes moist, but it was a happy moisture.

He leaned back, a little complacent, perhaps, even ridiculous, but none the less kindly; a man with possibilities.

The very next evening, Wednesday, he would seek Sally on the top of The Mountain and ask her to be his wife. Surely such a place as the scene of her great happiness would please her, and it would suit his glorified mood. It would make him pant a little to get to the top, but the coming down would be easy. They would descend hand in hand—if people saw them, well, let them!—the happiest, luckiest couple in the world, made for each other by God Himself!

They would be married the moment the unlucky month for weddings was out. The whole of Little Crampton would admire gallant groom, radiant bride. Never would there be such a wedding! He would give the school-children a treat. They should scatter roses for his bride, white roses. The fame of it would spread far and wide. Boliver, whom she had turned down, and rightly, would have to give them a handsome present—serve the fat fool right! Paton, that pernicious ass, could not do less than his usual silver salver accompanied with his cynical good wishes. Mr. Paton, who had been married twice, and would most certainly be married a third time if Fate permitted, did not believe in marriage, and had no hesitation in saying so. Bridegrooms always hated him.

Mr. Bingley decided to make a speech at the reception that would ring in the ears of all for days. Then he and Sally would fare forth on a honeymoon that would be all pure bliss. If people guessed them to be honeymooners, well, let them do that too. He did not care. He would have no reason to be ashamed of his choice. His wife would be absolutely suitable, a Mrs. Bingley with race and distinction in every line of her.

How the hours dragged till Wednesday evening arrived! He ate his dinner as usual, habit being second nature; besides, he needed fortifying against that steep climb, but it was still light when he got up from it. It would be light on the mountain-top for a long time, at least light enough. He smiled tenderly.

How different to that other time! How lovely she had looked by the fire. How lovely she would look to-night with a woman's greatest happiness shining in her eyes, when she saw him coming, her knight. He had a vision as of one setting forth clad in shining armour.

He settled a lily-of-the-valley in his buttonhole and looked at the sky. It looked clear, but one never knew. He took his rain-coat off the peg, throwing it lightly over his arm. It would not do to sit on a damp boulder; besides, it might be chilly, even damp, coming back.

He did not anticipate exactly hurrying home, though, of course, he would take care they returned in conventional time for newly-engaged lovers. Surely newly-engaged lovers were allowed a little latitude. He liked to think of himself and Sally seated on the mountain-top, looking down at the sea, knowing that they belonged together for always now, that she was absolutely his, had been created for him. He went forward exultantly ... he would feel her hair against his lips.

Then he suddenly thought of his goloshes and turned back and fetched them. He wrapped them neatly in brown paper and slipped them in the rain-coat pocket. It might easily be damp coming home. The Mountain had little damp hollows, and then one never knew about these dews.

He always wrapped his goloshes in brown paper before putting them in his pocket, first, so that they should not mark the silk lining of his coat—all his things were lined with the best silk—and, secondly, because there was something a little lacking in refinement about goloshes naked and unashamed.

He quite agreed that May, with its blaze of blossoms had a bridal air, he was conscious of it in all his being. For Sally orange-blossom, a foolish and extravagant habit, some might say, but after all, one only married once—at least that was his intention. He had it in him to be absolutely faithful to the memory of the one woman. If he left her a widow—almost as painful a thought—and she survived her crushing loss and grief, she also would never wish to marry again. For her own protection, and to make sure, and because well-endowed widows were got round by fortune-hunters, he would leave her penniless in case she tried to replace the priceless. Women must be protected from their folly for their own sakes. To think of another man spending his money, marrying his widow! It made Mr. Bingley's blood boil.

He folded the rain-coat more carefully, pushed the goloshes deeper into the pocket. Then, in complete readiness for the great event of his life, the carefully-considered proposal ready to his tongue, this modern Don Quixote set forth.

CHAPTER XXVI

"I am lower than the beasts that perish"

Sally awaited Robert Kantyre on the mountain-top. She had an instinct that he would come. There was something in the air that spoke of comings, of events.

It had been very hot all day, summer heat, and she had unearthed an old cotton frock and an old knitted coat. She glanced down at it discontentedly. How old-fashioned it was, and how shabby! How *outré* the fashions of 1914 were in 1915! Had there ever been such a *volte face*? Her conscience refused to let her ask Mr. Lovelady for another penny. She knew he would give her anything she asked for, and go without himself. His rule of life was very simple. When there was not enough for two, one must go without. He had always been that one; he accounted it a privilege.

"Oh, to be done with shabbiness," she sighed, with the petty little contrivances, the hateful stings! To be able to have this and that at last, to do this and that. To be looked up to, envied instead of half-pitied or half-despised! To be a success instead of a failure! It was time, it was time indeed, if she was ever to win out.

How she longed for home and place, to be able to meet Dinah Wilmot-Randal on equal terms, to have Jimmy realise she had done well for herself after all. Jimmy? She was startled. How long since she had given him a thought! Was that glorious, undying thing dead then? Had it not been so glorious and so undying, after all? Who, and what, had killed it? For it lay dead within her, that deadest of all things, a dead love. His happiness with another woman must have killed it, she supposed; it had not been able to look on that and live. Or was it his presence that had slain it? Was it of those things that throve in absence, but withered as under a rude touch before the face of reality?

"It was splendid while it lasted," she thought sadly, "but it is gone, and gone for ever. Must all splendour die, all great emotion just flicker out? Oh, what a ghastly, ghastly thought!"

She would not think of it. Rather would she think how much better it is to do without emotion, to be left unstirred, able just to enjoy; what money and ease and respectability could do; of how comforting to be on firm ground after hanging dizzily suspended over the abyss.

Of … how late he was! How uncomfortable he had made her feel the other night. How absurd to push a person on to a pedestal and insist on keeping the poor unaccustomed thing there! She was of the earth, earthy; no head among the clouds for her. One merely froze in high altitudes, lost one's breath. "God bless me, indeed!" She wriggled uncomfortably. "That's likely, that is!"

When he heard and realised that this was what she had been playing for all along, and that she had won, what would he do and think and say? He would say and do nothing, but he would probably think rather a lot. They would not be admiring or respectful thoughts. She wriggled again. Would he still wish her happiness always, still say, "God bless you!"

"Oh, what a silly ass I am!" she reminded herself sternly. "Stop it! Stop it, do!"

She lay back on the boulder, her arms crossed beneath her head. He was late. 'Late, so late, ye shall not enter now!' What made her think of that? "Comes of staying in a clergyman's house, I suppose. One of Lovey's texts." Did he mean never to come again? Had he realised? Better so, far, far better so, only … Well, one could not expect everything to be easy. After a while it would be pleasant enough, and he would be far away working out his salvation beneath the Northern Lights, and winning out, winning out like a man. It was easier for men, quite simple for them. For women it was entirely different; they were still tied. How lucky men were, and how little they realised it!

"The thing is to be sensible, *sensible*," she reminded herself, "not to think too much or worry, just to enjoy as you go along, getting as much of the smooth as possible. That's it, the smooth, the soft job."

She knew what the rough road meant only too well. The feet of eighteen could travel that way lightly enough, make a jest of it; not so the feet of thirty-one. They lagged a little, had grown a trifle heavy in those long thirteen years. They needed the easy way.

She looked up into the sky, and one by one tiny little pin-points of light twinkled here and there. It seemed to her that each had its friendly little face, that the heavens understood the turmoil and the stress of those below, and did not utterly condemn, while they counselled calm. It was austerity without hardness, purity without iciness; a vastness, a promise, and a peace.

Yet the same sky was looking down on the bloodiest battlefield of history, on a world in the anguish of travail, bringing forth not the living, but the dead. Nay, not peace, but a sword!

The stars seemed to run together into the shape of one, to shine blood-red, flaring across the sky, to shriek aloud of nations locked in a death-struggle, of the inexorable price that must be paid ere the sword was sheathed, paid by thousands and tens of thousands, by nations and individuals, by those that dwelt in palaces and those whose heads lay under a humble cottage roof.

The stars broke up, the sword dispersed. The lights ran hither and thither, playing at ships riding upon the waves. Sally watched them entranced—a great fleet with courage always at the helm. She blinked, and the stars were shattered, and there lay a mighty ship in the death-throes, sinking, sinking—death on every side of her, death beneath her feet, on her blistering decks the dying and the dead. She saw the living gallant band, their faces to the fore, meeting the end with a heroism and a sacrifice which lie beyond words.

All this—for what?

That one of the great nations shall go down into the very dust and raise her head no more till this generation shall have passed away; that here and there the map shall be painted in other colours; that the fair lands of pasture shall raise crosses instead of crops; that every village, every street of the many nations, shall know mourning and loss, and the Angel of Death be abroad in the land, his wings beating in sunlight and in shadow; that where there has been laughter there shall be weeping, and even the feet of children shall falter in their play. …

Sally hid her face in sore abasement. At such a time, in such a world, she was thinking of herself, of her own ease and her own comfort. She had put all her energies, all her thoughts into these things, and into the pursuit of Mr. Bingley.

"I am lower than the beasts that perish, infinitely lower," she thought, appalled at having to meet herself face to face and see what manner of person she was.

She dare look no more on the sky; she looked instead at the sea, and lo! out of that mystic sea visions came surging that would not be denied, a great throng. …

Here was martyred Belgium. The mailed fist held the cup to her lips, the voice of God's Anointed bade her drink to the dregs, and the Great Little Country, her head bloody but unbowed, drank … to the Resurrection.

Nuns, maids, wives trailed past her with veiled, bowed faces; they pointed to Sally, they seemed to say terrible things, terrible things … wondering, accusing. The little children came next, a great multitude, their eyes haunted; one small maid who had not even been left her eyes to weep with, a babe without the little hands to catch at the sunbeams; these were they whom war had crucified upon the iron cross. The homeless aged … things that could not be spoken of … on and on, a procession without a beginning, and without an end.

And one who stood apart, who had permitted these things, still sowing. Still far from his reaping, his last hour and his last cry, "Let the day perish wherein I was born, and the night wherein it was said, 'There is a man-child conceived.'"

And she was trying to marry Mr. Bingley for his money!

Her own men went by laughing, gallant and gay, an army growing week by week; sailors passed on ships, their eyes straining into the darkness for the hidden death. All these were fighting and dying, bearing the heat and the burden of the day, while she …

A shuddering sob shook her.

Then a foot struck sharply against a stone. The mist of these haunting visions cleared, and she knew someone was coming up behind her.

She turned to meet Robert Kantyre, her heart beating fast, her face a glory. Instead she found herself face to face with Mr. Bingley.

Mr. Bingley, pompous but passion-flushed, with a flower in his buttonhole, a little short of breath, but with a look of high resolve upon his face.

Then at last Sally knew that all she had schemed and hoped for, all the prosperity she ached for, everything—or almost everything—was within her grasp at last.

CHAPTER XXVII

"Sally? Sally!"

Mr. Bingley had his proposal at the tip of his tongue, something a little poetical, but at the same time sensible and suitable.

He would start by saying what a delightful evening it was, and then—letting himself go a little—go on to say that all evenings in Sally's company were delightful to him, come wet or fine, and from that come naturally to:

"I do not want to rush you, but if I might always have your company—as my wife? Will you do me the honour to marry me? I think we should be very happy together, and I need not say I would consider your welfare in every way."

Surely that was the perfect mean! Sober, loverlike, Bingleyish.

What happened, however, might be loverlike; it was certainly neither sober nor Bingleyish.

At sight of Sally with that strange, almost unearthly, glory in her face, all the carefully-prepared things fled. He just caught her by the sleeve and stammered like a schoolboy. His dignity was forgotten and dead; an absurd delirium shook him. He was shaken to the very soul of him where another Mr. Bingley, of whom he suspected nothing, lurked deep down. It was the case of the genii and the bottle all over again. The cork flew out of the cramped little soul and a giant arose, something far too vast to get back into his habitation.

"Sally," he stuttered, "I love you! Sally, I love you. Sally, Sally! I love you, Sally. Will you be my wife? Will you? Will you? Why don't you answer?

There was love and welcome in your eyes when I came. You knew—you knew! Sally? *Sally!*"

It was not a voice; it was a cry.

He tried to draw her to him. He was trembling, glorified, a strange and rather wonderful Mr. Bingley.

"I must keep my head," thought Sally, "I must remember to be sensible—sensible … all it means … the alternative."

But the man's passionate outburst frightened her. She had not thought to face this, to cheat it. The man had seemed so little, so mean; yet the thing he offered was neither. It was a big thing, far larger than the man himself, far more powerful. His very humanity startled her. The lay-reader, the typical Mr. Grundy, was almost primitive. He was no longer reader and bank-manager, but just a man who wanted her, needed her. He ceased to be a pompous absurdity, a figure to mock at; he was a man. This Mr. Bingley made her feel small and mean. He was only asking to give; she had only the mind to take, to take his money and possessions, and give him a half-mocking tolerance.

"Don't!" she cried, twisting away, "please don't! I—I—"

"I have taken you by surprise," he stammered, "rushed you. But I love you so. Oh, Sally, Sally!" His trembling hands closed round her arm.

"I—you must let me think. It's so surprising, so sudden!" she gasped.

"But you love me! I am sure of it. You will, you *must!* I should go mad if you didn't. I will give you everything, everything … you shall scatter the money, *scatter* it. My God, what am I saying? You shall have all your own way. Sally, Sally darling, don't look like that! I will be your slave. Yes, I know it's wrong, but I don't care. I don't care! I don't care about anything if only you will marry me!"

In that moment the giant Mr. Bingley out of the bottle spoke no more than the truth. He did not care. It was possible, of course, that later he would relapse, and relapse badly, and that his last state would be worse than his first, but he was far from that condition now.

"Marry me, marry me!" he cried.

"You must give me time," she got out. "I must think it over … such a big thing … all one's life—two lives. I can't decide in a moment."

She also was trembling, also torn, her soul divided against itself. All the time a little voice was urging, "Sally, you silly ass! Be sensible! Remember! Remember! Do you want to cut your throat? This is better than you dared to hope. You could rule him absolutely, get all you want. Such a chance, never to come again. Fool, oh, fool!"

"But I have decided, absolutely decided," he cried, "thought it all out. You have only just got to say 'yes.' Sally, my Sally, say it!" He pressed up against her.

Sally either could not or would not. Her throat went dry and she put her hand up to it as if she were choking.

"I c-c-can't, not to-night," she stuttered, "n-n-not to-night. So much has happened. Things are different. I must think, and—and try. Give me a little time, a day, a week. Yes, I insist. You must give me a week."

Mr. Bingley once more saw himself waking the instant too soon. He pressed closer. "No, no," he cried angrily, "it isn't fair, it isn't fair. Don't you understand? I am offering to marry you, to make you my wife—Mrs. Alfred Bingley of the Bank. How can you hesitate, how can you? I will not stand it. You are teasing me, naughty Sally; you shall pay me for that." His face was almost touching hers. "Now say 'yes,' darling. My little girl! My love, my angel, my all!"

Mr. Bingley had a still, small voice in his ear also. "You must be mad," it cried, shocked, "quite mad, man! Is this cool reason? Is this the way for a Bingley to propose? Is this the calm sea of matrimony upon which you seek to embark? Look closer, man; would you fling yourself into the maelstrom? Is this *respectable?*"

The giant Mr. Bingley did not know or care. He did not even listen. He was conscious only of an unbearable longing to hold Sally in his arms and kiss her again and again.

"Little torment, little torment," he went on thickly, "say you love me! Say it at once. Kiss me instead then, that will do. Kiss me!"

Sally shrank back. She could not take, just then, but she would not leave.

"I don't know," she cried wildly, "I can't think. I don't know. You must wait."

"Of course you know. Oh, you are wicked, cruel … I never think of anybody but you, never, never! Even in my dreams you are there. I want you dreadfully, dreadfully. You must 'yes,' you shall say 'yes'! Do you think you can just play with me—*me?*" He seized her wrists.

Sally turned white. This strange, insistent Mr. Bingley frightened her, yet she had never gone so near to liking him, almost to respect. The little tin god was made of flesh and blood; possibilities had materialised. He was even almost passable to look at just then; his love transfigured his face, gave him dignity and inches, manhood. He had shed the shibboleths.

She resisted him, but his grasp tightened. His eyes gleamed suddenly. He flung his arms round her, held her crushed against him, kissed her passionately on the eyes and on the mouth, pressed his cheek against the fine sheen of her hair.

"Now, Sally, now … now you can't say 'Give me time.' You must say 'yes' now. You are mine, *mine*, all mine!"

Sally tore herself away. "No, I can't! It is impossible now. I—I—"

He turned grey. "Impossible?" he cried shrilly. "What do you mean by impossible?"

The little voice grew louder in Sally's ear. "Oh, throw it away, throw it away! There are so many chances going, aren't there?"

She pressed her hands to her blazing cheeks. "I mean impossible to decide now. Time, I must have time. Just one week. That is fair—a week. I shall be sensible then; it will be easy. Only a week, but not to-night, not to-night!"

She began to shiver, though the night was warm and her body burning.

Something in her voice convinced him that to press the matter home now would be to lose. He turned cold all over; clammy fingers seemed laid on his heart. To lose Sally! It would be easier to lose life itself. She was his life. The glow of his ardour and the radiance of the vision faded. He had been a god, now he was a man again, Mr. Bingley of the Bank. The genii was being tricked back into the bottle.

He was shocked at himself. What had happened to him? He had really let himself go a trifle too much, been most undignified. He had lacked refinement, and refinement was a passion with him; he had positively been almost coarse in his love-making. Certainly he had been unseemly. He had shown his feelings with positive indecency; he had not only forgotten to be a Bingley, he had forgotten to be a gentleman.

He hung his head, abashed. "I am very sorry," he said humbly, "I—I quite forgot myself. I hope I did not startle you." He flushed as he remembered those kisses, but he did not regret them. He exulted in them.

Well, he was punished for his ungentlemanly conduct. Another week ere he could hold her again. Another week ere he could feel quite sure, own her before the world! A week, nay, a year, an eternity! He could not, would not wait. His passion surged up again. He should go mad. Why was she treating him in this cruel way? He had heard such ways were a woman's stock-in-trade, that she sought to enhance her value by such methods. But not Sally, not Sally, she was not like that. She was different from all other women. He could not bear to think of one speck upon her perfection.

Yes, this coldness, this drawing back and hesitation, was maidenly, womanly, tantalising. He was sure his mother would have approved of such conduct, and that she had acted just the same in her day. He never guessed that that great and wonderful woman had almost entirely conducted her courtship herself, and that one day she had just said to the man who was still thinking it over, "Well, Alfred, there's been enough nonsense and waste of time. We'll get married," and got married they had.

Yes, it was a beautiful attitude, so coy, so chaste! It would mean asking her twice, a thing he had certainly never contemplated. Still, a warm, glowing, blushing Sally clinging close was what he craved, a shy "yes," the yellow flame against his cheek. To think he must wait a whole week for this!

"Very well," he groaned, "if you really insist. But it's hard, it's awfully hard, darling. I—I don't know how I am going to bear it." He looked at her with pathetic little eyes. "I will come again for my answer in a week. Then it will be 'yes,' won't it, Sally?"

How that little voice echoed in her ear, reminded her of this and that, of black depths. …

"I think it will be 'yes,'" she said very low. "I—I hope so; only you must go now, at once, please!" How easy to accept Mr. Bingley at a distance!

He took off his hat mournfully and departed. A week to wait! A week to wait! Not thus had he thought to come from off the mountain-top. She should make up for that week she had stolen from him! Those lover's privileges should not be wasted; no, he would see to that. He would add them to the others. The little witch! His Sally, his very own Sally!

He went plunging on, not looking where he was going. Suddenly he plunged into water. Bah! *Damp!* He put on his rain-coat and undid the goloshes. He slipped them on and carefully buried the paper under a stone. Only trippers and such low abominations left paper littering the scenery. It made one think of oranges and ham-sandwiches, so disgusting out of their proper place.

A week! How many days, hours, minutes, were there in a week?

"Eternity!" groaned Mr. Bingley, "eternity!" He splashed again. "What a good thing I brought my goloshes this time!" he added thankfully.

CHAPTER XXVIII

"Then I also give you a week"

Sally stood very still when Mr. Bingley had gone. The little voice was screaming now, infuriated, "Oh, you fool, you fool! What have you done?"

Sally was frightened now the opportunity had gone. What had she done, indeed? She could only wonder at herself, only hope that the chance would be hers again.

"I am only giving myself a week, just a week's longer freedom," she panted; "seven more days to belong to myself. Of course next time—"

"If next time comes. Oh, fool!" The voice was mocking now.

"It will come. It would come to-morrow if I liked. Perhaps I shall—perhaps I shall. It was those … things that upset everything. They seemed so real, made me feel so low, but they've gone now, of course."

So they argued together, the two Sallies, one clinging to the lower road, the soft road; one reaching to the higher and the stony way. This way, that way! See-saw, Margery Daw! She could not afford to throw away such a priceless opportunity; she must; she must not.

Then her heart gave a great leap. Robert Kantyre was coming across the mists towards her, and had loomed up gigantic by her side. She knew now what she had really been waiting for all the time. She would see him again for the last time; then they must never meet again. His the stony road; hers the smooth. Far, far as the poles asunder! How her eyelids smarted!

"I had to come to-night," he said directly.

She did not move or turn and face him. "I knew you would come," she answered. "Why were you so late? Oh, why didn't you come first?"

"You wanted me to come? You watched for me?" His face lit up and he spoke rather breathlessly, moving nearer. "Oh, Sally, you cared whether I came or not?" Then he seemed to pull himself together. "I beg your pardon. I came to show you these." He held out a couple of letters. "Uncle Robert has written. He wrote at once when he heard, but the letter went astray, and I got both together. He—oh, he's the same Uncle Robert, thank God! He understands, and forgives. I want you to read them. They mean so much—hope, prospects, everything!"

"It's too dark," she said, moving away. "I—I really must go back."

"No, no, not yet." He barred her way. "You can see to read by this." He took an electric torch out of his pocket. "He wants me to go at once."

"To Canada?"

"Yes, to the Alberta ranch."

She did not speak for a moment, then she said a little dully, "It seems the best thing, I think. I—I am glad." She told herself fiercely she had *got* to be glad. Here was the last obstacle removed from her path. With him away it would be easy; of course it would be easy.

"Yes. Will you read what he says? This is the first one."

There was not much in the first letter.

My dear Robert (it began),

I have just got yours. Of course it's a blow, but I did not need to be told it was no question of cowardice—just a mistake for which you have paid the price, my poor lad. The greatest bitterness, to which death is nothing, is yours, but you will face it like a man, a Kantyre? Don't do anything rash; let the rest of your life make up. I wish you'd come out here; there's enough for three of us, and that three will soon be two. When I am gone Cecil will not grudge you your share. It wants two to work the place; there's a big job, and a fine job, to be done. So you never came across my boy? He's safe so far; please God he may remain so. We Kantyres are narrowing down a bit, just you and my boy's boy to carry on the name. Well, lad, if you will write or cable that you will come you'll make an old man very happy. I will then write, sending money and giving particulars, etc.

Your affectionate uncle,
Robert Kantyre.

"He sounds nice," said Sally.

"He's one of the best," asserted Robert warmly, "a splendid old man. This is the other letter."

The writing of the second letter lacked the firmness of the first; it seemed older, almost infirm.

My dear Robert (it ran),

I have just got the wire telling me my boy has followed his father and given his life for his country. I must not grieve, but it is difficult, difficult. Robert, you never answered my last letter, and I have been sick with fear sometimes lest you have taken the coward's way out, lest there is the worst grief of all coming to me. I pray God that is not so. Oh, Robert, you were always like a son to me; come and be a son in very truth. I am an old man now, I had not realised how old, and my days can't be long, but stand by me till they pass. I cannot work this place alone, and I cannot see it go and be wasted. It's very dear to me, the only home I have ever known, the home I built when my vagabond days were done, the home I brought my bride to, and from which she set forth on her last long journey, and her son, and her son's son. Old age is the greatest tragedy sometimes. All the faces are gone save yours; please God there is still yours. Oh, Robert, come to me, for pity's sake! All I have is yours. You had the right stuff in you. Come soon, come at once. I inclose all expenses.

Reference to a large cheque, and instructions, followed. Then the letter went on, and as Sally read this she felt Robert bend nearer, and was conscious of the tensity of his frame and face.

Bring a wife if you can, dear son. There's the house waiting, but it's not a home without the woman. It's a hard life, I know, so it will have to be the right woman, one you love with all your heart, one who loves you with all hers.

The girl's fingers shook as she held the letter, and Robert's closed over them. The two heads were very close as they went on with the letter.

It's right away from shops and play; just Mother Earth and Nature and work, and a little bit of the Old Country. You must not bring a girl who puts ease and luxury and the little things first, but a girl big and brave and splendid who puts the great things first, who is ready to give up luxury to make a Paradise for her man. Bring a mate worthy of a Kantyre and the Kantyres to be. I ask no more. If I could see your sons about my knees, and know there was the old breed to carry on, I could die happy indeed. Come soon, but don't come without her if you can possibly help it.

Sally gave the letter back, and found herself held by Robert's eyes.

"I suppose I shan't be able to help it?" he asked, very low. "It's a big thing to ask, a mighty undertaking … and for an outcast … isn't it, Sally?"

She looked round her a little wildly, but made no answer. The line of the sea had faded now in the gathering darkness.

"I've nothing to offer," he went on, "and the life you saved already belongs to you. Just work—and love. You know I love you, don't you, Sally? That I have loved you all along? If it's not you it will be nobody. Must it be nobody? *Must* it, Sally?"

He bent to look into her face, but he did not touch her.

"I don't know," she cried, for again she could say neither 'yes' nor 'no.' "Oh, I don't know about anything. Why must you come to-night, ask me now, when I—when I—" A sob escaped her. "Oh, how miserable I am!"

He put his arm gently round her shoulders. "What is it, dear? Oh, Sally! you are in trouble, unhappy? Am I making it worse for you?"

"Yes—no! I don't know." She leaned against him, sobbing. "Oh, Robert, Robert, life is very difficult, very hard. It tears one, tears one in two!"

He stroked her hair. "Oh, my poor Sally! You are thinking what it would mean. A grey life, the great loneliness, everything given up, and only me. How dare I think for a moment you could care even a little bit! And that would mean so much caring!"

"I am such a worm," she said abjectly, "such a low, mean, wriggling little worm. I want stepping on, cutting in two with a spade, flinging to that beastly Sapphira, the little cat! I like warmth and ease and softness, and shops and people and theatres, and pictures and books, and clothes and people to show them off to, and—and everything. But I do care, just a tiny little." She buried her head suddenly against his shoulder. "Only I do so hate washing-up—so greasy!—and cold and snow; and I always get chilblains in the winter, and my nose would be so red and horrid nobody would love me any longer, and my fingers blue and swollen, and—and—"

"Darling heart, I know, I know!" He pressed his lips to her wet cheeks. "My own precious Sally, anyway. I don't really expect it—how could I? Only I had to ask you. Bless you, bless you for caring that tiny bit! You don't care for that Bingley fellow, say you don't,"

"N-o-o, at least I—I suppose not," she stuttered, her face going hot; "but he—he—"

"He's rich. He can give you everything, while I can give you nothing save a hard life in a new land? That is it, eh, Sally?"

She clung to him closer. "I never pretended," she murmured, "I told you I was a little beast, and I am, I am!"

"No, you are not," he declared emphatically, "you are a perfect darling, a very human darling. Sally, it just comes to this: it's a question of caring not a little, but a lot, of caring … enough."

"It would mean caring so much that simply nothing else would matter. Oh, Robert!"

"Yes, it would mean all that," he agreed.

She was silent for a long time, and then she said wearily, "I cared like that once, years and years ago, but pain and regret came of it, and—and humiliation. I am afraid now. I don't want to care much ever again, though I would not mind being cared for. I only want to be comfortable and respectable and rich and in the thick of people and things. You do not know what my life has been, you do not know. If you did you would understand, not expect … And the life out in Alberta—"

"Only a great love could make possible. A woman will leave all for her own man, but I am not that to you yet. Perhaps I never could be, though to me you are the one woman in the world, and I would die for you. Do you think I would over-persuade you to your regret, see regret growing and growing? No, no, not by a word! I would do the washing-up for you," he laughed unsteadily, "if it happened to be necessary, but it is not quite as bad as that. My uncle has a man and his wife who do the roughest work. It would be hard, darling, but not drudgery or slavery. I could not take you to that. It would be lonely, and big and magnificent and beautiful. Oh, Sally, to go without you! Never to see you again! But—but this is hardly playing the game. Just think it over, and I promise you this—if you say 'go' I will go without a word."

"Yes, but you will despise me!" she cried chokingly, "not—not love me any longer."

"I'm afraid I shall love you a little longer—Heaven help me!"

"I don't know *what* I shall say," she said, panic-stricken, "I don't know what I *want* to say or do. I am just—muddled. Why didn't you come first?"

He stepped back from her. "Bingley has proposed to you? You have accepted him?"

"Not accepted him yet. I have a week to think it over."

Robert did not speak for a moment, then he said very quietly, "Then I also give you a week. Next Wednesday you will decide between us. I will come to you here that night."

"Yes, oh yes; I must decide, of course. Only I think I shall go mad. Go now, please, go at once."

He went.

CHAPTER XXIX

"Just fancy if there was a divorce in Little Crampton, Mr. Bingley!"

Mr. Bingley as a lay-reader was perfectly familiar with the love-story of Jacob—how he served seven years for Rachel, and yet again seven years, and how the fourteen years were as nothing to him owing to the love he had unto her. That Jacob could be content to wait fourteen years, while Mr. Bingley could not wait seven days—seven eternities they seemed to him—simply argued that Jacob could not have had it half so badly as Mr. Bingley. In fact, Jacob's passion was over-rated.

There was also the fact that even an Englishwoman waited for for fourteen years would be no longer in the first flush of youth and beauty, while the Eastern would be an old hag. No, it was a poor sort of love-story compared to his own; a poor sort of love compared to this rending, insurgent thing within him.

He counted the very hours till the longed-for Wednesday should arrive. Then, on the wings of love, he would fly swiftly to Sally's presence—in that hour usually devoted to the luncheon exercise. He left his mother's *Book* severely alone, but he read Tennyson's love-poems, and felt very much the lover, and rather a romantic figure. Nobody had ever loved like him before. Nobody else had ever married a Sally. How could she keep him waiting for a week, postpone her own happiness as well as his! Cruel! Cruel!

It was while the fevers of love and anticipation were at their height that he happened to run into Miss Maggie.

As a matter of fact it was, of course, Miss Maggie who ran into him, though she took care that it should seem otherwise. She never appeared to seek the people she was running down; she just managed that they 'happened' into her.

She held out her hand archly. "*You!* Just fancy, I thought it was Mr. Boliver. What a coincidence!"

Mr. Bingley did not see where the coincidence came in. His heart swelled within him. He, Mr. Bingley of the Bank, a young lover, gallant knight worth three thousand pounds per annum, taken for that short, fat, and long-married absurdity, whose income was as ridiculous as his appearance!

He looked in the light, piercing eyes, and smiled wryly as he said, "Honoured, I am sure, Miss Maggie. You don't *look* short-sighted!"

"I'm not. How quaint men are! Now the other day I took Mr. Boliver for you, and *he* said—but there," she broke off with affected embarrassment, "Mr. Boliver is a bold, bad man, and I can't repeat it. *I* think myself that it's the male sex that has most vanity; but then I never had anything to be vain of, not even a husband. Just a poor, plain spinster who never looked for one—and wouldn't have found it any good if she had!"

"You under-rate your charms, my dear lady," said Mr. Bingley in as nasty a tone as he could manage, "and the perspicuity of my sex."

"Oh, what a perfectly lovely word!" gushed Miss Maggie. "And does it only apply to your sex? If a woman had this perspicuity thing I suppose she would never be found out? How useful! *Dear* Sally!"

Mr. Bingley started nervously, and gulped. He was glad Miss Maggie noticed nothing. Sometimes her inconsequence was so very—well, consequent, so tricky. It meant she was leading up to something spiteful. He was not going to help her by making any comment.

"Too many scandals are bad for a woman. Don't you think so?" asked the spinster regretfully. "There always comes the one that matters in the end, smashes her up. I think a woman should be like What's-his-name's wife, poor fellow! simply unsmirchable."

"Some find it easy, I fancy," said the goaded Mr. Bingley.

What was she getting at now? The old moor story? But surely that had blown over, and it certainly would when the engagement was announced. Sally's too great kindness to the man of the moors? But that also would be put a stop to.

Miss Maggie smiled. She was not in the least offended. "Oh yes," she owned readily, "I was one of those kind of women. Very dull, but it can't be helped. It takes all sorts to make a world, and some of us must be respectable. I don't blame Sally in the least. Of course White of Moor-end Farm, gentleman or no gentleman, is a bit of a come-down after Mr. Boliver, and so on, but a handsome come-down, a big, fine, athletic and slim come-down, and that is always something, isn't it, Mr. Bingley? Then, of course, the Luntons always go their maddest after looks. Quite natural, I think. And after all, what's *one* scandal more or less?"

"There is no scandal," said Mr. Bingley firmly. "Miss Lunton has been quite too kind to White, but he's getting about again now—"

"Yes; so is she."

Mr. Bingley experienced a momentary pang of jealousy. "It would indeed need a depraved mind to suggest that Miss Lunton flirts with labourers," he said stoutly.

"Oh, hardly flirts, that's not quite the word, or 'labourers' either; a handsome gentleman-wastrel, you know. So fascinating. Women always begin by redeeming them, and then sometimes have to be redeemed themselves instead; but of course it's nothing compared with the other. I do wonder what Mrs. Wilmot-Randal will do about it. If she had had this perspicuity she would never have married Mr. Wilmot-Randal, considering. He was poor then, but I suppose she never suspected for a moment he was the sort that got led away. I don't suppose she'll take action now. After all, men with ten thousand a year don't find it so easy to get divorced from their wives."

Mr. Bingley pricked up his ears. A scandal at the Red House! He was glad to get away from the subject of Sally. He hated her name on Miss Maggie's lips; the bitter tongue made it sound like someone not in the least like Sally.

"Why, they are a most devoted couple," he exclaimed incredulously, "and nice and good and charming; quite suited to Little Crampton in every way. There must be some mistake. You have got hold of the wrong end of the stick this time, my dear lady."

He spoke in a tone of condescending reproof, which did not annoy Miss Maggie in the least. She had her rapier and some skill with which to confront his clumsy pinprick.

"Oh no, I've got all the letters somewhere." She brought a packet out of her bag, and he noticed without much interest that they all had the Italian stamp. "As a business man I should like your advice. Quite evidence enough for a divorce, I'm sure! Fancy if there was a divorce-case in Little Crampton, Mr. Bingley!"

Mr. Bingley could not fancy any such thing. The Little Cramptonians did not go in for such infamies, or else they worked matters so discreetly that none ever knew of them, which amounted to the same thing.

He laughed. "My dear Miss Maggie, what a mare's-nest! Oh, you women, fie! fie!"

"Fie, fie!" echoed Miss Maggie, tittering. "What a sensation, and the other person being in the place—though not, of course, a Cramptonian proper, or improper! Ha, ha!"

Mr. Bingley stared.

"People with pasts stay away as a rule," went on Miss Maggie, "and leave in a hurry when they are about to be found out, so really this is quite a new development. What a sensation it will make! Of course plain spinsters don't have pasts, poor things! but I've often thought it must be rather interesting. And she *is* interesting, isn't she, Mr. Bingley? So fascinating. Men always run after her—not that we have any men left here now, thanks to the war; but you know what I mean. She just finds *something*. That's Sally's way."

"Sally's way!" echoed Mr. Bingley palely. "*Sally's way!* I do not understand you, Miss Maggie. What has Miss Lunton to do with the Wilmot-Randal quarrel?"

"It's not a quarrel that I know of—just a scandal. But haven't you heard? Of course I took it for granted you knew all about it. I'm sure it's all over the place by this time. You know how people *will* gossip! What a hotbed your club is; everything starts from there, I sometimes think."

She turned the letters over and over in her hands.

The unhappy man plunged on to disaster. "I heard nothing at the club. And—and Miss Lunton could not possibly have anything to do with any scandal, not possibly!"

"Then you haven't heard?"

"Heard what?" His voice shook a little. His Sally! His Sally! Who dared to whisper falsehoods about her? The future Mrs. Alfred Bingley!

"That Sally ... Mr. Randal—when he was just Thompkins, of course—had a—a—honeymoon sort of thing in Italy six years ago." She seemed overcome with maidenly confusion. "So embarrassing, forcing me to tell you this, a bachelor too!"

Mr. Bingley reeled. "She's—she's married already?"

The spinster was confused again. "Oh, not *married* exactly; the unofficial kind of honeymoon, I mean. The—the other sort of thing! Oh, Mr. Bingley, you seem quite to forget that I'm not married, and haven't even a married sister. So shocking! Yes, Italy, six years ago. Quite common in Paris, I believe, among a certain set, and of course the Luntons were always like that, and her own parents too. ... To think that you never suspected ! How odd! What do you say?"

For the moment Mr. Bingley was incapable of saying anything. He was grey and gasping; he felt physically sick. He believed he was going to be extremely ill, and before a lady—surely the height of ungentlemanliness—and he did not care. He did not care about anything. If a breath of this hideous tiling were true, even the very bank became of little importance. Nothing mattered; nothing would ever matter again. He seemed rent by death-throes.

"No wonder you have lost your breath!" said Miss Maggie. "I'm sure I *almost* lost mine. I do wonder what Mrs. Wilmot-Randal will do, don't you? Forgive him, I should not wonder. You see, if she doesn't, Sally might get him, and there you are. They would just go off somewhere again, and she would have all that money, and such a fascinating young man. I suppose that's what she's been playing for all along."

"It's a lie," burst from Mr. Bingley hoarsely, "a damned lie! I don't believe a word of it!"

"Oh, hush, Mr. Bingley, and before a lady! I have always been so particular—comes of not being married, I suppose. And you our lay-reader, bank-manager. Everybody will have to believe it, anyway."

"I don't care, there's nothing in it, nothing. How could there be? Sally—and *that!*" He shuddered, for all the time he kept remembering hateful, horrible little things all pointing the one way. "I shall contradict it; I hope to be in a position to contradict it. I will knock down the first man who as much as whispers it to me."

"But, Mr. Bingley, suppose he is taller, stronger—and most of them are, aren't they? What would you do then?"

"Knock him down just the same," blazed the bank-manager. "I tell you it's a lie. I'd like to choke the vile throat that utters it!" He glared at her. Oh, to seize that scraggy throat and rend it! He had always hated Miss Maggie, but never more than now.

She began to sort out the letters. "But the hotel-managers say it's true; they recognised them, and speak of it quite openly. They pretend to think they were really married. One has to do that sort of thing in hotels—when couples come from Paris. Mr. and Mrs. Thompkins!"

"Thompkins! What Thompkins? Why?" he exclaimed, dazed.

"*Why?* A man of the world to ask a poor spinster a question like that! Oh, Mr. Bingley, how embarrassing you make my duty. Don't you remember? Why, they both owned to it, that tour in Italy. A whole month, just by themselves. Paolo and Francesca and that lot, you know. Quite the rage it used to be! Then all those naughty French pictures."

"A lie! A lie! Every word of it!"

"You had better see the letters for yourself—my questions, their replies. Everything quite clear, description, dates. Any court of law would recognise evidence like that. These are the originals. I sent copies to Mrs. Wilmot-Randal. I felt I hardly knew her well enough to trust her with these; women are so treacherous, so dishonourable, but you, of course, are different."

He took the letters with shaking hands; read them feverishly. The thing was only too plain. Not a glimmer of hope was left to him; he knew this devastating thing was true. He flung the letters on the road, ground them into the dust with his heel, as he longed to grind Miss Maggie Hopkins.

"My God! My God!" burst from his anguished lips.

"Oh, hush, Mr. Bingley; do remember the lay-reading, the bank, and me." The speaker retrieved the 'evidence.'

"You have done it, you have done it!" he cried. "Suspected, spied! Told poor Mrs. Randal, are trying to spoil three lives—"

"I have saved Mrs. Randal from her husband and Sally from deceiving hers—for of course she'll have to get one by hook or crook, take in some fool, make him a laughing-stock. And what thanks do I get for doing my duty? I am abused."

"It may have been no more than a harmless frolic," he said desperately; "she was young and reckless, he even younger."

"Yes, just led away, poor boy—"

"Very unconventional," he went on feverishly, "very rash, but not necessarily—not necessarily—"

"Well, she happens to be a Lunton," said Miss Maggie, as if that quite disposed of the case, as indeed it did; "and her bringing up and life generally and her ideas always rather loose. I don't think her eyes look like harmless frolics. I've seen a little devil there sometimes."

So had Mr. Bingley. He remembered it now, and how it had attracted him, lured him on. Oh, she was wicked, vile, his Sally, but he loved her still. How he loved her! It was jealousy that hurt most.

He looked at Miss Maggie, and rushing, bitter, wicked thoughts overwhelmed him, topsyturvy thoughts. Here was this acrid spinster, immaculate, a 'good' woman; there was Sally, kind and human, but 'bad'! So the world labelled such women and such things. Immaculate or the other thing; to be immaculate to be all. He was shocked to find himself asking if it were possible that the one virtue was exaggerated out of all sense of proportion, the others taken too light account of? No, no; and yet … There were the facts; Miss Maggie 'good,' Sally 'bad.' Nothing could ever alter them. Yet many loved Sally, always would love her, and nobody had ever even liked Miss Maggie!

His expression grew almost brutal; his thoughts entirely so.

That day had come news of the loss of some fifteen hundred souls on board the *Lusitania*, and the cry of the drowning children had not sounded sweet in Mr. Bingley's ears. This was the immunity of Britain; this was her sea-heritage! For a moment the war loomed nearer, seemed almost to touch him, to rouse him. It was becoming serious, one might almost say dangerous. Its poisonous breath hung over the inviolate land. On that ship good and kindly women had gone down, husbands and fathers, tender children, but Miss Maggie stood here in the road, safe and sound. Next, he thought bitterly, there would be some ghastly railway accident, and valuable and heroic lives meeting a terrible end, but Miss Maggie would not be there. The Miss Maggies of the world always were safe and sound, so it seemed to him. No house on fire, no railway accident, no shot or shell found them, they were as immune as he held Britain to be. Should they ever happen to be in a disaster they would be the sole survivors, and live to a ripe old age, the curse of their generation and a shame to the mother who had borne them. But they were 'respectable' women; the Sallies were—wanton.

He clenched his fists. Murder? What was murder? By God, there were times when it was justifiable!

Miss Maggie moved back a step or two. She was not afraid, but she was not unnecessarily rash. Her long, thin lips drew back over her sharp canine teeth; she looked like one who could inflict a dangerous bite. It is quite possible—had it come to it—that her bite would prove more dangerous than Mr. Bingley's blow, but it did not come to it. Mr. Bingley remembered himself.

"Men like women with the devil in their eyes," went on Miss Maggie, "only not for their own wives, do they?"

"You—you woman!" said the tortured man impotently. He did not know what he was saying; he only knew there was no hope, no longer any joy in life. His stable, orderly world was in ruins; the bricks crashing down upon his head left him sick and stunned. He had lost her—oh, what a blessed escape! If she had accepted him what a horrible situation now! Why hadn't she accepted him? Surely, surely she should have jumped at the chance! How puzzling it was! Was she playing for Wilmot-Randal all the time? Jealousy seared and rent him. Her first lover, if he were her first. That held with a woman. Perhaps she loved him still. She wanted him first; if she failed with him then she would take Mr. Bingley. Yes, that's what it had come to mean. Oh, horrible, most horrible! The woman he had thought of as an angel. She hoped for a divorce, a young husband with ten thousand a year. Oh, Sally, Sally!

"I wish I had never known," he thought, "then I might still have been happy. If only I had never known. O God! O God!"

"I suppose Mr. Wilmot-Randal must have been infatuated at the time," said Miss Maggie. "I always say Sally goes to the men's heads—unless, of course, they are well screwed on."

"Randal is a scoundrel. I should like to kill Randal!" muttered Mr. Bingley thickly, his eyes bloodshot.

"Then we should have a murder-case as well as a divorce-case," trilled Miss Maggie. "Just fancy, what a coincidence! But Sally would not let you kill him. She's in love with him. I saw she was in love with somebody, and I thought it was White; they met on The Mountain most evenings, you know, stayed there till late."

That too! That too! Mr. Bingley did not dispute it Oh, she was bad indeed, his Sally!

"Now I think it was Mr. Wilmot-Randal all the time—and his money. She loves money."

"I wish I had never come to Little Crampton!" burst out the tortured man.

"Oh, lots say that." She watched him as a cat watches a mouse, cynical amusement in her eyes. "But they come and go, Mr. Bingley, they come and go. I suppose the little boy can run the bank? How useful, to be sure!"

This did not sting as it once might have done, but it stung a little.

He turned on her with blazing eyes. "You—you have done this. If you had just let things alone we could all have been happy; now—now it's Hell. You are the curse of Little Crampton! I don't know how God can let you live. All those gone down on the *Lusitania*, and you here, always here, always safe, just going on and on, spoiling lives—"

"Dear me, you are quite excited, Mr. Bingley!"

"You are a beastly woman," he got out, "yes, a beastly woman, upon my soul, you are!"

He stumbled on, leaving Miss Maggie staring after him with open mouth. He was the first person who had ever taken the last word from her!

CHAPTER XXX

"I never guessed there were two of me"

Mr. Bingley went home. An outsider who knew not Alfred might have been excused for supposing him exceedingly drunk, so glazed were his eyes, so uneven his footsteps. His small mouth, so often buttoned up, hung slackly open, and over and over again a broken sound issued from it, "Not Sally, not my Sally! It can't be true."

But he knew that it was.

He went into his ponderous dining-room and shut the door. He sank down into his big arm-chair, leaned his head against the antimacassar that protected it from any possible hair-grease, and tried to think. Round and round went his thoughts like a squirrel in a cage.

A tap came at the door. If he heard he did not heed. Another tap, and then Vanner entered. "About dinner, sir," she began; "I've been thinking—"

Mr. Bingley looked at her with bloodshot eyes. "I don't want any dinner," he said.

Vanner's mouth came slowly open and she rubbed her eyes. "But, sir—"

Mr. Bingley gave a husky little bark; then he told Vanner to go to the devil and take his damned dinner with her.

Vanner staggered out of the room and into the kitchen, where she collapsed on to Kate Gillet and had an attack of hysterics, moaning:

"Damned me, he did, damned me to H—, me and his *dinner!* God have mercy on us!"

Gillet shrieked. "He's gone mad," she exclaimed, "and me just nicely settled and all. Aggravatin' critters men be, rich or poor."

It was all over Little Crampton next day that Mr. Bingley had called Vanner an unspeakable name, cursed her in language more lurid than that of any trooper, and otherwise behaved outrageously and unlike a Bingley. Miss Maggie sent her Gillet sister to demand of Mr. Bingley's, "And *where* did his boot strike Vanner?" Some people believed this, others did not; nobody believed Mr. Bingley had gone without his dinner.

Yet he had gone without his dinner. He sat there trying to think, trying to see some way out of this bitter *impasse*, trying to make up his mind.

She would marry him now if he asked her. There would be no question of wanting time or thinking it over. She would marry him gladly, gratefully, cling to him sobbing, say she was sorry, sorry, sorry, and would never, never so much as look at a man again; just devote herself to her husband, her brave, noble husband! Her wet cheek would be pressed against his. Mr. Bingley groaned aloud.

How she would adore him for his magnificence! He would be a god raising a Magdalene, redeeming her through his love, taking her to his compassionate heart. He would yet make her worthy of himself and all he had to offer. He seemed to stand on far mountain heights, head and shoulders above mere humanity, a giant among men.

If it came into his mind that a wife so raised from the depths to the heights, so nobly redeemed, would walk humbly all her days and adore her redeemer, and that she would be most malleable, well, even Mr. Bingley had a human side, and greatness has its limitations.

He would take her for his own, comfort her, see that she truly repented, stand between her and the whole world—and Little Crampton.

He winced. So easy to stand between Sally and the whole world, but when it came to standing up to Little Crampton, to Miss Maggie, *damn* her! to Boliver the fat fool, and Paton, that pernicious ass, well, that was rather different. He sickened, faltered, grew weak.

If he had been a nobody! How easy life was for nobodies, people without money or reputation or place. How difficult for those with a great career ahead, for personages, people in the public eye. A great career! Did men who married such a Sally, when they had been found out, ever 'arrive'? The thing could not be hidden. The corpse long buried was none the sweeter to look at when at last it rose from its grave; neither was it easily buried a second time.

Everybody would know and whisper and look knowing. Other women would look askance at Mrs. Alfred Bingley, turn coldly away. She would always be, even when quite old, "a woman of a scandal, a woman with a past." And he, her husband? The magnificent redeemer? The great man who had counted the world well lost for love? Oh no, that was never the judgment of the world. Just an infatuated husband, a man entrapped. A *fool!* Other men would snigger at him behind his back. His very clerks would talk of it, criticise. People would speak coarsely, say headstrong passion had destroyed him, whisper this and that. Mr. Bingley and headstrong passion! No, no! To look a fool, a passion-ridden fool …

He reached out his hands blindly and found his mother's *Book* within his grasp. The habit of years was not to be broken. How often had he looked for guidance! When had he ever failed to find it? If he had heeded her clear warning from the outset he would have been spared this terrible thing. She had warned him against Sally from the day he had seen her, pointed out what it must come to mean, and he had disregarded this genius, with the result that his whole life was shattered.

"Oh, mother, mother, forgive me!" he murmured abjectly. "Heaven knows I am punished!"

"*Don't marry a woman who has had an intrigue. She may make you quite happy and comfortable, but she must make you a fool in at least one person's eyes.*"

There it was, like that much-advertised medicament which always touched the spot.

"*Don't marry a woman with a past. Her past will be her own present and your future.*"

And finally:

"*Don't marry a woman because she seems a perfect angel; she is far more likely to be merely a clever devil.*"

"If only I had listened—in time!" groaned the reader. "Oh, my God! my God! what *am* I to do? I wish I was dead—or at least almost wish it!" The thought of his money being scattered by careless relatives, more than anything else, made life still the one thing to be jealously guarded at any price. He knew what he still wanted to do—to count the world well lost for Sally. He knew what he must not do—let passion decide.

Passion! The word had always had a very ugly sound to him, and he had never used it. He preferred to believe it seldom visited really nice people, and never the Bingleys of this world. His beliefs were being sadly battered about, not holding very firm. He once started to read a poem that began:

> Naught shall avail thy priestly rites and duties—
> Nor fears of Hell, nor hopes of Heaven beyond;
> Before the Cross shall rise my fair form's beauties—
> The lips, the limbs, the eyes of Clarimonde.*

He had read on no further, partly because he was shocked and partly because he was incredulous of such things. He was still shocked, but he was no longer incredulous. He thought of it as something akin to demoniac possession. He would and must drive it out. But how? How?

To think of Sally at all was to long for her, to crave fiercely, to feel that life without her was scarce worthy the name of life. 'If thy right hand offend thee, cut it off.' How easy he had thought that once! Such a little thing to do, to cut off the offending limb called Sally, bone of his bone, flesh of his flesh.

The Bingleys that were to be, that sacred trust—with Sally for a mother? No, no, that would be a crime! Sally, and no Bingleys? A crime again, wrong piled on wrong.

Again he felt her in his arms, the soft mouth against his. He had held her once, kissed her once; there was at least that to remember. If it meant Hell he would not repent of that; even if Little Crampton heard of it he would keep the memory, not cast it forth.

Sally of the mountain-top; Sally in the first short, wide skirt he had seen, with the arched feet, the slender ankles; Sally the fairy princess

---

* From *Poems of Passion*, by Ella W. Wilcox. With Messrs. Gay & Hancock's kind permission.

asleep by the rosy firelight—all to go for ever, all to be seen no more, thought of no more. *Sally the wife of some other man.* He could have borne it better had he felt sure that lonely repentance would be hers, but he was not sure. He was only certain that the Sallies did not repent in solitude. She would merely go and deceive somebody else, make him mad about her, marry him, and perhaps bring him happiness in spite of everything.

No, no, he would not let her go; by Heaven he would not! Some other man? Never, never! She was his, he had known her his from the first, ordained for him. Ordained for the little bank-manager? He groaned.

It seemed to him that in his big dining-room, handsome, stolid, and hideous, full of expensive Victorian furniture, very heavy, rather stuffy, and essentially commonplace and respectable, something very strange took place, and that like another he wrestled with one not of this earth in mighty conflict.

Backwards, forwards, first one gaining, then the other. Now failing, and perhaps not sorry to fail; one growing greater and stronger; the other smaller and weaker, dwindling and dwindling. … Who was this being who strove with him like the Son of God? Suddenly he saw him plainly, and the sweat burst from him. He was looking on his own face.

"I never guessed there were two of me!" he gasped, his knees shaking. Two Mr. Bingleys, and both so strong, so unconquerable. One for right and one for wrong; one for greatness, one for littleness. Which was right, which wrong? Which great, which little?

"I don't know," burst from him, "I can't think. I don't know." He never really knew; it remained one of life's unanswered questions.

The fight raged on, a drawn fight it seemed to him, for he could come to no decision. Eleven o'clock struck and the time-sense penetrated. He went upstairs to his room feeling as if the clothes had been torn from his back, and as if his face must be bloody and battered. He turned up the gas and hurried to the big mirror, expecting to look on he knew not what, but signs of the mighty conflict at least; perhaps to face a wreck. He looked, and gasped. Could such things be? His collar was not even crumpled; his coat 'set' as his tailor had to see to it that they always 'set.' His face was perhaps pastier than usual, his eyes smaller, puffy, his mouth and chins sagging, but that was all. No bloody nose, no broken crown, not even a tooth missing from the plate! He felt almost personally aggrieved. There should at least have been that missing tooth, so painlessly lost and quickly replaced, that streaming nose.

That a man could go through so much, and show so little!

Though he did not expect to sleep, he got between the sheets, and sleep was indeed long in coming. He tossed and turned, the bed-clothes grew hot and tumbled. His pillow burned like fire, and there was something else that burned like fire too, in eyes and on his cheeks, scorching, unmanly tears. Oh, Sally, Sally … to throw it all away! To spoil everything for both of them! No pair in the world would have been happier, no wife more beloved or more fortunate. And now—and now …

He gulped, a revolting and rather ridiculous spectacle, but spared that knowledge. He felt a martyr, a knight weeping on his ladye's bier, dignified, magnificent, solemn. He did not know that his rumpled hair looked dreadfully moth-eaten, and his second chin was merely ludicrous when he gulped.

He fell asleep at last, his real decision unarrived at, but memory picturing Sally by the firelight, something that could not be forgotten or foregone as duty told him it must.

When he woke at dawn there came a picture of Sally by its grisly grimness; duty seemed easier then. He would write after breakfast and tell her to forget what he had said, that it no longer held good, and why, but he would put it very delicately. It was a shocking thing to have to mention to an unmarried woman at all. Would she deny it? Oh, if she would—and prove that denial! Women always denied things; unfortunately they could not always prove them. Could Sally? He knew she could not. It only meant adding lying to the greatest of all sins a woman could commit.

As for that scoundrel, Wilmot-Randal, if he had twenty thousand a year instead of ten thousand he would never take his hand again, never greet him in friendship, never ask him to dinner. He would hate him as long as they both should live, and he would get moved from Little Crampton at once, even if it meant to a smaller bank.

When he had finished breakfast he still found it impossible to write to Sally. He could not hold the pen, and the words would not come. 'My dear Miss Lunton.' They seemed terrible words to him. He did not yet know what he had decided. To be the mockery of the whole world, but to have Sally? To be as admired as ever, but alone? The two Mr. Bingleys had another wrestle in that Victorian dining-room.

Again the striking of the clock recalled him to the habits of years. He rose and went into the bank.

The boy glanced at him. "Bilious," he thought, "been over-eating hisself, lucky old buster!"

The lucky old buster had given himself his solemn word that he would have his luncheon and then sit down and write to Sally. That was surely the most logical and the calmest time of the whole day. Turbulent passion did not raise its head at such an hour; neither did the grey of early dawn wither it.

Yes, that was the time to make a life's decision—and send it to Sally.

During an onerous morning—it happened to be the one busy day of the week—Mr. Bingley made no single mistake of any description; neither did he exhibit the slightest signs of flurry.

Miss Maggie cashed a cheque to see.

CHAPTER XXXI

"Even the 'soft job' has got to be paid for"

Sally too had to make her life's decision that week. She sought how she should do it, not knowing it had already been done for her, and that whether she should marry Mr. Bingley or not lay in his hands, not in hers.

What did she think of during that week?

It seemed to her that she had never thought so much in her life, or realised so much. She thought how easy the road of life still could be, at a price. She thought of those visions surging up out of the sea, and what others had sacrificed for their country, and the high ideal; of the gallant lives going and gone; of the thousands never to see the June roses blow; of those who had been faithful unto death, and on whose brows sat the crown of immortal life; of those left behind, no less brave, saddened, but proud.

'Be strong, and quit yourselves like men.' What a magnificent response there had been to those words!

And she thought of Robert Kantyre. She was always thinking of Robert Kantyre, tenderly, happily, restfully. If the other had been passion, a flaming fire, this was love, deeper, nobler, more lasting. One had led to the flame; this reached to the stars. One had been self—she knew that now—this was selfless. One was taking; this was giving.

The only thing she did not think of was Mr. Bingley himself.

She had no need to wait for the week. When she came down the mountain-top that night she knew. Clear before her lay the road—work and honour and love. Discomfort and sacrifice there must be, but that she would meet with a glad and cheerful heart. Her eyes shone and her breath came faster. Oh, to have found the way at last! To have the chance to make good!

The soft job! What a poor, backboneless thing it was when one came to analyse it—this desire of so many men and women. For it men fought, for it they lied and cheated and were unworthy. They clung to it through honour and dishonour, through cowardice itself; they even married for it. "God let my living be soft! God let me never be uncomfortable!" was perhaps their only prayer, as it was their only ambition. Was it worth it?

Surely even the soft job has got to be paid for somehow; even money has its price, the longest price of all. It is paid for in things that are more than money. This woman who had sold herself under the name of matrimony, this man who had lied and cheated, taken perhaps the unloved woman to his home: what did it profit them in the end?

Success and ease, most dearly bought, would be there; what of other things that would be there, and the things that never would? What of that illusive sprite called happiness? It did not wave its magic wand by that hearth; it had flown, for them it had no longer any significance; they did not know it by sight, save through another man's eyes. Instead of the fairy there was only a mocking little imp making faces in the corner, and it was no easier dispelled than happiness coaxed back. Most successful hearths knew this imp well.

That was what the soft job meant when men and women gave their all and their best for it, when self and greed were exalted, and the true things trodden into the dust.

Sally wondered why she had never seen it before. How plain it was now, and how near she had gone to making shipwreck of her life! She was thankful she had seen it in time. She had often heard that happiness came from within, never from without; that it lay in living for others, or another. She had not believed it then but she believed it now, for she knew that henceforth, for her, happiness would always lie where Robert was, and that no sacrifice would be too great for his sake. She loved him far, far beyond herself; she thought rather of making him happy than of being happy.

She had never been so happy in her life. Her heart was light, her feet danced, her eyes shone. She felt almost 'fey,' as if such joy was too great to be borne. She longed for the time when Robert would come to her, and she would hold out her hands, and say:

"I am all yours, and I will follow you gladly and proudly to the edge of the world and beyond."

She thought of those beautiful words, 'Thy people shall be my people, and thy God my God.' She was thrilled to think that she could echo them.

Then the old whimsical Sally crept out. "I will even add, 'and thy relations my relations,' for he has only one in Canada, and he's a dear, and I shall never have to see any of the others. I know I should have hated his horrid sisters."

When Mr. Lovelady looked at her, his own face, which had grown very white and weary, seemed to shine too.

"Ah, my Sallykin, you have found the real fortune?"

She told him all, even Robert's secret, for he had given her leave to do so.

Mr. Lovelady was silent for a long time, holding her hands in his, then he said thankfully, "Thank God for this. I can go happy now."

Sally clung to him with a cry. "No, no, you shall not even speak of such things. I could not bear it. You must rest more. Why, Old John still goes on, and you're not elderly yet."

Mr. Lovelady looked down at the dog, who raised faithful, glazing eyes to his. "He's not long to go either," he murmured, half to himself. "Who knows—who knows …"

On Wednesday Sally made up her mind that she must write and tell Mr. Bingley not to call, that it would be useless. She wrote her letter, making her decision quite plain, and feeling a little sorry for Mr. Bingley. After all, he was desperately in love with her, in his way. He was ridiculous, of course; he had been ridiculous upon the mountain, though not all ridiculous. Once or twice he had startled her and risen to real manhood. He had shown possibilities, almost greatness. He would make a better husband for Mrs. Dalton for it; they were really very well suited and might find happiness together. Mrs. Dalton would bring her credentials with her in the shape of plump Nina. She would probably give him the priceless little bank-manager, as that would be the shortest cut to many things, a car, for instance, and there was no reason why they should not be a very happy little family.

Yes, she could feel quite comfortable about Mr. Bingley. It was all for the best in every way. Of course he would be hurt a little, but his pride would suffer most. How astonished he would be that there could exist any woman who would refuse him! How astonished she would have been herself a few months back to see herself doing so!

Miss Maggie Hopkins would be disappointed that her little scheme had come to nothing.

Sally had written her letter, and was putting it on the hall table ready for posting, when a ring came at the door and a letter fell into the letter-box. She picked it out and saw it was addressed to her in Mr. Bingley's neat writing.

"The impatient lover," she thought, opening it. "Oh, poor man! Perhaps it will hurt rather a lot. I am sorry."

As she read, compassion turned to anger and then to fear. So he knew! It had got out! *Who else knew?*

Her hands shook. She would never, never have told Mr. Bingley. Would she have told Robert? Incredible to say she had simply never thought of it one way or the other, but she never had. She thought of it now, however, saw what she had to do. She should have told him that evening on The Mountain. Why, why had she never thought of it, seen the one course? She must tell him when he came for her answer that very night. She must not let him ask her, touch her, till he knew. Would it make any difference? It would make this difference, that it would be a very bitter moment for both; that what should have been all joy would be soured, spoiled. That he would be furious for the moment she felt certain, perhaps even hate her, shrink from her; but that his love was strong enough to conquer all, and forgive all, she did not doubt for an instant.

She would try and make him understand. Not even to him would she deprecate, seem to regret the passion that had swept her off her feet. It had been glorious, and it had been worth it—while it lasted. Not even now did she repent of it for her own sake, though for Robert's she was ready enough to heap the ashes upon her head. He would forgive, yes, but there would be that bad moment first, and the taste of the thing would he for ever between them. His pride of possession would be hurt, his love, his honour. He would suffer, and she would have to see him suffer. He would want to know why she had not told him at once, ask her if she would have told him at all if her hand had not been forced. Would she? She never knew. It was so clear now when it was too late. She had just forgotten Jimmy when her love for him died, forgotten the old story. It was as if the thing had never been, or as if she had been born anew—for Robert. But the stain was there all the time; must always be there, she supposed. Odd she had never thought of it like that before.

She read Mr. Bingley's letter again.

DEAR MISS LUNTON (it began),

I never thought to call you that again, and now I can never call you anything else, certainly never Mrs. Alfred Bingley, a tide I once thought you might be proud to bear. Oh, Sally! why did you deceive me so? Why were you so cruel? You have spoiled my life. I shall never really be happy again, not even when I am manager of the biggest bank of all. Miss Maggie Hopkins found out about everything, and told me all. *What* a woman! She showed me the letters. It's useless denying it. How you stayed with Randal in Italy six years ago—as Mr. and Mrs. Thompkins. Oh, Miss Lunton, what a terrible, terrible thing to do and be! Why were you not strong in the day of temptation? Then we could still have known happiness together, been worthy of each other; and now everything is over. I asked you to marry me, believing you to be what you are not. I cannot ask you again now, God help me, God help us both! Awful as this may be for you, believe me, it is almost as awful for me. There are times when it seems more than I can bear; but right is right, and the honour of the hearth must be maintained. I cannot put you in my mother's place, make you the guardian of the next generation of Bingleys. You must see that yourself. I do not know what is going to become of you, and I dare not think. I am crushed, yes, crushed; I wonder what my life will be now.

If lack of money stands in the way of a happier and better life for you, I beg you will think of me as a friend in that particular, and let me at least have the happiness of knowing I was some little help. As for myself, I have asked the directors to move me at once, anywhere; if I lose promotion I cannot help it. I can't stay in Little Crampton, where I have seen the possibility of my greatest happiness and known my deepest sorrow, and where people will hear, and talk and gossip. As for forgiveness, I forgive you—as I pray God may do. That you have wrecked my life is nothing, but that you should have wrecked your own in such a fashion is dreadful. I pray that henceforth you may lead a worthier life.

Good-bye, Miss Lunton, good-bye. Oh, it was not good-bye I thought we would be saying! I wish—but I must not think of that now. Perhaps this is the Divine Hand showing me I also have my weaknesses, my faults to amend; that all of us must be chastened. How true that mankind is born to sorrow as the sparks fly upwards! Good-bye, and let me know about the money—any *reasonable* amount I mean, of course.

Alfred Bingley.

"A chastened Mr. Bingley!" thought Sally, half-smiling. "Well, so much the better for Mrs. Dalton. But oh, that it was he that refused me, not I that refused him! Nobody, he least of all, will ever believe I meant to do that now. If only I had got my letter off first! Now I am just the unworthy cast aside by the good man. People will laugh and pity me!"

Certainly this was a bitter pill to swallow.

Then she forgot even that, for trembling, hoping, thrilling, she went up The Mountain and waited for Robert Kantyre.

Light faded into dusk, and dusk into darkness, and still he did not come. The twinkling lights of the village at her feet shone out and then disappeared one by one. The church clock chimed.

Sally's heart sank lower and lower, a fear and a poignant anguish gripped her; her soul and body seemed rent with agony. This was the punishment; this was the reaping, not of sin, but of being found out.

She waited and waited, but she knew it was vain. This time it was the man who had failed.

She crept homewards, her head bowed. She was humbled to the dust, beaten at last. She had learned to know the worth of love and sacrifice; that it should be snatched from her at the eleventh hour! He had heard and he would not come; he thought her vile. He had not even written like Mr. Bingley.

He would never come and he would never write. He would just go out of her life and she would never look upon his face again. He would go to Canada, to the new, free life, a man with the power of building up. She would remain in Little Crampton with her broken-hearted guardian—he would never get over this blow—and a soiled reputation: a woman who had been flung aside by three men, passed from one hand to another; a mockery, a byword.

She could not weep. It had gone beyond tears. "Sally on the rocks with a vengeance," she muttered shakily; "Sally on the rocks to the bitter, bitter end!"

CHAPTER XXXII

"In the midst of death ..."

The Reverend Adam Lovelady lay dead among the rose-trees he was never to see in flower, on his face that peace which passeth understanding. Old John crouched with his muzzle across his master's breast, moaning fitfully, the dog's eternal "Why?" in his piteous eyes.

Lads and lassies went romping down the lane, the children with shouts of glee, but the others quietly, and two by two. A laden bee fell heavily from flower to flower. The blossom lay on the ground in white sheets, for the time of flower was past, the time of fruit close at hand.

In the midst of death we are in life.

In the thicket, proud but puzzled parents contemplated a giant offspring in the nest; the mocking note of the cuckoo sounding from the pear-tree close by held no significance for them. Alone had they brought forth this marvel.

Ananias gazed with jaded eyes at the latest blatant matron flinging her golden balls at him. Same old business! Same old world! He was getting about sick of it. He made a sudden dart at Sapphira's private worm and secured half of it. Sapphira pecked him so fiercely that he was humbled, while his infatuation and admiration deepened. He found her another worm, a fatter and longer one, and in the finding trod one of the golden balls into the earth. *Squash!* One nuisance at least removed. Never-ending they were, always going on and on. ...

The spoiled cat sought Elizabeth's sympathy, but Elizabeth, leaving her new summer hat upside down on the rocking-chair, was coyly reposing in the arms of the porter whose ears she had once made ring, and being coaxed to name 'the day.' She named it for an even earlier date than he had anticipated.

The cat mewed piteously and trailed mournfully into the kitchen, seeking here and there … puzzled and distressed.

The woman from the cottage close by came to see 'The Reverend' about the christening of her first baby; 'The Reverend' delighted in christening first babies and always made quite a festa of it Her hand trembled with pride and triumph as she rang the bell.

It was this ring that reluctantly rent Elizabeth from her porter, and led to certain discoveries.

Sally returned that night to a house of mourning.

CHAPTER XXXIII

"I did some hustle for a husband"

The funeral was over; Adam Lovelady lay at rest. Old John was buried under the pear-tree. To Sally it was as if everything were over for ever.

She lay with face downwards on the mountain-top wishing that she had never been born, or that she could die. She had spoken of being broken; she knew what it meant at last.

It had been easy to preach to another, "Wealth lost, something lost; honour lost, much lost; courage lost, all lost." Now she had herself lost wealth and honour and courage, and the physician could not heal himself.

Home was gone, reputation was gone; gone also the only man who loved her and belonged to her—mercifully before he had learned the truth; gone, too, the man she loved. What was left? Perhaps a broken heart, but that was scarcely an asset. The country was full of broken hearts and broken lives; they were a drug in the market.

When the ancient cheap rubbish the vicarage contained was sold, and the few pounds her guardian had left were handed over to her, she might be worth some fifty pounds. Existence for a month or two, and then what? She had not the very faintest idea; she did know that her wage-earning capacity was *nil.*

She could not stay in Little Crampton when the new people came to the vicarage. The Bolivers had asked her to stay with them, but that was impossible; everybody knew that Mr. Boliver had proposed to Sally, and still had more than a weak spot for her, while his wife was jealous, and had been forced to the invitation by her husband. True, Miss Maggie Hopkins had asked her, but Sally had done with the woman who had ruined her out of sheer malicious curiosity.

It was a question not only of what to do, but where to go.

Britain was very much the tight little island at present, difficult to enter and difficult to leave. It was not easy to get away into some far country while war still had her strangling grip on the throat of the nations. Italy's flag flew with the Allies'. Even the neutral countries were finding that none could sit down and say, 'Let there be peace,' and there was peace; but that this priceless possession had to be bought and paid for. The whole world was in a ferment. It had no room or use for Sallies.

Yet go somewhere, do something, she must. London again; was it to be just drifting down and down? Never that now. The loss of home, reputation, and future was terrible enough, yet it seemed but a slight thing in comparison with the loss of the man she loved. That dagger was in her heart for ever; it was a maimed life she would have to drag about with her. Sally on the rocks! Deserted Sally! Worthless, repudiated Sally!

Her life and work in Paris were utterly swept away. The enemy still had their faces towards Calais, that city of their passionate desire. Not yet had men and munitions seen to it that there should go forth that irrevocable decree, 'Thus far shalt thou come and no further, and here shall thy proud waves be stayed.' The war that had raged with ever-increasing violence for ten months might rage for another ten or more. Ten months! nay, it seemed like ten years. Into household after household entered War's grim figure, saying to this one and to that one, "Follow me to sacrifice, to tragedy, to the last endurance," and follow they did, not because they would, but because they must.

Sacrifice! Endurance! Tragedy! Well, endurance and tragedy were hers, but the willing, happy sacrifice denied her.

She pressed her face deeper into the grass, wishing she could lie for ever beneath it.

She knew nothing of a man scrambling up from the other side. It was not till Robert Kantyre's voice struck on her ears that she recognised he had come at last. That he should come too late, and in such an hour as this! Why had he come? To mock her, perhaps; to throw her aside in actual words. Surely he might have spared her that; her punishment was already greater than she could bear, her head in the dust.

She did not raise it, but lay there a figure of utter abasement and despair.

Robert Kantyre knelt by her side and felt for her icy little fingers. "Oh, Sally, Sally, my dear—" he began with difficulty.

She shrank from his touch. "You might have spared me this. Please go away."

"Sally—" he began again.

She sat up, unbeautiful now, sallow and haggard. "Everything is finished, but I can't discuss it. I was to give you my answer; instead you gave me mine. It comes to the same thing, I suppose, but I don't want to talk about it. Please go."

"Forgive me! What must you have thought?"

"There was only one thing to think. You heard, and naturally you did not come."

"Yes, I heard. It—it drove me mad for the moment. I did not believe it. I went straight to Wilmot-Randal. He denied it, but I saw that it was true. Then I came here, but you had gone. I heard of Mr. Lovelady's death and I could not seek you till to-day. Sally, you might have told me, you might have told me."

"You will not believe me, but I forgot all about it. I just forgot Jimmy." She covered her face with her hands.

He made a little dive forward and caught her close in his arms. "My poor Sally, my poor little Sally! What you have suffered! And that Bingley brute threw you over, they say!"

She tried to thrust him from her. "I wrote and refused him, but his letter reached me first."

His arms tightened. "You refused him?"

"Yes, of course."

"Of course! Why of course, Sally? Sally, answer me!" He pulled her hands from her face.

"It doesn't matter," she returned with quivering lips, "you don't want me now … you never came. Nobody wants me now. How could they? Yet

I was not bad. I thought I loved him; I had not learnt what love meant then … and now—and now I suppose it's too late." She buried her face against him and began to sob. "You hate and despise me now."

"It looks like it, doesn't it?" he answered, smoothing her hair. "I loved you from the first moment I saw you. I couldn't live without you, and I won't, either."

"But—but—"

His face paled a little and his mouth set. "It hurts, of course, badly, but it is forgotten. You are my Sally, my all. You will marry me at once and let me stand between you and—and everything? I will book our passages. We will find a splendid happiness together, darling. I need you, need you desperately; can't you need me a little too?"

"Oh, Robert, I'm perfectly silly about you," she said brokenly. "I couldn't do without you now."

He drew her face against his, whispered foolish, broken words. They clung desperately yet happily together, two who alone had known disaster and anguish, but who together were to know a great joy, peace, and redemption.

Then soberly they came down The Mountain, not talking at all, but hand in hand. …

The news flew from house to house. Mr. Bingley experienced a bitter pang. So this was Sally's repentance! This was how she mourned the loss of the noble knight and the high ideals. The dead love was scarce cold in its grave ere she sought another. How like a woman!

He opened *The Book*. He would think no more of Sally, consider only the future now. Did Mrs. Dalton represent the future?

"*Don't marry a widow; she naturally prefers being a mother to her own children than to yours.*"

Mr. Bingley made a peevish sound. "Really, mother is a little too drastic," he thought, exasperated. Now she was disposing of the only alternative left.

He turned over leaf after leaf. Always the woman he must not marry, never the woman he should! A sudden suspicion gathered and grew. His mother had been a jealous woman; she would never have tolerated a daughter-in-law during her lifetime. Was it possible that she could not tolerate the thought of one even after she was dead? Was it all a cruel, selfish plot to ruin his happiness?

Another god gone! Another world in ruins!

August-May had turned to December-May, and a fire was burning in the grate. Mr. Bingley rose portentously. Deliberately he put *The Book* on the glowing coals; deliberately he held it in the heart of the fire with the poker till it was consumed to ashes, expensive binding and all.

Then he flung back his shoulders and drew a deep breath, for suddenly he realised that he was a free man, that his tyranny was overpast. He was at last captain of his soul—a man.

A few days later as he was walking with Mrs. Dalton, angrily discussing the iniquity of raising the age limit to forty, his heart gave a sudden jump. Alas! that it should still jump at sight of unregenerate Sally! He must put a stop to this at once; it was wrong, improper.

There must be a bulwark between him and danger, a substantial bulwark. Once married, any hankering after another woman ceased like magic; that was Bingley's belief and logic, the meaning of morality.

He turned to Mrs. Dalton. "Will you marry me?" he demanded gloomily, "and make me the happiest of men?"

Mrs. Dalton saw Sally approaching and understood. She murmured a radiant "Yes."

Mr. Bingley took her hand and drew it possessively through his arm. He had his bulwark; already he felt as one close to harbour, outside the storm.

It was thus they met Sally, who also understood and was glad. She bowed. Mrs. Dalton returned it. Mr. Bingley raised his hat with a funereal air. The episode was over.

On his return home he cancelled his June week in London. That the enemy would succeed in either gas-bombing it from above or blowing it up from Tube of Underground he knew to be both ridiculous and impossible; but he might as well go elsewhere this year. He hoped Miss Maggie would go as usual.

Sally and the widow met a few days later and congratulated each other. "I have what I want," said Mrs. Dalton frankly, "but you have the man. I think we shall both be happy, but yours will be the finer happiness."

"I am very fortunate," returned Sally, "and you—is it to be putting your foot down, and keeping it down, or womanly wiles?"

They both laughed.

"Womanly wiles," said Mrs. Dalton emphatically. "The shortest cut."

She was put to the test a few days later, for Mr. Bingley discovered that her income was a myth, and that she also had deceived him. He was shocked and a little dispirited. Did they *all* do it?

"It was very wrong, very wrong indeed," he said, pursing up his mouth. But what a little wrong compared to Sally's! Then he remembered not to think of Sally now.

Mrs. Dalton cried. She cried rather prettily. "What was I to do? You had become everything to me—someone to look up to … a widow … with *only* a daughter. …"

If Mr. Bingley was pompous he was also kind. He put his arm round her waist and patted her pretty brown hair, and remembered not to think of yellow hair.

"Well, well, but you must never deceive me again. Money isn't so much, after all." He spoke a little heavily. "I used to think it was, and of course one's glad to have it; but it's a little disappointing, I think, and there are other things. It doesn't bring happiness—" he broke off with a sigh.

They were married almost at once, not in the least in the fashion Mr. Bingley had once anticipated when he should be made into a benedict.

Miss Maggie was at the wedding, very much in her element. "He has given Nina a pony," she said, "but Mrs. Dalton, Mrs. Alfred Bingley, I mean, hasn't got her car—yet."

Sally and her husband stood together on the steamer, their happy faces turned towards the new land. A great vivid moon made a silvery track across the waters, turning the bride's flame of yellow to fairer gold. She leaned up against her husband and pointed to it.

"Robert, there was a time when I almost prayed for a moon, and it did not come, and now it's come without any asking, full measure and running over. It's just like a path to fairyland!"

He looked into her vivid black eyes. "Well, I've got my fairy princess, at any rate," he murmured contentedly, his arm holding her fast.

She began to laugh, a long, low, delicious laugh that floated out over the sea. "To think of it: I did some hustle for a husband—and caught the wrong one!"

Robert laughed too. "Of course I know you will always regret Bingley, and would have had him if you could!" he teased.

"Yes, it's been a bit of a fiasco. … Oh, look, look, how beautiful the sea is, how wide, how free!"

The ship seemed to give herself a little shake, and then she had plunged into the silvern way, on to the new life and the new land, to hope and happiness and achievement.

❂ ❂ ❂

Afterword

The opening of *Sally on the Rocks*, with its introduction to Little Crampton, might remind readers a little of Elizabeth Gaskell's 1853 novel *Cranford*. Here is a community where appearances are paramount and gossip is rife; where the calculated words of a powerful woman can forever determine your rank in the village, even if you hold the 'white flower of a blameless life' (quoted, on the first page, from Tennyson's *Idylls of the King*). But, unlike Cranford, here too are men.

No men are, none could be, as powerful as Miss Maggie – the first character we are introduced to, and of whom we are rightfully afraid. She is surely one of the most gently poisonous characters in fiction. As the narrator notes of the vicar, 'The Reverend Adam Lovelady did his best against Miss Maggie, but he was only a man, and she was a woman.' There is no defence against her determination to root out scandal – or create it, if need be.

> The sooner you discovered that Miss Maggie was neither to be defied nor ignored, but appeased, the better. Also that it would save time and trouble to tell her your own version of the worst. No matter how small the skeleton she pounced upon, the lady could make its bones rattle so loudly that you would be deafened yourself.

It seems right that, though Boggs puts Sally in the title, it is Miss Maggie we encounter first. We have learned something of the potential

❁ ❁ ❁

pitfalls in Little Crampton before Sally Lunton returns to live there. We know not to trust the letter that Miss Maggie sends to Paris, inviting Sally to return to the village where she had lived as Mr Lovelady's ward. The carrot she waves is Mr Alfred Bingley, the local bank manager and lay-reader – that is, someone who can preach and lead most of an Anglican church service but is not a member of the clergy. One of his chief characteristics is a severe and inflexible sense of morality and respectability. Miss Maggie refers to him as a 'Grundy-man', 'Grundy' being defined as 'a personification of the tyranny of social opinion in matters of conventional propriety' – proverbially referring to Mrs Grundy in Thomas Morton's 1798 play *Speed the Plough*.

But Mr Bingley has an advantage about which Miss Maggie makes no pretence: he is 'simply rolling, quite fifteen hundred a year, and most of it private means.' It certainly wouldn't come solely from his salary – the average salary for the period was £70 a year, and though a bank manager might expect to earn several times this amount, it would be a small percentage of £1,500. Today, this is the equivalent of approximately £90,000. His later windfall of £30,000 would be about £1.8 million today. You can see why Sally would have been prepared to compromise on love. One of her thoughts provides the key to understanding much of her motivation: "You're not out for romance at thirty-one; it's business". She is only five years older than the average age of first marriage for women, but those five years make all the difference in 1915.

When we do meet Sally – full name Salome – it is one of the few moments where the full force of the First World War is seen in the novel. She has been living in France which, in 1915, was well aware that it might be the next victim to the encroaching German army:

> "They may be here to-morrow" was in the eyes of all, though on the lips of none. They had heard what had been done in Belgium; they did not even whisper what might be done in Paris; they knew.

❁ ❁ ❁

'What had been done in Belgium' was, of course, the German invasion in August 1914 and subsequent occupation; an act that technically led to Britain's involvement in the First World War, bound by an 1839 agreement to protect Belgium in the event of war. What Boggs couldn't have known, in 1915, was that Paris would never be fully occupied by the German army during the War, though it did come under siege and was repeatedly bombed. As Sally receives her letter, the initial attempts at invasion by the German army have been called off – but Sally has lost everything. The temptation of a safe marriage, and the destruction of her current prospects, are enough to send her back to Little Crampton – and into Miss Maggie's clutches.

As Miss Maggie has predicted, a love triangle develops between Sally, Mrs Dalton and Mr Bingley. This is certainly not due to any personal charms of Mr Bingley. Finding eligible men was harder than ever in the midst of war – though conscription wouldn't come in until the year after *Sally on the Rocks* was published, there was certainly a dearth of men of marrying age, as so many had voluntarily gone to the front. Mr Bingley is a year too old to sign up anyway, and Boggs spears the delusional way in which he thinks about this:

> He was over the age limit and he had a conscience. To call himself an official thirty-eight, as many men well over forty were doing, was a lie, and one he would be no party to. Imagine being killed with a lie almost fresh on one's lips!

His chief anxiety about the war is that it costs him a small amount of his largesse. A reviewer in the *Times Literary Supplement* wrote that, to people like Bingley, 'the war is a grievance, a personal insult from that horrible Kaiser; it has upset their lives, it is sending up the income-tax "something awful," and they have had to give £10, out of £3,000 a year, to war funds'. This is precisely the amount he has given – 'and thought it liberal'. His view is not depicted flatteringly.

❁ ❁ ❁

So, Bingley is there, and marriable if not exactly desirable. What makes *Sally on the Rocks* so unexpected, and feel in some ways very modern, is the way in which the two women competing for the proposal refuse to become nemeses. The term 'love triangle' was first used in 1909, according to current *Oxford English Dictionary* research, but they were nothing new in fiction and continue to be a mainstay. But it is rare to see one so respectful of the women involved, so frank about the desired outcome, and where neither woman is cast as the 'bad' one.

> They knew it was going to be a grim struggle to the death, and yet they were attracted instantly, and wished it might have been friendship. How delightful to have laughed together over the situation, and that absurdity, Mr Alfred Bingley. [...] Fate had made them combatants against their will, and fight to the bitter end they must, but each knew the other would fight fair.

As Mrs Dalton says, they aren't fighting over Mr Bingley, as much – "only his things". Were he less objectionable, or the women less charming to the reader, we might feel sympathy for Mr Bingley. A couple of the early reviewers did. As it is, the reader only really feels sympathy for whichever woman ends up successful in her campaign. And there are no foregone conclusions. Mrs Dalton lays out what they each can offer: "It will be a close thing. You have the wit and beauty, but I am safe and domestic and have been through the mill, nicely broken in."

While this framing of the competition for Mr Bingley is quite progressive, Little Cramptonians are not. Sally falls in love with another man, of course, but the ultimate decider in Mr Bingley's mind is the revelation of Sally's sexual past. Miss Maggie asks, "Why shouldn't women sow wild oats too when they get the chance?" but she is being insincere; she knows full well why they did not or, if they did, why they did their best to ensure nobody discovered it. But Miss

Maggie discovers everything she wishes to discover, even if it takes a little time.

This moral disparity for men and women is spelled out clearly. It is a central theme of Thomas Hardy's novel of a couple decades earlier, *Tess of the D'Ubervilles*, but Sally doesn't have even Tess's fragile hope that she will be 'forgiven'. She explains the situation to Jimmy, the man with whom she shared an intimate relationship:

> "You are to be permitted to forget, but never I. Yet you have paid no price. Your wife forgave you and married you just the same, as women, wise or foolish, do the whole world over. You look at the matter one way and I the other—the man's and the woman's way. You ran no real risk of losing your wife by confessing. I lose everything in this world; some think everything in the next. No, such things are not on the same footing, after all."

As the narrative later adds, 'men could be thought "a little wild," even in Little Crampton, and still be asked out to dinner, and treated as admiringly as ever, perhaps more so—when they were unmarried.' Boggs does not rail against the injustice of these double standards; she holds them up close to the reader, and lets them draw their own conclusions. Feigning pity, Miss Maggie puts her finger on the pulse:

> "Too many scandals are bad for a woman. Don't you think so?" asked the spinster regretfully. "There always comes the one that matters in the end, smashes her up. I think a woman should be like What's-his-name's wife, poor fellow! simply unsmirchable."

'What's-his-name' is, of course, Julius Caesar – the proverb 'Caesar's wife must be above suspicion' coming from an occasion in 62 BC when a young man called Publius Clodius Pulcher entered a female-only party in disguise, apparently intending to seduce Pompeia, Caesar's

wife. While Caesar gave no evidence at the trial, he divorced Pompeia as his wife must not even be under suspicion. Or, as Miss Maggie says, unsmirchable. For women like Sally, one scandal made public is probably one too many.

A contemporary reviewer in *The Athenaeum* writes, 'The portrait of the arch-scandalmonger with her corkscrew methods of obtaining information is remarkably clever,' and it's a good description of her. Though Miss Maggie is a tyrant whom it is very easy for the reader to enjoy loathing, she is herself a victim of the 1910s treatment of women. Early in *Sally on the Rocks*, the narrative points out, 'But for the curse of sex she must have been famous as a ruthless criminal barrister or investigator.' *Sally on the Rocks* was published in 1915; it wouldn't be until four years later that the Sex Disqualification (Removal) Act 1919 enabled women to become barristers, among other new professions and entitlements open to them. In 1922, Helena Normanton became the first woman in the UK to practise as a barrister, having applied to become a legal student within hours of the act coming into force. Miss Maggie would perhaps have been reluctant to leave her domain of Little Crampton even if the option were there, but it remains true that the ruthlessness that would have been admired in a courtroom only makes her feared and disliked in her community.

Of course, there is a perhaps unrealistically happy ending for Sally – finding a man who does not share the widely held view of women's sexual morality, falling in love with him, and being one of the many Brits who emigrated during the first decades of the twentieth century. Perhaps Kantyre's own experience in the army, disobeying an order and thus losing many of his men's lives, is the male equivalent of Sally's 'shameful' behaviour in the eyes of their society – as well as contemplating suicide almost half a century before it would be decriminalised in the UK. Two people who face being shunned by the community around them can start again in a place where their past actions and decisions are not known.